### *"Aren't you going to give me some sugar?" Cody asked*

Three steps from the door, Laurel halted, turned and stared at him. "Sugar?"

Cody caught her face in his hands. He was smiling, his sleepy-looking eyes half-closed, but gleaming as if they were lit from within. "That's what you say when you want a kiss." And before she could think, his lips came down on hers.

Spontaneous combustion—that's the only way to describe it, she thought. Hot, wet and incredibly sweet. His hands raked up and down her back, then dropped to her hips, pressing her tightly against him. The bristles on his jaw sent shivers of excitement down her spine. His hair felt thick and warm and alive, and when she ran her hands down his back, sliding her fingertips under his belt, he shuddered.

"Now go to bed," he rasped, holding her away. "Or else."

"Or else?" she managed to croak.

"Or else neither one of us is going to get any sleep tonight."

Dear Reader,

The editors at Harlequin and Silhouette are thrilled to be able to bring you a brand-new featured author program for 2005! Signature Select aims to single out outstanding stories, contemporary themes and oft-requested classics by some of your favorite series authors and present them to you in a variety of formats bound by truly striking covers.

We want to provide several different types of reading experiences in the new Signature Select program. The Spotlight books offer a single "big read" by a talented series author, the Collections present three novellas on a selected theme in one volume, the Sagas contain sprawling, sometimes multi-generational family tales (often related to a favorite family first introduced in series) and the Miniseries feature requested previously published books, with two or, occasionally, three complete stories in one volume. The Signature Select program offers one book in each of these categories per month, and fans of limited continuity series will also find these continuing stories under the Signature Select umbrella.

In addition, these volumes bring you bonus features...different in every single book! You may learn more about the author in an extended interview, more about the setting or inspiration for the book, more about subjects related to the theme and, often, a bonus short read will be included. Authors and editors have been outdoing themselves in originating creative material for our bonus features—we're sure you'll be surprised and pleased with the results!

The Signature Select program strives to bring you a variety of reading experiences by authors you've come to love, as well as by rising stars you'll be glad you've discovered. Watch for new stories from Janelle Denison, Donna Kauffman, Leslie Kelly, Marie Ferrarella, Suzanne Forster, Stephanie Bond, Christine Rimmer and scores more of the brightest talents in romance fiction!

The excitement continues!

Warm wishes for happy reading,

*Marsha Zinberg*

Marsha Zinberg
Executive Editor
The Signature Select Program

Signature Select™

SAGA

# DIXIE BROWNING

## FIRST TIME HOME

Silhouette Books

Published by Silhouette Books

America's Publisher of Contemporary Romance

SILHOUETTE BOOKS

ISBN 0-373-28530-2

FIRST TIME HOME

Copyright © 2005 by Dixie Browning

All rights reserved. Except for use in any review, the reproduction
or utilization of this work in whole or in part in any form by any
electronic, mechanical or other means, now known or hereafter
invented, including xerography, photocopying and recording, or in
any information storage or retrieval system, is forbidden without
the written permission of the editorial office, Silhouette Books,
233 Broadway, New York, NY 10279 U.S.A.

All characters in this book have no existence outside the imagination of
the author and have no relation whatsoever to anyone bearing the same
name or names. They are not even distantly inspired by any individual
known or unknown to the author, and all incidents are pure invention.

This edition published by arrangement with Harlequin Books S.A.

® and TM are trademarks of Harlequin Books S.A., used under license.
Trademarks indicated with ® are registered in the United States Patent
and Trademark Office, the Canadian Trade Marks Office and in other
countries.

Visit Silhouette Books at www.eHarlequin.com

Printed in U.S.A.

Dear Reader,

This isn't about genealogy...honestly. It's about family and how a single link can reach out to other links, and before you know it, a chain is formed. That's what happened when one by one, members of the Lawless clan—who didn't even realize there *was* a clan—came in search of a bequest from an early Lawless rascal who happened to be a world-class moonshiner fielding a fleet of sales reps, aka bootleggers.

But that has nothing to do with our story, other than the fact that without old Squire Lawless's bequest, Laurel and her distant cousins would never have met. More importantly, Laurel would never have met her own special hero...although I have to admit that things didn't look too promising at first.

The fascinating thing, genealogically speaking, is how every link in the chain leads to other chains, ad infinitum. Harrison's Cleo was not a Lawless, but their children are. Same with Lion's Jasmine and Travis's Ruanna. Cody Morningstar is not a Lawless, but Laurel is. Imagine years in the future when the next generation tries to sort out relationships. Does that mean we're all related somewhere in the far distant past?

I sort of think it does....

Dixie Browning

To all the fans who made my writing life such a joy.
I can never thank you enough.

# Chapter 1

Laurel raced up the two flights of stairs, fumbling for the keys in her tiny purse even as her heavy tote banged against her hip. Today she was twenty minutes early, which gave her time to change shoes, do something with her hair and be seated at her desk looking cool, efficient and ever so subtly tempting by the time Jerry arrived.

She'd sprayed a whiff of Tea Rose cologne on her bare midriff after her shower. Nothing blatant, but as the day wore on and her body warmed up, it would offer a hint of what tomorrow held in store.

A weekend in the Hamptons. Possibly even a *house* in the Hamptons. She could hardly believe it, but Jerry had hinted that they might look at a few houses as long as they were there.

Not that he'd actually proposed, but a hint here, a hint there and pretty soon a woman might start dreaming herself a future.

He knew her weakness all right, she thought with a rueful little smile as she unlocked the front office of J. Blessing Associates, affectionately known as Jay-bass. If he'd offered her a tiny fixer-upper in Outer Suburbia she'd have been just as thrilled.

Okay, maybe not *quite* as thrilled, but all she really

needed was some place to put down roots and eventually start a family, preferably *not* here in New York City. Small was good. With a small house they could do most of the fixing-up themselves. A home was more than a house.

She was still lost in thought when she heard the clatter of feet racing up the stairwell. She quickly slid the tote containing sneakers, a bottle of water, an apple and a cereal bar in the bottom drawer and tried to look intelligent, industrious, sexy and temptingly kissable as she waited for Jerry to pop in to say good morning. She couldn't think of a better way to start the day, especially when she was running so far behind schedule.

The door burst open and a stunningly handsome, if rather wild-looking man stared at her. "You're already here? God—!"

Her temptingly kissable mouth fell open as she stared back at the man who had started out as her employer, recently become her lover and was hopefully soon to be her husband. "Jerry? What's wrong?"

Jerry Blessing raked a slender, manicured hand through his normally flawlessly groomed hair. "Look, I don't have time to explain, but I want you to go home. Now! I'm expecting—"

"Go *home?* Jerry, I've got three appointments this morning alone, and this stuff's due at the printers no later than noon today." She waved a hand at the mock-ups she'd done.

He was sweating. Jerry Blessing *never* sweated. From some distant Mediterranean ancestor he had inherited olive skin and the darkest of brown eyes, only now his face was the color of wet plaster and his eyes kept darting around her office, never once making contact with her own.

"Look, will you just do this much for me? Oh, and one more thing—" He held up a staying hand as he backed out her door and swung into his own corner office.

Laurel waited for several minutes, almost afraid to move. What "one more thing"? What was going on? She sniffed, wondering if there was a fire in the building. No smell of smoke. No alarms. The sounds outside were no more than the usual chaotic rush-hour traffic.

From the office next door she heard the slamming of several drawers and what sounded like a chair striking the wall. Jerry's precious ergonomic dark green leather roll-around?

Heaven forbid.

She didn't move a muscle, hardly dared breathe. If there was a terrorist alert, why hadn't he said so? In fact why hadn't he grabbed her and rushed her out onto the street? What was the alert status, anyway? Pink, purple, puce?

And then he was back, carrying what looked like the smallest of several paintings that hung on his linen-covered walls. "Mama's watercolor," Jerry said tersely. "I want you to take it home with you."

"You're giving it to me?" Totally at sea, she stared at the Jude Law look-alike—that is, if Jude were only two inches taller and Italian.

"For safekeeping. Look, you might as well know, we're being audited. I don't want to take any chances on some government goon damaging Mama's painting."

Government goon? Who, the IRS? Aggressive accountants, maybe—nosy, obnoxious nerds, quite possibly, but government goons?

She waited for more of an explanation. She waited for some word of…well, something. A reassuring embrace wasn't too much to ask, was it? She started to ask about their weekend trip when he cut her off with a flap of his hand.

"Go, go, go! For God's sake, Laurel, leave before they get here. It's only a fluke that I had this much warning."

Before she could move he wheeled away and the next thing she heard was the slamming of his office door, followed by what sounded almost like the click of a lock.

Laurel stared down at the amateurish watercolor in her hands. Not only was it not very good, it was poorly framed. Any value had to be the sentimental type, which said a lot about the man. He owned far more impressive art, both in his office and his upscale apartment.

Moving toward the door Jerry had slammed on his way out, which had bounced open again because the latch never held, she stared across the intervening few feet to his closed door.

"Well…shoot," she whispered. Turning away, she reached for the tote. Not bothering to change shoes again, she slipped the small painting into its commodious depths and scooped up the papers she'd placed on her desk only moments ago. If that was the way he felt, the heck with it. The posters would get done when they got done, and if that was too late, then too damn bad!

She was hurting inside as she waited for the ancient elevator to rattle its way to the third floor. No way was she about to tackle those stairs wearing five-inch heels.

On the way back to the apartment she shared with a friend, she stopped in her neighborhood bodega for something rich and sweet to hold off the jitters. She had a lot of thinking to do and food always helped. While she was there, she perched on one of the few chairs and changed into her walking shoes while she exchanged pleasantries with the proprietor, an elderly man with snow-white hair and coal-black eyebrows who called every woman younger than sixty-five *nieta.* Granddaughter.

She only wished she were. Life would be much simpler if she had grandparents. Any family at all, even an aunt and uncle and a few cousins whose big noisy home she could visit on holidays. Right now she needed someone honest and objective to tell her what the devil was going on, because she hadn't a clue.

The next day before she'd finished her breakfast, in what had to be the scariest moment in her life, she was invited downtown for questioning.

*Questioning?* Neither of the men who appeared at her apartment door with a polite request that she accompany them downtown was particularly scary. If anything, they were almost too polite. All common sense fled. She tried to find nerve enough to ask to see their badges again, but her brain was operating in slow motion. She didn't know these men from Adam, despite the fact that they had identified themselves as from some branch of government.

Which branch? Homeland Security? IRS?

Oh, God, she was hyperventilating. What if she opened the door and jumped out? Would they come after her? For all she knew, the doors might be locked. She didn't dare try them to see.

Not until they parked in an underground garage did the tall one offer her an answer to one of her questions.

"It's about finances, ma'am. J. Blessing Associates."

Feeling a giggle rise in her throat, she swallowed hard. With his hand on her elbow, she had no choice but to follow the man onto an elevator. "But I don't have anything to do with the financial end of the business. I don't even buy postage stamps." Jerry handled that by himself, serving as both CEO and CFO.

Once inside she was offered a drink of water and then the inquisition began. It was polite—she'd give them that much. But afterward, she couldn't remember a fraction of what they'd covered. The tall one, whose name was Willoughby, offered to drive her home. She declined but quickly wished she had accepted the offer when she stepped outside to face at least two film crews and several reporters, two of whom she knew personally.

All she needed was a pair of orange prison coveralls. Before she could signal a cab she was hit with a barrage of questions, reminding her of the coverage she'd seen and dismissed so many times on the news. People surrounded by men in dull suits, the perps—that was what they were called—laughing and trying to pretend they weren't scared out of their Gucci loafers.

Recovering her wits, she remembered the standard response. "No comment."

For the next several days whenever she ventured outside, one or two flashbulbs went off in her face, a few microphones were poked at her. "Is it true, Ms. Lawless—?" "What can you tell us about—" "Is there a direct connection between Jerry Blessing and Al Quaeda?"

Crazy. The world had gone absolutely bonkers, that was all she could conclude. Thankfully, it hadn't lasted long. Evidently another scandal had come along and she was off the hook. The oddest thing, though—ever since her fifteen seconds of infamy she had occasionally had this spooky feeling of being…watched. Her roommate,

Peg, said it was all in her head, but Laurel was not the imaginative type. Anyone who knew her knew that despite a job that entailed hobnobbing with minor celebrities, she was a certified, card-carrying pragmatist.

All she could conclude was that a few people in the neighborhood had seen her picture in the news and later, seeing her again, wondered where they'd seen her before. That had to be it, because she was definitely a low-profile type.

With no particular credentials except for writing book and movie reviews and ad copy for a small upstate weekly, she'd been hired to do public relations when J. Blessing Associates' former PR person had been fired for some indiscretion or another. Jerry had never said what the guy had done. Another mark in his favor—he didn't gossip.

Thanks largely to her contacts in the print media, limited though they were, she'd been hired to get—as Jerry put it—the biggest bang for the buck. In other words, scrounging freebies by dropping the names of minor celebrities who agreed to appear at a fund-raiser into the right ears; composing cheap but effective ads and placing them where they would do the most good. She liked to think that all sides of the equation benefited—the celebrities, Jay-bass and the charities they served.

It hadn't taken long for the IRS gestapo, or whatever they were, to catch on to the fact that she didn't know beans about the financial end of the business. All she knew was that every penny saved in overhead went directly to the charities for which they raised funds. But try telling that to humorless creeps who seem convinced Jay-bass was funneling money to terrorist groups. Granted, the world was a dangerous place, but there was such a thing as being *too* suspicious.

She had expected to hear from Jerry, if only to find out what she'd been asked and how she'd answered, but no such luck. A brief phone call—was that too much to ask? Laurel checked her cell phone battery. Almost a full charge. Did a cell phone ring when it was being charged? Funny...she'd never thought to find out. But if he couldn't get her on her cell, surely he would call her other number.

So she waited. And waited.

A week later she was still waiting; almost too stressed to settle down to any task more demanding than folding laundry. She had tried several times to call Jerry, leaving messages which he never returned. With her salary on hold and her bills piling up, she needed answers, and she damn well needed them now!

And she knew where to get them. At least it was a starting place.

By the time she reached the old renovated office building that housed J. Blessing Associates and two other small businesses, she was steaming, and not just on account of the weather, which was the typical mid-summer, mid-Manhattan steam bath. Her hair was sticking to her face and she'd just reached up an arm to brush it away when someone called her name.

She turned her head just as someone stepped in front of her and poked a microphone in her face. "What—who—get that thing away from me!"

"Ms. Lawless, is it true that—"

She darted up the steps, ducked inside, slammed the heavy door and leaned against it. What in the world had happened now? Jay-bass, the downfall of, was yesterday's news.

"Is *what* true?" she muttered to the dark, dusty-smelling entrance hall.

She took out her cell phone and punched in Jerry's cell on her quick dial. Nothing. Not even an invitation to leave a message. Maybe he was upstairs. She considered using the cranky old elevator that took forever to groan its way up two flights, but then she thought, maybe this wasn't the swiftest idea she'd had. Wearing a white cotton shift and red sneakers, minus any makeup and with her hair looking like a hawk's nest, she was in no condition to confront anyone. She certainly didn't want Jerry seeing her like this, even if he happened to be here.

Okay, so it had been a really lousy idea. What had she hoped to accomplish?

Improvisation wasn't her long suit.

Once she was certain the reporter was gone, she let herself out and hurried away, wondering what to do next. She had to do something, only what? Nothing she tried was working. Nothing even made sense anymore.

Later that evening she was comforting herself with a chocolate éclair and a glass of wine while she watched the evening news coverage of parents picketing a local school. Three commercials later, she watched as a vaguely familiar-looking woman hurried along the sidewalk. She was wearing red sneakers and a white shift, carrying a familiar envelope-size shoulder bag.

Laurel watched herself spin around, saw her own lips moving, but no sound emerged. At first it didn't quite register, but then it did. Oh, God—this morning! The camera didn't flatter her at all. She looked angry and hot and sweaty, not to mention frightened.

"Oh, no," she whispered.

"D'you say something?" Peg called from the kitchen.

Before she could answer, another talking head appeared. The camera cut away briefly and she saw Jerry hurrying across the same section of sidewalk, followed by the same reporter who had cornered her. Time must have elapsed. Jerry couldn't have been there when she was, or else she'd have seen him.

He turned to face the camera and she read his lips when he said, "No comment." Then he said something else, only the remote was on the other side of the room with the volume turned all the way down.

"Isn't that Jerry?" Peg appeared in the doorway that separated the small living room from the minuscule kitchen. She was munching on a strip of bell pepper.

"I think so." Laurel knew so, she just couldn't talk about it. Even without seeing his face, she'd have known his walk, his build. She even recognized the tie he was wearing, a limited edition designer model he got from the tailor who fitted his suits.

What was going *on?* If he was still considered a person of interest after all this time, it had to be more than a simple accounting glitch. She retrieved the remote while she watched Jerry's lean backside disappear through the front door. The spokesperson was saying, "Blessing has been accused of funneling money to terrorist organizations. According to a spokesman for—"

Furious, Laurel snapped off the sound and then fumbled to raise it again. Even maddening misinformation was better than no information at all. She found the volume control again just in time to hear the spokesperson saying something about a landslide in California.

"Wow, is that what's going on?" Peg stared at her as if she'd never seen her before. "No wonder you're pissed."

"I'm not pissed, and that's not what's going on."

But was it? Could it possibly be true? Jay-bass raised funds for worthwhile causes that were too small to rate celebrity telethons. Jerry had lost friends in 9/11. He would never, ever help any terrorist group. Not knowingly, at least. "You know the gutter press. These people build their reputations on other people's misfortune. Believe me, they never let the truth get in the way of a good story."

Peg eyed her with open sympathy. "Have you talked to him lately?"

Laurel only sighed.

The next day she faced the fact that her salary was probably frozen for the foreseeable future, or at least until Jerry was cleared. Meanwhile, she had bills to pay. Rent and health insurance were the two biggies, but she still had to eat. So far, her attempts to find temporary work had netted her exactly zilch.

To keep from going crazy, she cleaned the tiny apartment, getting down on her hands and knees with an old toothbrush to scrub the corners of the base molding where the vacuum cleaner wouldn't reach. She removed the bulbs from the light fixtures and vacuumed the bugs from the socket and climbed up on a chair to dust the blades of the ceiling fan.

She did endless online job searches. And still she had energy to burn. Energy that was eating her from the inside out so that she was practically living on antacid tablets.

"Look for a serious job, not just something to fill in," Peg suggested.

"Ha! Easy for you to say, you've got a marketable degree."

"Dust off your old résumé."

"Fine, that'll make a great impression. From copy-writer and book and movie reviewer for a small upstate paper no one in Manhattan ever heard of to public relations director to a fund-raising firm that's currently suspected of supporting terrorists. Besides, nobody uses résumés anymore. Whatever any prospective employer wants to know is online, right down to when you had your last period."

"No kidding. Then I can dump my calendar?"

"Oh, hush up. Last week I checked in at a temp agency, offering to do anything from housecleaning to office work to dog walking."

"And?"

"Don't call us, we'll call you." She made a face. It was better than crying.

By mid-August nothing had changed. Laurel had worked two days at a Greek restaurant and was fired when the owner accused her of stealing from the cash register. His own son had done the filching, but she wasn't about to tell the old man that, so she'd walked out without even asking for her pay. Pride was something she could no longer afford!

At least news coverage had moved on to the latest scandal. Jerry had called once while she was out looking for a job and left a message saying he would let her know when to come back to work.

Nice. Really thoughtful, considering all the times she had tried to reach him. She'd even tried calling Kirk, the other partner, who spent most of his time on the road signing up almost celebrities for their fund-raising affairs.

Evidently he'd lost his cell phone again. It happened regularly. The guy was a real loser…literally.

It was Peg who came up with the only sensible idea she'd heard in nearly two months. Sensible at least for Peg, who wasn't known for her practicality. Or maybe it only seemed sensible because Laurel was going crazy trying to find out what was going on, what to do about it, whether or not she had any future at Jay-bass…or with Jerry.

"Go check out that land you inherited. At least you can put a For Sale sign on it."

Now, after glancing at her packing list, she held up a neatly folded gray cardigan she'd had forever and considered the remaining space in her largest suitcase. It was August, hardly sweater weather, but the sweater was so good to snuggle in when she was tired or PMS-ing, or coming down with a cold. "Why can't I make the simplest decision anymore?" She'd never been one to dither. Her method had always been—at least for the past twenty-odd years—to think a thing through, come up with a plan and then follow it to the letter.

"Take it," Peg advised.

"Thanks, I needed that." At least she knew what Peg's angle was. The sooner Laurel moved out, the sooner Peg's boyfriend, Dan, could move in.

"Hey, you might as well do it, as long as you're temporarily unemployed," she'd reasoned. "Once this mess at Jay-bass gets settled and you go back to work, you'll never take time off to do it. Someday you'll look back and wish you had."

If there was one thing Laurel needed now, it was a chance to get rid of at least one loose end, never mind that the rest of her life was like ten yards of tangled fringe. So she'd surprised herself by agreeing that it might be a good time to check out whatever it was she'd inherited in North Carolina.

"You know what?" Laurel said now, her hands going still. "I'm feeling really weird."

"I know you are, but look, everything happens for the best."

"Peg, the eternal optimist," jeered Laurel, and she placed the last item in her suitcase, folded with military precision and closed the suitcase.

When the letter had come shortly after she'd gotten back from Atlanta, where she'd gone some months ago to arrange for her father's burial, she'd still been grieving in her own quiet, unemotional way. Busy trying to play catch-up at work, she had scanned the letter, which was written mostly in legalese, filed it under *P* for pending and forgotten it until Peg had reminded her of her so-called interests in North Carolina.

How big was a quarter-interest in a tract of land? How big was a tract? Bigger than a city block? If so, she probably owed a fortune in taxes.

John James Lawless, the father she had barely known, had been brilliant, impractical and largely absent from her life. As his only child, Laurel had given him due respect. As for love, that was one of those messy emotions that defied definition. She knew like from dislike, but love was more complicated.

At least she'd done her duty. As he'd allowed his insurance to lapse, she hadn't thought twice about dipping into her meager savings to pay his burial expenses on top of her travel expenses to and from Atlanta. Since then she had consoled herself with the thought that her parents were together again, traipsing around unhampered in Heaven. Or wherever.

Orderly by nature, Laurel had managed her grief by rationalizing it and then setting it aside. She had a life to get on with. Now, after seven months and one week, the occasional sense of emptiness—it felt more like rootlessness—had lessened, but she still missed knowing he was somewhere in the world, and might drop in on her at any moment. He'd usually managed to visit once or twice a year, with no regard at all to her own schedule.

In some ways she missed her mother, too, although Elizabeth Lawless had died a long time ago. Actually, neither of her parents had played a large part in her upbringing. She had more or less raised herself, and done a pretty good job of it, if she did say so herself.

Holding in her hands the watercolor Jerry gave her, Laurel wondered not for the first time what had her father been doing with property in North Carolina. With property anywhere, for that matter. If either of her parents had had a theme song it would've been "We're Movin' On."

"Oh, go ahead—pack the damn thing," Peg exclaimed. "You never know how long you'll be gone. What if they've found a few oil wells your father owned but forgot to include in his will? He was in oil, wasn't he?"

"He designed software for petroleum companies, he wasn't *in* it. People don't own oil, corporations do. Stockholders…I guess."

"You don't know that for a fact."

Laurel would be the first to admit that there was a lot she didn't know as fact. She did, however, know better than to believe in fairy tales. At the end of probate, her father's estate had pretty much balanced out, credit-and-debit-wise, except for this one loose end. Before leaving Atlanta she had donated his clothes to Goodwill, including two pairs of size twelve snake boots, a fedora she'd almost been tempted to keep and two Italian silk suits. The letter concerning the one-fourth interest in an undivided tract of land in northeast North Carolina had come a few weeks later. She was pretty sure the property was worthless, as whoever owned the other three fourths hadn't even bothered to get in touch so that she could pay her share of the taxes.

But Peg was right. As long as her career seemed to have slid down a storm drain, there was a certain appealing logic in turning a negative into a positive by winding up this last loose end. Ever since Jay-bass had been shut down, Laurel had been—as Peg's jock friend, Dan, put it—off her game.

In a state of shock was more like it. It was all a ghastly mistake, of course. They'd probably latched onto Jay-bass because it was so small. It must have looked like an easy target. Well, this time they were dead wrong, because Jerry, for all he could be exasperating, was one of the good guys. Smart, handsome, and the sweetest man she'd ever met. She was lucky he'd hired her, luckier still that he'd fallen in love with her, because while she was considered fairly attractive, she'd be the first to admit she could be cranky. And to be honest, she was also something of a control freak, a trait she was trying hard to…control.

# Chapter 2

Driving again after so many years demanded most of her attention. After moving to Manhattan nearly four years ago, crossing the street had been a major under-taking, but she'd survived. Now she just had to keep the vehicle between the lines.

Not until several hours had passed did she allow her mind to stray from between the lines to Jerry. One of the things she liked about him was that he valued fam-ily things. With a fancy apartment full of really im-pressive art and antiques, he treasured that tacky little watercolor enough that he'd brought it in recently and hung it directly across from his desk. Most men were afraid to let their softer side show, but not Jerry.

*Jerry who wouldn't return her calls. Jerry who wouldn't e-mail her—who wouldn't even scribble a few lines and send them by snail mail!*

The SUV that had been riding her bumper whipped out and passed. Irritated, she switched on the radio to hear someone talking about Homeland Security. Great. According to Dan, that was probably what was behind the Jay-bass investigation. She switched to an all-music station and after several miles, managed to relax her death grip on the steering wheel. She was half tempted

to turn around and go back. She could sell the secondhand car Dan had helped her buy last week—the first
one she'd owned since her junior year in college. She
could have bought a complete outfit for what it took to
fill the gas tank.

What was almost as bothersome was the fact that she
didn't know whether she was running away from something or running toward something. Hadn't a clue. And
that alone was totally out of character because being in
control was important to her—probably because it was
the one thing she'd lacked as a child. Move here, move
there—one semester in this school, another in that
school. The daughter of a mostly unemployed anthropologist and a petroleum software designer who occasionally popped in unannounced for a brief visit, she'd
barely known her parents. Occasionally they'd allowed
her to tag along for a few weeks during summer vacation, but for the most part she never knew if she was
going to end up in a Middle East desert, sleeping on a
pallet in a neighbor's house, or in a summer camp in
the Poconos. The closest thing to a permanent home
she'd ever had was the house in Connecticut her parents had rented for several years. She'd been in grade
school at the time, while her mother had been writing
her second book.

So far as she knew, neither of them had ever actually
owned any property, which was what made this so-
called inheritance such a hoot. Imagine—Laurel Ann
Lawless, landed gentry.

Well, maybe not "gentry."

Probably not "landed," either. She'd just have to see
about that.

At least she hadn't forgotten how to drive. Her middle-aged red Honda performed beautifully. Dressed for the road in her most comfortable jeans and a sleeveless top, she drove no more than four miles above the limit—which might be the reason she was always being passed by impatient motorists who honked and occasionally flipped her the bird.

After stopping roughly every three hours to stretch and breathe, her tension headache gradually faded and her trapeziums no longer felt like granite. By the time she crossed into Virginia she was physically exhausted, but mentally relaxed to the point where she actually found herself singing along with Sarah Brightman. Fortunately, Sarah couldn't hear her.

If her left brain hadn't completely ceased functioning, she would have made reservations online before she'd left home. On the other hand, who knew how far she would get the first day? After checking out motel prices, she was tempted to save a few bucks by sleeping in the car, but she really needed a shower. The cheapest room she could find was twice what she'd hoped to spend; the bed nothing to brag about, but by that time she could have slept on a bed of nails.

So it was a day and a half after she left her Murray Hill apartment that she peeled off I-95 and headed east toward the town of Columbia, North Carolina. The letter from her father's executor had mentioned Columbia as being the jumping-off point to her property.

The jumping-off point? That didn't exactly sound encouraging. Nevertheless, she braced herself to jump.

Using only the light of a LED flashlight, the stocky red-haired man prowled through the trashed offices. It was the first time he'd felt safe coming back. Even now, he didn't care to advertise his presence by turning on the lights.

According to Jerry, all the copies had been destroyed except for one, but Kirk didn't trust the bastard. It was Jerry's name on the ATM card when he'd told him—dammit, he'd *told* him they both needed a card in case something happened to one of them.

There *had* to be another copy somewhere—someplace the Feds might've overlooked. The place was still a wreck. Some jerk had spilled ashes on Jerry's precious Oriental rug and the drawers of his fancy-ass desk had been pulled out, dumped and left on the floor. Even the crummy gold-framed art he was so proud of was lined up on the floor, face to the wall.

Kirk raked back his hair and swore. Dammit, if Blessing thought he could cut him out of his share, he'd turn in the bastard himself. What could they do to him? It was Jerry's name on the account.

"Cool down, I told you it's in a safe place," Jerry had said the first time they'd been able to talk after the initial inquisition. "Once they call off the dogs we're good to go."

The dogs were gone, but Jerry still wasn't talking. "Just wait," he kept saying, as if they had all the time in the world.

Blessing could hang around if he wanted to, but the minute Kirk got his share, he was out of here. Gone, like yesterday.

His own office was little more than a closet, which suited him fine, because he rarely used it. Jerry could put on the dog with his fancy pictures and his big, shiny furniture, but they both knew who did all the work.

Opening the door to Laurel's cubbyhole, he had to

laugh. Damn bitch. She didn't like him any more than he liked her. Whenever he got a chance he liked to mess up her desk, toss a few pieces of scrap paper on the floor, as if it had missed her trash basket because he knew it drove her nuts. Now someone else had done it for him. Posters and flyers all over the floor as though a hurricane had blown through.

"Serves you right," he muttered.

Back in Jerry's office, he got to thinking about how tight those two had been right up until the shit hit the fan. Could they be playing him for a fool? Jerry said he'd hidden the single copy he hadn't flushed and handed it off to Laurel in a way she wouldn't even know she had it. She'd been hauled in for questioning same as the rest, right down to the part-time bimbo who ran errands and handled his paperwork.

"Jerry, you gold-plated jackass, what the hell were you thinking!" he'd said the first time they'd managed to talk after Kirk had been called back from Nashville.

"What she doesn't know, she can't tell."

Kirk had wanted to wipe that smug look off his face, but when Jerry had finally told him where he'd hidden the thing, he had to admit, it was clever. Inconvenient, but damned clever.

"Look, she thinks my mother painted the damn thing. She'll guard it with her life, believe me."

"Where'd it come from?" Kirk had asked at the time.

"Bought it at a yard sale. Impulse—you know how it is."

Kirk didn't know how it was, but he knew his partner. Jerry never did anything on impulse. In his own way he was as anal as the Lawless woman.

Thinking about it now brought on a fresh surge of acid to his gullet. Could the two of them be…?

Nah. Jerry wouldn't do that, not when they'd planned everything so carefully, skimming the cream in small enough amounts to pass under the radar. Took longer that way, but it was a hell of a lot safer.

At least, that had been the plan.

The door opened cautiously and Jerold Blessing slipped into the room. He switched on a table lamp. "I thought I'd find you here. I called Taylor to see if I could start cleaning up the mess they left." Sam Taylor, the agent in charge of the investigation that was all but finished, had given him the all clear. That didn't mean they weren't still watching for any sudden affluence or any break in their usual habits.

Kirk studied the man with whom he'd joined forces nearly eight years ago on the West Coast. There were dark shadows under Blessing's eyes and he was about three weeks past needing one of those two-hundred-buck haircuts he liked to brag about.

"Look, there's nothing here, I told you that," Jerry said tiredly. "If I'd left a copy here, they'd have found it. They reamed out my apartment same as they did yours, same as they did this place."

"You weren't even going to tell me where you put it. What—were you going to wait for the all clear and bug out?" Kirk Candless didn't know which hurt more: the loss of all the money they'd been stockpiling or the loss of his best friend.

Jerold Blessing, self-styled CEO and amateur crook, closed his eyes. They were shadowed against the pallor of his face so that he looked dead…or dying.

He was neither. What he was, was in way over his

head. "I told you, I didn't have time to think, I just acted."

"Right. You handed everything off to your girlfriend."

"I told you Laurie doesn't even know she has it, but I made sure she'll keep it safe."

"Yeah? Well, your little pigeon's flown the coop, so now what do we do? Twiddle our goddamned thumbs? I *told* you to stash it in at least two places! Didn't I tell you? But oh, no—you always know best! Don't put it in the computers," Kirk Candless mocked, "that's the first place they look, and no hard copies, oh dear, no!" He swore again. "I hope to hell you're satisfied, because I'm sure as hell not. I want my share and I want it yesterday!"

Under a rumpled Armani suit, Jerry Blessing's shoulders sagged. "Look, I'll get it back, all right? I had all of, what—twenty minutes notice? What did you want me to do, memorize all those numbers and swallow the paper it was written on? And do what with the ATM card?" He bent over and picked up an autographed photo of a third-rate rock group that was lying under a chair. "At least I knew better than to leave a computer trail. If I'd burned the damned thing, they'd have smelled smoke. If I'd tried to flush it, the damn john would have stopped up. I'm telling you, it's safe where it is, all right? Now get off my back!" He ran a hand though his lank, black hair.

"I don't care how you do it, just get it back. I'm not hanging around here until some smart-ass decides to ream me out again, I want my share now!"

"Shut up! Just shut the hell up!" Jerry shrilled. "I had the place checked for bugs, but that doesn't mean they couldn't have planted a few more since then. If you think we're off the hook, you're the one that's crazy."

"Yeah, well—all I'm saying is, you can play their game if you want to, but count me out." The red-haired man stalked to the door.

"Kirk, wait! Don't do anything stupid, dammit! I'm telling you, we're in the clear—just give it another week. I'll call her tonight and tell her we're back in business. She'll be on her way back tomorrow, I guarantee."

"Yeah, like you guaranteed that as long as we kept every transaction under the limit we wouldn't have to worry about getting nailed." Candless stalked out, slamming the door behind him.

Leaving the tax office in the small riverside town, Laurel struggled to readjust her expectations to fit reality. Only minutes after leaving the air-conditioned office she was drenched with perspiration. She opened both car doors to let the heat escape, gazing around at the sluggish dark river, the cypress-lined banks, and that droopy kind of moss that always reminded her of the cover of a Gothic Romance. Control freak or not, one thing she'd never been able to control was her imagination.

Okay, so she hadn't inherited a Tara-style mansion. Not that she'd actually expected anything so grand. So far as anyone in the tax office knew, the only building on the property had sunk into the mud decades ago. The Lawless tract, originally several thousand acres—she still couldn't believe it—several *thousand!*—had been logged out some fifty years ago. A large portion was now owned by one of the federal wildlife organizations, which made her wonder if any of the other three owners had been paid, or if the government had simply condemned what it wanted and moved in. Evidently it had occurred at least a generation ago. For all she knew, her father's share of the proceeds could have paid for her years of boarding school. At this point, it hardly mattered.

Far more interesting was the fact that a portion of what was left was currently being considered by yet another government agency as an OLF. According to a woman in the tax office, that meant an off-landing field or out-lying field—something or other to do with flying and the military.

Best of all, she had learned that there was another Lawless heir living only a few miles away. He had to be a cousin, probably a dozen times removed, but Laurel was almost more excited about that than she was at being landed gentry—or whatever they were.

So she did the logical thing. At least it seemed logical at the time. Hungry, butt-weary, and totally out of her element, she looked up the man's number and called him.

Genealogy had never particularly interested her, probably because it was one thing over which she had no control. Both her parents had been only children and to her knowledge, neither had ever expressed any interest in extended family. She couldn't even remember her grandparents, other than as photographs—although she seemed to recall hearing that one of her grandmothers had taught school in Tennessee and a grandfather had done something on Wall Street and later drowned when a ferryboat sank somewhere in the Gulf of Mexico.

As unlikely as it was, at the age of twenty-nine, Laurel Ann Lawless was beginning to feel an urge to discover her roots.

* * *

Harrison Lawless hung up the phone, absently stroked his jaw and then called through the screen door to his wife. "Company coming."

Cleo had been hosing off the deck where seven-year-old Jimmy had built a mud condominium for homeless mud daubers, modeling it after the ones plastered up under the eaves of the shed roof. He'd poked holes in the wet mud with a pencil for easier access.

"Oh, phoo," she called back. "How many? Do I need to cook something?"

"Just one, and we've got some ham left over, haven't we? I'd better shower and put on a shirt." He'd been weed-whacking earlier. Wild grapes, briars, Virginia creeper and honeysuckle would climb right through the windows if he didn't keep the vines in check.

Cleo came inside, shoving her straw-colored hair off her face. "Who is it? Should I change clothes?"

"Don't bother, you look good enough to eat."

"Then I won't bother to slice the ham. Is it a he or a she?"

"It's a she, and she's apparently my cousin. Claims to have inherited a quarter interest in our swamp." Harrison smiled whimsically at the thought. "Be something if we could finally clear up the title to that damned piece of property we've been paying taxes on, wouldn't it? Not that it's worth anything, but…"

"I know," said his wife, sole owner of his heart and the luxurious log house on the banks of the Alligator River. "You just can't stand having unfinished business hanging over your head. You've come a long way, babe, but you still have a few control issues."

By the time they heard a car pull up outside, Harrison had showered and changed into cargo pants and a clean shirt. Cleo had made pasta salad, iced tea and sliced the ham. There was blackberry cobbler left over from last night and ice cream to à-la-mode it.

"Oh, my…she's pretty, isn't she?" Cleo murmured as they watched through the front window.

Harrison stepped out onto the front deck to greet the woman who claimed to be a distant cousin. So far as he could see there was no sign of family resemblance, not to him or to either of the other present-generation Lawlesses.

Having been born in a suburb of Atlanta, lived in Stamford, Houston, Galveston, Buffalo, and for the past few years, Manhattan, Laurel would be the first to admit she was far more at home in the city. But she had come too far to turn around. She would accomplish what she'd come for and by that time, maybe the whole Jay-bass mess would be cleared up. When that happened, Jerry had a lot to answer for. To say she was disappointed in him was an understatement.

Before leaving the security of her familiar little Honda, she took a moment to admire the rambling log house. Set on a broad, calm river, it had three visible wings, each with its own deck. She tried to picture it in the Hamptons, Jerry's old stomping grounds, but she had a feeling Jerry would prefer something more…polished? Whatever. She was beginning to believe she didn't know him quite as well as she'd thought.

While she was still trying to get her bearings, a man and woman emerged to stand on the front deck. As neither of them looked particularly intimidating, she hooked her purse over her shoulders, took a deep, bracing breath and opened the car door.

The man—that would be her cousin Harrison—was probably in his midforties. A much younger Richard Gere, she decided, only taller and with broader shoulders. His wife—at least, Laurel assumed the woman was his wife—could have passed for Nicole Kidman in the latter part of *Cold Mountain.*

I've got to stop thinking in movie terms, she thought. It was a habit she'd fallen into during her early career as a reviewer. She knew better than to judge a book by its cover, but then, who didn't occasionally make snap decisions?

The tall, dark-haired man came out to meet her, wearing a smile that warmed his dark gray eyes. "Laurel? I'm Harrison. Come on inside. Cleo's set out a cold supper. This is my wife, Cleo—honey, this is Laurel. You haven't eaten, have you?"

Actually, she was starved, as she hadn't stopped to eat since leaving the interstate. "Oh, please—don't go to any trouble. I just thought we might…"

We might what? Now that she was finally here, all the questions about family relationships and fractions of inherited property were caught in a mental logjam. Besides, she needed to use the bathroom.

It was her cousin-in-law, Cleo, who came to her rescue. "You probably want to freshen up. Come on in, I'll show you around, then we'll all have something to eat while you and Harrison catch up."

Again Laurel looked for a family resemblance, but then, as she and her father were the only Lawlesses she'd ever known, she might easily have missed it. Before it had turned gray, her dad's hair had been medium brown, several shades lighter than her own, his eyes more blue than gray. Basically, Harrison and she were both gray-eyed brunettes, but his hair was sprinkled with silver and her own eyes were actually greenish gray if you looked close up.

In the bathroom she took a few minutes to revive herself. Not only was she totally out of her element, but her knees felt wobbly from having been cooped up in a compact car for nearly two days. Besides that, she had no idea what questions to ask without sounding like an opportunist. *I came down here to claim my inheritance, but I'm even more interested in learning about my family?*

Oh, sure. As if they'd believe that.

She emerged from the bathroom somewhat refreshed, but still unsure of what to expect. These people were strangers, but they seemed pleasant enough. Following the sound of voices, she joined her hosts in the kitchen. "Thanks, I feel like I might survive," she said, taking in the attractive blend of rustic and modern. Log walls, stainless steel appliances, several childish drawings on the refrigerator door.

Following her gaze, Cleo said, "My son, the artist. You've got to meet Jimmy. He's actually mine by my first husband, but he might as well be a Lawless, the way he tries to imitate Harrison."

Harrison tapped her playfully on the arm as she dumped a handful of silver on the table. He let his hand linger to stroke her there. "When did I ever pile a bucketful of mud on your front porch?" he teased.

Alone and hundreds of miles from all that was dear and familiar, Laurel envied them their obvious closeness. She had never felt that close to anyone, not her parents, not Peg—not even Jerry.

As it turned out, the whole evening was like that. Easy and surprisingly comfortable, talking about this and that while they ate ham and pasta salad with feta cheese and homegrown onions and peppers. As Harrison was originally from New York, they had lots of notes to compare. And though he'd obviously traveled in loftier circles than she did, they found several places in common to discuss.

All the while Laurel searched for something familiar—the way he stroked his chin when he was considering something. Her father had done that. And the way he sounded when he laughed.

During a lull in the conversation, Cleo mentioned that she grew the vegetables they were enjoying out on the deck in planters because of the deer and rabbits. "Even alligators," she claimed.

"I didn't know alligators were vegetarians," Laurel said.

Harrison shook his head and said, "Knock it off, honey, she believes you."

"Do I look that naive?" she asked.

When they both nodded, Laurel had to laugh. It occurred to her that she hadn't laughed in weeks.

The tract of land that had brought her down to North Carolina was never mentioned and Laurel didn't know how to bring it up without sounding crass. Actually, it no longer seemed as important as getting to know someone who had the same genetic roots, however many generations ago.

After yawning twice over supper and again over postprandial decaf, she apologized, blaming it on Hondalag. Actually, it was more like endless weeks of shock and uncertainty that included searching for a temporary job in a down-turned economy and waiting for a phone call that never came.

They both insisted she stay overnight, as the nearest motel was miles away and probably booked solid. "We have lots of empty rooms, and besides, you need to meet Jimmy," Cleo reminded her. "He's spending the night with another of your cousins, but they'll be here early in the morning."

*Another* cousin? Had she landed on an anthill of Lawlesses?

But by that time Laurel was too tired to argue. Cleo led her to a guest room in what she laughingly called the west wing. Varnished log walls with white chinking, wide plank floors, crocheted rugs and country antique furniture. All Laurel was interested in was the big sleigh bed.

Actually, that was not quite true. There were at least a dozen watercolors hanging on the walls, each one far better—in her estimation, at least—than the one Jerry's mom had painted, that was safely shrouded in her old gray cardigan.

Harrison brought in the suitcase she'd indicated and Cleo lingered to be sure she had everything she needed before saying good-night. By that time Laurel was too tired even to ask questions about this other cousin her son was visiting.

Family, she thought drowsily. Sounded lovely…especially if the other cousin turned out to be as nice as Harrison. She'd withhold judgment until tomorrow.

Tomorrow…

## Chapter 3

Breakfast was whole-grain cereal, decaf and lots of fresh fruit. "Sorry if the menu doesn't suit," Cleo said. "I try to take care of Harrison's health, whether he likes it or not."

Harrison said, "He likes it," and winked at his wife. There was a closeness between them that Laurel envied with all her heart. Was this what a real family was like? She thought that happened only in old TV shows.

Cleo explained that it had been a heart attack that had pried Harrison off the fast track and sent him south in search of the fabled family property. Laurel made a mental note of the early heart attack. That kind of genetic information was important. Her dad had died of a heart attack, too, her mother of a killer flu bug. From now on she might switch from éclairs and Danish to granola bars.

Or not...

Before she could ask about their jointly owned property, her cousin said, "You'll like Travis." He continued to slice figs over his cereal. "His mother was a Lawless." He glanced up, his quick smile a flash of white teeth in a tanned face. "Did Cleo tell you there's another cousin living up in Virginia? Lyon's wife used to be an actress, I believe."

Laurel perked up at that. "An actress? Would I have heard of her?"

"Jasmine Clancy. The name ring any bells?"

"Mmm…not really." After a dreamless eight hours on the world's most comfortable bed, her body had recovered from the trip, but her mind was still scattered like confetti after the Thanksgiving Day Parade.

"I don't think she did anything major, mostly walk-ons back in the early to midnineties."

Cleo said, "Anyway, maybe you'll get to meet the entire clan while you're here. You know you're welcome to stay for as long as you like. As you can see, we have plenty of room."

Laurel stirred her second cup of coffee while she tried to sort out priorities. As crass as it sounded, money was right up there near the top. Her father's funeral expenses plus her round-trip flight to Atlanta, plus her car and its operating expenses, plus her share of last month's rent and utilities, had soaked up most of her savings. She had three hundred and eleven dollars in checking, fifteen left in her savings account to keep it active. Gas was expensive. So was lodging. Maybe she should check out this Virginia connection and see if he could put her up overnight.

"You don't happen to know of any short-term jobs in the area, do you?" she asked, and immediately regretted it.

Cleo raised her eyebrows. Harrison looked thoughtful. "Not right around here, but maybe Trav knows of something down his way. The last time we drove down the banks, I seem to remember seeing Staff Wanted signs all over the place. Most of the jobs there are seasonal."

Cleo said, "He's talking about the Outer Banks in

case you wondered. The trouble is, there's lots of low-pay jobs, but no low-cost housing. How are you with retail?"

"Inexperienced, but a hard worker and a fast learner."

She didn't know if she was a fast learner or not, but she was definitely motivated. She had too much pride to abuse her cousin's hospitality. "What about camp-grounds?" she asked, thinking maybe she could get a temporary job and rent a tent.

Feeling about as secure as a blindfolded trapeze art-ist, she reminded herself that it had been her own deci-sion to come South to check out her inheritance. She could turn around and go back anytime she chose, but once she was back at work again, who knew when she'd find the time? Jay-bass was too small an outfit to offer much in the way of paid vacations.

A few minutes later as they were examining her dis-mal prospects, one of those gutsy-sounding SUVs pulled into the yard. They had taken coffee out onto the front deck where a light breeze off the river kept away the mosquitoes.

"Here's Jimmy now." Cleo went down to meet the lit-tle boy who opened a door and jumped out, waving his hands and talking a mile a minute.

"Mama, Mama, Unca Trab says I'm a good paddler!"

By which Laurel deduced that this was her cousin Travis and he had a boat. Harrison explained the early arrival by saying, "Monday's Trav's day to volunteer at the Aquarium over on Roanoke Island. Did I mention he's a diver? He cleans everything underwater from shipwrecks to tank walls to shark's teeth." He grinned. Laurel was coming to appreciate that easy smile of his.

Both her parents, but especially her dad, had been adventurers. She hadn't inherited that particular trait, but evidently a few of her cousins had.

Jimmy would be a natural for TV commercials. He had that captivating wide-eyed look the cameras loved. Before he even reached the front steps he was bragging about how many fish they'd caught in Unca Trab's net last night and chattering about how humongous someone named Aunt Ru was. "She stays in bed all the time, did you know that? Unca Trab says it 'cause she's nesting, like that ol' duck in the black pond."

Laurel took in the information as it was relayed.

With Jimmy hanging on to one hand, Cleo reached out to hug Travis. "How's she doing?"

"Pretty good. She's bored stiff—read everything in the library, hates daytime TV, picks fights over nothing. Having young James around helps distract her."

"In small doses only," Cleo said, laughing.

Distract her from what? Laurel wondered, but didn't feel free to ask.

Travis Lawless Holiday was about Harrison's age, completely gray, and another young Richard Gere look-alike. Obviously, Laurel mused, the Lawless men shared some pretty fine genes. Her father had been handsome, too, in a mature way.

When they were introduced, Travis took her extended hand, then pulled her into his arms and said, "Hey, cous. 'Bout time you decided to look us up."

By this time she was feeling so much at home, she came right back at him. "You've got that monster truck out there—why didn't you come up to New York and look *me* up?"

"We thought there might be another relative out there in the boonies, we just didn't know who or where."

"The boonies? I happen to live in Manhattan."

"So?" They all laughed as they trooped inside. Travis lingered long enough to nibble on a whole-wheat muffin made with sweet potato instead of shortening, although he turned down a cup of coffee. "A smart man learns not to drink and dive."

Then Cleo said, "Trav, Laurel's going to need a job if she's going to stay around for a while. How's the job market down your way?"

"Plenty of construction work, but I guess that's not what you're looking for, right, Laurel? How about retail? I happen to know of a high-end craft gallery that's losing half its staff now that school's about to start. They're mostly college students."

"She can stay here, but that's a pretty long commute," Harrison said. Evidently her two cousins had taken over planning her immediate future. Was this what families did?

She had to admit that it felt good, as if a weight had slid off her shoulders and onto theirs. And as theirs were much broader than hers, Laurel let them run with it, knowing that at any time she could take back control by getting in her car and heading north again.

*Oh, yeah? And do what?*

"You know the old place Cody was living in?" Travis was saying.

Cody who? she wondered. Not another cousin, surely.

"The guy that rented it back in April moved out last week. Cody was planning on having it reroofed before he rents it out again, but that can wait."

Harrison stroked his jaw. "You need to run it by him first?"

"He's gone to Richmond. I'm not sure when he'll be back, but as long as I'm acting as rental agent, I say, let her have it. It's furnished. Mostly old odds and ends, but we can piece it out."

Laurel moved to stand between them, looking from one to the other. "Run what by who? Whom? Let who have what? How about telling me what you're talking about?"

It was late in the afternoon when Travis came back to the log house on the river after a day spent doing underwater window washing or shark dentistry or whatever it was he really did. By this time Laurel had fallen in love with seven-year-old Jimmy, who'd taught her, among other things, how to spit on a straw, dip it in the dirt and poke it down what he called a doodlebug hole. As they'd never caught anything, she had no idea what a doodlebug looked like, much less why anyone would want to catch one. But she'd had fun. And by late afternoon, she was more relaxed than she'd been in weeks— in months.

As her apartment building rented mostly to young couples and single professionals, Laurel had had little exposure to children since she'd been one herself. Obviously, she'd been missing something. It occurred to her that if she'd gone for a teaching degree instead of ending up with the patchwork career path she had followed, she might not even be here. Which meant she might never have met her two cousins.

The first thing she planned to do when she got back to her old life was to find out how Jerry felt about children. They had never discussed it. Actually, they'd never discussed marriage; it was just sort of taken for granted.

Laurel wanted at least two, though, because she knew what being an only child felt like. Not that Jimmy seemed to be suffering.

Besides, if Cleo's loose shirts and the sounds she'd heard coming from the bathroom in the other wing early this morning were anything to go by, that situation might change in another six months or so. Cleo hadn't mentioned it and Laurel hadn't asked, but early-morning barfing usually had only one cause.

Hugging her newfound family goodbye, her eyes burned and her throat felt so thick she could hardly speak. She put it down to allergies, as she'd never been sentimental. Or it might be the fact that she was about to head off to an unknown destination, based solely on a decision between two men she barely knew, involving another man who wasn't even related. For all she knew they could be selling her as a sex slave to some potbellied potentate instead of merely setting her up with a temporary job and a leaky roof over her head.

Talk about being in control!

Before they left, Travis gave her a map, pointed out where they were headed and gave her directions for finding his house in case they got separated. Not until after they had crossed two bridges and were headed for a third did Laurel realize that she had a death grip on the steering wheel. She deliberately forced herself to relax.

*Breathe slowly,* she commanded silently. She was not jumping off the ends of the earth, it only looked that way. She was among family. Her friends knew where she was.

The trouble was, she read too much suspense and not enough poetry. Bad stuff happened just when you let your guard down.

By the time they'd crossed Oregon Inlet Bridge her shoulders had stiffened up again. Traffic was surprisingly heavy on the narrow two-lane highway 12 with everything from monster trucks to convertibles hauling surfboards to SUVs bristling with fishing rods. Nothing at all like back home, but then, the streets were wider there.

Rolling down the window, she allowed the salt air to whip over her face. Her last beach vacation had been eight years ago when a group of college friends had spent a week in Daytona. She had sweated off her sunscreen, blistered her thighs and shoulders, lost her favorite charm bracelet and been sick as a dog from something she'd eaten, probably the sushi. She'd give it a try, but she wasn't promising anyone anything. Her real life was back home in New York, no matter that she'd hit a snag.

Some forty minutes later she followed Travis's Suburban up a steep driveway to a plain shingled cottage surrounded by live oaks, overgrown shrubbery, bird feeders and masses of flowers, none of which she could identify. She set the parking brake, forced herself to control her breathing while she listened to the tick of cooling metal. Maybe she'd crawled too far out on a limb of the family tree. What if she couldn't find her way back?

Panic threatened. She regulated her breathing and controlled the direction of her mind. She still had a little money. She had her own wheels. She had road maps. She could back down the driveway right now and retrace her route off the island. By tomorrow night, or the next one, she could be back in her own cramped apartment, waiting for the phone to ring.

Travis unloaded two large sacks of sunflower seed and propped them against the house. Then he sauntered back to where she was parked and opened her door. "Ready to risk getting out? I hope you weren't expecting anything fancy. I was single again when I built this place." He indicated the rectangular, one-story shingled cottage with a variety of antennae sprouting from the roof.

*Single again?*

"Then I met Ru and everything changed. I've added on so we have plenty of room for guests, even a nursery." It occurred to her that he was giving her time to adjust. Had he guessed at her insecurities?

God, she hoped not. Being reserved was okay. Falling apart whenever she was out of her comfort zone was embarrassing.

As soon as she released her sweaty grip on the door, Travis swung it open. "I guess Harrison told you about Lyon and Jasmine. Lyon's another cousin. Second, I think. I've been meaning to sort us all out, but you know how it is…."

Laurel nodded as if reaching out to kinfolk was something she did all the time. "He mentioned him and his wife. I'm trying to keep all the limbs and branches and twigs straight, but coming all at once, it's not easy."

Before Travis had showed up to lead her home with him, Harrison had told her something about the property that, as it turned out, had finally succeeded in bringing them together. "Travis is the only one of us who's always lived in the area," Harrison had said. "Lyon lives in northern Virginia, but he has a place at Hatteras, a few miles from where Travis lives. We usually manage to get together at least once a year."

A family gathering. She had dreamed of something

like that, but it would be a long drive, and besides, she wasn't sure how Jerry would like Hatteras Island. It wasn't exactly posh.

"So, who actually lived in our swamp?" Laurel had asked. She'd been fascinated to learn that the property had originally belonged to a mutual ancestor whose name was Squire Lawless, Squire being his given name, not his title.

"That was old Squire. He built a house there, but it sank in the mud. You do know, don't you, that he was a moonshiner and a bootlegger? That's manufacturing and distribution, in case you were wondering. They say he had sales reps covering a route that ran all the way up to the Canadian border."

"Nice to know we're descended from a successful entrepreneur," Laurel had quipped at the time. "Now I know where my father got his wanderlust."

"You mentioned your father was involved in oil production."

"Software. He could do incredible things to make the stuff go where it was supposed to go or something. He was never good at explaining, and frankly, I'm not technically oriented."

"What about your mom?"

"Oh, she was almost as big a traveler as Dad was. She was an anthropologist. She wrote lots of articles and was working on a book when she died. I'm not sure what became of her notes—I guess Dad has them. Had them," she amended, knowing that her father had rarely kept anything he didn't actually need in his own work.

So much for family keepsakes.

"How did she die? You said your dad died of a heart attack."

"She was in Ireland while Dad was doing something on one of those huge North Sea oil rigs. She caught a cold or maybe flu and ignored it, and within a week she was gone. I was in boarding school in Connecticut at the time."

Harrison hadn't said anything. Instead, he'd reached across the table and laid a hand over her knotted fists in a gesture so easy and natural it had made her eyes water.

She *never* lost control of her emotions, having learned a long time ago that the only thing crying ever accomplished was clogged sinuses and a red nose.

That was this morning. Now she stood beside another cousin on the high wooded hill where his house was located, wondering what, if anything, to take inside. Decisions, decisions…

Pointing to a white house half-hidden by trees on the other side of the narrow highway and down a few hundred feet, Travis said, "There's your place, the one you'll be renting. The tall house over there—" he pointed to a shingled double-decker with white trim "—belongs to the owner, Cody Morningstar." He looked at her as if he expected her to say something.

"That's nice. It looks like something Grandma Moses might have painted, doesn't it?"

"Grandma who?"

Evidently, he wasn't into art. "Painter who liked old houses."

"It's old, all right. This the bag you want?" He reached for her largest suitcase. "What else?"

"Oh, no, just the little one." She had organized her packing the way she organized everything else. Once she settled down long enough to rinse out a few things, she might not even have to unpack the bags in the trunk of her car.

At the moment she was half tempted to crawl back in her car, lock the doors and stay there for the foreseeable future. Or at least until Jerry called to tell her to come back home.

Of course, her car didn't have a bathroom....

"Come on inside and meet my wife. She, uh—I guess they told you she's majorly pregnant. Actually, she's been having a few problems, so mostly, she stays in bed or on the couch."

Great. Just what she needed—two strangers, one of them an invalid. "Look, I can easily go to a hotel. I don't want to be a bother."

"You're no bother at all. Ru needs a distraction— that's why I took Jimmy home with me overnight. You're just what the doctor ordered."

"Travis, are you sure?"

Travis leaned against her car, his arms crossed. In no way did he let on that she was a pain, although he must have thought it, because she was. Exhibiting far more patience than most of the men she knew, he said, "Laurie, I wouldn't have offered if I didn't think it would do Ru good to have company."

She'd told him her friends called her Laurie, not Laurel. Some did, some didn't, but she liked it. He said, "I do the cooking and clean-up. All you need to do is entertain your hostess, take her mind off her problems. My son's away visiting his mother, so you can have his room until I open up your place and turn on the utilities."

His son. Another cousin?

Her brain was beginning to feel like a pinball machine.

Travis's wife was named Ruanna. She said to call her Ru. She was beautiful in the classic style of movie stars back in the fifties and sixties, with expressive eyes and gorgeous cheekbones.

She was also *extremely* pregnant.

Of course, Travis Lawless Holiday was no slouch in the looks department, either. Not for the first time she thought that when she and Jerry got around to starting a family, their children stood to inherit some pretty fine genes.

"Move those magazines and sit down and tell me everything," Ru said, and then she chuckled. "But first, if you travel like I do, you'll want to freshen up. Help yourself—towels in the lower cabinet. Then come back and tell me all about yourself. D'you mind if I'm terribly nosy?"

Laurel laughed and said she didn't mind at all. While she used the bathroom, Travis called the owner of the crafts gallery and set up an interview for nine in the morning, an hour before the place opened.

"All set," he said when she rejoined them in the living room. "You're a shoo-in, they're desperate."

"Thanks…I think."

Ru laughed and said, "That's my husband, tactful as always." Did she imagine it or was there a little grit in her voice? "Trav, did you tell her about Cody?"

Evidently, Laurel thought, she'd imagined it. "Tell me what about Cody?" All Laurel knew was that a man named Cody Morningstar was hopefully going to be her landlord.

Travis said, "He can tell her if he wants to. It doesn't matter."

"Tell me what? That he's a werewolf? That he has three eyes? That he plays trap drums and likes to practice between the hours of 4:00 and 6:00 a.m.?"

Travis said gravely, but with a twinkle in his eyes, "I

happen to know he likes his beef well-done. He has the normal quota of eyes and if he plays any instrument louder than a pennywhistle, I've never heard it, and I'm usually up before daybreak if I've got any nets out."

A few minutes later Ru was telling her about the best places to shop when she got this funny little smile on her face. "Laurie, do you believe in ghosts?" Turning toward her husband, "Trav, did you tell her that her house is supposed to be haunted?"

"Aw, come on, Ru—don't start that."

"Hey, I adore ghosts!" Laurel could dish it out as well as she could take it. She'd had some practice, especially with Jerry's partner, Kirk, who didn't like her any more than she liked him. But then, she didn't have to work with him. Kirk rounded up the so-called talent, Jerry signed them on and booked the hall and Laurel took over from there.

"That reminds me," Laurel said. "How's cell phone reception down here?"

"Depends on your service. We've got a few iffy spots, but if your cell phone doesn't work you can use our landline until we get your utilities hooked up."

After explaining that she wouldn't be here long enough to hook up a phone line, she excused herself and went outside to try the cell phone she'd left in the car. Now that she knew where she was going to be for a week or so, she could call Peg, who could pass the word to Jerry.

Of course, Jerry could have called her anytime on her cell phone, only he hadn't. Peg said he probably had this crazy idea about lines being tapped and about not wanting to involve her in his problems. Which was a bit paranoid, because she was on record as an employee.

Besides, surely by now he'd been cleared of anything other than careless bookkeeping.

Peg picked up on the fifth ring. "Yeah?" Her phone manners were casual, at best.

"Peg, turn down the noise." A ball game was playing full blast on Dan's big speakers. Laurel shuddered, thinking of how her living room must look after only a few days. "Look, I need you to tell Jerry that I'm staying in a place called Frisco—it's on Hatteras Island, on the Outer Banks in North Carolina. He can get me on my cell phone here. At the moment, I'm staying with a cousin, but—"

Peg tried to interrupt, but Laurel needed to get her message across first, because once Peg started talking, she never knew when to stop. "Starting probably tomorrow I'm renting this old house, and I'm interviewing in the morning for a temporary job, and I guess that's about it, except that like I said, my cell phone works here, so Jerry can call me anytime he wants to."

Peg finally broke though. "Oh, God, Laurie! I've been trying to call you ever since yesterday."

"I forgot to turn it on after I recharged."

"Someone broke in!" she exclaimed in a voice that didn't even sound like Peg.

"Broke in what?"

"The apartment, silly! I got home from work yesterday and the door was unlocked, and everything was dumped out all over the floor—even the stuff in the kitchen, like sugar and salt and even my herb tea!"

It took a moment for it to register. That's what distance will do for you, Laurel mused before she could pull herself together. It puts you in a totally different reality. "You didn't lock the door?"

"Well, of course I locked it, I *always* lock up!"

She wasn't about to accuse Dan, who was casual, to put it kindly. "Where was Dan?"

"At work! Anyhow, I called the police, and they came and did whatever it is they do, but as far as I can tell, nothing was taken—not even Dan's sound system, and that's worth a small fortune."

Laurel took a deep, controlled breath. Break-ins were a fact of life, even in the quiet neighborhood where they lived. But it had never happened to them personally.

"Do I need to come back?" she asked quietly, shocked at how much she didn't want to return yet.

"To do what? Play *CSI* and dust for fingerprints? I told you, nothing was taken! The lock wasn't even broken, so that means somebody has a *key!*"

"Peg. Stop shouting. It's over now. Calm down."

She heard her friend draw in a deep breath and expel it in a single gust. "Okay, but look, I'm in the process of getting the lock changed."

Laurel started to say something about the horse and the barn door, but decided flippancy wouldn't be appreciated.

"Talk about a mess, it took me all day to clean up. I didn't even go in to work yesterday, and I'm still pissed about my tea. Did I mention that every single one of Dan's CDs was taken out of the case and dumped on the floor? He cussed for a solid five minutes, I kid you not."

Feeling helpless, and even a little guilty because she hadn't been there to help with the cleanup, Laurel ended the call and stood for a few minutes, staring out at a colorful sunset that was reflected perfectly on the still water of the Pamlico Sound. From inside the house she could hear the quiet murmur of voices. Ru sounded snappish.

Trav said something short and then she heard a cabinet or a door slam.

So much for sweetness and light. Evidently they had a few issues, and rampant hormones probably didn't help. Laurel didn't know much about it, but it must be like mega PMS.

Leaning against her car, she watched the first few stars emerge, giving them time to cool off. One night and then she'd be under her own roof. They could have as much space as they needed to work out whatever problems they had.

She had problems of her own. If she were back in New York, she'd be having to deal with a break-in on top of everything else that had gone wrong in her life. Not that she particularly believed in astrology, but had every single planet suddenly gone retrograde?

Her whole life seemed to have gone retrograde.

Sighing, she willed Jerry to pick up the phone and call her, if only to tell her how he was holding up. Or to ask how she was doing. To give her some idea of when things would settle back to normal and they could be together again.

*What am I doing here? I don't really know these people, and besides, who cares about a few acres of swamp?*

# Chapter 4

By nine-forty-seven the next morning, Laurel was gainfully employed and feeling vaguely guilty about it because she'd just promised to stay on through the Labor Day weekend. Which meant that if Jerry called and wanted her back at work tomorrow, she would have to choose, and at this point she wasn't sure she was capable of making a fair choice.

Damn Jerry, anyway, for putting her in this awkward position!

When the doors opened at Carolina's Craft Gallery, she was standing behind the counter, trying desperately to assimilate all she'd just learned concerning computer codes, various artists and store policy. The owner's name was Caroline, not Carolina, but as she'd explained, in a high-end gallery a bit of artistic license was permissible.

It was after six when the Open sign was taken down. Laurel didn't know which was more exhausted, her brain or her body. I can do this, she assured herself as she eased under the steering wheel, leaned her head against the headrest and closed her eyes. The pay was pathetic, but at least if she lasted through the end of August she could add it to her résumé.

Just in case....

Travis was up on the roof doing something to one of his antennae when she pulled up into his driveway. His rangy silhouette blended with the gray-green oak limbs that surrounded his house. Shading her eyes, she watched him for a moment, half tempted to ask him if one of his antennae could get in touch with the nearest satellite and find out what the heck was going on up there that was screwing up stuff here on planet Earth.

"How'd it go?" he called down, and when she assured him that it had gone well, with no real disasters, he said, "Your house is all ready for occupancy."

"Right. My haunted house." Squinting against the sun, Laurel watched him climb down the ladder. Cousin or not—married or not—he was a man worth watching. Lean, broad-shouldered, his prematurely gray hair was a striking contrast to his darkly tanned face.

"Hey, a few friendly ghosts never hurt anybody." He grinned, and she almost forgot her aching feet. "Come on inside," he said, "it's a lot cooler. Ru's waiting to hear all about your first day."

He was right about that. Ru was reclining on the sofa, nursing a tall glass of chocolate milk. "It's about time you got here," she greeted. "Now, tell me everything. Who bought what? Were they locals or tourists? By the way, Trav baked a big flounder with salt pork on top and potatoes and onions around the sides, and you're invited. One thing he knows how to do is cook fish."

One thing? Was that a compliment or a snide remark? Having skipped lunch because she hadn't known to take her own, but pretended she had, she could eat sawdust with chopsticks. "I really should move in while there's still some daylight left." She inhaled the fragrance drifting in from the kitchen. As much as she liked both her cousin and his wife, she didn't want to be a burden. Ru had confided that she'd had trouble in the past carrying a baby past the third month. This time they were taking no chances.

"Hate to tell you, but your cousin is a dictator. He allows me to walk around outside for a few minutes every day, but he's threatened to hide all my clothes if I even look like I'm going any farther than the bottom of the driveway. I told him I'll just rent a tent—if I can find one that fits."

Travis came in with a handful of tools in time to hear his wife's remark, and they all laughed. Whatever issues they might have, Laurel thought—and she might have only imagined the earlier tension—she envied them their relationship. Dinner—or supper, as they called it—was a given.

Trav said, "After we eat I'll go over and help cart your gear inside. I left all the windows open to air the place out, so it'll be hot. You can turn on the bedroom window unit or use the ceiling fans."

"Use the AC," said Ruanna. "With all this water around us, the air never cools down more than a few degrees at night."

Laurel placed her cutlery across her plate and laid her napkin aside, the way she'd been taught at boarding school. "That was delicious! What's your recipe?" Not that she was ever likely to try it.

"If you don't have a gill net and a license to use it, you set out once it's good and dark with a lantern and a flounder gig," he said gravely.

Ru said, "Oh, hush! Laurie, cooking fish is easy. If I can do it, anyone can, believe me. Although I have to admit, Trav's pretty good."

After Laurel washed the dishes and Travis dried and put them away, he led the way to the house that would be hers temporarily. It was that evanescent time of day when the very air seemed to glow with an amethyst light. The sound of insects and tree frogs was loud, but far more pleasant than the traffic noises she was used to.

More than once as they were carting boxes and suitcases inside, Laurel wondered what she'd been thinking when she'd packed practically everything she owned for what was supposed to be a brief trip to check out an inheritance. She hadn't packed any linens, but Ru had lent her more than enough to last and offered the use of her washing machine in case the one there didn't work. Evidently there was no laundry on the island.

"Cody should be back in a few days. That'll be soon enough to sign whatever rental agreement you two settle on."

"I thought you were his rental agent."

"I vet the tenants, he takes care of the paperwork. You all set for the night? I turned on the water heater this morning and you've got my phone numbers if you think of anything you need."

She thanked him and promised to call if anything came up. "Does that include things that go bump in the night?" She was only half joking. The old place might look like the quintessential haunted house, but everybody knew…

"Hey, you're wiped out. Kick off your shoes and turn in, why don't you? You need a wake-up call for in the morning?"

What she needed was a wake-up call retroactively. *Hell-oo. Is there a brain anywhere under all that shaggy hair?*

What the devil had she been thinking?

Answer: she hadn't been thinking; she'd been reacting. That was just one of the things that was going to change. Time to take control again.

Before leaving, Travis insisted on showing her through the house that had to be at least a hundred years old. Evidently it had once been owned by some distant relative of Travis's mother, which gave her an odd feeling. Someone had once told her that life was like a crocheted doily, full of tiny links that were endlessly connected.

She was beginning to believe it.

"It might be noisy," Travis apologized for the third time. "Creek out behind the house…bullfrogs."

"Let 'em croak, I could sleep through anything." She was just grateful to have a place of her own, even if the kindest word she could think of to describe it was picturesque. "And before you warn me again, I don't believe in ghosts. On the other hand, old plumbing and old wiring, not to mention leaky roofs—those are another matter."

"Just stick your head out the door and holler if you run into any trouble. If I'm home, I'll come a-running. Or you can come on over. Like I said before, company helps keep Ru's mind off her problems."

They had both joked about her problems over supper. Ru had complained about having to stay off her feet for the last few weeks before she was due to deliver. "If my ankles weren't so swollen I think he'd use leg chains to keep me prisoner."

Travis had said, "I'm considering using an anchor." He'd made it sound like a joke…almost. It was probably only her overworked imagination that made her think there might be more that neither of them wanted to bring up.

Laurel had rushed to fill the uncomfortable silence. "What about books? I brought along a few of my keepers."

"Just drop by when you have time, that'll be even better," Trav had said. "She's heard all my stories by now. All I can do is keep her supplied with chocolate and rub her back."

"Oh, poor thing!" Laurel had said.

She thought now she must have imagined it. The tension. They were sweet together, she thought wistfully. She should be so lucky.

It was almost dark as she stood on the front porch watching Travis lope down the road. His place was on the Pamlico Sound, across the island's only highway, within easy walking distance, which she found comforting. Not that she intended to make a nuisance of herself.

She'd noticed as they'd driven down the rutted driveway the difference in the neatly mowed lawn surrounding her absentee landlord's house and the scraggly, weed-filled yard surrounding the old house. Then she'd caught a glimpse of an intermittent sweep of light across the treetops. It had to be the lighthouse she'd seen while driving down the beach. Neat, she thought. Maybe she would even climb to the top before she went back, just to say she had.

Taking one last look at the scrubby forest that was punctuated with the pale ghosts of dead pines—victims of earlier hurricanes, according to Travis—she thought that if ever there was a place where ghost stories seemed plausible, this just might be it.

Good thing her head had been screwed on tightly at

an early age. She'd been called a few unflattering things, control freak being the most frequent. The one thing she'd never been called was fanciful.

She had also never been called house-proud, but the furniture was pathetic. The first thing she would do was rearrange it.

No, the first thing was to touch base with her real life. Dropping down onto a tapestry-covered sofa that had aged to a nasty shade of gray-green, she punched in Jerry's cell phone number. It rang three times and cut off. Damned inconsistent high-tech gadgets.

She whacked it on her palm a few times, as if that would jump-start it, then laid it aside. Just as well he hadn't answered. She was so exhausted she probably wouldn't have been able to carry on a rational conversation, much less explain why she was calling when he'd all but ordered her not to.

But she so needed to hear his voice. After all these weeks of silence, she was beginning to wonder if she'd imagined him.

"Ho-kay, let's look on the bright side," she said standing to survey her new living room with its white-painted wooden walls, dark-varnished floors and collection of junky furniture. The sofa should be on the other side, the table moved to the far end of the wall, and the ugly recliner over in the far corner. And that was just for starters.

On the plus side, she had a roof over her head, even if according to Travis, it leaked like a sieve whenever it rained. She had a job with the promise of a modest paycheck at the end of her first full week. She'd met two cousins and their wives and liked them all. Better still, they seemed to like her. The one she had yet to meet was married to an actress, and according to Trav, they had a cottage on the island they visited several times a year.

Next on the list was to meet and deal with her absentee landlord. According to Travis, he was in Virginia visiting his daughter and his ex-wife. She told herself that any friend of Travis's, especially one who was on visiting terms with his ex-wife and cared enough to visit his daughter, couldn't be too bad.

At the end of her first full week on the job, Laurel collected her first paycheck in nearly four months. She was starting to wonder if she would ever collect the salary Jay-bass still owed her. So far she had arranged the living room furniture more to her liking. It was still ugly, but at least it was harmoniously arranged. She had dealt with spiders, a small snake in the bathroom and a crazy noise that sounded like a convention of hyenas, all without indulging in a single paniç attack.

But she was still worried about Peg and the break-in that had occurred. The more she thought about it, the more she wondered why none of Dan's electronics had been stolen. Because it was too bulky? Too heavy? A couple of scrawny kids with a habit to support couldn't easily cart it off without arousing suspicion?

As August was the busiest month of the season and the shop was desperately shorthanded, she lacked both the time and the energy to worry about small details, such as not having paid rent, much less paid a deposit or signed a lease. She had yet to meet her landlord.

Retail was rough duty, and by the time she got home each day her feet ached all the way up to her armpits. As a remedy, she'd quickly fallen into the habit of shedding her clothes, pouring herself a glass of wine from the local grocers, filling the claw-foot bathtub with lavender-scented water and sinking into the rust-stained depths, where she remained until she all but fell asleep. After that she dressed and hobbled to the kitchen to rummage for supper. Back home she'd relied heavily on takeout, but takeout was expensive and she was hoarding her pennies for the trip home.

Then, too, as soon as her landlord showed up she would have to pay for the privilege of sharing this old house with various undomesticated creatures.

Most days she managed a brief visit with Ru, sometimes after work, sometimes before. Occasionally both, if there was some tidbit she wanted to share. She'd learned to enjoy a glass of sweetened iced tea while they chatted about who'd been in the shop, how they looked, what they'd said and so on.

Still no word from Jerry. She was rapidly running out of patience. She'd spoken to Peg several times to see if she'd heard anything from him, or if there'd been any leads on the break-in.

"I left a message with your phone number and address and stuff. I guess he got it—I don't know why he wouldn't," Peg said. She'd sounded worried.

"Anything more about the break-in?"

"Uh-uh, but since they didn't take anything, I doubt if it's a priority."

Laurel doubted it, too. All the same, even though she hadn't been there at the time, she felt as if her privacy had been invaded. As if being hounded by the media and having strangers ask all sorts of intrusive questions hadn't been bad enough, someone had actually dared to break into her apartment and touch her personal belongings. Thank goodness she had cleared out as much as she had to make room for Dan.

Poor Peg. In the nearly three years since they'd moved into the tiny two-bedroom apartment, they'd never had a speck of trouble. Odd that it should happen only a day or two after Dan had moved in. She'd occasionally suspected he had friends in some pretty low places, but as she didn't know that for a fact, she hadn't mentioned it to Peg.

As it was a great beach day, business was slow the next day. According to Caroline, rainy days were standing room only, and since no rain was in the forecast, Laurel was able to leave in time to reach the post office before the window closed. As there was no home mail delivery in any of the villages on the island, she'd had a choice of renting a box or collecting her mail from the window. She wouldn't be there long enough to rent a box. Besides, the only mail she could expect was forwarded bills.

On top of the usual junk mail addressed to box holder, there was a fat envelope from Peg that felt like clippings. Hopefully, there'd been more in the papers concerning what was going on with Jay-bass.

Damn Jerry for not bothering to keep her up-to-date, she thought resentfully as she dumped the flyers in the recycle bin and shouldered her way out the door. She had a few bones to pick with that gentleman once things got back to normal again.

Tossing the envelope onto the passenger seat, she peered around a dark-windowed van that had pulled in too close beside her and cautiously began backing out of the parking slot. She was barely moving when there was a loud crunching noise. Her head flew forward and then hit the headrest.

Cody swore. Becky screamed. BooBoo yapped frantically and hurled his hairy body against the back of the front seat. "Shh, calm down, it's all right," he said to his daughter.

The devil it was. This had been the trip from hell even before some damn fool had backed out without bothering to look and creamed the right front end of the Range Rover. Gripping the steering wheel, he clung to the last slender thread of patience he possessed. The car reeked of vomit, which didn't help. Becky had never been a good traveler, which was only one of the reasons he'd driven instead of flying, the damned mutt being the other.

But far more worrisome was the fact that his daughter had evidently entered a new stage of development where fathers were considered *persona non grata*. Instead of telling him when she needed to stop, she'd held it in and then barfed all over herself.

At least the air bags hadn't deployed.

"My chest hurts, Daddy," the eight-year-old whined. It was the first time she'd addressed him directly in hours.

"Loosen your seat belt, but stay put." Ignoring the yapping dog that kept lunging at him from the backseat, Cody swung open the door. He took his time climbing out until he was certain he could hang on to his badly frayed temper.

He watched as the driver of the other car emerged from a middle-aged Honda. Lucky she was a woman. He'd never struck a woman in his life, never even sworn at one...although he'd been tempted more times than he cared to recall.

He turned to survey the chrome rod holder on his front bumper. It was a write-off, but he hadn't used the thing in over a year. Seeing no apparent structural damage to the front end of his vehicle, he turned back to the woman.

Oh, hell. She looked as though she was about to pass out. The milk of human kindness having long since soured, Cody couldn't dredge up much sympathy, especially considering which one of them was responsible for this mess. She'd come charging out of her parking place like a bat out of hell. Someone, including his daughter, could've been hurt even though he'd been barely crawling, having just turned in off the highway.

The woman had a white-knuckle grip on the door of her faded red Honda. She glared at him. "Where did you *come* from?" she demanded. Her skin was the color of raw dough.

"Where did *I* come from?" What the hell did she think—that he'd dropped from an alien spaceship? "The stork brought me. How about you?"

No sooner did he utter the words than he regretted them, but dammit, he wasn't about to apologize. From force of habit, he took in and cataloged every single thing about her, from her shoes to the top of her dark brown, windblown hair. She was probably attractive enough under normal circumstances. What little he'd heard of her accent placed her well north of the Mason-Dixon Line; he couldn't pin it down to any one locale. Clothes, casual—high-end but definitely not designer.

It was a writer's trick. He never knew when he might need to pull a character out of his mental filing cabinet, so he kept it well stocked.

"Oh, shut up," she said, interrupting his silent inventory. "You were nowhere in sight when I started to back out! Why didn't you stop when you saw what I was doing, or at least blow your horn?"

Flexing his shoulders, he absently massaged the back of his neck with one hand. The post office was located at one end of a small shopping center. There were nearly a dozen vehicles scattered haphazardly along the small parking area, including a couple of pickups and a Jeep pulled up at the gas pumps. There were two entrances to the lot. The first one—the one he'd taken—was located directly across a busy two-lane highway from the entrance to the island's only airstrip and a Park Service campground. The nearest traffic light was half a dozen miles away in another village.

The lady was on a rant. It wasn't the first time he'd been called names, usually involving his parentage and certain animals. This time it was pretty mild. He was stupid, blind, an arrogant jerk who thought that just because his car was bigger than hers, he had the right of way.

Cody figured the least he could do was to let her get it out of her system. To be fair, they were both victims of a population explosion on a small, eroding island that was never meant to hold so many people and their paraphernalia. Which, under the circumstances, was about as charitable as an exhausted, pissed-off and put-upon guy could be.

Not that she appeared to appreciate his tolerance. Her chin was starting to wobble and her eyes had a glittery look. *Just don't start crying, lady. I've had all the tears I can handle for the next few decades.*

"My car didn't have a single scratch on it until you rammed into my rear end," she claimed. "I've had it less than two weeks!"

The thing was at least ten years old, but he waited

while she got it all out of her system. Pale, with blotches of red in her cheeks and the tip of her nose, she might easily have rated a second look—maybe even a third, under normal circumstances.

This wasn't a normal circumstance. Normal meant pounding a keyboard roughly six hours a day, breaking to swim a few miles in the summer, jog along the beach or on various woods trails during the winter. It meant freeing his mind by clearing another half acre or so of the encroaching maritime forest. Normal meant studiously avoiding reading his reviews and jotting off a few scrawled lines in answer to the fan mail his publisher forwarded in batches every week or so.

Normal meant trying to figure out what the hell had gone sour in his relationship with his daughter between now and the last time he'd brought her down here for a visit.

None of which could be blamed on the woman, who looked as if she was about to blow steam out her ears. In direct contrast to her strident tone, he softened his response. "Technically, your right rear collided with my right front end."

Eyes the color of Spanish moss on a rainy day. He tucked the fragment into his mental file. She was hopping mad, and he grudgingly admitted that she looked almost as tired as he was. She had New York plates, so it couldn't have been her first fender bender, regardless of the act she was putting on. But if this was a scam, she could find herself another victim. He wasn't interested.

Becky was still whimpering, but at least she hadn't thrown up again. BooBoo was yapping his fool head off. Did Afghans ever do anything else?

Yeah, they did. That was how he'd got his name.

A few of the onlookers wandered away while a few more emerged from the sporting goods store to assess the damage and offer words of advice.

"Man, tha's gonna cost you," said a shirtless, shoe-less kid with a purple Mohawk. "How much one of them things cost, anyhow, much as a Hummer?"

"It didn't hurt his wheels, man. That rod rack's shot, though. Them things'll rust once the chrome wears off. Me, I go for plastic. Plastic don't rust."

Ignoring the ensuing quality comparisons, Cody reached for his wallet. "Look, I don't have time to hang around, but the highway patrol knows where to find me."

Shaking visibly now, the woman fumbled in her purse for a card. "I really think we should call some-one—at least wait for the police."

"You wait right here, then. Like I said, they know where to find me."

"About insurance…" She drew in a deep, shudder-ing breath, and then another one.

Ah hell, he thought. Any other time he might be a lit-tle more cooperative, but not after five days of doing bat-tle with his ex-wife, her fiancé and her lawyer over custody rights. At the time of the divorce he'd been forced to compromise on too many issues. Thanks to the exaggerated and largely fictional background his pub-lisher had put out, things had threatened to go public in a big way, and that was the last thing any of them—es-pecially Becky—had needed.

Even after he'd got all that straightened out, a bach-elor living alone didn't stand much chance against a beautiful woman who had total command over her tear ducts. One who happened to be engaged to a well-con-nected West Coast lawyer with political ambitions.

"Do you think you can drive?" he asked, too tired to play the role of reckless bastard she'd obviously assigned him.

"Of course I can drive! You're the one who came charging in like—"

He cut her off with a gesture. "A bat out of hell. Right. Message received." He leaned over to see if her rear fender was touching the tire. It wasn't. She was good to go.

"Your thingee is crooked." She pointed to his rod rack.

"Don't you worry about my thingee." Cody had a nasty smile when he cared to employ it. Today, he cared.

Arms crossed, she patted her foot—about a size six, in a light blue suede with a three-inch heel. Writers' minds were reservoirs of trivia.

She continued to glare at him until he turned away. "Dammit, like I needed this," he grumbled as he swung up onto the seat and slammed the door. Speaking quietly, he told Becky to stop crying. He snarled at the dog and then popped him on the nose. The dumb mutt was so startled he actually shut up.

"You hurt BooBoo's feelings," his daughter accused.

"If I'd known it was that easy to shut him up, we wouldn't have had to contend with his yapping all the way from Richmond."

"You hit him with your hand! Mama never hits him with her hand, even when he poops on the floor."

"Your mama—"

What could he say? He was pretty sure Mara considered the overbred Afghan as more of a fashion accessory than a pet, but he wasn't about to criticize his ex-wife in front of her daughter. Pulling away without bothering to pick up all the mail that would have collected in his absence, Cody told himself that just because he'd failed miserably as a husband, that didn't mean he had to fail at fatherhood. At least she was talking to him again.

The first few years, they'd had a pretty fine relationship, if he did say so himself. It was only recently—this particular trip, in fact—that the job of part-time fatherhood seemed to require the patience of Job and the wisdom of Solomon. At the moment, six months behind on a deadline, Cody possessed neither.

Except for the occasional times when she forgot herself, it was almost as if his daughter, the child of his heart, was afraid of him. Each time he tried to find out what was going on in her head, she clammed up. Bribery hadn't helped, it had only made her sick to her stomach.

He would tackle the problem tomorrow, to hell with his deadline. Tomorrow they could cook out on the beach and she'd beg him to let her ride a wave and cover him with sand, and insist on racing him along the beach. It was damned hard for a guy who stood six foot two to race with a kid and allow her to win. Pratfalls usually did the trick. She would giggle and fall down on his back and tickle him….

Dammit, he had to find out what was bothering her. Granted, there were times when her constant chatter got on his nerves when he was trying to concentrate. But her natural curiosity was part of who she was—her creative take on the things he'd always taken for granted. Even the hundred or so questions she used to ask before, worn out with play, she fell asleep before he finished reading her whatever story she'd demanded.

*Mara, what the devil have you told her? What bunch of lies have you fed her now?*

# Chapter 5

Laurel crept home—a matter of less than a mile—at twenty-five miles an hour while a long line of impatient traffic built up behind her. For several minutes she sat in the car in front of her rental house, trying to talk herself out of being upset over a dented fender on a secondhand car. She had insurance—liability, not collision.

"Whatever," she muttered, gathering up her mail and her purse. She was not a "whatever" kind of person.

As a child she had learned that, while she couldn't always control what happened, she could learn to control her reactions. Such as the times when her parents, who were supposed to pick her up at school for the holidays would arrange instead for her to stay with a classmate or a teacher. Probably paid them to take her, too, which made her feel like an object of charity. She'd worn herself out being helpful and polite, but mostly staying out of the way while the family did whatever it usually did on holidays.

It might even be the reason she'd gone to work for Jay-bass at barely a living wage. Help those in need; who knows when you might find yourself in that position.

She had handled it then, just as she'd learned to handle the situation when the main attraction at a fund-raiser showed up drunk or stoned to the gills. Or when the kid she'd paid to put up posters put up a few and dumped the rest. Or when the stringers who'd promised to cover an event failed to show up.

Peg's jock boyfriend used to say that when it came to dancing out of trouble, she was better than Mike Tyson ever was. She didn't know about that, but as catastrophes went, a dinged fender barely rated. Even so, she automatically lapsed into the old even-breathing regime while she stared at the shadowy woods behind the house and went over her options.

*In with the good energy, out with the bad.*

At least the car was still drivable. And fortunately, it had happened close by. What if it had happened on the interstate, miles from anywhere? What if the other driver had been a thug instead of a family man? A murderer, one of those creeps who preyed on lone women? How many cars would've whizzed right by before one stopped to help, and could she afford to take a chance even if one did?

Actually, she'd been pretty lucky.

Not that her opponent wasn't a real jerk. The fact that he was strikingly attractive didn't change that one bit. That monster SUV he'd been driving with the cow-catcher on the front had barely been scratched. What did *he* have to be so upset about?

*Breathe, Laurel.*

She breathed. Okay, it had happened. It was over. No one was hurt. She had his card; she could call her insurance agent and let them deal with his insurance agent. Once she got back home she would sell the car or donate it to one of the charities that accepted old cars. Let some poor guy learn a new trade by whacking the dings out of her fender.

Digging into her soft leather tote bag, she found the card her opponent had given her, read the name and frowned.

And then a ton of bricks came down on her head.

Cody Morningstar? The Neanderthal who had creamed her car was her *landlord?*

"No way," she whispered. No matter how many planets went retrograde, fate couldn't be so perverse.

She knew for a fact that some people loved being seen as the victim in any traumatic situation because it kept them from having to assume personal responsibility, but she was no victim. While she might not be able to control every single aspect of everything that happened around her—well, recent events had proved that beyond any doubt—she could and would control how she reacted to it.

"I am damn sure not a victim," she muttered.

All the same, if there was any way to turn a fender bender involving a nasty landlord into something positive, she was going to have to dig deep to find it.

This one might take a bit of finesse.

She dropped the mail and her purse onto the sofa that was every bit as uncomfortable as it was ugly. Normally, she would have sorted the mail, placed it on the dresser in her bedroom to be dealt with later, and put her purse on the closet shelf.

Here she didn't even have a real closet, only a makeshift corner of the bedroom.

What she needed now was caffeine. The ritual wine and the lavender-scented soak would have to wait. She had some serious vertical thinking to do.

More than an hour later she was still thinking. As frustrating as her current situation was, not knowing what was happening with Jay-bass was even more maddening. She really, *really* needed to talk to Jerry. She'd spoken to him exactly once since the big hoo-ha. He had told her not to call him, that he would call her when things got settled.

At this rate, Hades would be fielding an ice hockey team.

Frowning, she was still turning over various parts of the puzzle when she heard the scrape of sandy feet on the front porch. As hot as it was, the bedroom air conditioner couldn't handle the whole house, so she relied on open windows and doors and ceiling fans.

She heard a dog bark; someone tried to shush it, and then she heard a timid knock rattle the screened door.

"Travis?" She was too tired to move. "Come on in, it's not hooked."

"It's not Uncle Travis, it's me—Becky."

The dog was still yapping. When the childish voice registered, her feet hit the floor. She set her coffee mug down, wondering if her cowardly landlord could have sent his daughter as a peace emissary.

The minute she opened the door, the dog raced in, tried to stop and skidded on the varnished floor, knocking against a coat tree that remained naked in the heat of August. The child slipped inside, lunged after the dog, scolded him and set the rack upright again. "I'm sorry. I told him not to follow me."

She had big, solemn, honey-brown eyes and a lopsided blond ponytail that was coming undone. There was a smear of something that looked like chocolate on the cuff of her grimy yellow shorts. Laurel put her age at a year or two older than Jimmy, but when it came to children, she was no expert.

"Won't you come in and sit down, Becky."

The child regarded her gravely. "I'm already in, but could BooBoo and me pick some figs?"

"Figs." Had she missed something?

"Out in the backyard? Daddy always lets me pick figs when I come to stay with him just before school. He says to leave some for the mockingbirds, but I can't reach the high ones, anyway, so could I pick some for us and some for you?"

Which is how Laurel and the landlord's daughter came to be picking soft, wine-colored fruit from a huge tree that she hadn't even noticed as it was surrounded by knee-deep weeds that scratched and caught at her clothes.

At some time in the past, an attempt had been made to landscape the front yard, but behind the house, the jungle had taken over. Through the wild, vine-covered growth she'd caught what looked like the glint of water and something grayish-white and rectangular, possibly old abandoned beehives. They had lived near a bee-keeper for a few months when she was about Becky's age. And while she liked honey, she wasn't particularly eager to encounter any bees. The mosquitoes and biting flies were bad enough.

Waving away a swarm of the things, Laurel reached for a huge, lopsided fruit. She slapped at another bite. Before coming outside she had changed out of her work clothes into a pair of old tennis shorts.

Now Becky frowned at her bare legs. "Did you spray?"

"Did I spray what?"

"Your legs."

"Oh, you mean insect repellent? I meant to get some,

but I—" Before she could finish, she heard the voice of doom calling from the front of the house.

Becky answered, sounding almost defensive. "She said I could have some figs." She scowled at the grim-looking man rounding the corner of the house.

"Run along home, Rebecca. I'll be there in a minute. Take the dog with you. Give him some water."

The dog was one of those gorgeous creatures you saw in the AKC shows loping arrogantly around a ring, looking as if its handler was merely a servant. Which was probably true from the dog's perspective.

The man was something else. She'd been too furious—okay, too shaken—to take complete inventory when they'd met only a short time ago.

Becky called the dog, which at the moment was stalking a dragonfly. "Come *on,* BooBoo!" Without looking at her father, the child grabbed the red collar and tugged the dog toward the narrow path between the two houses.

Laurel braced herself to hear that he'd already contacted his insurance agent and given him a one-sided version of the truth. Instead, he said, "She won't bother you again."

Laurel tried to pretend she was wearing her gray silk jacquard and her new slingbacks, dealing from a position of strength instead of being hot, sweaty and on the defensive. She was probably already coming down with whatever disease you got from mosquito bites. She'd been vaccinated years ago for any number of nasty diseases, but her immunity had probably long since worn off.

"Who, Becky? I assure you, she wasn't bothering me at all." Most of the time she was pretty good at projecting authority. Cowering in a weedy backyard with scratches and bites on her naked legs and sweat filming her face was not one of those times. Besides, it wasn't worth the effort.

"I believe we have some business to discuss."

"Business?" She swallowed in an effort to calm the butterflies in her stomach. So much for projecting authority.

Dammit, he's dressed no better than I am, Laurel told herself, tugging at her shirt to make sure it hadn't ridden up over her waist. Compared to Jerry, the man wasn't even particularly good-looking. Compelling maybe, but hardly handsome. None of his features seemed to go together. And yet…

Consider him part of the local scenery, she told herself. Just one more in a long line of tourist attractions.

And stop gawking, you are *not* impressed!

His thick hair was sun bleached on top, darker near the roots and about two weeks overdue an appointment with his stylist—or in his case, probably a barber. As he was still wearing the same aviator sunglasses he'd been wearing when he'd come barreling into the post office parking lot, she couldn't tell about his eyes.

Knowing that there was an advantage in forcing your opponent to speak first, Laurel crossed her arms, clamped her lips shut and waited.

"We need to talk. Did Travis tell you I'm getting the roof reshingled?"

First point goes to me, she thought smugly. "He did."

"Did he explain why you can't stay here while the work's going on?"

"He did not." Succinct answers. That much she'd learned from having recently been interrogated by professionals. As to who had the advantage at this point, it was probably a draw.

"How long were you planning on being here?"

Were, not are. There was a subtle difference. Before she could come up with an answer, Becky came racing around the corner of the house. "I can't find a water bowl!" She addressed the words to Laurel, not to her father.

The dog galloped after her, trailing a red leather leash that matched his studded collar. He skidded to a halt mere inches from Laurel's body. Not that she had anything against dogs, but never having owned one, she was not sure what to expect.

"Back, BooBoo," snapped Cody.

"Go home, BooBoo," urged Becky, trying to step on his trailing leash.

Ignoring them both, BooBoo stood on his hind legs, braced his big front feet on Laurel's bosom and slapped her in the face with a long wet tongue. She backed away, tripped on a root and ended up on her butt in a patch of knee-high weeds, shielding her face with her arms as well as she could.

The dog was all over her until Becky managed to grab the leash and pull him away. Shaking her finger, she shouted, "Bad dog, bad dog!"

Actually, Laurel admitted to herself, the only thing hurt was her dignity, but that was in ruins. Ignoring Cody's extended hand, she got up with as much grace as she could muster…which wasn't a lot, considering she'd had three and a half years of ballet training in her prepubescent years.

At least she didn't trip over her own feet and sprawl at his.

He was wearing cargo shorts beneath which his muscular thighs, which had been roughly at her eye level a moment before, were tanned and furred with dark golden hairs. Shaking off the minor distraction, she told herself that looks were irrelevant. And anyway, she'd always preferred dark-haired men with polished manners. If he had any manners they were not only tarnished, they were rusty.

Gingerly, she picked a sandspur from the cuff of her shorts, then tried to shake the thing off her fingers. It refused to let go. Scrooge took her hand, plucked the prickly thing from her fingers and tossed it aside.

"I'll pay for the damage," he said tersely.

"I should think so, since you're the guilty party," she retorted.

"Only indirectly." Now he sounded amused, and that *really* ticked her off.

"That's a matter of opinion," she retorted. Not quite the admission she'd hoped for, it was better than nothing.

Only then did it occur to her that Scrooge wasn't looking at her injured car, which was parked in front of the house, he was looking at her. More specifically, at her bosom.

Instinctively, she glanced down at her old yellow camp shirt. The bottom button had been missing for years. Now the top flapped open, revealing more cleavage than she was comfortable showing.

"Oh, shoot," she muttered. "That blasted dog!" Snatching the two sides together, she turned and headed for the house. And then she turned back. She had him on two counts now—the car thing and the dog thing. When it came to bargaining, she was very good at taking advantage of the smallest opening.

Before she could launch her first offensive he said, "Ms. Lawless, we still need to talk."

Not the most advantageous position for striking a

bargain, nevertheless, she gave it her best shot. Holding her shirt together, she confronted him. If he thought he could intimidate her with a scowl and a pair of Oakley sunglasses, he was dead wrong. She'd been scowled at by experts.

Actually, as much as it pained her to admit it, Cody Morningstar's scowl was almost attractive, bristly square jaw and all. That mouth, with the full lower lip and the curved upper one, had never been designed to look grim, it had been designed for—

Never mind what his mouth was designed for, you dunce.

But before she could refocus her thoughts she had him pegged as a cross between George Clooney and a young Redford, with Hugh Grant's mouth.

*Oh, for Pete's sake, woman, if you have to think in movie terms, at least think of someone truly gross!*

She pictured Dr. Frankenstein's monster. It didn't help. Head high, she said coolly, "Have your people contact mine. Tell them to let me know where and when the work can be done."

"You're talking about your car? Aren't you taking a lot for granted considering you didn't hang around long enough for an official report?"

"*I'm* not the one who refused to hang around," she exclaimed. "*You're* the one who ran away first!" She was practically shouting. She *never* shouted. It indicated a loss of control.

"Dammit, I didn't run away! I had to move so you could back out, didn't I? And then you kept on going."

"Well, excuse *me* for not knowing proper protocol. You're the one who decided not to wait for the police because—" she made quotation marks in the air with her fingers "—they know where to find me. You must do this sort of thing often."

His arms were crossed over his chest. So were hers. From what she could see behind those damned sunglasses of his, he looked almost as if he was holding back a smile, and that *really* ticked her off.

Ignoring the twitch at the corner of his mouth, she said, "Just tell me how to get in touch with your insurance agent and I'll tell them exactly what happened. How I was carefully backing out of a legal parking place after looking in both directions and suddenly, you came barreling in off the highway as if you owned the planet and everything on it."

"The hell I did!" Any hint of a smile was gone instantly. "I signaled a right turn. There wasn't a damn thing blocking my way when I pulled in. That's when you came backing out of there without even looking."

"I did not! I looked both ways!" She slapped another mosquito, dropping one hand to do it. Next time she'd spray.

Was there a spray that would repel landlords?

He started to say something, but she cut him off. "All right, I'll agree to a compromise. My insurance will straighten up that chrome gadget on your front bumper and your insurance can replace however much of my car needs replacing, but I want it thoroughly checked over because I have to drive it all the way back to New York."

She thought she heard him mutter something about "the sooner the better," but she couldn't be sure.

Aloud, he said, "I gave you my insurance card, remember?"

Oh, shoot. He had. She'd forgotten it, which was totally unlike her. Talk about your organized minds.

"As a matter of fact, it wasn't your reckless driving I was talking about when I said I was partially responsible."

It wasn't? Then what? Laurel waved away a mosquito that was buzzing around her left ear.

"Go on inside before you get eaten alive. I'll check on Becky and come back. We still need to sort out this rent thing. Obviously, Travis wasn't thinking straight when he gave you permission to move in."

Oh no, she thought, you're not getting away with that. Hurrying after him, she caught his arm. "Look, what happened at the post office has nothing whatsoever to do with—with anything else. Travis is my cousin and he said he was acting as your agent."

He slowed up enough to look at her. His gaze fell to the hand on his arm and she jerked it away as if his flesh burned her fingers. One dark eyebrow lifted above the rim of the Oakley shades.

Hastily, she said, "Yes, well—well, since he had the keys and was able to get the utilities turned on, he obviously has the proper authority. So exactly what is your complaint?"

She didn't say, "what the hell are you bitching about?" Even angry, frustrated and itching from mosquito bites and lord knows what else, she knew better than to engage in an inflammatory exchange. That old flies and honey versus vinegar thing.

He continued to walk, but slowly; she kept on following several paces behind, her gaze unwittingly focused on his backside. All of it. Her legs itched and the air was so still she could hear the insects buzzing around her head. For all she knew, trained snakes could be creeping through the weeds, ready to take her out at his command.

Not until he reached the place where dense wild

growth had been allowed to form a hedge between the two houses did he turn and confront her. Quietly, he said, "Travis knew I was planning on having the place reroofed. It needs a termite inspection, new gutters, new wiring and plumbing before it's fit for long-term occupation."

"I'm short-term. Extremely short-term. You can have all that done after I leave. My *cousin*—" she got that in again for what it was worth "—assured me that for the length of time I plan on being in residence, it wouldn't be a problem." A slight oversimplification, but hardly a lie.

"Exactly how long had you planned on staying?"

*Had she planned on staying?* If he was subtly trying to make a point, he could consider it made. "How long? Two weeks, possibly longer. It all depends." Considering the fact that her life was in total free fall at the moment, she thought she was handling things rather well.

"This is August. We're getting into hurricane season. That roof won't stand another bad storm."

"Travis said he had buckets I can borrow if it rains."

"The attic's already full of buckets. Emptying them out is a lot of trouble, starting with hauling a ladder upstairs."

"I'm sure Travis has a ladder I can borrow, too." This was beginning to feel like a game, the way they were feeling each other out, probing for weaknesses, hopping from one square to another. If Cody Morningstar had a single weakness, it wasn't visible from where she stood.

But there was his daughter. Laurel hadn't seen enough to be sure, but she'd always been good at reading people. Sensing that their relationship wasn't all a father-daughter relationship should be—as if she would know—she moved in for the kill. She managed a smile that was probably about as convincing as a Halloween mask. "Tell Becky to come pick figs anytime she wants to, whether or not I'm there. In fact I'd appreciate it. The birds are so noisy just before my alarm clock goes off, you'd think there was a wild party going on back in the woods."

*Your move, Mr. Morningstar. Are you going to keep your daughter on a short leash? You can't even keep that monster dog of yours on a leash.*

Hoping it wouldn't occur to him that Becky could pick figs whether or not she was still there, Laurel crossed her arms, holding her ruined blouse together with one hand. Cody Morningstar crossed his arms, showing to advantage a pair of tanned, muscular forearms. Whatever he did for a living must require physical strength. Construction, maybe. She could easily picture him up on top of one of those tall, fancy palaces that were sprouting all up and down the beach like mushrooms after a three-week rain.

"I wouldn't get too comfortable if I were you, Ms. Lawless. I'll be back." The warning was made all the more ominous for the smile that accompanied it.

For several minutes after Cody left, Laurel stood in the opening in the wild hedge. And then she heard it again. A flock of gulls? Wasn't there one called a laughing gull? Because that's what it sounded like—laughter.

That had to be it. This close to both the ocean and the sound, noises were deceptive. Either that or she had an unseen neighbor with a rowdy sense of humor.

# Chapter 6

Standing in the middle of his top-of-the-line, largely unused kitchen, Cody wondered which to tackle first—the daughter who had turned into a stranger; that damned dog she'd insisted on bringing along, or the woman who had moved onto his property. Laurel Ann Lawless, according to the card she'd given him. Public relations director of something called J. Blessing Associates with an East 31st Street address.

All of which told him nothing except that she was the cousin of a friend and the kind of trouble he didn't need, not with the worst case of writer's block he had experienced since his marriage had ended. Usually at this stage of a work in progress, he'd be on a second, if not a third draft, tying up loose ends, making sure he had solved all the problems he'd laid out for himself.

When it came to real life, his record was less impressive, starting with his beautiful and greedy ex-wife. On the verge of a second marriage, Mara had agreed to discuss renegotiating their custody agreement in exchange for his keeping Becky and the mutt while she and whatsisname honeymooned in Paris.

And while there was nothing Cody would like better than to have Becky live here permanently, even if it meant keeping the dog, something had happened between now and the last time she'd visited him. Usually, she chattered away a mile a minute, to the point that occasionally his mind would wander, especially if he happened to be at a crucial point in a plot. And face it—a writer's mind was never a hundred percent detached from his current work in progress.

Now she wouldn't even look at him directly. She barely spoke to him unless that damned dog needed something. She couldn't have spoken more than a dozen words the whole trip.

And on top of all that, he had to deal with this woman, Laurel Lawless. His unwanted tenant, who was sleeping in the bed he'd slept in before he'd moved into his new house, picking his figs, eating her meals at the round oak table that had been there, for all he knew, since whoever had built the house had first furnished it.

Staring at the teakwood table he'd had delivered along with enough other stuff to set up housekeeping, he visualized her stepping into the rust-stained bathtub that was probably only seventy or eighty years old, testing the temperature of the water with one toe while she stood there, looking like Botticelli's Venus on the half shell, only with darker and shorter hair.

As if he really needed that image burned into his consciousness.

She was hardly the most beautiful woman he'd ever seen. Smallish, dark brown hair, gray eyes—the kind of face you might not notice at first glance because she did little if anything to call attention to her looks. Given a second glance, you couldn't help but admire the flawless bone structure. Her figure, even in shorts and a torn shirt, was almost as subtle. It occurred to him that subtle was a hell of a lot more intriguing than blatant. When it came to women, his standards had changed since his early rutting years. For the better, he liked to think. Picturing Laurel Lawless in his mind's eye, he felt another shift coming on.

Cody had been in the air force when he and Mara had married after knowing each other for all of three weeks. A multiple beauty pageant winner, Mara had been easily the most beautiful woman he'd ever seen. The moment they'd been introduced at a private party at an officer's club in Oceana, he'd gone down without a whimper. Gradually, over the next few years he had learned how little substance there was underneath her flawless features and her surgically enhanced figure.

A few years later Mara had been managing a high-end dress shop in Richmond while he, once more a civilian, worked for a small airline during the day and struggled with his first novel at night. *Dealer's Choice* was eventually published and promptly fell off the radar screen. He hadn't given up.

By the time his writing career took off with a new agent and a different publisher, his marriage had effectively ended. He'd moved into a residential hotel while Mara had stayed on at the house they'd once shared. It was shortly after his third novel had made the *New York Times* list and he'd signed a lucrative new contract with his publisher that they'd got together again. Mara had started dropping by his hotel, inviting him to spend weekends with her in the Midlothian house they'd bought long before they could afford it. When she'd begged for a second chance, Cody had tried to focus on the things that had once drawn them together instead of all the little things that had driven them apart.

One of which was a total lack of anything in common.

In the early days he'd had trouble believing a woman with her looks would marry someone like him, the son of a small-town Oklahoma building contractor who grew up mostly in foster homes after first his mother and then his father had died before he was twelve years old. He figured it was the uniform and the fact that he was a pilot.

The split had been a reprieve. His writing had taken off. Not unexpectedly, it had slowed down once he'd moved back home again. Nine months after their reconciliation, Becky had been born. Mara swore she hadn't deliberately gotten pregnant, and Cody had to believe her, if only because she'd hated every minute of her pregnancy.

He hadn't been wildly enthusiastic about the idea, himself. Hell, he had enough trouble being a husband—at least the kind of husband Mara wanted—without having to learn to be a father. But he'd fallen for his daughter the moment she'd come kicking and screaming into the world. Bald head, red face, squashed nose and all, she'd been so damned wonderful he had cried for the third time in his life.

But the marriage had quickly started going downhill again. Cody had stuck it out for a few more years for Becky's sake, but in the end they'd agreed to call it quits. Guilty over his part in the breakup—he'd never been unfaithful, but neither had he been entirely blameless—Cody had let Mara call the shots. She'd ended up with the house, the Jaguar, half their investments and custody of Becky with limited visitation privileges on his part.

He'd drifted for a few months and ended up buying a piece of land on the Outer Banks. As there was already an old house there, he'd moved in, updated a few things—mainly the wiring, to support his computer— and spent the next few years writing the best work he had done to date. Meanwhile, with Becky in mind he'd hired a local contractor to build him something a lot more comfortable, with a lot less maintenance. If he ever hoped to reclaim his daughter—and he damned well did; he'd been working on it ever since the divorce—he needed a clean, safe place to bring her.

Now Mara was about to marry again; this time instead of a veteran with a crazy ambition to write, she'd chosen a West Coast lawyer with political ambitions. If he knew his ex-wife, she was already planning her wardrobe as first lady of California.

As for Becky, he'd noticed a difference within the first half hour after picking her up. She'd been much quieter than usual, but as Mara had said she was just getting over a summer cold, he hadn't thought much about it until they'd been traveling nearly three hours. Only then did it occur to him that she was addressing all her remarks, when she was forced to speak at all, to the dog and not to him.

Cody would be the first to admit he spoiled his daughter, probably because he tried so hard to make the most of their brief times together. Last year he'd taken her to Busch Gardens. Knowing she was fascinated by his computer, he'd bought her one and taught her to use it. She was so damned quick he'd been amazed, but then he'd heard that kids were born knowing how, even when their hands were too small to manage a keyboard.

The summer she turned six he'd bought her a boogie board and taught her how to use it under his close supervision. They'd cooked hot dogs and blackened marshmallows on the beach, after which he'd nursed her through sunburn and stomach upset. When Travis had showed her how to find clams in the sound, he had cooked the two small ones she'd brought home so proudly, just as he'd cooked the whiting she'd "caught" when they'd gone surf fishing. He had hooked it, reeled it in and let her race down to the surf to grab the line and bring it up onto the beach. He'd even taken her picture with it. Framed it and hung it in his office.

Now for some reason, he couldn't even get a smile from her. Not even after he'd agreed to bring that damned dog along. The dog was one of Mara's recent acquisitions. More like an affectation, he thought now, knowing his ex-wife. The first thing the crazy mutt had done was pee on the floor and then skid through the puddle as he galloped around exploring the house. Becky had raced after the dog, then stopped and looked back at him almost as if she expected him to grab the dog and beat some manners into him.

"I'm sorry, Daddy." It was the first time she had addressed him all day. "He knows he's not supposed to do it on the floor. Mama hits him with a newspaper when he messes up."

"It's all right, hon, he'll learn." Maybe bringing the mutt along hadn't been such a bad idea after all. A few puddles were no big deal, especially as he'd never gotten around to buying any rugs. The place was still only half-furnished, but then that kept housework at a minimum. All he had to do was rinse out his few dishes, occasionally wield a broom and toss a load of laundry in the machine when he ran short of clothes. He lived out of the dryer—it saved a lot of work, all the folding and sorting and putting away. His office tended toward organized chaos, but the rest of the place, largely unused, remained neat enough.

He had a feeling that was about to change.

Cody believed in discipline, but he also knew it had to be carefully and consistently meted out. He was a bit short on parenting skills, but on-the-job training had taken care of it until recently.

*"Dear, the baby needs changing,"* Mara would call up to the third floor, where he'd be sweating over his work in progress. Still on maternity leave, she'd spent most of her time watching TV from her bed or going with a friend on shopping marathons. Instead of waiting until her body settled down after childbirth, she'd used a few lingering pounds as an excuse to replace everything in her walk-in closet.

So he would shut down his computer and jog downstairs to take care of whatever needed doing. Bottles, diapers, trips to the pediatrician and, later on, the play school Becky attended three mornings a week. Even after the divorce when he was allowed to have her one weekend a month, alternate holidays and two weeks in the summer, he'd done pretty well, if he did say so.

Last year had been his turn to have her for Christmas. He'd still been living in the old house as his new one was just being finished. Becky had helped him pick out a shapely cedar in the nearby woods, supervised chopping it down. *"Don't cut it there, Daddy, cut it higher up! Does it hurt the tree when you cut it down?"*

She had helped decorate it with ornaments she'd made using colored paper, glue and glitter. Becky had wanted to take them home to her mother, but Cody had begged her to let him keep them, telling her how fragile they were. Mara would have trashed them. Cody had saved every one.

So where had he screwed up? By letting her eat all the junk food she wanted on the trip here until she got sick to her stomach? As if he was trying to buy her affections? Hell, he knew better than that. The only kind of affection that mattered was the kind that couldn't be bought.

But what, then? She seemed willing enough to talk to the Lawless woman, but when he'd asked her a simple question about breakfast cereals or whether or not she still needed a night-light, all he'd got was a shrug.

Of course, the last time she'd come for a visit he'd still been living in the old house while his new place was under construction. Maybe that was why she'd gone racing over there first thing. On the way from Midlothian he'd explained about his new house, and how she'd be sleeping in a brand-new bedroom he'd had built especially for her instead of the old one that she always claimed was too noisy.

He couldn't figure out the noise part, unless she'd been dreaming. Maybe owls or chuck-will's-widow. Tree frogs. Fish crows liked to congregate in the dead pines on the other side of the creek. They could raise a hell of a ruckus. According to Travis, some guy who lived half a mile or so away kept peafowl back in the woods.

But at night…?

Travis's wife had always been a big help during Becky's visits, but Ru was in the last stages of a difficult pregnancy. As there was still a chance she could lose the baby, even after carrying it this long, he wasn't about to burden her with this new situation.

Besides, how complicated could it be, figuring out the mind of an eight-year-old?

At the moment, his eight-year-old was feeding her accident-prone dog the fresh tuna he'd planned to grill for supper. After first emptying out two onions and last week's mail, she'd served it up in a raku bowl that a fan had given him after a book signing he'd done a few years ago at Greenbriar Mall in Norfolk.

One more reason for moving to Hatteras Island: the island's only bookstore was smaller than his den, giving him a ready excuse not to do signings. He also didn't do interviews, didn't have a Web site and no longer even had a secretary, though there were times when he could have used one. But secretaries, even the best of them, talked. Since a particularly ugly situation a few years ago, his publisher had agreed not to use his photo on the back of his books, or in any of the advertising. The brief bio stated only that mystery writer Lee Larkin lived on an island in the southeastern United States and was currently at work on his next novel. All true, but deliberately ambiguous. Too many female fans seemed to confuse him with his studly fictional hero, Detective J. Smith Jones.

As for the stormy-eyed woman who had backed into his rod holder and invaded his property, he thought now with wry amusement, she was obviously not a fan. What she was, was a thorn in his side, one he didn't need at the moment.

Over a tall glass of iced tea, Laurel sat at the kitchen table in front of an electric fan and scanned the brief clippings Peg had sent, most of which she'd read before leaving New York. There were ceiling fans in the living room and bedroom, but not the kitchen. Anchoring the scraps of newsprint with a plate to keep them from blowing away, she checked the datelines and reread only the most recent. After all that had happened since she'd collected her mail, she had almost forgotten tossing it onto a kitchen counter.

Evidently there was nothing new. Before she'd even left town the coverage had degenerated to a smattering of letters to the editor, pro and con, concerning Section 215 of the Patriot Act that allowed for searches without warrants or probable cause. Since the first flurry of coverage, J. Blessing Associates hadn't rated more than a few brief mentions in the business section in the *Wall Street Journal*—hardly surprising, since it was barely a blip on the business horizon. Even Peg claimed the only reason they were being investigated at all was that the Homeland Security thing had gotten out of hand. Since 9/11, all the fund-raising businesses were suspected of funneling money to terrorist groups.

"Special Olympics? The Salvation Army?- I don't think so," she muttered now. Shoving the clippings back into the envelope, she brushed her hair back and lifted her face to allow the hot air stirred by the fan to cool her damp brow. She'd rarely read the editorial page of the *Wall Street Journal.* Aside from her own personal budget and the one she adhered to at work, finance had never interested her. The entertainment pages of the smaller dailies, those she read regularly—not that many of Kirk's so-called celebrities rated much coverage even there.

Looking back at all the times she'd been forced to play nursemaid to some no-talent, lip-synching wannabe, it occurred to Laurel that she'd never particularly enjoyed her job. The pay was nothing to brag about, either. Better than what she was earning now, but then, the cost of living was much higher in New York.

In a way, she almost dreaded going back to the same wheedling and manipulating, trying to appear impressed by someone who, without the benefit of major electronics, had a voice like a wounded duck, not to mention the personality of a turnip. Back to buttering up stringers who might be persuaded to cover an event for a dozen free tickets and a personal interview with the "star."

Time and distance had a way of putting things in perspective. Any glamour she might once have expected had yet to materialize, but there was still the satisfaction of helping those who needed help. And there was Jerry, whose picture was in a few of the early clippings Peg had sent, along with Kirk's and her own. Dark-haired, dark-eyed Jerry Blessing, who managed to look both stoic and melodramatic. Even the way he said "No comment" in that chocolate-covered voice of his had been a major turn-on.

*Why don't you call me, dammit? Enough of the strong silent treatment!*

Retrieving the oversize envelope, she checked the postmark. It had been mailed three days ago. Could there have been any new developments since then? If so, would Jerry have bothered to let her know?

On the off chance that something had happened in the past few days, Laurel reached for her cell phone and punched in Peg's number. After five rings, her friend answered, sounding breathless. They chatted for several minutes about Laurel's job, Peg's wavering decision about whether or not to have liposuction and the possibility that ESPN was interested in Dan.

"Nothing new," Peg admitted when Laurel asked about the break-in. "Oh, I need to send you the new key before you head back. I'll do that tomorrow, but look—what have you found out about your property down there? You don't want to leave without getting every-thing settled, like how much you're going to get for your share, right? If you don't get things settled now, it's not going to get done."

In other words, Laurel interpreted, don't hurry back. Oddly enough, it didn't hurt quite as much as it should have.

"There's a bunch of acres involved, but on the tax map," she explained, "it's designated as mostly swamp-land." She had already explained about the wildlife ref-uge. "According to my cousin Harrison—I told you about him, remember?—it's too wet to plow and too dry to nav-igate. In other words, whatever's left is pretty worthless."

"Hey, take some pictures while you're there, okay? Dan knows these guys who like to go hunting. Maybe he could get up a party and hunt on your property. Like, maybe they'd even be willing to chip in and build some kind of a hunting lodge there. That'd be cool, wouldn't it?"

"Next door to a wildlife refuge? I don't think so. Uh…look, Peg, can I call you back? I think someone's coming up my front walk."

Walk was a euphemism for the sandy, weedy space between what had probably once been shell-lined flower beds. Among the thriving weeds were a few things she vaguely recognized, but as the only plant she'd ever per-sonally owned was a potted cactus, she was no expert.

Peering through one of the double-hung front win-dows, she felt a combination of dread and anticipation. The wavy old glass badly needed washing, but there was no mistaking either those broad shoulders or the muscular stride that fell just short of being a swagger.

Touching her hair on the way to the door, she reminded herself that she needed to stay on his good side until she had a signed short-term lease in her hand. "You might as well come in," she said grudgingly. She had a feeling she was going to need all her negotiating skills this time.

He stopped just inside the screen door, glanced into the living room and lifted one dark brow. "I see you've already rearranged things."

Recognizing the challenge, Laurel responded in kind. "Is that a problem?" So she liked to put her mark on any space she intended to occupy for more than a few days, what was so wrong with that? Peg called it staking a claim and teased her about it, but all she'd done was to rearrange the few pieces of furniture and hang Jerry's mom's watercolor. It looked a little lost, as it was far too small for the space, but at least it was safe…although she'd noticed when she'd unpacked that the masking tape that held on the cardboard backing was starting to come loose.

Her reluctant landlord launched his offensive. "You mentioned you'll be leaving in a couple of weeks."

Refusing to be intimidated, Laurel countered with, "I'll be here through the end of August and a few days into September. According to the owner of the shop where I work, it's the busiest part of the year and she's desperately shorthanded. I'd hate to be forced to let her down."

She waited. Behind those shades he wore indoors and out, he was about as easy to read as a sphinx. If he was trying to make people think he was a celebrity pretending not to want to be recognized, she could have told him that was definitely not the way to go. At least he wasn't wearing a ton of gold jewelry. "She's Caroline Danvers—a local? You might know her." In other words, if you don't give a darn about my needs, at least consider your neighbors.

He stroked his jaw, remaining silent, so she hit him with a flank attack. "Your daughter seems really nice. How old is she? Nine? Ten?"

"Eight."

Ha! He took the bait. "She seems mature for her age."

In another man, that slow release of breath might be considered a sigh. A sighing man had vulnerabilities. Now all she had to do was poke around until he yelled ouch. "Did you give her my message about the figs? Tell her if she needs a basket, there's one on the back porch. I think it used to hold clothespins since there's a coil of rope hanging on the same nail. Oh, and while I have you here, what about that iron stove in the kitchen? It doesn't work, does it?"

"There's no stovepipe, in case you hadn't noticed." His tone implied a lack of respect for her mental acuity. "Usable woodstoves affect insurance rates."

"How interesting," she murmured. Not. "Then I wonder why it's still taking up space, since the kitchen's not all that roomy."

"In case the bridge goes out again and we lose power for a few weeks, I can hook up the stovepipe and burn wood."

"Ahhh. Good idea." Scary idea, losing power for a few weeks. She distinctly remembered crossing at least three bridges, although what any of them had to do with electric power, she couldn't say.

She was beginning to wonder if perhaps the man had just had an eye exam and his eyes were still light sensitive when he whipped off his dark glasses and hooked them in his shirt pocket.

In a face that was strikingly attractive, if hardly Hollywood handsome, his eyes were deep set, thick lashed and far too intense. If she'd had to name a color, she'd have said hazel, but with late-afternoon sunlight streaming through the open back door, they looked almost gold.

"The rent is five hundred dollars a month," he said brusquely. He skipped a beat, probably waiting for her to protest.

It was far less than she'd expected to pay...on the other hand, the place was a dump. She murmured something that could be taken any way he wanted to take it.

"I have a crew ready to start on the roof as soon as they finish up the job they're on now. If you can't stand the noise, you're free to move out, otherwise, you owe me two-fifty for two weeks."

Doing the mental arithmetic, she arrived at two days before the Labor Day weekend. Not good enough, but it would do for a starter. She didn't know if she was getting a break on the rent or not. She did know that rates varied wildly in different parts of the country. Compared to what she paid for her half of the tiny Murray Hill apartment it sounded like a very good deal, even with a leaky roof and a noisy neighbor.

She said smugly, "Fine. I'll write you a check, just let me get my checkbook." At least he hadn't asked for first and last month, which was standard in all the places she'd ever lived.

When she came back to find him studying the watercolor, she felt compelled to defend the poor thing. "It was painted by the mother of a dear friend of mine— my fiancé, in fact." She hid her ringless hands behind her back. "Jerry let me bring it with me for, um—sentimental reasons."

"The paper's buckled. This climate is rough on paper goods—too much humidity. If you want to get it reframed, there's a place up in Avon that can do it for you."

Or it could wait until she got back home. She really didn't need another expense. On the other hand, if it fell apart, she'd just as soon not have to explain to Jerry that she hadn't bothered to get it fixed when she'd noticed the backing coming loose.

"Thanks," she said coolly. "I'll consider it."

Okay, so she would probably end up having it done. By the time she had to pick it up and pay for it, she'd have received at least one paycheck.

Wincing at the remaining balance—four figures only if you counted the seventy-three cents—she wrote out a check and handed it over. He barely glanced at it. Instead, he continued to look at her as if…

As if what? As if he knew just how uneasy she was? How far out of her nice, neat, orderly element? What did he expect her to do now, genuflect?

She stared right back at him, forcing herself not to be impressed by his gorgeous tan, his athlete's build and a face that seemed to have been put together from spare parts, but was none the less riveting.

Dammit, her feet ached! In just the past few days she must have collected roughly five hundred mosquito bites, every one of which suddenly started itching.

She flat out refused to scratch. "The check is good," she said, sounding defensive, which was not at all the way she felt. Really, it wasn't.

Then Cody suggested—ordered, was more like it—

a walk-through. Laurel knew the drill, having rented all
her adult life. Knowing it was for her own protection as
well as his, in case anything later turned up missing or
damaged, she turned and led the way.

"You'll notice that there's only a single flimsy lock
on the two doors," she reminded him. She was accustomed to at least two, with a sturdy chain.

"Never been a problem, but if it bothers you, maybe
you'd be more comfortable somewhere else."

*Oh, ho! Nice try, but you won't catch me that way.*
"It doesn't really bother me, I just thought I'd mention
it." She could always shove a chair under the doorknob.

She followed him up the stairs to the two bedrooms
and a bath that had probably been added at some point
after the house had been built. As had been the meager
bedroom closet. The first room they glanced into was
vacant except for two buckets in the middle of the floor.
In the room where she slept there was a dark oak dresser
with three stubborn drawers, a straight chair, an iron-
frame double bed with a surprisingly good mattress and
a rickety little table she'd brought up from the living
room to serve as a bedside table.

The inspection didn't take long. She followed him,
trying not to notice the easy way he had of moving. "The
furniture is all yours, I presume." He could take it for
what it was worth. The stuff was junk.

"Most of it was here when I bought the place. Ask
your cousin if you want to know who to blame. I bought
the property from him."

She would hardly bother Travis over something so
trivial.

Following him downstairs, Laurel did her best to ignore his narrow backside in a pair of cargoes that had

faded from khaki to cream and a black knit shirt that was faded to brown across a pair of shoulders roughly as wide as a yardstick—maybe a few inches less. Her heart might belong to Jerry—well, of course it did—but no woman with a viable hormone in her body could fail to notice so much masculine pulchritude.

With one hand on the screened front door, Cody turned to confront her. "Any questions? If not, you're set for two weeks."

He had her over a barrel and they both knew it. She merely nodded. Possession was nine-tenths of the law. By the time her two weeks was up, she would have thought of something to allow her to stay on through Labor Day.

"See you later," he said as he loped down the three wooden steps.

*Not if I see you coming first.*

## Chapter 7

To learn more about the high-end crafts and handmade jewelry sold in the shop where she worked, Laurel went in half an hour early for the next few days. On the way home she usually stopped in to see Ru and report any gossip she'd heard, but the visits were always brief because by that time she was truly bushed, her feet swollen from standing all day. They commiserated on the problem they both shared.

At least there'd been no sign of Cody or his daughter, although it was obvious that someone—probably Becky—had been visiting in her absence. The lower branches of the fig tree had been stripped of fruit and someone had left a few figs in the basket to draw fruit flies.

Someone—again, probably Becky unless the laughing ghost was a gardener—had straightened the row of bleached conch shells that lined the front path. A section of one flower bed had been weeded, and something that looked like wilted bok choy had been planted there.

The sun was still high, the house stifling even with the windows all open for any ephemeral breeze. There simply wasn't one. After changing into a pair of shorts and a tank top Laurel quenched her thirst with a glass of iced sun-tea and wandered outside. She pulled up a few weeds, then raked the sandy soil with her fingers into waving patterns around the bok choy that probably wasn't. She'd always loved the calm orderliness of Zen gardens. Pebbles, a few perfectly placed rocks and a shrub or two...

The next day her patterns were gone. The wilted bok choy had been dug up again, along with several of the conch shells. This, she mused, was beginning to look like the work of a certain dog—definitely not a ghost.

On Saturday evening she had supper with Ru and Travis. Over the tastiest fried fish she'd ever eaten in her life, Travis told her about his home-based marine electronics business. She didn't pretend to understand. "Cell phones and PCs are the extent of my knowledge," she admitted.

He laughed and said he understood. Ru said, "Honestly, it's not a chauvinistic thing. He has to keep Becky out of there. She's fascinated by anything she doesn't understand. I think she's going to be another—"

"How about dessert? I made lime pie," Travis said.

"*You* made?" Laurel said.

He held up both hands as he rose from the table. "Hey, you won't find any chauvinism around here, on either side—right, hon?"

"Right," Ru said dryly, and Laurel looked from one to the other, wondering if she'd missed something.

Over delicious key lime pie and coffee the talk skipped from one topic to another, including storm season, tourist season and tick season. Not until Laurel mentioned Jimmy, Harrison's stepson, did the conversation seem to fall apart. She sensed some sort of tension between the Holidays, which was both puzzling and unwelcome. Now that she had found her nice little family circle, she couldn't bear for it to be split apart by dissension.

It was nearly dark when Laurel said good-night and drove the short distance to her rental. Even so, there was enough light to see that her ghostly gardener had been at work again. Where the wilted bok choy had once stood there was something that might be either a palmetto or a pineapple.

In case her reluctant landlord was trying to make amends for creaming her car, she might point out a few improvements she would prefer over landscaping. The window unit in her bedroom, for instance, had two settings—steam heat and Arctic blast. And the kitchen sink took forever to drain. Those were things she should have thought to mention during their inspection tour, but hadn't because at the time, she'd had too much else on her mind.

Including the man, himself. She'd heard about personal magnetism—who hadn't? But she'd never been close to any man who could mess up her brain waves and her breathing without even cracking a smile.

Unfortunately, moving was not an option. She had quickly learned that any rentals still habitable after the last hurricane were already taken. In fact, Cody could probably have gotten twice what she was paying if Travis weren't her cousin and his friend.

After first unlocking the front door, she followed what had quickly become a habit, stepping out of her shoes on the front porch and clacking them together to shed any sand before going inside. Dropping her purse on the stairs to go up, she glanced through the few pieces of junk mail Travis had collected for her at the post office before tossing it in the waste can. Not that she'd expected a letter from Jerry, but still…

Feeling oddly restless, she went back outside and settled cautiously in the old-fashioned swing to watch the last few streaks of color fade from the sky. She'd asked Travis to check the rusty chain the last time he was there, and since he'd assured her it was safe, she kicked the thing into motion, stirring up a gentle breeze.

Actually, the rhythmic squeak was rather relaxing. Ignoring the lights that shone from Cody's windows, she concentrated on counting the seconds between sweeps of the lighthouse as the beam skimmed over the treetops.

Lulled by the creak of the chain, she allowed herself to fall under the spell of the light. It was as effective as any hypnotist's watch and chain. She felt more relaxed than she had in months.

Had whoever built this house and lived in it nearly a century ago sat on this same front porch—maybe even in the same swing—and watched the same beam sweep over the treetops? Cody had said he bought the property from Travis, which meant it might even have been family property, but which side of the family? Holiday or Lawless?

Wouldn't it be something if…

"If nothing," she muttered aloud. Time to quit daydreaming about the past and start thinking about her immediate future. What she needed was a contingency plan. Turning a negative into a positive by tying up the loose end of her father's estate had seemed like a good idea at the time, but so far, no one else seemed interested in title searches, deed writing, or whatever was involved in dividing up a property.

So what now? She was fresh out of ideas.

Sooner or later, Jerry had to call her. She would give it another week, she told herself, and then she would call him and tell him she was committed to staying through Labor Day, but after that, she was free for…whatever.

Free of her newfound cousins. Free of her sexy and far too attractive landlord and his adorable daughter.

After a few more minutes of watching the stars come out, listening to the deafening sound of frogs and insects, she went inside, locked the front door and checked to be sure the back one was secure. Home sweet home, she mused, taking in an assortment of the world's ugliest furniture and one small, amateurish watercolor that was lost on the ten-foot expanse of empty wall. Tomorrow, she decided as she switched on the radio Travis had lent her, she would take it to the framer.

Decision made, she felt marginally better. Before lowering herself carefully into the lopsided recliner, she opened the window and switched on the ceiling fan to stir the muggy air. That way she could hear the ocean. She only hoped her noisy neighbors, whoever, wherever and whatever they were, would keep it down. It didn't happen every night, but often enough so that she woke up feeling irritable. Ru claimed it was her ghost, but she'd laughed when she'd said it. Big joke on the city slicker. Having moved around so many times growing up, Laurel knew all about that sort of thing.

She'd come back the first time with, "Thank goodness that's all it is—a ghost with a sense of humor. I was afraid I had some rowdy neighbors. The last time that happened and I called in a complaint, they put a dead rat in my mailbox."

After going through her nightly ritual of shower, flossing, brushing and moisturizing, plus a few half-hearted yoga exercises designed to help her relax, she settled against the pillows and punched in Jerry's number.

"To heck with waiting a week, dammit. If you won't call me, then I'll call you." She let it ring until his message machine clicked on, listened to his familiar voice and hung up, more frustrated than ever, without leaving a message. No wonder people were warned against office relationships.

The beam from the lighthouse swept across the far wall, momentarily distracting her. She took a deep breath, then tensed up again. *Dammit, Jerry, where are you? Are you all right? Are you—?*

Well, of course he wasn't in jail. She'd have heard by now if anything that drastic had happened. Peg kept reminding her that court cases took forever, with all the hearings and delays and appeals. But then, Peg was a big fan of the high-visibility trials that seemed to go on forever. She even had a tape of OJ's famous forty-five-mile-an-hour car chase.

But this was nothing like that, for Pete's sake. It was simply an unfortunate combination of an overzealous auditor and sloppy bookkeeping. To cut down on overhead, Jerry kept the books himself, which was pretty darn decent of him in her estimation. Maybe not very smart, but certainly well-intentioned. A penny saved and all that...

At half past eleven, unable to fall asleep, she punched in the number again. This time she left a message. "Jerry, please let me know what's going on. I'm stuck here until after Labor Day, but I'm really anxious to get back to work. I need to see you again."

She ended the call, immediately wishing she could erase that last part. She'd sounded needy and insecure, and really, she wasn't.

* * *

Sometime after midnight Jerry returned her call. Laurel woke slowly, entangled in the remnants of a dream.

"Jerry?" Smothering a yawn, she sat up in bed and clutched her cell phone. "Well hi, stranger," she said, trying to sound nonchalant rather than half-asleep.

"Hi, sweetheart, sorry I missed your earlier calls."

Of course he would've known that all the hang-up calls were hers, too. A dozen times at least she'd called and then lost her nerve at the last minute. "That's all right, I probably shouldn't have bothered you but it's been so long since I've heard from you. Haven't they taken off the thumbscrews yet?"

"Hey, you know how these things are. These guys aren't satisfied unless they can justify their bloated salaries by bringing in as many scalps as possible. I guess they were a little short of their quota when they decided to go after me. My lawyer filed another appeal last week, so things should be cleared up sooner rather than later."

Laurel interpreted the news as meaning they could soon pick up their relationship where they'd left off—although at this point, she was no longer quite certain where that was. Had he actually proposed, or had they only discussed marriage in general terms?

"How long do you think—"

Ignoring her unspoken question, he said, "So how are you doing, darling? Miss me?"

"You know I do," she said, her voice low and husky. She *needed* him, darn it! Needed him to remind her of why she was so crazy about him. Because she was… surely, she wasn't so fickle she forgot her own feelings. Out of sight, out of mind.

"So tell me about this place where you're staying. Peg says it's a swamp."

"Actually, the swamp is what I inherited. The place where I'm staying at the moment is this old house in the woods with a cast-iron stove and no air-conditioning." Wriggling up to a sitting position, she leaned back against the wrought-iron headboard. Not the most comfortable position, but it helped to wake her up. "I'm on Hatteras Island in a village called Frisco, didn't Peg tell you? It's part of the Outer Banks—the National Seashore Park. The island, not the village."

"You inherited a piece of a national park?"

"No, I inherited a swamp," she snapped. "Sorry—we still haven't straightened out the property mess." So then she told him about her so-called inheritance and where it was located, and how she'd accompanied one of her newfound relatives to his home and ended up with both a cheap rental and a temporary job. "This house where I'm staying now? It's at least a hundred years old, and they say it's supposed to be haunted." She laughed to prove she didn't believe in any such nonsense. "I've actually seen something that could be an old cemetery back in the woods, but it's all grown over with trees and vines and I left my machete at home, so I haven't investigated. Travis—that's one of the cousins I was telling you about? He says, they're all over the place. Family graveyards, I mean. Maybe before I leave I'll hack my way over there, jump a creek or two and scrape away the vines and see if there are any Lawlesses buried here."

Ha-ha. Big joke. She was chattering like a monkey and couldn't seem to stop. She was known for her cool composure, but unfortunately, she seemed to have left it somewhere between New York and North Carolina.

"Sounds creepy. Do you have a street address?"

"I have an address, but no street. I'm staying just off something called Ridge Pond Road, but I get all my mail in care of general delivery. I didn't even bring my laptop because it's in quarantine."

He said, "Hmm," making her wonder if he planned to surprise her with a visit. Or maybe a floral delivery.

"By the way, how's Mama's watercolor? Did you take it with you?"

Peg must have told him. "I was afraid Dan would take it down to hang all his jock posters. I thought it would be safer with me." No point in telling him that the poor thing had started to self-destruct from the shoddy materials used by whoever had framed it, probably his mother. Sentiment aside, Jerry, with his impressive art collection, should have known better.

"Good, good. Well…I guess I'll be seeing you soon," he said.

"Jerry, I promised to stay through Labor Day, but I'll be back home the first week in September. By that time—I mean, with the new appeal and all…?"

With a wrought-iron rosebud digging into her spine, she willed him to tell her whether or not Jay-bass would soon be back in business; whether or not he was free to leave New York in case he wanted to visit her and meet her new family.

Just tell me something, at least, using simple, declarative statements, she willed silently. She tried to picture him and failed. Even his voice sounded…different. Those crazy sound waves Travis had mentioned, probably. Something to do with being surrounded by water.

"Things are looking up," he said cautiously. "Kirk

has a couple of tentatives on the hook for late in April. He's handling everything now that Doris is gone."

Laurel only hoped the secretary, a single mother of two, had had better luck at finding another job than she had. They talked for a few more minutes, and then Jerry claimed an incoming call.

At this hour of the night? Laurel wondered who might be calling him. Probably Kirk. Whatever else he was, Kirk was a hustler. She had no idea what his salary was, but by now he was probably as broke as she was, on top of which he probably had a heaping pile of legal fees.

She whispered good-night after Jerry had already hung up, and put her cell phone on charge—something she was prone to forget with her life so disorganized. For a long time after that she lay awake, thinking about all she'd been missing since Jay-bass had been shut down. Full, exciting days—okay, busy, exasperating and often frustrating days, but at least her feet hadn't hurt quite so much.

And sometimes those days would be followed by dinner out and a sleepover at Jerry's place, which was more than just a place, actually. Her employer-lover lived pretty high on the hog, as her new Southern friends might say. She should be grateful he managed to make as much room for her as he did in his busy schedule instead of resenting the fact that it wasn't more.

It was a long time before she fell asleep again.

Having fallen asleep with Jerry on her mind, Laurel wondered why she woke up thinking of Cody and his piercing eyes, his bronzed, easy-moving body and his hostile attitude. Their relationship had been doomed from the first. She did her best to avoid him, but as theirs were the only two houses served by Ridge Pond Road, an old one-lane sand road that had existed long before the highway was built back in the late forties, avoidance was next to impossible. Especially when his daughter seemed so attached to the old house.

She showered, brushed, moisturized and applied a discreet amount of makeup consisting of tinted lip balm and stick blusher. Her eyes were already shadowed by another largely sleepless night.

It would help if he weren't so strikingly attractive. Peg would've called him a babe magnet; Laurel was in no position to disagree. Even seeing him from a distance he was hard to ignore. She'd all but quit using the front porch swing, because her front porch faced his house and he seemed to spend a lot of time in his yard building something—maybe a pen for the dog. If she leaned just so, she could see through the gap in the hedge.

Three days after her late-night call from Jerry she came home to find Becky and the dog working in her flower bed. The conch shells were scattered and her newest plant had been dug up and was lying on its side, covered with sand. It was the top of a pineapple. Who knew the things could be planted?

"I'm sorry." The child started apologizing even before Laurel emerged from her car. "Daddy built him a pen but he dug out and ran away. He doesn't mean any harm, he just likes to play in the sand."

Bless her solemn little soul, Laurel thought as she tried to reassure her. "Let me change clothes and I'll help you line up the shells again, all right?"

"You're not mad?"

"Not at all. In fact, I think I owe someone a big thank-you for straightening my conch shells and planting a—a surprise."

"That was me. Picola—she's mama's housekeeper—she said you could plant the top off a pineapple and it would grow to a real tree."

"How exciting," Laurel murmured. She was pretty sure pineapples didn't grow on trees, but it was the thought that counted.

She looked for a resemblance between Becky and her father, but found little. The child was a whole lot nicer than her father was—at least she wasn't looking for the first excuse to kick her out.

"It was a lovely gesture, Becky. Maybe if we replant and water it, it will survive...you think?"

Becky brightened and started to speak, but just then the dog came racing around the corner of the house, ears and tongue flying, and before Laurel could back away, he had both front paws on her shoulders and was bathing her face with his foot-long tongue.

Laurel dropped her purse and tried to shove him away while Becky shouted, "Stop that, BooBoo, get *down!*"

"Step on his toes," Cody Morningstar said calmly.

Well, shoot. Of all times for her landlord to come calling. "Do what?" she managed, backing up to try to escape the canine attentions.

Becky was dancing around trying to grab the leash. Sounding hopeful and slightly apprehensive, she said, "He likes you. BooBoo, get *down!*"

"His toes," Cody reiterated. "Once he associates pain with jumping up, he'll quit doing it."

Standing upright, the dog was tall. Laurel wasn't.

"*You* step on his toes," she exclaimed, trying to cover her face with one arm. "He's your dog!"

Becky made another lunge for the leash and missed. "He's not Daddy's dog, he's mine. Mama said I could have him. Quit that, BooBoo!"

"Oh, yuck!" A big wet tongue slipped through the crook of her arm and caught her on the cheek. Laurel reached out one leg and tried to step on the dog's hind foot. She missed. He licked her again. She cried, "Will someone *please* get this creature away from me?"

Cody took control. Laurel could almost swear he was smirking, in which case she was going to kill him.

Becky picked up the pink purse and brushed off the sand. "I'm sorry, Laurie, I was only trying to make things nice. I thought BooBoo was playing in the creek."

Cody handed the leash to his daughter. "We don't want him playing in the creek, either." He sounded tired. So maybe he hadn't been smirking. Maybe he was only worn-out with trying to keep up with the crazy, four-legged clown. "Take him home, honey. Put him in the house."

"But Daddy, what if he has to go to the bathroom?"

Cody gave her the oddest look. Laurel would remember it later and wonder. "Just put him in the kitchen and—no, not the kitchen. Put him in the laundry room and shut the door."

"But he'll cry." Becky looked close to tears, herself.

"Let him cry, there's nothing in there he can hurt."

Reluctantly, the child left, tugging the unrepentant Afghan along behind her. Watching her retreat, Laurel wanted to put an arm around those frail shoulders and tell the child that she and her mutt could dig up her yard any old time they felt like it. What did she care? As much as she'd enjoyed her first attempt at gardening, she wouldn't be there long enough to see anything take root, much less bloom and bear fruit.

## Chapter 8

"Are you all right?" Laurel likened his voice to chocolate-coated gravel. Dark and smooth on the surface, but rock hard underneath. Unlike Jerry's, which was dark and smooth all the way down.

She turned her attention from the child to the man. Arms crossed over his chest, Cody was frowning at the ruins of what had probably once been a neat, well-tended flower bed. "It won't happen again," he said grimly.

"Oh, for goodness sake, lighten up. So your dog dug a few holes. I seriously doubt if this place was up for any landscaping awards."

"That's beside the point. I'll see that they don't bother you again."

"You're going to lock Becky in the laundry room, too? What a lovely relationship you two must have." She didn't bother to hide her unflattering opinion of the man. From what she'd seen so far, he didn't deserve a child, much less someone as sweet as Becky.

He started to speak, changed his mind and turned away. A moment later, he turned back and pointed his finger at her. "You don't know a damned thing about me or my daughter—or my dog, either. So don't bother to try and analyze any relationships. One more week and you'll be out of here. I've got the roofers scheduled for the third."

Laurel could only stare. In other words, she interpreted, work Labor Day Monday, come home and pack your bags and get the hell off the island.

We'll just see about that, she thought as she watched him stride off across the straggling mixture of sandspurs and Bermuda grass. She'd seen plenty of disagreeable men in her life—definitely more than her share—but this one was in a class by himself. She'd been judged and found wanting from the moment he'd come barreling in off the highway, creamed her poor rear fender and then tried to pin the blame on her.

Watching as he disappeared through the gap in the hedge, she muttered, "You just try and evict me—we'll see who wins that case. Possession is nine-tenths of the law, you jerk."

She knew something about the law pertaining to rentals. He had accepted her check for two weeks rent. It would take at least another thirty days to evict her. Her actual stay would be closer to three weeks if she kept her promise to Caroline, and she wasn't in the habit of going back on her word.

"You just try kicking me out, Morningstar," she addressed his back as he reappeared again, loping up the outside stairway that led to his upper deck. "I'm a hell of a lot tougher than I look."

Feeling irritable and unsettled, she let herself inside. Her dress would have to be hand washed and dried flat. She'd already discovered that there was no dry cleaner on the island, and things that usually dried overnight back home took forever down here. She was tempted to call Travis and tell him what was going on, but she'd never been one to whine.

Besides, according to Ru, they had lost three babies in the first trimester. The last thing they needed was to have her dump her troubles in their lap when they evidently had a few of their own. Having just discovered the joys of having an extended family—just how far extended, none of them seemed to know—she wasn't about to impose on the relationship.

Once inside the house, she dumped her purse and a small sack of groceries from Conner's Market. After a few moments of indecision, she put away the milk, the sandwich meat and the bagged salad. She was tempted to call Jerry again, but what could she say that she hadn't already said? He knew how she felt. The next move was up to him, workwise and otherwise.

She punched in Peg's number and waited through seven rings before ending the call. If there'd been any news, Peg would have let her know. She thought about calling Harrison, but that was crazy. What could she say?

She was antsy. Under the circumstances, it was no wonder. Talk about being a stranger in a strange land…!

She straightened the few dresses hanging in the makeshift closet, then lined up the small row of shoes, checking the soles for sand. She rearranged the things on top of the dresser with mathematical precision and looked around for something else she could bring into order. The bedroom window was curtainless, so there were no drapes to straighten. The bed had already been made. It would pass a military inspection.

Needing something to do, she changed into her grungiest clothes and went back outside. The rake was lying on the ground where Becky had dropped it, so she picked it up and began raking the conch shells back into line. It was nearly seven and still hot as blazes without so much as a breath of wind.

According to Travis, a southeast wind brought out any latent disagreements. Tempers flared at the least excuse. She wondered which way the wind had been blowing when Cody had run into her car. Travis was right. To be perfectly honest, she wished she had someone to yell at, if only to relieve the tension.

After the first few minutes she was dripping with perspiration. She managed to line up some dozen or so conch shells, all bleached bone-white. She wondered who had collected them from the beach and arranged them so carefully. Her ghost?

*Stop it. Just stop that!*

If there was a ghost anywhere around, it had a terrific sense of humor. Travis said the only two houses within shouting distance were his and Cody's, but that wasn't Ru she'd heard cackling in the middle of the night. And it definitely wasn't her landlord.

*Deep breath. In with the positive, out with the negative.*

Leaning on the rake handle, Laurel caught a glimpse of the winding, half-hidden creek in the woods near where she'd spotted what Travis said was an old family graveyard. If she'd inherited her mother's interests, the first thing she'd have done was hack her way through the bushes, wade across the creek, examine the surrounding land for signs of unmarked graves and take rubbings from those that were marked. She'd gone with her a few times as a child, and knew the drill.

Although her mother would be disappointed if the graves didn't date back at least a couple of centuries. Elizabeth Redd Lawless had been exploring an ancient

burial mound in southern Ireland when she'd caught a
cold or flu that had turned into pneumonia. She had
died within a week's time. The curse of some ancient
entity?

"I don't think so," Laurel muttered, raking her hair
off her sweat-filmed forehead. She wasn't in the least
bit superstitious. She prided herself on her pragmatism.

Still, she had to admit she felt oddly drawn to this
particular patch of unkempt land for no discernible reason. The tall, twisted live oaks, the cedars and bays and
various hollies—even the ghostly dead pine trees that
Travis said were hurricane victims—they all appealed
to a side of her nature that must have lain dormant for
nearly thirty years.

As a result of having moved so many times while she
was growing up, Laurel had never let herself grow attached to any one area. It hadn't particularly bothered her.
In fact, she'd never even thought about it until she found
herself here in the northeast corner of North Carolina.

Maybe it was hearing the local legends, first from
Harrison and then from Travis, many of which involved
their mutual ancestors, that had triggered her imagination. "Two Lawlesses were light keepers," he'd told
her. "You know about old Squire, the bootlegger, but did
you know we had a pirate in the family chain?"

That's when he'd told her about Blackbeard's second
in command, whose daughter had reportedly married
one of her ancestors. Ru had scoffed and told him not
to spread it on too thick.

"Hey, it's the written record," he'd claimed.

"Says who?"

"Says all the genealogists who study that kind of
stuff. There's folks down here who've read just about

every family Bible on the island, not to mention all the court data—wills, deeds, that sort of thing."

They had bickered for a few minutes more about what constituted a legitimate source, and then Laurel had gone home and dreamed a series of what might have been outtakes from *Pirates of the Caribbean.*

Probably only the peppery clam chowder Travis had served that evening. Hatteras style, he'd called it. No milk, no tomatoes, only salt pork, onions, potatoes and clams, and tons of black pepper. And while it was certainly tasty, she'd had to take an antacid before she could sleep.

Now, unwilling to go back inside and face an empty house and an empty evening, she continued to rake neat patterns in the sand until it was too dark to see. Only when the mosquitoes began to hunt in earnest did she prop her rake against the porch and hurry inside.

Oddly enough, her inheritance no longer seemed quite so important. According to Travis, the taxes weren't much. The three known heirs had split them, and if it suited her, he'd just as soon wait until after Ru had the baby to clear up the title.

It suited her just fine. She would make sure they knew where to find her before she left. She had offered to reimburse them for her share of the taxes, which would mean starving for the foreseeable future, but Trav said they weren't worth mentioning.

"It's all in the family," he'd told her. "Maybe next time Lyon and Jasmine come down here to visit, we'll get together and sort things out."

Only she wouldn't still be here then, she thought as she washed her hands at the sink before heading upstairs to clean up properly. As much as she would love to meet another cousin, her real life was back in New York. And she could hardly wait to get back there.

Honestly, she told herself.

Laurel's next run-in with her landlord was precipitated by Becky and the dog. As the shop was closed on Sundays and Mondays, the shorthanded staff badly in need of the two-day break, she had planned to spend all day Sunday at the beach with a good book. After a restless night she'd slept late and then sleepwalked through her morning ritual.

She blamed the weather for her lethargy. Hot, still and dripping with humidity, it was what Travis called storm-breeding weather. She could vouch for the fact that it was also energy-sapping weather.

It was past one when, armed with sunscreen, beach towel, a book and a cold drink, she locked the door behind her and headed for her car. That's when she spotted Becky racing toward her, waving her hand.

"Wait, Miss Laurie! Are you going to the beach?"

"How'd you guess?" She was wearing flip-flops, a bathing suit and a man's dress shirt for a cover-up. "Would you like to join me?" she invited, knowing Cody wouldn't allow it. Poor child.

"Me and Daddy are going to the beach, too, so you could come with us. Daddy can drive in the sand. He said your car can't, so you'd have to walk and the sand burns your feet, and we're gonna cook marshmallows."

Later, Laurel would wonder what had prompted her to accept the invitation. Mark it down to sheer wickedness, to knowing how her presence would irritate her landlord and how hard-pressed he'd be to hold his tongue in front of his daughter. She simply couldn't resist the temptation.

Cody was waiting in the fork of the driveway, the powerful engine of his SUV throbbing like a sleeping dragon in the stillness of the August afternoon. "Is it all right?" Laurel asked, daring him to say no.

Watching Cody's eyes flash, his lips tighten, set off the oddest kind of excitement inside her, as if she'd turned into an adrenaline junkie.

At least things seemed to have smoothed out in his relationship with his daughter. The first few times she'd seen the two of them together, Becky had looked almost fearful. Cody had called her *honey*—she'd heard him do it at least twice.

But then, even ant poison was sweet.

Becky was in the backseat. Laurel slid in beside her and a silky-haired canine head came over the back of the seat to rest on her shoulder. She was afraid to pet him for fear he'd end up in her lap.

They passed up two beach ramps in favor of one that appeared comparatively unused. There were several vehicles scattered along the beach, but Cody found a spot some distance from fishermen and surfers. A lazy surf frothed at the edges of the water, lacy ruffles on a turquoise sea that eventually shaded to royal blue.

"This suit everybody?" he asked, setting the parking brake.

Without answering, Becky loosened her seat belt and reached for the door handle. "Come on, Laurie, let's go in the water."

"I guess it does," Cody answered his own question.

Becky grabbed Laurel's hand and tugged her out of the car. "Come on, I'll show you how good I can swim."

"Is it all right?" Laurel asked as she kicked off her sandals and shed her cover-up.

"Yeah, go ahead, I'll keep an eye on things. You can swim, can't you?"

"Oh, sure." She could. Not stylishly, but barring rip currents, she could hold her own. So she raced after the eager child, leaving him to deal with the dog and all the paraphernalia piled in the back of the vehicle.

"Waist-deep only," Cody called after them. At least, that's what Laurel thought he said. She waved a hand to show she understood.

Evidently, Becky knew her limitations. "Daddy says I can only go in waist-deep. Can we use your waist instead of mine, since I'm with you?"

"Only if you hold on to my hand," Laurel replied, uncomfortably aware of the man watching them from the shore. "How about my hips instead of my waist?"

Holding hands, they waded out, with Becky jumping over the gentle waves, giggling breathlessly. "Daddy says you can only see the top of a boat that's three miles out on account of…of something, I forget what it's called. Can we ride a wave?"

The waves were hardly big enough to float a paper boat. "We can try," Laurel said. Holding hands, they turned toward the shore and looked back over their shoulders, ready to catch the next decent wave. Cody had tied the dog to the bumper. He was watching them again. Watching his child, she hoped, instead of checking out her unexciting figure in the modest tank suit.

"Here we go, hold on to my hand," Laurel cautioned, launching them on the brief ride to shore.

"I told you I could do it," Becky proclaimed breathlessly a few moments later as she blinked away the saltwater and fingered the sand she'd collected in the seat of her bathing suit.

"You certainly did," Laurel replied, wishing she could clear out her own seat as unselfconsciously. It had been years since she'd been to the beach. She'd forgotten that particular aspect of washing ashore on her belly.

After wading back out again, Becky demonstrated a few strokes and Laurel dutifully admired them, watching to make certain they didn't stray too far out or get smacked by an errant wave. They stayed in the water for perhaps half an hour, every minute of which Laurel was conscious of Cody, watching from the shore. BooBoo, on a long lead attached to the bumper, exhausted himself barking at seagulls, then seemed content to lie on his side and gnaw at the various stickers in his once silky coat.

Slogging ashore, Laurel found it next to impossible to ignore the man who was wearing only sunglasses and black boxers, his bare skin gleaming like polished bronze. Not until much later did it occur to her that not once all afternoon did Becky respond directly to a single one of her father's remarks. Instead, interspersed with commands to the dog, which BooBoo ignored, she directed her remarks to Laurel.

"BooBoo's afraid of the water," Becky confided breathlessly after racing along the surf and belly flopping on something called a boogie board. "Daddy said if he had a dog he'd get a—a some kind of a retriever, because they like to swim, but Mama likes BooBoo 'cause he's won lots and lots of ribbons. He even has a handler."

Laurel had a vague idea what a handler did after watching a few dog shows on television. She had never owned a pet, much less personally attended any dog shows. The Afghan hound had given up yapping at ghost crabs and seagulls and was peacefully working on removing something from the bottom of his big, hairy foot. He jumped up at their approach, a goofy grin on his canine face.

While Becky collapsed on her knees, throwing both arms around her dog and telling him all about her swim, Laurel avoided looking at Cody while she spread her beach towel on the other side of the small fire he'd built. He offered her the low beach chair he was using, but she no-thanked him, settled on her towel and began rummaging in her beach bag for sunscreen.

"Can we go swimming again after we cook marshmallows?"

The question was directed at Laurel, but it was Cody who answered. "Why don't we look for shells while the fire burns down?"

Ignoring her father, Becky jumped up again, scattering sand. "C'mon, Laurie, I can show you which shells are best. There's pigs and sheep and eyeballs, only sheep are real hard to find."

Seeing Cody's mouth tighten, Laurel felt a surge of unexpected sympathy. Evidently, his daughter was paying him back for some real or imagined wrong. She had no idea how these father-daughter relationships were supposed to go because her own father had rarely been around when she was Becky's age.

Toweling her hair, she said, "Let me catch my breath first, all right?"

Becky dropped down on her knees between Laurel's feet. Without looking at him, she tipped her head toward Cody. "He can go swimming while you and me and BooBoo find shells."

Laurel was getting just a tad irritated by such open rudeness. "Why don't you and your father go collect shells? I'll keep an eye on BooBoo." Talk about your sacrifices.

"Daddy can swim till we get back. I've got a bag we can put shells in, so are you rested now?"

It wasn't so much sympathy for Cody as it was a dislike of rudeness that made her say, "Only if your father agrees. After all, he was kind enough to bring us here and build a fire so you could toast marshmallows."

Becky lifted her skinny shoulders in a long-suffering sigh. "Can I, Daddy? We won't go out of sight, I promise."

"Yeah sure, run along."

Oh, for heaven's sake, Laurel thought as she stood and brushed off the sand Becky had scattered in her lap, how could any man so big and virile elicit such a feeling of sympathy?

And it was sympathy she was feeling. That's all it could be. It had nothing to do with his golden eyes or his sun-streaked hair, much less his bronzed, virile body.

Before she could stop herself, she pictured Jerry's lean, white body. Elegant was the word that came to mind, not sexy. But a man, she reminded herself, was more than the sum total of his parts.

*And dammit, you will* not *think about his parts!*

"C'mon, Laurie, I'll race you to that sign on the post." Thank God for the distraction.

Laurel jogged because she needed to get away from the man who, without lifting a finger, was complicating her already complicated life. "You're not looking for shells," she called to the child. She'd been stuck with the leash while BooBoo chased low-flying beach birds, sniffed at piles of seaweed and generously marked his territory. "Come on, you clown," she muttered. "Heel!"

Responding to her voice, the big clumsy hound raced back and jumped up on her, his toenails raking her shoulder. Laurel nearly tipped over backward trying to stomp on his foot.

And then Cody was there. So much for getting in a swim. He hadn't even gotten his trunks wet. "Rebecca, come take this dog before I drown him." To the dog, he said sharply, "Heel!"

This time the dog heeled, if that meant plopping down on his wet, sandy butt and grinning as if this were some new game and he awaited only the next move.

"We need to put something on those scratches," Cody said. "I can drive you up to the medical center or you can settle for what's in my medicine cabinet."

"Oh, for heaven's sake, it's just a few scratches," she objected. Among numerous other scratches, mostly inflicted by briars in the course of her unsuccessful attempts at landscaping.

"Left alone, even minor scratches have a way of getting infected."

At his grimmest, the man still got under her skin. Talk about getting infected! "I'll take care of it as soon as I get home. I promise." If the thing needed cauterizing, his touch alone would do that. He was standing so close she could feel his warm breath on her face, smell the sunbaked, masculine scent of his skin. The effect was dizzying.

Something was definitely affecting the emotional control she'd always prided herself on maintaining. She wanted to blame the salt air, but self-honesty got in the way. Fortunately, before she could say something stupid, Becky raced up breathlessly and grabbed her hand. "I'm sorry he scratched you, Miss Laurie, he didn't mean to do it. Daddy's medicine doesn't burn, does it, Daddy?"

Cody's eyes briefly met Laurel's. Was the fact that this time the child had addressed him directly responsible for that warm glow?

Surely it was. What else could it be?

"Then why don't we just wash me off in seawater for now, and when we go home, I'll borrow your daddy's medicine. Now, did someone promise me a roasted marshmallow, or did I just dream that?"

Which was how they all came to be seated around a small campfire just as the sun settled behind the dunes, layering the sky with streaks of brilliant color. The dog, finally exhausted by the day's activities, was content to sleep on Laurel's beach towel. Cody had stridden out into the water up to his hips, dived under and come up long moments later where the water changed from pale green to deeper blue. Laurel had watched as he shook his head, then set out to swim to Bermuda. She watched, hardly daring to breathe, until he turned and began swimming back toward shore, powerful arms flashing like bronze pistons.

"I'm the one who remembered to bring the sticks," Becky confided later as she offered the first marshmallow to Laurel, who accepted the blackened confection, ignored the grit and the stickiness and professed to enjoy it enormously.

Again Laurel caught Cody's eyes. A silent message passed between them, but for the life of her, she couldn't have said what it was. She knew only that this was a moment she would not soon forget. Someday, when she had children of her own...

"Tomorrow we'll bring hot dogs," Becky said earnestly when eventually they began to gather up their belongings.

Laurel pretended she hadn't heard. She hadn't intended to stay this long—nor, she suspected, had Cody. She wondered if he'd been reluctant to end the peaceful outing because in the past hour or so, his daughter had actually directed the occasional remark his way.

Whatever was going on between them, it was none of her business. The last thing she needed was to get in the middle of a family situation and give him an excuse to kick her out.

Cody spread a plastic tarp over the rear end of the SUV and signaled for the dog to jump in. They covered the fire pit with sand, collected the small cooler and wet towels, and then Laurel slipped into the backseat beside Becky. She was starting to feel slightly foolish for avoiding the front seat, but if Cody noticed, he didn't mention it.

By the time they pulled up in front of her house, Becky was all but asleep. Cody helped sort out the soggy towels and sandy gear and she said, "Thanks. And thanks for letting me share your outing. I had a wonderful time."

Cody nodded. Becky opened her eyes and said sleepily, "I'm going to plant something pretty for you tomorrow. I found it in the woods. It's got purple berries. Daddy, can we have hamburgers for supper?"

Progress, Laurel thought tiredly as she carried her small bundle up the front path. That made at least four times today that Becky had addressed a remark to her father.

She was almost too tired to let herself inside, but it was a good kind of tired. Salty, sandy, relaxed, she was reminded of something her employer, Caroline Danvers had said recently. After an amicable divorce, Caroline had moved to the island eight years ago, bought a business and settled in. "I'm what's called a local," she'd said. "Down here you have the natives and the locals— that's the ones who buy a house and settle here. Then there are the transients who come work for a season or two and then move on. And of course, the tourists." She'd been trying to explain various relationships about who was kin to whom among the natives, some of whom were customers. "I've quit trying to figure it out. Half the people who move down here have folks who came from the island. As for the rest of us, some stay permanently, others pick up and leave after a few years. Maybe it's a chemical reaction, ya reckon?"

Now, dumping a handful of lavender bath salts into the tub as she adjusted the yellowish water to luke-warm, Laurel wondered where she fit in. According to Travis, she probably had dozens of distant relatives here, since the Lawlesses were among the first families to settle on the island long before the American Revolution. Evidently they'd been prolific. Maybe that was why she felt so comfortable here, she mused. It was almost one of those déjà vu things, as if she'd been here before, a long, long time ago.

An examination in the clouded bathroom mirror revealed two red streaks across her right shoulder, but nowhere was the skin broken. The scratch didn't even sting when she ducked under the water to wash her hair. After giving her hair a final rinse under the faucet, she found the energy to climb out of the tub, towel off and slip into a J. Peterman caftan. Barefoot on the cool, gritty floors, she headed downstairs to heat a can of

## Chapter 9

Cody held up the tube of Neosporin, waiting to see if she was going to let him in. "I see you got some sunburn, too. I have calamine lotion if you need it."

"It's not a problem. Neither is the scratch. Really. The skin wasn't even broken. But thank you." Short, clipped sentences. It was the way he'd have written dialog if he wanted to express irritation.

"I always believe in playing safe," he said solemnly. "No point in risking an infection. By the time I got Becky settled for the night, I was afraid you'd be in bed, but I took a chance."

As she still hadn't invited him in, he tried a different tactic. "You might have noticed that my daughter and I have a slight problem communicating. She really likes you, though. Normally, she's shy around strangers." Without giving her a chance to speak, he went on. "So I was thinking—now that you've been around her a while, have you picked up on anything? I could really use some objective insight here."

Even as he asked, he was wondering why the devil it suddenly seemed so important to involve his tenant. The same tenant he'd done his best to evict. Still waiting for a response, he told himself it had nothing to do with the fact that she was an intriguing, not to mention a damned attractive woman. "I'm speaking strictly as a clueless, frustrated father here."

When no response was forthcoming, he flashed her a smile, the practiced version he used to use in publicity stills. His hair had been darker then, and he'd had a mustache. "Tell you what, if you can find out what the devil's bugging her, you can stay here rent free for as long as you like."

Talk about your great opening lines, he thought as she unhooked the screen and held it open. He stepped inside quickly, before she changed her mind.

"If you mean she rarely addresses you directly, I did notice that."

"Actually, the situation's improved just today, but on the way here from Virginia, she didn't speak more than half a dozen words, not even when she needed to stop. The way she won't even look at me, it's almost like she doesn't trust me." He followed her into the living room and dropped the tube on the coffee table. When she still didn't speak, he said, "I don't mind telling you, I'm at a dead loss here. Just when I think things are starting to improve, she clams up again."

And it hurt like hell. His own daughter—the child he'd worshipped from the moment she'd been born. He'd done his best to shield her from the divorce. Mara had, too. He could give her credit for that much at least. But when you take away everything in a child's small world, break it into pieces and throw it all away, you had to expect repercussions. Counseling had helped. Up until this trip, he'd thought they were handling things pretty well, although he would admit to being a little too indulgent.

Cody waited for her to sit, then lowered himself cautiously onto the sofa. He knew where the wild spring was located and avoided it. "So like I said, she seems to be going through a new phase, and damned if I can figure it out. It's not like she was openly defiant or anything like that." He shook his head.

Hands clasped in her lap, Laurel said cautiously, "I really don't know much about children."

"Yeah, well I thought I did—I mean, I've got one, right? But evidently, I was wrong. It's like we're strangers. Like we don't even share an eight-year history anymore. Has she said anything at all? About me, I mean?"

Maybe it wasn't fair, laying so much on a woman he'd done his best to evict, but he didn't want to burden Ru with his problems; she had enough of her own, with the baby and whatever was going on between her and Travis. He could write to one of those syndicated advice columnists, but chances were Becky would be in college before he got an answer—if he ever did.

The room smelled different. Felt different, too. Maybe it was the woman herself, or maybe it was just him. Dammit, he felt different, too. He hadn't come here because she was a fine-looking woman, an intriguing woman, and he was…intrigued. One way to put it, he thought with wry amusement. Intrigued, as in he couldn't look at her, sunburn, scratches and all, without wondering how she'd be in bed. Quiet and controlled?

Or wild as a tiger that had just been released from a small cage…

"Place looks good," he said, looking around the small room. "Stuff fits better. I didn't do much while I was living here, just left things pretty much the way I found them."

The truth was, the place was no more attractive now than it had been when he'd lived here, but it felt roomier. He noticed the picture she'd hung on the far wall was missing. Evidently she'd taken his advice.

"Heard any ghosts lately?" he asked, and could have kicked himself for bringing it up. Half a dozen people had filled him with the same old blarney—probably their way of having fun at a newcomer's expense. Like the guy who swore he'd been attacked by a giant stingray, twisted off its stinger and used it to stab the poor critter to death.

What the hell, he'd made up a few wild tales himself back in Oklahoma when he'd been a kid. Some pretty gory ones, too. Probably what eventually led to his present career.

"Cody, I wish I could help you, but honestly, Becky hasn't even mentioned you to me. Nothing that would hint at what's bothering her, at least."

It took only a split second to remember his earlier question. Too much to expect she'd come up with a tidy answer right off the bat. "What happened to your painting?"

She looked at the bare west wall. "I took it to a framer. The woman there said the moisture had already attacked the paper. Little brown flecks in the sky. I thought they were supposed to be there."

"Humidity's rough on paper goods. Mostly it hangs around the eighty percent range, depending on the season and which way the wind's blowing. I keep an AC on in my office to dry it out, even when the rest of the house is wide-open."

"In case you hadn't noticed," she said dryly, "I don't have one downstairs."

"You could've hung the picture in the bedroom. I

happen to know there's a working unit up there." He assayed a grin, wondering if her eyes were green or gray? Or did they change color depending on what she was thinking?

What *was* she thinking? Something about that steady regard, so different from the way Becky avoided looking at him lately, was starting to get under his skin. She had the kind of looks that were all the more effective for being understated. The small sunburned nose, the full, firm mouth—those high cheekbones.

He cleared his throat and tried to remember what he'd been about to say.

"About Becky," she said, interrupting his silent inventory somewhere in the region of her small, high breasts. "Do you mind her coming over here?"

"The question is, do *you* mind? I think I mentioned that I was still living here the last time she visited, so I guess it seems natural for her to run over here to play. My house was being finished up inside and I didn't want her over there where she might get hurt."

"She certainly doesn't bother me. Most of the time, I'm not even here, but when I am, I enjoy her company."

"What about the dog? He's pretty obnoxious." Cody was glad he'd taken time to shower and change while Becky fell asleep over her untouched hamburger. He'd chosen a lousy time to try and bribe her with marshmallows on the beach so close to supper time. While she'd rinsed off in the solar-heated outdoor shower, he had taken a ready-made burger from the freezer and popped it into the microwave.

He'd ended up putting her to bed, wet hair and all, and waiting a few minutes to make sure she wasn't going to wake up. Watching her, he'd wondered for the millionth time what he had done to deserve anything so perfect.

And what the devil was going on inside that beloved head.

"I'm okay with dogs," Laurel said in answer to the question he'd all but forgotten asking. One of the reasons he was so far behind on his work in progress—he couldn't seem to concentrate. Brain cells scattering like a load of buckshot.

She was still talking. He tuned in as she was saying something about never having owned a dog. "He seems harmless enough. Some breeds scare me just by their reputations. Rottweilers, Dobermans—I don't think I'd recognize a pit bull if I met one face-to-face. But you know what?" She flashed him a quick smile that hit him square in the solar plexus. "The only time I was ever bitten by a dog, it was a toy poodle."

He chuckled; her smiled faded, and the atmosphere grew strained again. Cody cleared his throat. "About Becky—like I said, we've always gotten along fine before this trip, but I doubt if she spoke more than a dozen words the whole way from Richmond. Midlothian, actually. I might have mentioned that my ex-wife still lives there?"

He didn't want to get into Mara and the custody thing with a woman who was essentially a stranger, even if she didn't feel like a stranger. Not when he'd seen her mad as hell, watched her throw back her head and laugh at something the damn fool dog did. Not when he'd seen her both dressed for work with her hair gleaming like mahogany, and wet, sandy and tousled.

He'd watched her exclaim over the broken shells

Becky collected while that clown of a mutt pounced around, kicking up sand and peeing on every pile of seaweed.

But yeah…she was still basically a stranger. In another week or so she'd go back to wherever she came from and he could get on with the business of finishing his book, reengaging in the ongoing custody hearings and either bringing this old house up to standard or razing it to build a larger rental.

"Becky did mention that she's going to have a new daddy," Laurel said quietly. She cut him a sidelong glance, as if wondering if she should bring up something that was none of her business.

"She told you that?"

"Indirectly. That is, she mentioned something about her new daddy not liking animals. I take it that includes BooBoo?"

"I've met the guy, but the subject of dogs didn't come up."

"You think he might not let her keep BooBoo?"

Cody shook his head. "Could be, although technically, he's Mara's dog. I still don't see how it involves me, unless she wants me to adopt the mutt and is afraid to ask." Reticent by nature, he hesitated, and then he said quietly, "If I didn't know better, I might even think she was afraid of me."

Silence was a vacuum. Laurel leaned forward in the ever-so-slightly lopsided recliner. She crossed her ankles, her gaze fixed on her small bare feet.

Cody said, "Dammit, Laurel, I've never laid a hand on that child! She can't be afraid of me!"

"Then it's obviously something else. Not all threats are physical." She looked up at him then. "If I had to guess, I'd say it has something to do with this new man in her mother's life. You say they're engaged?"

"By now they're already married. Mara wanted to be married in Paris, of all the crazy notions." He shook his head. "Too much red tape. They were married in Richmond and took off the same day for France. Why do you think I got to keep Becky for an unscheduled visit?"

"Well, I wouldn't know, would I? Really, this is none of my business, but if you're worried about her coming over here to play, please don't. Not on my account, at least. She's more than welcome to dig up my yard—actually, your yard—and plant anything she wants to in the flower beds."

Cody figured he'd pushed it as far as he dared. He stood, and then Laurel did, too. The top of her head came just to his chin. She gave the impression of being taller, but he figured that was mostly attitude. The lady had that, all right. Although in her softer moments, he suspected she might be…softer.

Before his baser impulses could get him in trouble, he said, "Do me a favor. Keep an ear out for any clue about what's eating on her, will you? Because something definitely is, and the more I try to find out, the more she clams up."

At the door, Laurel said, "I will. And thanks for the antibiotic. I'll return it tomorrow." From somewhere nearby came the sound of a hoarse croak.

"Night heron," he said.

She nodded. "That's what I thought it was."

On his way home, Cody let his mind range free. Ideas, new and old, mingled with fresh impressions. So Laurel had picked up on this new guy Mara had married, same as he had. Cody had met him only briefly, but he'd heard more than enough from Mara about her reasons for marrying a man nearly twice her age. Although she hadn't put it in so many words, the clear attraction was money and political ambitions, starting with the state senate.

Just where Becky fit into the equation wasn't clear, but something was going on. Something that had started between the time he'd dropped her off after her last visit and the time he'd picked her up for this one. Mara hadn't even been there at the time. Picola, whom he liked and trusted, had Becky packed and ready when he'd pulled up in front of the house.

"I think she might be comin' down with a cold, Mr. Cody. You see she gets enough sleep now, y'hear? And don't let her take that computer game to bed with her, either. Blessed things, they're ruinin' all the young'uns's eyes. My nephew's already wearin' glasses, and he's not but seven years old."

At his sliding glass door, his mind wandered back to the woman he'd just left. She smelled like coconut. She had a cowlick on one side of her crown that she probably lacquered down every morning. After a rough toweling on the beach earlier today, it had stood up like a cock's comb.

The exhausted dog barely lifted his head when Cody let himself quietly inside his plain, practical, three-quarters-of-a-million-dollar house. "Good boy," he murmured as he silently climbed to the second floor to check on his daughter.

"Your mama's not the maternal type, honey," he murmured, gazing down on the tangle of straw-blond hair, which was the only thing she'd inherited from him. "Never was. The only reason she fought so hard for custody was that she knew how much I wanted you."

As for what happened once the newlyweds got back to the States, that was anyone's guess. But one thing he vowed: his daughter would be spending a lot more time with him than she had in the past. He had already marshaled an army of arguments to that end, beginning with the fact that Picola, who was more like a mother than a housekeeper, would not be making the move to the West Coast. Which meant that except for photo-ops, Becky would probably be left in the hands of strangers while Mara and her new guy launched his senatorial campaign.

On the other hand, she had a perfectly good dad who worked from home and could be with her 24-7.

"Meanwhile, sugar, any cooperation on your part would be greatly appreciated," he whispered, leaning over to kiss his daughter's cheek before pulling the top sheet over her delicate shoulders.

Once upon a time back in Oklahoma—he must have been about her age when it happened—he'd found an unfledged bird that had fallen from the nest during a hard blow. Ugliest critter he'd ever seen—gray skin with the innards showing through, big yellow mouth and no feathers. He had cradled it briefly in his hands before placing it back in the nest, then hunkered down and watched to see if mama bird was going to take over her duties again.

By nightfall, she still hadn't, so he had taken the bird home with him and made a nest from a shoe box and several T-shirts. Using tweezers, he fed it earthworms, but it had died the next day. He had bawled his eyes out, and then he'd buried it in the woods and put a brick over the grave so the raccoons wouldn't dig it up.

The young were so damned fragile. He would just

have to wait and see if Mara intended to fight him over their fledgling. As a single male, he was at a disadvantage, but if he knew Mara, her new role as the wife of a senate candidate would appeal to her far more then the role of mother.

He thought about turning in, but it was early yet. With a few uninterrupted hours before he crashed, he headed to his office, trying to focus on something over which he had at least some semblance of control.

Trav sorted through boxes of old radio equipment, his mind not really on finding the part he needed to repair a thirty-year-old transmitter. Dammit, the last thing Ru needed at this point was a teenage kid who was hell-bent on doing what he wanted to do instead of thinking about his future. The first time he'd ever met the boy it had been after one of the worst weeks of his life, when Matt, the son he'd only recently heard about and had yet to meet, had run away from home. Sharon had called from California where she lived with her second husband and their two kids, frantic to know if Matt was with Travis.

Eventually, after making his way across country, being involved in a bus wreck, ending up lost in a rare island snowstorm with no way of finding the man he'd considered his father—still did, because Trav had never told him otherwise—Matt had turned up here. Ru had found him and brought him home.

Once he'd recovered from his initial shock—again, thanks to Ru—Trav had accepted the boy and never let on for one moment that Matt was a younger replica of one Luis Galanos, a civilian base-worker who'd had all the single women—and some of the married ones—in Wildwood, panting after him.

Sharon included. It had led directly to their divorce.

Matt had finished school at Cape Hatteras High and been all set to go to college when he'd got this crazy bug about being in the way. As if there was only room in the house—in their lives—for one kid.

Both Ru and Trav had racked their brains trying to recall anything either of them might have said to give Matt the idea that he was no longer welcome. Trav distinctly remembered telling him that the new baby was mighty lucky to have a ready-made big brother.

His school friends had probably teased him. Kids made a lot of thoughtless remarks. Trav had set about planning to build another room onto the house. They could have managed without it, but he liked to build. He'd even taught Matt a few skills as they added on another bedroom the summer after Matt had showed up.

Where the hell *was* the boy? He could at least have called to say he was all right. It was eating on Ru, bigtime. She figured since she was a stepmom, she must be responsible, but that was a bunch of hooey. She was a better mom than Sharon would ever be. Without once seeing Matt and his mother together, Trav knew that much.

He reached for the antacids that sat on top of an old CB radio, the first one he'd ever built. It was housed in a flowered metal cake box. Matt had been interested, having picked up a lot of the trucker lingo on his way across country a few years ago. Trav had encouraged him to study for his ham license instead, but then he'd started mating on one of the charter boats, and the next thing, he was going to work toward getting a captain's license.

Trav wondered, not for the first time, if he should have told the kid about his true paternity. Every instinct said no. For all intents and purposes, Trav was his father.

On the other hand, if he ever needed an organ transplant, something critical like that…

Lying wasn't something he did well. Or at all, if he had a choice. But he'd lived with a lie of omission for the past six years, ever since Ru had dragged in a scared, half-frozen kid she'd found hiding in the woods. Not once had he ever let on to the boy that his paternity was in question. He hadn't once questioned it himself when Sharon had called and told him they had a son who was going on twelve years old. His first impulse was to rush out to meet the boy, to bring him back home.

Sharon had shot down that idea right away, saying it wouldn't be fair to her husband—Matt's stepfather. Instead, he'd arranged for child support payments and sent fishing gear, computer games, baseball gloves—anything he figured a kid that age would enjoy.

He should have suspected something was off base from the way he kept just missing him. "Oh, my heavens," Sharon would say, "You should have called. Matt's gone fishing off Baha with this friend of his—they're classmates."

"I called," Travis reminded her.

"Well, yes, but that was last week. This trip just came up day before yesterday when another boy came down with a strep throat."

Trav had studied her for a long time—the woman he'd once been married to. She hadn't invited him inside. "And you couldn't have called and let me know?"

There'd been a couple of near misses before Trav had finally caught on. For some reason, Sharon didn't want the two of them to meet.

Why? Because she was afraid he would insist on joint custody?

Damn right, he would. The only reason he hadn't was that he was still in the process of building his house and a homeless, unmarried retiree was in no position to take on the care and feeding of a kid.

Not until they had finally met did Trav learn the truth. All it had taken was one look at the dark-haired, dark-eyed, olive-skinned boy who claimed to be his son.

# Chapter 10

"It's officially a tropical storm," Ru announced the minute Laurel walked into her cousin's house on Monday. She switched off the TV. "They're calling it Helene."

"Whoa, back up. What's officially a tropical storm?"

"Sorry, I've gotten hooked on the weather channel ever since I've been in protective custody. It's still pretty far out in the Atlantic, so we don't have to put up the storm blinds quite yet." Ru motioned to the kitchen, only a few feet away. Travis's house was nothing if not compact. "Pour yourself a glass of sun-tea. I used a couple of mint tea bags and real sugar."

"Does Travis know you've been cooking?"

"I ran water in a pitcher, added a few tea bags and set it out in the back porch. It's not cooking unless you use a stove."

Laurel knew the limitations; Travis had spelled them out. No sudden moves of any kind, no lifting anything that couldn't be lifted with one hand. According to Ru, the trouble was remembering all the restrictions.

They talked about the possibility of a storm, and about a few of the locals who'd been in the shop that day. Laurel found herself wondering whenever anyone who sounded local came in whether or not they could be a distant cousin. Silly, but harmless. She had to have something to occupy her mind, else she'd worry herself sick about Jerry and her old job and the fact that their apartment building was suddenly turning into a crime area. Not that a single break-in meant anything, but when it happened to you, it was different.

Ru mentioned a video Travis had rented for her, and they discussed the movies Laurel used to review. They both loved the older ones and spent several minutes trying to remember who had starred with Gene Wilder in *Young Frankenstein*. When Laurel described a few of the so-called-celebrities she had shepherded through public appearances for J. Blessing Associates, Ru had never heard of a single one.

"I'm not surprised," Laurel said, laughing. "The surprise is that most of them actually drew large enough crowds to make a decent profit for whichever charity we were raising money for. As a good friend of mine says, any old excuse to party, especially when it's for a good cause."

Shortly after that, Laurel rose and took both glasses to the kitchen and rinsed them out. "I'd better run along and see what my neighbor's daughter's planted today. Stay put. You only have what—three more weeks? I'll get you some books from the library if you'll tell me who your favorite authors are."

Ru made a face. "Surprise me. I've already read all my favorites. Now I'm reduced to reading essays and editorials. If there's anything scarier than pregnancy, it's politics."

The first thing Laurel noticed when she pulled into her yard was that three new plants had materialized in her flower beds. Pokeberries? She was no expert. At least her conchs were all in a row and BooBoo hadn't thrown sand all over her front steps.

The old house still smelled somewhat musty, but the bouquet of Cape jasmine Caroline had given her from the bush in her yard helped, as did the lingering smell of coffee.

From the coffeemaker.

Which she'd forgotten to turn off before leaving for work.

"Well, shoot," she muttered, tossing her purse onto the detached woodstove, which currently served as an additional table. She punched off the appliance and wrinkled her nose at the half an inch of sludge in the bottom of the glass pot. What could have been a disaster had been avoided—*this* time. But it just went to show how far she'd fallen from the orderly, make-a-list-and-check-it-off type of person she'd been all her adult life. She could have burned this place down. Where was her brain, anyway?

The answer eluded her. All she knew as she changed out of her work clothes and set to scouring her inexpensive coffeemaker, was that ever since she'd lost her job—

Make that ever since she'd come South and started meeting relatives she'd never even heard of. And then heard of more she had yet to meet.

But even then she'd been doing just fine, taking it all in stride, until she'd had that run-in with her irritating, puzzling, too-sexy landlord.

Not to mention her landlord's daughter, who at the moment was picking her way through the sandspurs toward the back porch.

Laurel called through the window. "Come on in, I'm in the kitchen."

"Can BooBoo come in, too?"

She sighed. "Sure." What did she have to lose? The furniture wasn't hers, and she was getting used to walking on gritty floors. Sand seemed to seep through the walls.

Becky insisted on showing her the bedroom upstairs where she'd slept before her daddy had built his new house. The only thing in the room was a worn-out broom and two buckets.

"Daddy took my furniture to the new house because I helped him pick it out when we went shopping. I was real little then, only just a child."

She said it so seriously Laurel wanted to hug her. Instead, she gave the blond ponytail a gentle tug. "I'll bet it's pretty," she said.

"Mama got me pink. I like purple better than pink, but Daddy said furniture doesn't come in purple so he got me a purple bedspread and a purple chair that's stuffed full of little plastic beads. BooBoo chewed it and some of the beads came out, and Daddy said don't put them in my mouth 'cause I might choke. I promised him I wouldn't, and he let me keep my chair. He sewed it together, but he didn't have any purple thread, so it shows real much."

Laurel tried to picture the big, muscular man on his knees with a needle and thread, repairing a child's chair. Something tightened in the region of her chest. It was just the opening she'd needed. She was all set to steer the conversation around to the issue between father and daughter when a crash came from downstairs.

"BooBoo, get down!" Becky shouted before she even reached the stairs. Laurel was right behind her.

The dog cowered in the door of the kitchen, looking

as guilty as it was possible for a once elegant but now bedraggled show animal to look.

"At least now I won't have to finish scouring the thing," Laurel said when the child looked ready to cry. "I burned coffee in it. I was going to buy a new one anyway."

She wasn't—it would hardly be worth it for the time that she would be here, but that didn't seem important now. She could make do with instant.

Becky wanted to help pick up the big pieces, but Laurel made her go outside until she ran the upright vacuum cleaner she'd found in the pantry over the floor. "All clear," she called as she put away the ancient appliance.

"Did you see what I planted? I looked it up in Daddy's plant book and it's called a cali—cali-some-thing. It starts out with lots of eency white flowers and then it has purple berries."

That is, if it survived, which Laurel seriously doubted. Together they admired the landscaping, and then Laurel mentioned planning to visit the library in Hatteras village, several miles down the island. "Why not ask your daddy if you can go with me?"

It was the best she could do at the moment. If Cody happened to have a library card, that would be even better. He might not be much of a reader, but at least he had a "plant book."

"He might not let me. I better go home or he'll be mad."

"I thought he gave you permission to come visit anytime."

Becky dug her foot in the sand. "Yes, but he's got a— a artistic temper. Mama says I'm not s'posed to bother him or he'll get real mad."

Laurel knew all about artistic temperaments. She'd

seen no sign of one in Cody Morningstar. "Is your father an artist?"

"Uh-uh, he just writes books."

Aha. She'd begun to wonder what he did for a living. Travis hadn't said, and she hadn't wanted to pry, but he must be fairly successful if he could support himself and a part-time daughter. Maybe he even wrote "plant books."

"C'mon, BooBoo, there's snakes in there!" she yelled as the dog galloped toward the creek.

Something else she needed to watch for, Laurel thought, more amused than irritated. Mosquitoes, sandspurs, ghosts and now snakes. She would almost rather have housebreakers, high traffic and higher taxes. Although she was counting the days until she could get back to her old routine, she had to admit that even with a job that required her to be on her feet for hours at a time, she was rather enjoying the break.

"Now, let's see," she said, back in the kitchen again. Somewhere she seemed to recall seeing one of those cordless three-part coffeemakers. If she could just remember where she'd seen it and then figure out how to use the thing, she might not have to resort to instant for her morning dose of caffeine.

It was on a high shelf over the washing machine. The washer itself was old and noisy, but at least it worked. Travis had tested it. With any luck, the coffeepot would, too.

She was rinsing the aluminum pot under the faucet when her cell phone rang. Quickly, she dried her hands and snatched it off the countertop. Even before she picked it up, she knew who it was. Call it instinct—call it wishful thinking.

"Jerry?"

"Hi, love. Did you think I'd forgotten you?"

"Are you all right?" Laurel blurted. Of all the questions she needed to ask, that was the most important.

"Couldn't be better," Jerry replied promptly. A little too promptly, which made her think he was hiding something, trying not to worry her.

"Then we're back in business again?" she ventured.

"Getting close," he said, but she detected a note of caution. She knew him too well. "Kirk's managed to re-sign the Blue Bazookas."

"What about that group he had on the string for the Friend In Need Fund?"

"Friend In Need signed with Leinbach." Jerry considered Sid Leinbach a competitor, but when it came to raising funds for worthy causes, Laurel considered competition a good thing. Neighborhood bake sales on a case-by-case basis just weren't enough.

"So look, the Blues are tentatively rescheduled for mid-November, but you need to get back long before then to start building the buzz."

"Jerry, that's not much lead time. I could e-mail my usual contacts from here if I had my office computer." She broke off, frustrated. "I could even start designing ads, but darn it, I need my programs, not to mention my address book."

"It'll wait till you get here. You'll be back in another few days, right?"

Talk about being between a rock and a hard place! Ignoring his question, she asked one of her own. "Then you got it all back? Our office computers and everything else they confiscated?"

He groaned. She could picture him with one long, pale hand on his brow. Jerry tended toward theatrical gestures. In person, they worked. Long-distance, they weren't quite as effective.

He said, "Oh, God, don't ask. Those pigs probably lost half my files, the way they rooted through everything. I can reconstruct most of it, but it'll take time."

"Did they ever say what it was they were looking for?"

"Put the IRS together with this Homeland Security thing and they don't even need any evidence. First they go after the 501C3s, then they turn on people like me."

She could picture him raking his hair off his forehead. One of the more endearing things about Jerry Blessing was also one of the most irritating. He might look like the hero of a Shakespearean melodrama, but he was about as organized as a box of Cracker Jacks. He was forever jotting down important information on the backs of envelopes while he was talking on the phone. Then he'd forget and trash the envelope and have to turn the place upside down looking for it. She had to remind him regularly to put his cell phone on charge. Half the time, she had to locate the thing for him, which she usually did by punching in his number on her own phone and waiting for his to ring. As meticulous as he was when it came to his surroundings and his personal grooming, he was a train wreck when it came to keeping track of details.

"Is Doris back yet?"

"She signed on with a temp agency. Once we're ready to start up again I'll give her a call."

"Then you don't really need me yet, either?" If she could just stay through Labor Day, she could leave with a clear conscience.

"Oh, no—I'd say the sooner you get here, the better. I'll need you to help put things back together again. The place is a wreck and you know how much I depend on your organizational skills."

Is that all you depend on? she wanted to ask, but didn't. Somewhat to her surprise she realized that it was no longer quite so important.

As Tuesday was a perfect beach day, meaning low traffic in the shop, Caroline told her to take a few hours off. "We can handle it. You've done a great job, but it can get to you, and believe me, the worst is yet to come."

Laurel didn't doubt it. By now she was beginning to catch on to the traffic patterns. Rainy days were hectic; beach days far less so. Just as she pulled into her yard she saw Becky and BooBoo cutting through the hedge. "Perfect timing," she called, gathering up her purse as she swung open the door of her car. "How'd you like to visit the library with me today? Did you ask your father?"

Twenty minutes later they were shown a section of local interest. "Everything from John Lawson's *History of North Carolina*, if you're interested in the Algonquin culture, to books about all the pirates that used to hang out around these islands. Everybody knows about Blackbeard, but did you know he had a place just over on Ocracoke Island?"

"What about genealogy?"

"Whose, Blackbeard's?"

Laughing, Laurel shook her head. "Just general. As it relates to the local people, I mean. I've been told some of my father's family might have come from around here."

"Who were his people?"

"The Lawlesses?" For no real reason, Laurel's heart tripped into double time. She wasn't all *that* hard up for roots. Still, as long as she was here…

"To tell you the truth, I've only lived here a few years, but I've certainly heard the name. Other than yours, I mean."

Her heart had settled down, but her palms were damp. "It's not important, I just thought as long as I was here I'd check it out." She glanced around to see Becky studying a shelf of children's books.

The librarian said, "We don't have a whole lot here in the library, but I can tell you who knows just about everything about the original families. They're still here, you know—their descendants, at least." The librarian's name was Helen, according to her lapel pin.

"Thank you, Helen. Then I'll just browse if that's all right."

She was still considering the heady thought of being descended from an "old family" when Becky snatched a small volume from the shelf. "Look, Laurel, I know who this man is," she crowed. "It's Blackbeard—see? His beard's all braided and he's got burning candles stuck in the ends. I don't think he really did that, though, do you?"

"Not if he had a brain in his head," Laurel said dryly. She was searching the local-interest section for anything pertaining to local history. Once she was back home she could go online and Google the areas and the names she was interested in, but since her office computer had been confiscated along with everything else and her laptop had succumbed to a virus, any search would have to wait.

Actually, she didn't really need to know anything more than she already knew, but as long as she was here with nothing better to do with her unscheduled half day off, she might as well see if Squire Lawless turned up anywhere in the history of the Outer Banks. According to Travis, the Lawlesses had started out right here on Hatteras Island nearly three centuries ago. Later on, a few of them, including Squire-the-bootlegger, had migrated inland.

"That's my daddy's book," Becky announced as they made their way to the checkout desk.

Laurel spared a glance at the Lee Larkin mystery on a shelf with several others bestsellers. She knew the name, of course, but as she read romantic suspense and not the hard-edged stuff, she'd never read one of Larkin's.

Evidently, her landlord was a fan.

She nodded, wondering how she was going to be able to take out the three books she'd selected without a library card.

"Oh, I know you," said the woman behind the desk. "You work at Caroline's place up in Frisco. I used to work there ages ago when they first opened. You want these?"

"I don't have a card."

"Not a problem. I'll just sign them out to the shop. If you don't get a chance to return them before you leave, just give them to Caroline. She's a regular here."

"Could I take this home to read it?" Becky added the pirate book to Laurel's small stack.

"Sure can, hon. My, he's ugly, isn't he? Did you know he used to hang out around these parts? In fact, he was killed just a few miles away from here. Lost his head, you might say."

Laurel frowned. "Maybe you'd rather have the latest Harry Potter," she suggested, but Becky shook her head. "I've read all those. Daddy buys them for me. I want Blackbeard. Maybe it'll tell us where he buried his treasure."

Laurel shook her head. Helen, the librarian, smiled and handed over a slip of paper for Laurel to sign. "If you get any clues, honey, let me in on it, will you? Folks have been hunting pirate gold around these parts for a hundred years. Mostly all they turn up is potsherds, pop-tops and arrowheads."

"Going on three hundred years now, isn't it?" Laurel remarked as she turned to go.

"Lawsy, isn't that the truth. Time really flies. Y'all come back now," the friendly librarian called after them.

Once they left the village behind, Becky said, "We're going to cook hot dogs and stuff on the beach again as soon as I get back home. Want me to ask Daddy if you can go, too?"

Laurel started to tell her not to bother, but by that time, she was amused to see that Becky had her nose in the book of pirate lore. From time to time she looked up to ask a question. "How do they know what he looked like? They didn't have cameras then, did they?"

"No, but people drew pictures. Some were quite good at it."

"Oh." And a few minutes later, "He could've buried his treasure right here, couldn't he? If he lived in Ocracoke, he prob'ly wouldn't bury it there, 'cause then everybody would know where to dig it up."

"Sounds reasonable to me," Laurel murmured. As she turned off the highway into Ridge Pond Road, her mind was too scattered to concentrate on where some legendary bad guy might have buried his equally legendary treasure. "Just don't get your hopes up, honey. Whatever he buried has probably washed out to sea by now. Travis said there are tree stumps out in the water on both sides of the island where the woods used to be. The island's gradually washing away."

"Not where Daddy's house is, though. It's on a hill. Our old house where you live now used to get wet inside when it rained real hard and the creek came up too high. That's why Daddy built his new house up on long legs."

*Over to you, Cody. What do I know about pirates and storm tides?*

"So can we go looking for gold?" Becky said anxiously. "Since he rode a boat, we can dig near the water. That's prob'ly where he buried it. I bet he jumped out and waded ashore and dug a deep hole when nobody was looking."

Laurel figured she'd brought it on herself. "Why not?" she said. "Ask your daddy first, though. Since you're going to the beach today, maybe we can do it after I get home from work tomorrow."

"I want you to come to the beach with us," Becky yelled over her shoulder as she ran through the split in the hedge. "I'll tell Daddy to wait while you put on your bathing suit!"

"Better yet, why don't I stay here and get ready for our treasure hunt tomorrow?" Laurel called after her.

She should have thought before she'd promised. It wasn't like her to be so impulsive. But then, it wasn't like her to spend her free afternoon with an eight-year-old child, either. The surprising thing was that she had enjoyed every minute of it. Whatever problem Becky might have with her father obviously didn't extend to other adults.

She'd almost forgotten the impromptu invitation to a wiener roast when Becky came racing back to ask if she was ready. "Daddy says you can come with us, 'cause he has plenty of food, but if we want to go swimming, we have to do it today 'cause it's going to rain tomorrow, so tomorrow we can put on our raincoats and look for pirate treasure."

Laurel had just changed into her caftan. She sighed. There wasn't a cloud in the sky, but she knew better than to argue. If the weather guru told her before she left for the office that it was going to rain, she might take an umbrella. She might even take a cab, although in her neighborhood, cabs were an endangered species once it started raining.

It occurred to her as she changed into her swimsuit and a cover-up that once she got back to New York she was going to miss her trusty little Honda with its wrinkled rear fender.

She really had no business being here, Laurel told herself some half hour later as she climbed down from the high SUV onto the pale pink sand. On the one hand, the more time she spent with Becky, the better chance she had of finding out what was bothering her. She already had a clue.

The sea was much rougher today. According to Cody, the tide was on its way in. He pointed to the position of the moon, a white orb low on the horizon, and Laurel learned something about the relationship of the moon and the tides. Tired after what had already been a long day, she would just as soon lie back on the beach towel and doze in the warmth of a sinking sun, but Becky was full of energy.

"BooBoo and me can dig a hole, Daddy, and while Laurel and me swim, you can build a fire, all right?"

Catching Cody's eye, Laurel saw a look of surprise

and something that looked like appreciation. Neither of them bothered to correct the child's grammar as Becky fell on her knees and began scooping up sand to form a fire pit. While Cody brought firewood from the SUV and Laurel carried a basket of food and an armload of beach towels, BooBoo did what dogs do best—he marked the growing sand pile as his own.

As it turned out, the three of them went for a brief swim while BooBoo, anchored to the contraption on the front bumper, barked enthusiastic encouragement. With Cody and Laurel looking on in approval, Becky swam a few strokes before being tumbled by a small wave. She came up sputtering and laughing.

Laurel said to the man standing beside her, knee-deep in the surging water, "She's a terrific little girl."

"Yeah, she is, isn't she? I owe you, Laurie." Evidently he'd picked up on the diminutive from his daughter. "Whatever was going on with her, she seems to have gotten past it. At least she talks to me now."

"Daddy, look at me swim!"

"Head toward shore, hon, that fire looks about ready."

"But, Daddy, I haven't even showed you how I can ride a wave yet."

Cody said, "Surf's not good for riding today. You don't see any boarders out there, do you?"

"Besides," Laurel called, "I'm getting hungry, aren't you? Swimming always gives me an appetite."

And so the cookout proceeded, if not exactly according to plan. Ketchup, but no mustard for the dogs. Slaw, but no onions. Probably just as well, Laurel thought. She loved onions, but not on a date.

Not that this was a date, she hastily amended.

BooBoo shook sand and water over them all and

then plopped down on the dry clothes they'd brought along to change into. Becky slapped at a blackfly that bit her on the ankle and dropped her hot dog in the fire. Dark clouds quickly built up, covering what had promised to be a colorful sunset.

Disorganized or not, Laurel told herself with a rare sense of contentment, I could get used to this.

"Laurie and me are going to look for pirate treasure tomorrow, aren't we, Laurie?"

"I expect Miss Laurie will be tired when she gets home after work tomorrow," said Cody as he threaded another wiener on a stick.

"You can sit down while I dig, can't you, Laurie?"

Before Laurel could think of an excuse to beg off, her landlord answered for her. "Why not do some studying before you go into the field? With so much territory to cover, the search might take years if you don't narrow it down to the likeliest places."

Laurel shot him a look of gratitude while she spread ketchup on her bun. He winked at her, and she felt a surge of some unfamiliar emotion. Trying without much success to ignore the bronzed masculine body within touching distance if she'd cared—or dared—to reach out and touch, she put her feelings down to being tired and out of her element.

"It's starting to sprinkle," Cody said a little while later. "Time to put out the fire, cover the hole and gather up the remains. Wake up, honey."

It was only then that Laurel noticed that Becky was almost asleep. She'd been lying on her stomach watching a flock of tiny beach birds probe for supper between waves that washed higher and higher on the shore.

Quickly, they covered the fire and carried the remains back to the car. "I really enjoyed this," Laurel said softly as she buckled the sleepy child into the backseat.

"Yeah, me, too."

Not until Cody dropped her off at her house did it occur to her to wonder why she enjoyed spending time with a quarrelsome man who had dented her fender and then tried to evict her. She enjoyed spending time with his daughter, but it was more than that. Today had felt almost like family.

Not that hers had ever felt so comfortable and undemanding.

She tried and failed to picture Jerry wet and sandy, playing on the beach with a child and a dog, but her imagination wasn't up to the task. Besides, what difference did it make?

Oddly enough, she had no trouble picturing Cody in Manhattan, or any other big city. What *was* it about the man that set her off on a wildly erotic journey of the mind? She didn't even know enough to imagine such things.

# Chapter 11

The treasure hunt was postponed when the rain that started late that afternoon continued into the next day. Before she left for work, Travis brought over four plastic buckets and told Laurel where any leaks would be likely to show up, and sure enough, the ceiling was stained in those places.

"How's Ru?"

"Ready to pick a fight if I so much as look at her."

Laurel dared to ask a personal question. It was all in the family, after all. "Was your first wife the same way when she was expecting your son?"

He hesitated, then shook his head. "Tell the truth, I wasn't around a whole lot. I was still in the service back then. Make sure all your windows are closed before you leave, y'hear?"

"I hope your son comes home before I have to leave—I'm looking forward to meeting him. What is he, a third or a fourth once removed?" She laughed because it really didn't matter. A cousin was a cousin, as far as she was concerned, regardless of the degree of kinship. She was still enjoying the novelty of having family connections.

The shop was jammed with frustrated vacationers,

and Laurel quickly discovered that being too busy was every bit as tiring as not being busy enough. By the time she got home after the first full day of rain, kicked off her shoes and emptied the buckets under the upstairs leaks, she was ready to collapse.

When the rain continued into a second day she detoured by the local grocer's after work to pick up a few cans of soup and something from the deli. It was while she was looking over the display of books and magazines that she felt something she hadn't felt in weeks— more like months.

That creepy back-of-the-neck feeling.

She glanced over her shoulder, thinking it might be Travis. Or if not him, someone she'd seen in the shop who was trying to place her, the way people did.

There were three people in line at the checkout, none of them looking at her. Two teenage boys were smirking in front of the magazine rack. There was no sign of Travis, or anyone else she knew. There was, however, an elderly woman pushing a shopping cart along the produce aisle, who seemed to be staring at her.

When Laurel caught her eye, the woman smiled and came toward her. "I've seen you around with Travis," she said in a friendly tone. "They say you're working at Caroline's place now."

*They* say? *Who* says? Laurel smiled back, not altogether comfortable with being the subject of gossip. "That's right, I work at Carolina's Craft Gallery."

"I don't shop there, but Caroline goes to my church. She's a real sweet girl."

Caroline Danvers was closer to fifty than forty, but then the older people she'd met since coming to the island seldom bothered with political correctness.

At a loss for an appropriate response, Laurel fell back on the weather. "Is it going to rain forever?"

"Well, my bones has stopped achin' so I reckon it'll clear up directly. Who did you say your people were? I 'clare, you've got the look of somebody I used to know."

Laurel managed to close her mouth before she could be accused of gaping. She'd always considered it rude to ask personal questions of strangers, but evidently age had its privileges.

Or maybe it was a Southern thing.

"Travis is my cousin," she said, thinking that if he wanted to fill the old woman in on his family history, that was his business. "It looks like it's starting to slack up now. I'd better hurry. I didn't bring an umbrella. Nice meeting you."

They hadn't met, not technically, but at least she no longer had that creepy feeling that someone was watching her. The store was crowded, but she got through the checkout line and hurried outside. Dropping her sack of groceries onto the passenger seat, she looked both ways, then looked again before backing out of her parking place. After pulling out onto the two-lane highway she took a deep, steadying breath. For a minute there, she'd wondered if some tabloid reporter had tracked her down, looking for a "Whatever Happened To…?" story.

On impulse, she turned into Travis's driveway instead of her own. If Ru needed distraction, Laurel could provide it. At the moment, she had a few questions. She grabbed a can of Manhattan clam chowder out of her sack as an excuse for stopping by.

"Oh, you're just what I needed! I've got a low-pressure headache and Trav won't let me dose up on painkillers."

"He wants you to hurt?"

"No, he rubs oil of peppermint on my temples and applies wet heat to the back of my neck."

"Does it help?" Laurel asked curiously as she reached inside the kitchen to leave her store-bought treat.

"The peppermint makes my eyes water, but the wet heat really does. Before I got as big as the Goodyear blimp, he used to make me stand under the shower and drill the back of my neck with hot water whenever I got one of these nagging headaches. I'm not even sure I could get through the shower door now."

Both women laughed, and then Laurel described her encounter at the grocery store. "I actually felt someone staring at me, you know? Did anything like that ever happen to you when you were going through that awful mess about your stolen identity?"

"Oh, yeah, I was paranoia personified, right up until I looked at the map and headed for what looked like the far edge of the continent. At the time, I thought I had a job here."

Laurel slipped her feet from her shoes, which she should have done on the porch to save Travis from having to sweep up after her. "Sorry about the sand," she murmured.

"No problem, it'll give Trav something to do to keep him from driving me crazy. Like I was saying, I actually thought I had a job waiting here. Turns out, I didn't. Anyhow, I didn't even make it as far down the Banks as Kinnakeet before my car broke down. It was raining like the devil, the sand was blowing so hard I could barely see, and there wasn't a village in sight, not so much as a single house."

"And then…?" Laurel prompted. She'd heard the story before, but if telling it took Ru's mind off her headache and whatever else was bothering her, she didn't mind hearing it again as long as she could listen sitting down.

"Well, you know the rest. Anyway, what happened at Conner's?"

"This woman—" Laurel described her as elderly, with short gray hair, blue eyes and the accent she had come to recognize as native Banker. "Anyway, she said she'd seen me with Travis and then she asked me who my people were."

"Did you tell her?"

"Well, what could I say? As far as I know, Travis and Harrison are it, not counting Matt and the other cousin, whom I've never met. Anyway, I was so relieved that I wasn't being stalked by some weirdo that I didn't even resent the personal question."

"Oh, honey, she wasn't prying. It's just that so many second- and third-generation Bankers move back here after living away that the ones who never left have to put them in context. All you had to do was tell her you were a Lawless and she'd have indexed you into the proper slot right away. I think Travis has a batch of genealogical information somewhere on his computer that he's never had time to go through. If you ask me, it's because all the oldest families are connected, and there might be a few links he doesn't particularly care to claim. Anyway, I'll remind him that you're interested, shall I?"

Laurel murmured something noncommittal, knowing she wouldn't be here long enough for it to matter. At least she had a few people to exchange Christmas cards with, which was more than she'd had before. "Have you heard anything from Matt? I hope he comes home before I have to leave. I'd love to meet him."

Ru picked at the fringe over the lightweight throw. "I could kill that husband of mine," she said in a tone that was totally un-Ru-like.

Laurel sank slowly back in the chair she'd been on the verge of vacating. "Um…any particular reason?"

Ru sighed. "Just hormones on the rampage. Don't worry, he's in no danger. Who else would I get to wait on me hand and foot?"

Laurel rose again. "That reminds me, I brought you a can of *real* clam chowder. It's on your kitchen counter."

At least it brought forth a laugh. Laurel had told Travis that the local version was probably an acquired taste. "Then you'll just have to stick around long enough to acquire it," he'd teased.

It must be true that blood was thicker than water, she mused as she hurried out to her car. Already she felt closer to Travis and Ru—and even to Harrison and Cleo, where she'd spent only a single night—than she'd felt to anyone in years. To think there were two more cousins—Matt and the one in Virginia, not to mention all the ones who went by different names.

A few minutes later she let herself in her front door and discovered that not only had the tooth fairy emptied her drip buckets, he'd left her a small television. "Whoa," she murmured, staring at the dark screen. If there was a TV antenna on her roof, she'd missed it. She definitely hadn't signed up for cable.

She started to turn it on to see if it worked, but first she needed to put away her purchases and change out of her good clothes. She was already unbuttoning as she headed to the kitchen when Cody appeared at the front door.

"What do you think?" he called through the screen.

"Without an antenna you won't be able to get much, but rabbit ears should allow you to keep up with Helene's progress."

She dropped the grocery sack on the cast-iron stove and quickly rebuttoned her top. "Helene," she repeated. Another cousin?

Never one to stand on ceremony, he let himself inside. "Right now it looks like it's targeting the Gulf Coast, but we're still not out of the woods."

"I don't have a clue what you're talking about. Thanks for emptying my buckets, by the way. That was you, I take it?"

"I dumped. Becky replaced. Figured I owed you a favor for breaking through that wall she threw up to keep me out." He shook his head. With his rugged features and his tousled, sun-bleached hair, he reminded her of a puzzled lion. "Something's still bugging her, but at least we're starting to communicate again."

Laurel wanted coffee, and she wanted it now, but there was no way she could make a pot without inviting him to stay. "I really didn't do anything," she demurred.

"Yeah, you did. I'm not sure what, because I still don't know what had her in such a bind, but you notice she's addressing me directly now? She even let me comb the tangles out of her hair this morning." He looked so proud of the small triumph that Laurel wanted to hug him.

Far too smart to come anywhere near him physically, she said, "I think I've mastered this three-piece coffee-pot of yours, if you care to risk it. I've gone as long as I can without caffeine."

"The dripolater. It was here when I bought the house. Sure, I'll risk it. While you get it started, I'll check the latest reading on Helene, okay?"

Helene, of course, was the hurricane. "I knew that," she muttered as she put on a kettle of water and filled the basket with grounds. Then, while Cody fiddled with the rabbit-ear antenna, she dashed upstairs and changed into something dry, something that was flattering, but subtle about it. No point in giving him any ideas.

She fluffed her hair, added a bit of tinted lip balm and spritzed her midriff with body spray. Not that she was trying to impress anyone.

"Where's Becky?" she asked when she rejoined her landlord downstairs. He had poured two mugs of coffee and set them on the table along with the carton of half-and-half and her sugar, which she kept in a screw-top jar sitting in a saucer of water because Ru had told her it kept the ants away.

"Buried in her pirate book, waiting for the rain to stop."

"It's already slacking off." She doctored her coffee to suit her taste and studied the grainy picture on the twelve-inch television screen. "Is that Helene? It looks like a soufflé someone poked a hole in."

"I'm keeping up with the coordinates on a tracking map. I'd feel a lot better if she headed north in the next couple of days instead of waiting."

"Because?" Laurel tried to imagine him living in this old house. He simply took up too much room. And until recently, he had slept in the bed she was sleeping in now. Which *definitely* didn't bear thinking about, she told herself, knowing she'd think about it every time she crawled under the sheets.

"Because I'd rather see her on a heading that would take her east of Bermuda instead of taking dead aim at the mid-Atlantic coastline."

As she had nothing intelligent or even speculative to

add, Laurel sipped her coffee and waited for him to get to the point of his visit. Granted, her imagination had been acting up lately, but she sensed there was something else he wanted to say—the way he was looking at her, as if trying to gauge her mood.

She could have told him that while she was physically tired and somewhat emotionally confused, she was ready to take on anything from insurance adjusters to hurricanes. Helene didn't worry her. By the time it was a real threat, if it ever was, she'd probably be back in New York.

"About Becky? Do you think what's bothering her might have something to do with this guy Mara's marrying? Not that she's said anything directly. Guy by the name of Clyde Everstone—a lawyer with some pretty heavy political connections on the West Coast. According to Mara, he walks on water."

"Could be dangerous unless he wears a life jacket," she remarked, earning a chuckle that raked along her nerves like velvet-sheathed claws. "Still, you could be right. A new father…" She had already drawn the same conclusion.

"Stepfather," Cody corrected.

"All the same, family relationships can be confusing to a child."

He lifted an eyebrow. "Yours?"

She hesitated, then said, "Mine was…atypical. Good, I guess, but confusing, too. And no, I didn't have any steps, just mostly absentee parents. Mom and Dad loved to travel, and as I was usually in school— boarding school for the most part—I was rarely included. But we had some wonderful times and I definitely learned a lot of weird stuff when things worked out so I could go along." She shrugged. "Not that any of that relates to what's going on now with Becky."

"Mara and Everstone are due back next weekend. They're flying into Norfolk and driving directly down to pick up Becky and the dog. Before then, I'd like to find out exactly what's bothering her, but whenever I touch on the subject, she clams up again." He set his empty mug on the coffee table and stood, hooking his thumbs in his front pockets, square-tipped fingers splaying over a flat abdomen. "Would you mind keeping an ear open? I could use a disinterested opinion."

"She mentioned the fact that you have what she called an artistic temper. I think maybe she was warned not to bother you when you're trying to work."

He nodded slowly. "Maybe."

God, the man was gorgeous. Did he have any idea how he affected her? A few times he'd looked at her as if he were seeing her for the first time all over again.

"You never got around to telling me about what you do. Or for that matter, why you rented a house and took a job while you're here on vacation." He lifted one thick brow that was two shades darker than his hair. "You are on vacation, aren't you?"

She sighed. "Not now, do you mind? I've been on my feet all day, talking to customers. I'm plum out of steam, as you Southerners say."

At any other time, his smile might have ignited another rush of forbidden fantasies, but she was wilting fast. Besides, something just outside her consciousness kept nagging at her…something she had either seen or heard that hadn't registered at the time.

"Pull up a stool when you get a chance tomorrow,"

Cody advised. "If you're behind a counter, the customer won't know whether or not you're standing at attention."

"A lot you know about it. You've never worked retail in your life, have you?"

"Lemonade stand when I was Becky's age. Does that count?"

He was chuckling when he left—they both were. His was the kind of laughter that registered on parts of her body she could have sworn were immune to aural stimuli.

Hers was merely tired...tired and somewhat frustrated.

She watched him out of sight, then closed the door. The rain had slacked off to a light sprinkle, but the dampness was blowing through the screen. She had already discovered that dampness made drawers swell and doors refuse to shut tightly. "Helene, if you're out there, do me a favor, will you? Head for the Devil's Triangle and get lost."

Someone, she couldn't remember if it was Harrison or Travis, had mentioned that the most dangerous place on the Atlantic seaboard was not the so-called Devil's Triangle, but right offshore, where the Labrador Current met the Gulf Stream. It was called the Graveyard of the Atlantic.

Great. Just what she needed—another graveyard.

She tugged at the screen to close it and then shut the paneled door. On impulse she turned the single latch, hoping it was sufficient to fend off ghosts and hurricanes.

# Chapter 12

Cody typed in *Chapter Twenty-One*. For several minutes he stared at the letters on the blank screen, then he leaned back in his ergonomic chair and swiveled around to stare into the darkness outside the window, waiting for the sweep of light that came every few seconds. How the devil could he concentrate on the placement, layering and infiltration involved in money laundering when he couldn't keep his mind off the subtle and not-so-subtle infiltration that was taking place in his own life?

Instead of trying to figure out what was going on in his daughter's head since her last visit, he kept seeing Becky and Laurel giggling in the surf after a ten-foot ride on a three-foot wave. Or wandering up and down the beach collecting shells, chattering away as if they were two kids who'd been friends forever.

A couple of days ago he had finally brought up the subject of her mother's remarriage. "Think you're going to like living in California?" *Over my dead body,* he'd added silently.

Avoiding his eyes, she'd concentrated on scratching a pink streak that might or might not be poison ivy. "So what's he like? Your new stepfather?"

"He's allergic to dogs," she'd whispered.

"Then maybe BooBoo can have his own outdoor house and playground," Cody had suggested. The dog belonged to Mara, but Mara's enthusiasms had a short shelf life.

At least the mutt was no longer doing his business on the furniture. He'd been trained not to go on the floor, which meant if he couldn't get outside in time he jumped on the handiest piece of furniture and cocked a leg.

Becky had agreed to take full responsibility, and he'd held her to it. Responsibility was good for a kid, only not too much, too soon. He didn't kid himself that it was going to be that easy, dealing with the various stages of childhood. Especially if he won the current custody battle they were engaged in. And as Mara had bigger fish to fry, it just might happen.

One of these days in the not too distant future he'd probably be vetting her dates. He didn't look forward to it. Unless she changed in the next thirty or so years, she'd be a formidable opponent. She'd insisted on bathing herself when she was five, but she'd still allowed him to brush the tangles out of her hair and braid it for her.

Now that she was nearly eight she claimed she was too old to wear pigtails. Instead she used some sort of fancy rubber band to hold it up in a ponytail. At least she hadn't tried soaking it in purple Kool-Aid. That was probably the next stage.

God, she was growing up. Changing almost daily.

Turning back to his computer, he scrolled down and followed the heading with a five-sentence paragraph, knowing he would probably change every word the next time he sat down to work. At least now he wouldn't have to start with a blank screen.

Shutting down his computer—with the fluctuations

in power, he didn't dare leave it on if there was even a chance of an outage—he switched off the light and padded silently down the hall in his bare feet. On the way he opened Becky's bedroom door and waited for his eyes to adjust to the darkness. She was curled into a fetal ball. The mutt was sprawled across the foot of the bed, one leg twitching. He must be dreaming of whatever show dogs dreamed of. Not hunting. Trotting in circles with a handler before a row of judges, probably.

"Some disciplinarian you are," he muttered and closed the door.

"Who called?" Ru asked as her husband emerged from his home office. "Was it one of your so-called sources? Did you learn anything?"

"It was Pete, and all he knows is that if Matt's anywhere in the area, he's keeping a low profile." They both thought there was a chance Matt Holiday was in the coastal town of Wilmington, as he'd been accepted at UNC Wilmington. It was a slim hope, but at the moment it was all they had.

"If you hadn't—" Ru broke off. They'd been over this particular battleground too many times, getting nowhere. Regardless of who was to blame—and she wasn't yet willing to assign blame, nor to accept it herself—the boy was missing. Gone without a word of goodbye, much less a hint of where he was going and whether or not he'd be back.

"At least he has enough money to last for a while," Trav said. Matt had worked as a mate aboard one of the charter boats ever since he'd graduated.

He sighed. Standing with his back to his wife, he stared out over the sound, as if the answers could be found on his homemade tidemarker or the net floats just offshore, or the distant channel marker a thousand or so feet away.

And then Ru said, "Travis, I'm worried about Laurel, too."

She shouldn't have mentioned it. They both had enough on their minds, with Matt's running off and her own precarious state. Trav's hair was no longer salt-and-pepper, it was pure salt. The fact that he had the face and body of a far younger man only made him look sexier—something else that added to the constant tension between them. They were both counting down the days. Six weeks after delivery, if all went well.

With another heavy sigh—and Travis Holiday wasn't the sighing type—he turned and began gathering up her breakfast tray. After setting it in the kitchen he returned to help her to the bathroom for her shower.

Neither of them mentioned Laurel. She would wait for a better time to broach that particular subject.

Meanwhile, he insisted on standing by, even though he'd provided her with a bench and a handheld shower attachment. She blamed it on his Coast Guard background. Always prepared for trouble.

"She's worried about something," she blurted out. So much for waiting for a better time. "Has she said anything to you about—well, about anything? The last time she was here I got the feeling she was looking over her shoulder. Figuratively, if not literally."

"Yeah, something's going on there," her husband agreed. "Next time she drops by, get her to talking about her old job. Harrison said she mentioned something about some trouble—the reason she was laid off temporarily. All I know is that she definitely plans to head North again once she gets the all clear."

"All clear from what?" Ru's sense of balance had been shot from the seventh month on, but the way Travis babied her, you'd think she was carrying triplets instead of one big, miraculously healthy baby girl.

"That's for you to find out. Harrison seemed to think the outfit she works for is in some kind of legal trouble."

"A charity fund-raising company? What, they left the glue off the address labels? They dipped sticky fingers into the kettle?"

Travis eased the robe from her shoulders and supported her while she stepped over the low shower rim. "Hey, just because our local charities are pretty transparent, that doesn't mean the possibility's not there. Exaggerating overhead, underreporting profits—it doesn't take much in the way of brains if you're small enough to go under the radar."

"How do you know so much about it?"

Travis poured liquid soap on a loofah, and began to stroke his wife's back. As much as she resented his constant mollycoddling—especially when they'd been bickering—she had to admit it felt good.

"Because when he's in a jam, Cody bounces things off me. Right now, he's staring at a blank wall."

"What, he's trying to compose some bestselling graffiti?"

Grim-faced, Travis ignored the gibe. "Money laundering, gunrunning and dirty politics, among a lot of other stuff. Want me to do your front?"

"Go away. Even my stretch marks have stretch marks."

"Hey, they look like that fancy tablecloth of yours that has patterns woven into it. What d'you call it—damage?"

"Damask." She laughed, then growled, "Quit being a pain in the bohunkus and leave me alone. If you want to do something useful, go make me some hot tea with lots and lots of sugar."

Used to his wife's mood swings by now, Travis filled the kettle and set it on low, then headed for the office that had been compared to the control room of an early World War II submarine. As his specialty was marine electronics—designing them, repairing them and collecting older models, it wasn't too far off the mark.

He was also a ham operator, but this time he used a protected line to leave a message for Lyon Lawless, Director of Operations for one of the under-the-radar government intelligence branches.

He needed him now on two counts.

The rain had stopped, the sky layered in shades of copper, gold and deep purple by the time Laurel rapped on her cousin's door the next day and let herself in. "Stay put, Ru, it's just me. Oh, I like that shade of lipstick on you," she said.

"Raisin Red. Tomorrow I thought I'd switch and try using it around my eyes and use the Wild Grape eye shadow on my lips. Pull up a chair and tell me every teeny little thing—I am just so bored!"

"No word yet from Matt, I take it?" Laurel stepped out of her mules, wriggled her toes and settled into Trav's favorite armchair. Seeing him working in the shed out behind the house, she had waved to him on the way up the driveway.

"Nothing. It's driving Trav quietly mad, I can tell you."

"But he left of his own free will. That's a good sign."

"Is it? Oh, I guess so, I just wish he'd call. I'm afraid it's about the baby—you know, not exactly jealous, but…"

What could she say? She'd never even met the boy, who had left a few days before she arrived. Not until recently had anyone let slip that there was anything irregular about his leaving.

"Look, I can't stay but a minute, but I thought I'd catch you up. Not that there's much to report, but there was this woman in today who said I looked just like a picture of her grandmother. She was sixty if she was a day."

"Who, the grandmother?"

"No, the woman. That would make her grandmother probably at least a hundred years old. I didn't even try to work it out, math's not my thing."

"Women used to marry young. What was her name?"

"Which, the grandmother's? Heywood. Miz Missouri Heywood. Ring any bells?"

Ru shook her head. She looked amused. "Not a dingy-dong thing. Sorry. Trav says that back when there were only a dozen or so old families living on the island, so many people shared the same surname that married women used to go by their own first names and their husband's first names. I'd be Ruanna Travis, not Ruanna Holiday, only there aren't any other Holidays here. Any other clues?"

"Missouri whatever-her-name-was used to make something called yaupon tea for her husband to sell across the sound. She dipped snuff."

"So did a lot of other women. Both the tea and the snuff."

"You think there's a chance—?" Laurel shook her head. "I'm reaching for straws, I know. But you know what? She could be my great-something or other. Wouldn't that be super? To know I actually had great-grandparents?"

"Well now, I was under the impression most of us had ancestors. It's sort of a chain thing. You think you're a product of spontaneous combustion?"

Before Laurel could come back with a suitably snide response, Ru placed her palms on her rounded belly and winced. "Ballet practice. The pirouettes are the very devil. But look, if you're not going to stay around much longer, I guess it doesn't matter how many relatives you dig up, right?" She snickered. "I don't mean that literally."

Rising, Laurel moved to stare out the window overlooking the sound. Only a few coral streaks now, in a lavender sky that was flawlessly reflected in the still water. A single white heron stalked the shoreline, and while she watched, a squadron of pelicans winged clumsily past. "You do have the most spectacular view," she said enviously. "My front window takes in the top floor of my landlord's house, and my back window looks out over a jungle and a few ancient gravestones. I think. So far, I haven't worked up the courage to explore beyond the fig tree."

"Have you heard anything more about your job? I mean your old job," Ru asked when several minutes passed in comfortable silence.

Laurel turned away from the peaceful scene outside. "Jerry called. My boss, who's probably going to be my husband, we were sort of headed in that general direction when all hell broke loose."

At least I think we were, she added silently.

"And?"

"And he wants me back there ASAP. I owe him, Ru. He never lost patience with me, not even when I messed up getting an interview or getting the posters out on time, or ran late reserving ad space. Which I hardly ever did, because I'm meticulous about details, but still, things happen."

Ru nodded as if she understood. Laurel paced between the front window that looked out over a sloping, wooded front yard to the highway, and the back window that looked out over a wooded backyard and the Pamlico Sound. Her Murray Hill apartment looked out on the brick facade of another apartment building.

"Did I tell you about his marvelous apartment? Those places are impossible to find, even if you can afford them. Jerry's never mentioned it, but I think his folks must be loaded. Silver spoon syndrome, you know?"

"Yeah, I sort of do," Ru said with a wry smile, no doubt thinking of her own background. She'd said a little, but not a lot.

"Honestly, Ru, he's so special."

And honestly, he was, Laurel told herself, trying to picture that aristocratic face and those dark, penetrating eyes. She had occasionally wondered if two equally strong-minded people could find happiness together, or if one of them would be forced to hand over control.

Oddly enough, it no longer seemed so pressing. She had other concerns at the moment.

Ru waved an impatient hand. "Okay, so now I know all about tall, dark and handsome Jerry with his Italian suits and his designer ties and his fancy address. Now tell me about all hell breaking loose. I need something gritty to think about besides the fact that my stepson has disappeared and my own perfect husband is starting to get on my nerves. He won't let me do a blessed thing! He even folds my bras and underpants, can you believe it? Like I couldn't sit right here and fold laundry, for lord's sake!"

Laurel had to laugh at the thought of her big, masculine cousin folding his wife's delicate lingerie. "As for hell breaking loose, I still don't know exactly what started it. Jerry said it was a disgruntled ex-employee who tipped off the IRS, and they brought in Homeland Security. All this hush-hush stuff about national security, as if little old Jay-bass was out to conquer the Western world. My God…!"

"Is it over, then?"

Laurel shook her head. "But Jerry says it will be by the time I get back." Did she believe him? She wanted to, but then, everything seemed to have changed since she'd left New York to come to this funky little island with its beautiful, natural beaches and its mixture of new and old, tacky and picturesque.

She said thoughtfully, "So far as I know, nobody's been convicted of anything. At least if they have, it never made the papers." And Jerry hadn't mentioned it. "I was questioned by these guys who wouldn't crack a smile if you pumped them full of laughing gas. Not that there was anything to smile about. I couldn't seem to make them understand that my job was simply to get all the publicity I could for our celebrities du jour. They might threaten a few eardrums, but I'm pretty sure they never threatened our nation's security. Try telling that to all those stiff-upper-lip types."

Holding the sides of her stomach, Ru shifted her position. "What kind of celebrities? Anyone I'd know?"

"I doubt it. Like I said, we're pretty small potatoes. Kirk—he's Jerry's second in command—he's in charge of signing up names that might draw a crowd. Usually the under-thirty crowd—not the biggest givers, but good enough. I wanted to shoot for the boomers, but even yesterday's stars are out of our reach budgetwise." She paused to scratch a rash on her left ankle with her right toe.

Ru laughed. "I get the picture. What ever happened to—you know, the Mothers and the Fathers?"

"Mamas and Papas? Weren't they the ones with the great harmony?" They discussed a few more musical groups before veering back to their childhood experiences. Laurel had already heard part of Ru's story— what it was like to grow up in a white brick mansion with a maid and a butler who taught her to roller-skate on a circular driveway. What it was like to be plagued by scandal, to have her marriage go down the drain and to lose not only her job but also her identity.

"As if that weren't enough," Ru said, "when Trav— this perfect stranger, mind you—when he rescued me off the beach and took me home with him, almost the first thing I did was throw up. I was sick as a dog for the next three days."

"Oh, wow," Laurel said softly, although she'd heard it all before. "That's a tough act to follow. My problems don't even rate a mention beside yours."

"Hey, I never got called in for questioning by the FBI."

"IRS, FBI—I'm not even certain who it was now, the way all those acronyms were floating around. I was so scared it was all I could do to breathe." She chuckled and felt on the floor for her shoes.

"Oh, don't run, you just got here," Ru protested. "I'll just start worrying again, imagining poor Matt sick to death in some seedy motel, unable to call home. In some ways he's still just a child, even if he is eighteen."

"Oh, I know, hon. I'm sorry, but I've got a date to go

digging for pirate treasure now that it's stopped raining. Travis said we could explore along his beach, but it'll be dark in less than an hour. Becky's probably been camped on my doorstep for the past two hours."

"I haven't seen much of her this trip, but Trav says Cody's got his hands full. I've heard all about the terrible twos. If I get through those, I guess I'll have the enigmatic eights to look forward to next."

"Don't look to me for advice." Laurel slipped on her mules and collected her purse. "I was an only."

"Me, too." Ru sighed. "It gets lonesome sometimes, doesn't it?"

"You learn to live with it, since it's hardly something you can change retroactively." She'd often thought that the lack of siblings might help explain why she had trouble compromising. "I'd better run if we want to get any digging done before dark."

"Save me a piece of eight, will you? Call it a baby present."

"How about a gold necklace? Gold doesn't rust, does it?"


"What took you so long? It's almost dark!" Hands on her narrow hips, the child stood to greet her. Wearing shorts, an outgrown tee and a pair of red canvas sneakers, she'd brought along a shovel and several plastic bags. "These are to put things in," she said, indicating the grocery sacks.

Laurel wondered if she had ever been that young and optimistic.

"Daddy said don't go in the water, but he said the tide's out, so we can dig on the shore today, and if we find any clams, he'll make fritters."

Today? Did that mean she expected to go again to-morrow? And the tomorrow after that, until they found something?

Laurel had a feeling that digging up a few pop-tops and a corroded penny—or even a few clams—wouldn't be enough to cool the treasure-hunting fever. Next she'd be begging her father for a metal detector.

"Just give me time to change clothes and get us something cold to drink, okay? Treasure hunting is thirsty work."

Not to mention boring. Laurel had been allowed to tag along on a few summer digs with her mother. She'd nearly died of boredom as she hadn't been allowed any-where near the actual work areas. Not that they'd been digging for treasure, only artifacts and possibly bones.

Leaving her tools on the porch, Becky trooped up-stairs behind her. "This is my daddy's bedroom." She looked around curiously. "The bed used to be over there and the dresser was right here. You moved it."

She had moved most of the furniture. It was what she did, no matter where she was. Peg called it compulsive meddling, but Laurel needed to put her own stamp on her surroundings, if only to prove that she was in con-trol of her life.

Ha. As if!

"Daddy sleeps with the window open, even in the winter. I know, 'cause I used to sleep with him when I had a bad dream."

Like I really need to know that, Laurel thought. She was having enough trouble with her own dreams. Now she'd probably dream about snuggling under a layer of down comforters, pressed against a hard, warm body while a cold winter wind blew in through the window.

Tying on her walking shoes, she told herself that Jerry's lean body was more than enough to keep her satisfied. He was a fastidious lover on the rare occasions when they were able to schedule a weekend together. Somewhat less than spontaneous, but then, she'd never been the spontaneous type, either, which was what made them so perfect together.

Right, she thought before she could stop herself. They were perfect together as long as she allowed Jerry to take the lead.

*I'll think about that tomorrow.*

*Sure you will, Scarlett.*

# Chapter 13

The walk to the sound shore took only a few minutes, following Ridge Pond Road, crossing the highway and then taking the twisted path through Travis's wooded acres. At the top of the ridge, Laurel paused to look down on the narrow white-sand beach. She felt some of her tiredness fall away. Talk about your low-tech splendor. No special lighting display could come close to competing with a colorful sky reflected on mirror-calm waters. The distant mainland was too far away to be seen, leaving her feeling as if she were truly on the edge of the earth.

She wondered if Cody appreciated the quiet splendor of a perfect sunset reflected on still waters. She could almost imagine herself standing here with him, holding hands—better yet, his arm across her shoulder and—

"Come *on*, Laurie!" Becky grabbed her hand and gave it a tug. "I think we ought to dig over there where that tree root sticks out of the sand. Maybe it was a marker or something."

Judging from what was left of the stump, the tree couldn't have been much more than a foot or two around. She seriously doubted if it had been even an acorn back in the time when pirates roamed the sounds, but try telling that to a child whose eyes were filled with visions of doubloons and pieces of eight.

They dug for several minutes, finding nothing between the tangled roots but a few broken shells. The hole filled with water almost as fast as they dug.

Then Becky chose another spot. "That looks like a place where a pirate might bury his treasure," she said, her small face pinched in a thoughtful frown.

"Shall I dig this one?" Laurel tried to follow the child's line of reasoning, but her own childhood was too far behind her.

"No, me." As they had only one small gardening spade and Becky refused to relinquish it, Laurel, still tired but pleasantly relaxed, wandered along the shore under the guise of searching for further clues. Now and then she waved away a mosquito, but for the most part she simply allowed her mind to range free, for once making no effort to keep it under control.

She thought about Ru and Trav, and Matt, the missing son. She had an idea there might be a bit of jealousy involved with a new sibling on the way, but she couldn't know for sure, as she'd never met the boy.

She thought about Jerry and the virtues she had described to Ru. Were they really all that impressive? Thinking back to the words she'd chosen, it occurred to her that she'd made him seem almost materialistic. And truly, he was not, she assured herself. It was only smart for a man in his position to dress well, to live at the right address, to frequent the right restaurants and the right hair stylist. As the JB of J. Blessing Associates, he had an image to maintain.

And he was sentimental; she had definitive proof of that. With the wolf practically at the door, his first thought had been to protect both her and his mother's painting. He couldn't possibly have had any other reason to value the little watercolor, because even without a background in art, Laurel recognized mediocrity when she saw it.

Becky gave out a squeal, breaking into her somewhat troubling thoughts. "Laurie, come look! I found a secret message!"

It was an exhausted child who insisted on dragging Laurel home with her when it grew almost too dark to see. "I want you to 'splain to Daddy why we have to go back tomorrow, 'cause now we know where to dig. Can you get off early?"

"I'm afraid not." After a day that seemed endless, Laurel could barely drag herself up the stairs leading to the deck, some ten feet off the ground level. Silhouetted against the light shining through the sliding glass doors, Cody was leaning over the railing, waiting for them.

"I'm returning your daughter. I think she has something to show you." Why was it that her heart did that crazy little flutter-dance whenever she saw him, even when she was angry and irritated?

"I was about to call out the rescue squad."

"Daddy, Daddy, we found something important! Laurie says it's an Indian sharp, but it looks like there's some secret writing on it, so it could be a pirate message, couldn't it?"

"A shard," Laurel said. The last thing she felt like doing was visiting the lion in his den, but Becky had insisted, and as it was nearly dark now, she felt better about handing the child over to her father in person. Chalk it up to city living.

So then they all had to go inside so that Becky could show off her fragment of pottery under a good light. Laurel took time to glance around at the leather-covered sofa and matching reclining love seat, the child-size chair and table and the massive, overloaded bookshelf. Even with bare floors, bare walls and bare windows, the room looked comfortable and inviting.

"I've got a book," Cody said, and reached for a thick volume with several bookmarks protruding from the pages.

Laurel thought, amused, that he had more than a book—he had thousands of them. Either he did exhaustive research, or he was a marathon reader.

The potsherd was quickly identified as net-incised and probably Algonquin. Cody explained the process that produced the texture, and pointed to several illustrations.

"Convenient that you had a book," Laurel said dryly.

"Research," Cody replied.

"Thought so," she said, stifling a yawn. She backed away. Standing too close to so much masculine pulchritude could be hazardous to a woman's health. Even a woman who was sensible enough to know better.

Becky was still studying the illustrations, comparing her find to the ones displayed in the book, as if reluctant to give up her pet theory.

Cody had that quirky kind of half smile that she wanted to think of as a smirk, only it probably wasn't. "That's right, you're a writer, aren't you?" she said. "What sort of thing do you write?"

"Fiction."

"Historical?"

"Mostly crime."

"Oh." She didn't read crime fiction. Didn't read historicals, either, except for the occasional historical romance. "Is Cody Morningstar your real name or a pen name?" She yawned again, and this time she wasn't quite as successful covering it.

"Real name. Would you like a plate of bacon and scrambled eggs before you go? That's what I plan to cook for Becky and me."

"No thanks. Becky—" she managed a tired smile "—I enjoyed your company today. Maybe we can do it again before you leave."

"Tomorrow! Now we know where the Indians lived, we can find lots of stuff and look it up in Daddy's book."

With an expression that was part amusement, part sympathy, Cody caught Laurel's eye. "Honey, they probably lived all over these woods," he told his daughter. "Why not dig right here in the yard?"

Dig up his beautifully grassed lawn? Laurel gave him points for tolerance.

"But Daddy, we found our sharp on the beach," Becky protested.

"Then how about waiting until the weekend," he countered.

Becky did something with her fingers and said, "But that's two whole days away. What if somebody else finds it? Besides, Laurel has to work Saturday, she said so."

"Becky. Go wash up for supper."

The child sighed heavily. She said, "Yes, sir," and headed for the stairs, sandy shoes and all.

"Thank you," Cody said when they heard the sound of water running upstairs. "You've been more than patient. Sure you won't join us?"

Laurel shook her head. "Tell me something. Why don't you take her treasure hunting?"

He looked away. It was several moments before he spoke, during which time Laurel studied his strong profile, including the lines that feathered out from the corners of his eyes. Lines and all, he was the most strikingly attractive man she had met in a long, long time. Like maybe ever.

"I offered. She said you'd promised. I didn't push it."

Laurel felt sorry for the big, rugged man. He might be successful enough to afford an expensive house and drive a top-of-the-line SUV, but evidently he had his own set of problems.

Accustomed to placing the people she met in neatly labeled slots, it dawned on her that she hadn't the least idea of how to file Cody Morningstar. Under *S* for Scrooge? Under *H* for Hottie? Or *F* for Father without a clue?

Cody watched until he lost sight of the slight figure disappearing through the tangle of vine-choked scrub oak and yaupon that formed the hedgerow between the two properties. He should have lent her a flashlight. There was a light on her front porch, but with Becky camped on her doorstep when she got home from work, she'd evidently forgotten to turn it on.

But then, she probably hadn't realized she'd be out this late. Once the sun went down—always a spectacular display—there was very little time before it grew too dark to see in these woods.

Might be a good idea to have a security light installed between the two houses. He'd miss being able to step out on the deck and view the sky from horizon to horizon with no city lights to interfere.

On the other hand, why bother? She wouldn't be

here much longer, and he still wasn't entirely certain what he was going to do with the old place. He'd contracted to have it reroofed, but with property values and taxes as high as they were, it didn't make sense to renovate a shabby old two-bedroom house when he could raze it and build something that would quickly pay for itself in rent.

Still, there was something about the few old houses left standing. Character, dignity. A sense of continuity that appealed to him far more than was practical.

Meanwhile, he would put a bigger bulb in the porch light and turn it on for her if she forgot.

As he leaned against the railing, waiting for Becky to come back downstairs, something Trav had said recently came back to him. Laurel had mentioned to Ru that her apartment in New York had been broken into shortly after she'd left town headed South. Break-ins were hardly a rare event, especially in a big city. But then she'd said something about feeling as if she were being watched recently.

He told himself it was a quirk of his, something to do with the way a writer's mind worked, yet he couldn't quite bring himself to dismiss it entirely. Whether or not people realized it, the gut was a powerful antenna. Crime on the island was minimal, most of it either drug or traffic related, but she could have brought trouble with her. It happened occasionally. He didn't know her background, only the few things Trav had let slip. Damned few, come to think of it.

Bottom line—he'd keep an eye on her until she left. As his office faced the old house, it wouldn't be hard to do.

Not that he needed the additional distraction.

* * *

"I didn't realize kids had obsessions," Laurel said as she shoved a wiener on a stick and held it over the bonfire the next afternoon. Becky had grudgingly agreed to postpone the treasure hunt in favor of another cookout, as the weather was threatening to close in.

"No stuff? You mean you didn't look under your bed before you climbed in? You didn't step over cracks in the sidewalks to protect your mother's health?" Cody in a teasing mood was a little more than she'd bargained on. He was downright…likable.

"Not the sidewalk thing, but I did go through a stage of seeing boggeymen in every shadow. I think I might have been younger than Becky, at the time. I'd just discovered ghost stories."

"Those have been around forever. What about pirates? Are you the one who's responsible for Becky's newest interest?"

"Not unless you count taking her to the library where she found the book on Blackbeard." She wriggled uncomfortably, wishing she weren't wet and sandy, and that her tank suit wasn't quite so revealing.

"She already knew who he was. Mr. Teach is a local hero, in case you hadn't heard."

"Not my kind of hero." She grinned. "Although I admit to seeing *Pirates of the Caribbean* three times." Okay, not for the story; not even Jerry could hold a candle to Johnny Depp.

Although, come to think of it, Cody easily could….

While Becky and the dog romped on the beach, they continued to talk idly about nothing in particular. Small talk. She'd never been good at it, but somehow, with Cody, it was easy. Sharing a laugh now and then, she wondered idly which felt better—the warm sun on her shoulders, the fresh breeze blowing off the water, or the easy camaraderie. They were only neighbors. Only landlord and tenant. So how come she kept feeling this tingle of something more? She'd never been the imaginative type.

"Heard anything lately from your resident ghost?" Cody asked as he held a bun open for her to slide a wiener in.

"Oh, so you know about him?"

"Her. Not that you can prove it by me—I happen to be immune."

"Her, then. Funny, you didn't mention her. What were you afraid of, that I'd ask for a break on the rent?"

"Hey, you got a break. Do you have any idea what that much square footage costs down here, even out of season?"

"Yes, but as I'm having to share, I should only have to pay half as much," she teased, casting him a sidelong look. "Why'd you buy a haunted house, anyway? Thinking about the great Halloween parties you could have?"

He waved away a greenhead fly. "I didn't hear the rumors until after I closed on the property."

"And?"

He shrugged. "And I was…mildly intrigued. Since there's no such thing as ghosts, you have to wonder how such rumors get started. Kids, probably. Halloween stuff."

"Or cavemen huddled around campfires trying to explain things like thunder and hailstorms and the occasional earth tremor? I have to admit that since people started asking me if I've heard the ghost, every little noise sounds spooky."

He cut her a teasing look. "Natural causes. Loons out on the reef. Mourning doves sound kind of spooky, too, come to think of it. Even crows."

"There are plenty of those back in the woods, big ones, too."

"Fish crows." Cody flicked a bit of gravel from her shoulder.

She shivered, not from cold but from his touch. "What's the difference between fish crows and common crows?" she asked, not from any real interest, but because she suddenly felt too aware.

If he felt it—the awareness—he hid it well. "There's this test," he said. "What you do is, you ask a crow if he's a common crow. If he's a fish crow, he'll say, 'Unh-unh!'"

"You're kidding, right?"

"Dead serious," he replied. "Which reminds me, you do know there's a graveyard just on the other side of the creek, don't you?"

"Thanks," she said dryly. "I was hoping those grayish-white rectangular things were beehives."

"Nope." The greenhead returned, looking for a landing site on her face. She blinked. Cody brushed it away and his hand lingered on her cheek for a moment too long before falling away.

Before she could catch herself, Laurel touched the place where the heat of his hand still lingered. For several seconds neither of them spoke. Then Cody said, "In fact, that's supposed to be where your ghost was buried."

"I could have gone all day without hearing that," she said dryly, reaching for another bun. "Are you going to cook another one for Becky?"

"She's had two already. Any more and she'll have another nightmare."

"Evidently nightmares are endemic around here."

"You, too?"

Intent on putting things back on an impersonal level, Laurel busied herself with her hot dog. Taking a bite, she nodded and waited until she could speak. "Stuff on my mind." She waved a hand dismissively. "Sometimes it follows me into the night. You know how that goes."

Impersonal? It occurred to her that the relationship that had started out on the wrong foot little more than a week ago was making remarkable progress. She was telling him things she'd never even told Jerry. Next thing she knew, she'd be admitting that she was scared of lightning to the point of covering her head with a pillow; she was that relaxed in his company.

Or as relaxed as a single woman with a full complement of hormones could be around a sexy, somewhat mysterious man.

"With me," he said, as if exchanging such personal tidbits didn't bother him at all, "it's insomnia. I lie awake creating whole brilliant scenes complete with dialogue. Then I stay awake worrying because I know it'll all be gone by morning."

"Get up and write it down," she suggested.

"It disappears the minute my feet hit the floor."

"Then keep a pen and paper beside your bed and scribble it down without getting up." Or take a secretary to bed with you. Unfortunately, her secretarial skills were on a par with her cooking skills. Less than impressive.

"Sleep-writing. I tried that, but I have trouble reading my own writing at the best of times." He leaned back on his elbows and his bare foot accidentally brushed against hers.

"Tape recorder?"

"Comes out gibberish. I thought about hiring a stenographer to sleep with me, but…"

"I know. Risk of sexual harassment charges." She actually felt herself blushing and hoped that if he noticed, he'd put it down to sunburn.

Slanting him a sidelong glance, she saw that he was smiling.

Somewhat to her surprise, so was she. They were veering into some risky conversational territory, but she had to admit it was fun. Besides, where was the harm? With Becky and the mutt as chaperones, nothing could come of it. Even if she'd wanted it to.

*Did* she want it to?

Time to steer the conversation away from the personal. "I don't mean this in a derogatory way, but your dog's looking a little shabby. Have you thought about having him shorn?"

Cody chuckled. "Yeah, he's pretty bad, isn't he? I'll have to do something about it before Mara picks him up."

His wife was coming here? His ex-wife and her new husband? That was pretty chummy, Laurel mused, wondering if the couple would stay with Cody or at a motel, or in one of those monstrous beach castles.

"Place is full of wild cactus and sandspurs, not to mention fleas and ticks. I'll probably give him a scrub and a trim tomorrow. If you'd like a ringside seat, I'll schedule it for after you get home from work."

"I think I have a standing appointment with your daughter for after five."

"Actually, I could use some help. I tried rigging up

a running line and the clown nearly hanged himself. I even threw together an outdoor pen from lattice panels, but he dug under it."

"He ran away? Becky didn't mention it."

"Nope, just dug out and flopped down outside the pen. I could almost swear he was laughing at me."

Laurel laughed, too. It occurred to her fleetingly that she hadn't laughed so much in months—maybe even years. The one thing Jerry lacked was a sense of humor.

Finishing her second hot dog, she leaned back on her elbows and watched mutt and child cavorting on the beach, daring the waves that washed up on the shore. The sun seemed to leach any lingering tension from her very bones. Still living in the moment, she allowed her mind to roam free until Cody rolled over onto his side to face her. He was so close she could see the rapid darkening of his gold-shot eyes.

"So…you're still planning to leave after Labor Day?" He reached out and began to trace circles on her sandy shoulder.

If she'd needed a downer—and she probably had—that did it. Still, she couldn't make herself move away. "My lease here is up then, remember?" Before then, actually.

His fingers traced her shoulder bones, then slipped up her throat to her hair. "That's negotiable. Caroline stays open through the end of the year."

"I have a job in New York." One that might still be in limbo. Jerry hadn't actually said they were free to start up again, not in so many words. "I also have an apartment there." One that she couldn't afford until she went back to work at a better salary. "And friends. Good friends."

"You have friends here, too. What about family?"

She shook her head and sat up on the rumpled, sandy bedspread they shared. His hand fell away and she missed it sorely, but evidently his touch had the capacity to short-circuit her common sense.

"Nope," she said in a squeaky voice that reminded her of a cartoon character. "My, the ocean's rough today, isn't it?" She made a big deal of brushing the sand off her legs.

"Turn around," said Cody.

"Why, have I got sand there, too?"

"A currycomb might come in handy," he said as he brushed off her back, using his fingernail to dislodge bits of broken shell that stubbornly adhered. "Did you know you've got a mole right…here?" He touched a place on her lower back.

"Mmm, hmm," she murmured, hoping the goose bumps his touch set off weren't visible on her back. "Had it for years, it's nothing to worry about."

Gently, he turned her to face him. "Got another one right here." He touched her left cheek. "They're called beauty spots. Used to be, anyway. Women used to fake 'em by using stick-on patches."

"Imagine your knowing something like that." She found herself unable to look away from his eyes, her peripheral vision taking in features that could hardly be called handsome, yet were all the more arresting for their irregularity.

"Writers' bag of tricks." His smile was self-deprecating, calling into prominence the laugh lines that bracketed his wide, firm mouth. "We writers know a little bit about a lot of stuff."

She scooted back so that his hands dropped to his knees. "Okay, then tell me this…" But to her acute embarrassment, she couldn't think of a single thing to ask him. She was still trying when Becky and BooBoo raced up, scattering sand and drops of cold water.

As a mood-killer there was nothing like a spray of cold water.

# Chapter 14

"Daddy! Daddy! Guess what!"

Cody broke away to tug on the child's bedraggled ponytail. "Do I get three guesses?"

"BooBoo dug up a piece of wood and I think it's from a pirate ship. You wanna see it?" She held out a piece of dark wood that was roughly the size of a loaf of bread.

He took it and examined it carefully on all sides. Bless his heart, Laurel thought—she was picking up a few Southernisms—he was treating the find as seriously as if it had been stamped with a skull and crossbones.

"You might be right," he said. "It's definitely old wood, been underwater a long time. When we get home, I'll show you another clue."

Becky was practically jumping up and down. "Now, tell me now!"

"When we get home. How'd you like to help pack up? You and BooBoo can cover up the fire pit, you can put the sticks in the truck, I'll carry the cooler and Laurie can bring the rest of the stuff."

It was that evanescent period called dusk when Cody pulled up in front of the old house. Becky insisted on helping Laurel carry her few belongings inside while Cody took care of the dog. He called after her, "Don't bother Miss Laurie, honey. She's tired. You come on home directly, y'hear?"

"I will, Daddy!"

Laurel dumped the damp sandy pile on top of the washing machine. She would shake the sand out tomorrow. "Shouldn't you run along home? You want me to walk partway with you?"

Becky was standing in the doorway of what had probably once been a pantry, but had since been converted to a laundry. There was something almost conspiratorial about the way she was regarding her. Laurel said, "Honey, as impressed as I am with your beach find, I don't have a clue. My mother could probably have told you something about it, but I didn't inherit that particular gene."

She halfway expected a question about her mother. Or about genes. Becky was intelligent, inquisitive and imaginative. Looking forward to a warm shower, Laurel said, "I've had fun today. Thanks for inviting me."

Taking a deep breath, Becky tilted her head and said earnestly, "You know what? If you married my daddy, I could live here all the time and not have to move to San Francisco with Mommy and Mr. Everstone. Then you and me could play while Daddy worked."

It was several hours later when Cody came over. Somehow, Laurel was not particularly surprised when he rapped on the screen door and came on inside. "I took a chance you weren't in bed yet."

"If I had been, the screen would have been hooked, the door locked and the lights would be off. Did you need something?"

"I wanted to thank you for all the help you've been. With Becky," he added when she didn't say anything.

What could she say when all she could think of was that his daughter was actively matchmaking? Should she be flattered? Probably.

Should she be interested?

No way. She had her life all planned, and it didn't include leaving her job and her friends behind to take on the care and keeping of a ready-made family.

*Was* she interested?

What woman under the age of ninety wouldn't be interested in a man whose simplest touch made her bones melt—a man who was patient and kind when it came to dealing with children and nutty dogs, if not with tenants? "I guess she's pretty worn-out by now. I know I am."

"Then I won't keep you," he said quietly.

Her inner rebel cried, *Keep me, keep me!* "She was really excited about that chunk of wood. Is it really from a shipwreck?"

*If you married my daddy, I could live here all the time and not have to move to San Francisco with Mommy and Mr. Everstone.*

Distracted by the faintest hint of soap and some subtle masculine fragrance, Laurel only half listened as he told her about the distinct cut on one side that was part of a hole made for something called a tree peg. "Before iron bolts came into use, ships' hulls were pegged together with wooden tree pegs. Bolts eventually rust away once a ship goes down, but there's usually some residue. When a peg rots out, all you have left is the hole."

"Amazing," she murmured, trying to sound amazed instead of bemused. *If you married my daddy…*

"What's sad is how much history gets tossed onto bonfires by people who don't know what it is they're burning and don't really give a damn." Cody spoke about beach wood while his gaze moved over her face.

It was all Laurel could do to breathe.

"I, uh—what I came over for is to bring you a flashlight," he said finally, fracturing the silence as if it were a thin sheet of ice.

She drew in a deep gulp of air and smiled broadly. "Thank you," she said far too enthusiastically. "I have one...somewhere. I just never can find the thing when I need it." Another sign that she'd parked her left brain somewhere north of the Mason-Dixon Line.

There were dark rims around his golden irises. Odd that she'd never noticed before. If his pupils expanded much more, his eyes would be black instead of golden-hazel.

Without breaking visual contact, he said, "I've got a book. On shipwrecks. If you're interested."

She managed to break the spell by distractedly waving at the stack of books she'd borrowed from the library. "Thanks, but I've got more here than I'll be able to finish before I leave."

Cody picked up a slim paperback from the stack. "*Local Legends,* hmm?" He glanced at her over his shoulder. She hadn't moved. "Searching for your resident ghost?"

Grateful for anything that would take her mind off the man and his daughter—*If you married my daddy*—Laurel spoke quickly. "Not that I believe in ghosts, but even if I did, I wouldn't know what to do about it. Light a candle? Burn incense? Hire a witch doctor to cast a spell?"

"Nix on the candles and incense, but if you can find a witch doctor..." His grin deepened the laugh lines that bracketed his mouth. It only made him more attractive.

Damn. To think how much she spent on trying to prevent lines… "Actually, I planned to check the index to see if there were any Lawlesses listed. So far I haven't had time." She waited for a comment. When none was forthcoming, she flashed an insincere smile and said, "Some of them spell it differently, but Trav said half the population of the northeast corner of the state is related, way back."

At least, this time he nodded. "Did he tell you that a couple of your ancestors were lighthouse keepers? At least, his were. I assume they were yours, too."

"I heard about that!" She clapped a hand to her chest. "Oh, my—oh, wait till I tell…"

Tell who? She couldn't think of a single person who would even be interested. Jerry? Hardly. Peg? Only if they'd also happened to play professional sports.

"Ask Trav about Blackbeard's second in command while you're at it. Oh, and before I forget, Becky's got some bulbs she wants to plant in your flower beds. I think Ru gave 'em to her last time she was here. I suspect it's the wrong time of year, but I told her I didn't think you'd mind."

"It's your property. If nothing digs them up she can look forward to seeing them bloom next spring." They were standing in the living room that had, until recently, been Cody's. If there was an unseen presence haunting these rooms, it was his…her reluctant landlord's. She could easily picture him lounging on the lumpy old couch, his bare feet on the scarred coffee table while he read the daily paper. Or sleeping in her bed, eating at her kitchen table. Standing in the old rust-stained bathtub while he tried to inveigle a trickle of water from the clogged showerhead.

Enough, already! Obviously, all this salt air had corroded her few remaining brain cells.

He laid the book aside and glanced out the front window toward his own house, some two hundred feet away. "I'll put a larger-watt bulb in your porch fixture, speaking of bulbs. Anything else you can think of that needs doing? This landlording business is still pretty new to me."

"I thought you'd rented this house before."

"Travis knew this couple who needed a place, so while I was getting settled in my new house, he moved them in here. They stayed less than a month before the guy got transferred."

"Maybe your ghost chased them away."

"You're still here, aren't you?"

"I'm tougher than I look. Or maybe she just likes me."

Cody turned away from the window just as a beam from the lighthouse swept over the treetops. *My* lighthouse, Laurel marveled silently. No wonder the place was haunted, given how many generations had lived in the same small area. It occurred to her that she might have inherited something from her mother after all, if only a growing interest in the past.

"I expect you'll be rushed off your feet these next few days, judging from the way traffic's picking up." Turning to face her, Cody flexed his shoulders and crossed his arms over his chest. There were faint shadows under his eyes, shadows that did nothing to lessen his good looks.

"I noticed. It's nothing like what I'm used to back home, but then, I don't drive there."

"It'll drop off after Labor Day, then we'll start getting the fishermen. Come late January and February, we'll have things pretty much to ourselves for a few weeks."

Laurel looked away, blocking thoughts she would

prefer not to deal with. Cody expressed them for her. "But by then you won't be here."

For the life of her, she couldn't tell if it was relief or regret she heard in the brief statement. She could only nod. "Oh, long before then," she agreed, wondering if coming South hadn't been the biggest mistake of her life. Whatever happened in the future, whether or not she married Jerry, she would always feel a link with this place and these people, and not just her newfound cousins, either.

She led the way to the door, wishing she could lock him inside for the foreseeable future. Just as he brushed past her, he paused, placed his thumb under her chin and studied her face. "Did you know your eyes are the exact color of Spanish moss when it's wet?"

A long time later, as she watched him disappear through the hedge, she remembered to breathe.

The next day marked the start of the three-day holiday weekend. Caroline had warned her, but no warnings could prepare her for the reality of hundreds of customers, all demanding attention of one sort or another.

Caroline saw the last one out, leaned against the front door and closed her eyes. "And this was just day one. If tomorrow turns off rainy, I'm not even going to open up, I swear."

Dead on her feet, Laurel stayed forty-five minutes past closing time to help restock and reassemble displays. Fashionable or not, she intended to wear sneakers for the rest of the holiday weekend. Retail was a killer profession!

Becky was waiting on her front porch, shovel at hand, when she got home. Oh, damn, Laurel thought, remembering the promise she'd made yesterday. Wanting nothing so much as to flop down across the bed and stay there until hunger drove her in search of food, she managed a cheerful greeting. Fortunately, there wasn't all that much daylight left.

"Just give me a minute to change clothes and grab a banana. I didn't have time for lunch. Want one?"

Becky shook her head. "Daddy cooks better than Picola. She's Mommy's cook, 'cause Mommy doesn't cook at all. That man takes her out to eat and Picola makes me eat gunky stuff like cauliflowers and oatmeal."

A few minutes later, while they followed the now-familiar path to the soundside, Becky chattered about her beach find. "Daddy says it's a shipwreck on account of the hole. I think it was a pirate ship, don't you? Daddy said it was old enough."

Daddy says this, Daddy says that. Quite a change since she'd first met the Morningstars, Laurel told herself. She wanted to take credit for the gradual thaw in their relations, but then, how could any female, even an eight-year-old one, hold out long against a man like Cody Morningstar? Even she, who was supposed to be in love with another man, wasn't as immune as she should be to a sexy blend of physical strength, emotional vulnerability, with a tad of mystery thrown in.

They took the path that led behind Travis's shed, so at least Laurel didn't feel obligated to stop by and visit. Carrying the shovel and several bags for whatever loot they collected, she picked her way through sandspurs and trailing tendrils of beach grass while Becky ran on ahead. She envied the child her energy, not to mention her dogged optimism. Her own was beginning to waver like a feather in the wind.

Go or stay. Stay or go. Once she left, she would probably never come back, even though she had family here. So far, she didn't even know what degree of kinship she shared with the cousins she'd met, much less those she had yet to meet, like Lyon and Trav's son, Matt. Travis had promised to check with his genealogical friend and get back to her, but with his work and his concerns about Ru—and now with Matt gone missing, even though he was eighteen years old and had probably gone ahead to the college he'd be attending next month—she hadn't wanted to add to the pressure.

She tried to picture Jerry in a place like this. He had mentioned loving Captiva Island and Hilton Head. She had a feeling that Hatteras Island wouldn't quite meet his exquisite standards. Although maybe if he rented one of those monstrous beach palaces...

"Laurie—hurry up!"

"Coming," she called out, and picked her way across mounds of dead eelgrass to where Becky waited impatiently, squinting against the lowering sun.

"Daddy said I could wade, so come on. I'm going to dig right out there where that chunk of grass sticks up." Becky pointed to a bit of grassy turf a few feet out from shore.

They ended up wasting more than the promised hour, but Laurel had to admit she was coming to enjoy it. Not so much the ever-present mosquitoes or the small blue crabs that challenged intruders before darting away to safety, but the gulls that soared overhead—the fish crows and their raucous cries that sounded eerily like laughter.

"Water keeps filling up my hole." Becky complained.

"How about we try for five minutes over on that

sandy point, and then we'd better head back before it gets too dark to see our way home."

A few minutes later, as the sun disappeared below the horizon, Laurel called time. Becky was reluctant to leave, but the promise of another dig tomorrow had her skipping up the path, swinging today's prizes, which included several more potsherds, one perfect arrowhead and half of a thick white mug that had been broken neatly in two. Laurel decided to let Cody be the one to tell her that it was probably of Coast Guard rather than pirate origin.

Becky chattered all the way home. Lost in her own thoughts, Laurel only half listened. They waited for a break in traffic, hurried across the highway and parted at the cut in the hedge. Laurel was thinking longingly of sinking into a deep, cool bath with one of the library books.

On second thought, better make it one of the paperbacks she'd brought with her. The way she felt now, she could easily fall asleep in the tub and drown herself and whatever book she happened to be reading.

Unwilling to risk drowning, she settled for a quick shower, a single-serving can of soup and two glasses of grocery-store merlot. She slept dreamlessly through the night, oblivious to the intermittent beam of light that brushed over the foot of her bed like a benevolent night watchman.

Cody caught her halfway down Ridge Pond Road on the way to work the next morning. There was barely enough room for two vehicles to pass without both edging over into the boggy weeds. "Need a favor," he said when she rolled down her car window. He glanced at her as yet unrepaired fender and grimaced. "Yeah, well…I'll see that it's taken care of before you head north again."

"Thanks. What's the favor?" About time he owned up to his responsibility, Laurel told herself—although it no longer seemed quite so important.

"I need to run up to New York for a few hours today, so if you wouldn't mind, could you collect Becky from Trav's when you get off from work? He'll be home all day, so he'll see she doesn't worry Ru."

"Well…I guess. Of course, but…*New York?* Is this about…Matt?"

"Sorry, it's personal. Look, I'll be back before dark. Our airport's not rigged for night landings."

"You're flying?" The nearest airport of any size was Norfolk International; she did know that much. It had never occurred to her that he had his own plane.

"Anything I can pick up for you while I'm there? I don't plan to go into town. My party's meeting me at JFK, but I'll be glad to do courier duty if you can set it up."

What she needed was information that couldn't be had at the airport. "Thanks, but I can't think of anything. I'll take care of Becky, though."

He was a pilot. A writer and a pilot and…what else?

She had a quick vision of him wearing boots and riding pants and flying one of those open cockpit planes, à la Ralph Fiennes in *The English Patient*.

Customers were lined up on the ramp waiting to get in when Laurel parked behind the shop and went in through the back door a few minutes before ten. She took a minute to stash her purse and the sandwich and bottled water she'd brought for lunch, and another to comb her hair.

Caroline emerged from her office just as she turned away from her locker. "You need to get a Hatteras haircut. With this wind, it's easier in the long run." She tilted her head. "You know, for a second there you reminded me of someone I know. Give me a minute, I'll come up with a name."

But neither of them had a minute. Eight hours later, after she stepped outside to flip the Open sign to Closed, it was all Laurel could do to limp out to her car. Every bone in both feet radiated pain—and today she had changed into her sneakers.

"Oh, shoot." She'd forgotten her promise to collect Becky and keep her until Cody got back. She would probably expect another soundside dig unless she'd prevailed on Travis to take her exploring. And even if she had.

Laurel had really been looking forward to a candy bar and a three-hour nap, but a promise was a promise. A few minutes later, after changing into her grungies and eating a banana, she climbed the hill—Travis called it a ridge—and called softly through the screen door in case Ru was dozing. "Anybody home? Becky?"

"Mmm, oh…hi, Laurel." Sound of a yawn. "C'mon in, it's unhooked."

"I came to relieve you of your playmate. Oh, those are gorgeous!" She sniffed the air, fragrant with the scent of stargazer lilies.

"Trav thought I needed cheering up. For all he drives me nuts, he really can be sweet."

"Can't argue with that. It must be in the genes."

For a woman who was enormously pregnant, Ru managed to look surprisingly wicked. "Spelled with a *J?* Oh, yeah…big-time."

Laurel laughed as she was meant to do. "No word

from Matt, I guess. If he calls, tell him he has a cousin from up North who really, really wants to meet him." She laughed again. "Like that would be an inducement to an eighteen-year-old boy. Where's Becky?"

"Out back with Trav, I guess. I turned on the TV and fell asleep just before the hurricane update. Call out the back door."

"I just found out Cody's a pilot. Why didn't he fly Becky here instead of driving all the way from Richmond?" She answered her own question. "Oh yeah…the dog."

"That and the fact that she gets horribly airsick." Ru shook her head. "After months of morning sickness, I can sympathize."

Laurel hurried around to the shed where Travis kept everything from fishing gear to surplus lumber to antique radios. He looked up from a trotline he was rigging with floats. "Hey, cous. You want to put in your seafood order?"

"Can you catch me a shrimp cocktail with that thing?" When he chuckled, she asked where Becky was.

The tall, prematurely gray-haired man straightened up, glanced around and called, "Becky?" To Laurel he said, "She was here a minute ago, going through a box of old radio tubes. Kid has more curiosity than a roomful of cats."

The box was on a bench just outside the shed. They both called a few more times, then Travis moved to a spot where he could look down on the soundside. "Becky, your playmate's here to go digging! Come on, honey, before it gets too dark!"

"She wouldn't have gone back home, would she?" Laurel asked anxiously. "Maybe to check on the dog?"

"She knows her dad would skin her if she crossed the highway by herself. Nah, she's probably just off exploring—wandered a little too far. You know how kids are. No matter what their age," he added ruefully.

Actually, she didn't. She had certainly never had two parents, plus a stepfather, fighting over who got to keep her.

Increasingly worried, she said, "Cody says there are snakes—poisonous ones, I mean. What about rabid animals?"

"None so far this year, at least not that I've heard of." Travis cupped his mouth and called again, first in one direction, then another. "'Course, we do have a few 'gators and a caiman or two."

Laurel gaped at him. "Don't even *joke* about that!"

He shook his head. "Sorry, honey. I'm not joking, but I seriously doubt if she'll run into anything bigger than a rat snake—at least not on this side of the highway." His frown deepened.

"On *this* side of the highway?" Cody's house and the one Laurel was renting were on the *other* side of Highway 12. The alligator side.

"They usually hang around freshwater ponds. Actually, the creek-fed ponds are brackish. You'll find blue crabs and bluegills sharing the same water." He called a few more times, then swore quietly. There was a sudden tension in his face that made him look a decade older. "Look, let me call a friend of mine. He's got an old hound dog that can track a shadow at midnight."

Which only served to remind them both that it was rapidly growing dark. Laurel felt a chill come over her. Reminding herself that this wasn't the big city, but a small neighborhood where everyone knew everyone else, she took a deep breath. "You go call. I'm going down to the shore and see if I see any tracks while there's still enough light."

Above the tide line there were deer tracks, dog tracks and something that looked like the tracks of a small cat, but then she was no Daniel Boone. She found a few footprints from the past few days, but nothing she could pick out as recent. "Becky? Where are you, honey? If you're playing hide-and-seek, I give up!"

Searching the shoreline, she quickly lost track of time. When she came to a marshy point jutting out into the water, she removed her shoes and waded in the warm shallow water, calling loudly as she hurried along. *Oh, God, oh, God, please…!*

Slogging back to shore, she picked her way across the mounds of eelgrass that Trav said had washed ashore after the last big storm. It was booby-trapped with all manner of trash, which she ignored.

She didn't ignore the snake she nearly stepped on. Although she was no expert, she didn't think this one was a rat snake. Short, thick bodied, it opened its mouth wide, showing her the white mucous lining.

Laurel backed away. The snake held its ground.

"I don't have time for you now, fellow," she muttered, giving it a wide berth as she edged around and kept on calling, growing more frantic by the moment. What if Becky had been snake-bitten and was lying somewhere in agony, unable to call out? *Oh, God, please…!*

# Chapter 15

Dodging the ghosts of dead trees near the water's edge, Laurel waded through thickets that were probably full of poison ivy, not to mention a variety of bloodthirsty insects. No more snakes, though. Not that she saw, anyway. "Becky, if you've gone and got yourself lost, your daddy's going to skin us both!"

Panting, she braced her hands on her knees and hung her head for a moment, trying to think. Trying to catch her breath. *Please, please be safe!*

A small plane flew low overhead and she glanced up, wondering if it was Cody. Half an hour past sunset—he'd told her that was the rule. No flying in or out except during daylight hours. And daylight was rapidly fading.

Oh, God, he's going to kill me, she thought, but her worst fears were for Becky, not herself. Renewing her efforts, she cupped her hands and called in all directions. Once she thought she heard a faint response, but then a dog started barking and a truck roared past out on the highway several hundred feet away through the woods. She decided she must have been mistaken.

When she came to a dense section of bog filled with the tall, plumed weeds Travis had called phragmites, she turned back. Becky wouldn't have gone through them; they were taller than she was. Besides, there'd have been no incentive in the child's mind. Becky had earnestly explained that pirates always buried their treasure on the beach. Ignoring all the erosion that had taken place over the past few centuries, that was where she'd insisted on digging.

Retracing her steps, calling every few yards, Laurel tried to think of anything the child might have said that would offer a clue. There were several houses along the ridge overlooking the water. Should she have stopped off at one of those and asked if anyone had seen a small child with a shovel?

Actually, ever since Becky had found what she'd thought was secret writing, she'd seemed almost more interested in Indian artifacts than in pirate treasure. Which cast a slightly different slant on the matter.

"The shell mound," Laurel whispered, peering along the shoreline to an area roughly a thousand feet in the opposite direction from the one she'd been searching. Travis had mentioned it when he'd given her a condensed version of local history.

Did Becky know about it? The mound wasn't on Travis's property, but storm tides and erosion had probably distributed any artifacts all up and down the shoreline.

What if she'd decided to explore the mound itself, even though it meant climbing over a low breakwater and wading through several hundred feet of turf riddled with mussels and sharp saw grass?

Turning back, she passed by her cousin's small boat landing and called again, not waiting for a response. The more she thought about it, the more certain she was that the fearless, imaginative child had decided to explore ground zero—the low hillock littered with huge, bleached shells that according to Travis indicated an early Native American settlement.

From several hundred feet away, Laurel spotted the huddled figure and hurried toward her, oblivious to her own cuts and scratches. One of her sneakers came off in the mud. She didn't stop to retrieve it. "Oh, Becky—oh, honey, we were so worried!"

Becky stood and then ran to meet her, crying noisily as she stumbled over the uneven turf. "Please, I just want to go home. I'm sorry, I'm sorry."

"I don't know whether to hug you to death or put you on a diet of bread and water," Laurel scolded, embracing the child. "You had us all so *worried!* Didn't you hear us calling?"

Briar scratched, mosquito bitten and filthy, Becky sniffed and said, "Daddy said not to go off Uncle Travis's property, but there's not a fence, so I didn't know. I was coming back, but I saw a snake and he looked at me."

"Oh, honey, we're just glad you're all right."

Smearing tears and a runny nose across her dirty face, Becky attempted to make light of the situation. "I bet BooBoo's peed on Daddy's chair again. He knows not to do it on the floor."

"Don't change the subject, young lady. Do you have any idea how many people were worried sick about you?"

"I'm sorry," the child whispered, waving away a swarm of mosquitoes. "Can we please go home now? My feet hurt. I lost my shoes."

"Yeah, me, too. This muck owes us, right?" Turning her back, Laurel leaned over and grasped her knees. "Up you go. Grab my shoulders, wrap your legs around my waist and then give me your hands."

Becky scrambled up, nearly strangling her in the process. "Watch out for the snake," she warned as they set out through the sharp, knee-high grasses.

"Let him watch out for me," Laurel retorted. Nevertheless, she stomped and made as much noise as possible on her way back to Travis's beach. If she could just get home before Cody discovered his daughter was missing, maybe he wouldn't kill her after all.

Of course by then her feet would be beyond help and her back would be broken, so what did it matter?

Following the narrow path from Trav's boat landing to his house, she called through the back screen door. "I found her, Ru. Get Trav on his cell phone and tell him to call off the dogs. She's fine."

"Oh, thank God." Ru appeared at the door, clutching her swollen belly. Suddenly she started to cry. Shaking her head, she said, "I'm sorry, it's just—everything. Matt and—I'll go call Trav. He'll be so relieved."

"My foot hurts. Why are we going to your house?" Becky whined when they reached the end of the Ridge Pond Road and turned toward the old house.

"Because your father's not home yet and I'm not about to take my eyes off you until he gets back. Besides, we need to clean you up some before he sees you."

"I 'speck BooBoo needs to go out," Becky said almost too softly to be heard.

"Why didn't you take him with you?"

"'Cause I can't hold on to him and dig, and if I let him go he runs away."

"Re-ally," Laurel drawled, and instantly felt

ashamed. "Well, what's done is done. Now let's do some damage control."

They went directly upstairs to the bathroom, where Laurel examined the child for ticks, something she'd quickly learned to do after plowing through the weeds to pick figs. Next she ran a tub full of lukewarm water and tossed in a handful of bath salts. Short of doing a load of laundry—there wasn't time for that—there was nothing she could do about Becky's filthy clothes. "Want me to wash your hair for you? Maybe we'd better use the pruning shears. I doubt if those tangles are going to comb out anytime soon."

"Are you going to tell Daddy?"

"Tell him what?" She reached for the bottle of shampoo and knelt beside the tub.

"That I ran away."

"That you wandered off?"

"Uh-huh."

"Without asking permission or telling anyone where you were going?"

Becky's slight chest lifted and fell in a sigh. Laurel lathered, scrubbed and then lowered her and rinsed. "Stand up and we'll rinse you again under the shower. Then we need to look at those scratches. *Then* we'll think of what to tell your daddy. The truth always works best in the long run."

"What's a long run?"

Before Laurel could formulate an explanation she heard the familiar sound of Cody's SUV. She needed to catch him before Travis had time to talk to him. If there was one thing she'd learned over the past few years, it was how to spin the news. For the sake of all concerned she'd just as soon Cody not learn that the child he'd left in their charge had been missing for nearly an hour.

Half the time when she'd been growing up, even when her parents had been around, they'd been too caught up in their own interests to worry about her if she didn't show up on time. She might decide to stop off to play with a friend after school and walk the rest of the way home, taking her own meandering time.

Her friends had envied her freedom.

She'd envied them their caring families.

"All I have is this tube of stuff your daddy lent me for scratches. I'll use it on yours, and that cut on your foot, but it needs a bandage and I don't even have any Band-Aids."

"I could put my shoes on, only they came off. I think they might be near the place where I found…" A stricken look came over the child's small face. "My stuff! Laurie, I left my stuff there! What if someone steals it?"

"What kind of stuff?" Laurel finished anointing her scratches, then sat her on the commode and examined the cut on her foot again. It wasn't as deep as she'd first thought, but it probably needed more attention than she was prepared to offer. "Wait here, you can borrow a pair of my socks to wear home."

They were miles too big, of course, but Becky pulled them up on her legs and examined the effect. "If I had something to tie around the tops they could be pirate's boots. I found a really old doorknob, prob'ly off an old ship, and some more sharps and a piece of bone that might even be Blackbeard's leg bone."

"We'll have to settle for rubber bands." No doubt about it, the child was going to write fiction, just like her father, only with a definite slant toward fantasy. "Okay, you're as good as I can get you, so let's go face the music."

"Are you going to tell him?"

"Tell him what?" Laurel asked as she led the way downstairs. "That you wandered off without telling anyone where you were going, even though you were supposed to stay with Travis until I came for you?"

Becky's limp suddenly grew more pronounced. She hung her head and Laurel relented. "Okay, so maybe I'll edit it some so he won't lock you in the basement on a diet of bread and water."

The limp forgotten, the child looked up and giggled. "Daddy doesn't have a basement, 'cause if he did, water would get in it. If I promise never, ever to run away again, do we have to tell him?"

"Why, will he spank you?"

"He doesn't do that, he just *looks* at me. Like this." Becky pulled a long, sorrowful face, which is why they both happened to be laughing when Cody stepped out onto the lower deck to watch them climb the stairs.

"Nice boots, kid," he said dryly.

Becky galloped up the last few steps, her injured foot obviously forgotten. "Daddy, Daddy, if you got me a pony, Mama would prob'ly buy me some riding boots. Did you see the man?"

What man? Laurel wondered.

"Yep."

"Is he going to put my picture on your books?" She giggled.

"Nope."

"Is he going to put *your* picture on your books?"

"Nope."

"Is he going to tell everybody that my daddy is really Lee Larkin so the kids at school will want to come to my birthday party and bring me lots of presents?"

Laurel did a slow double take. Cody swore quietly.

Becky looked remorseful. "But Mama tells all her friends who you are, so why can't I tell mine?"

Cody glanced over at Laurel, who was still standing at the top of the outside stairs. He nodded toward the sliding glass doors. "Come on inside, we need to talk."

"Oh, I—that is, I need to clean up, I'm filthy."

"Laurel, come inside. Becky needs to eat her supper and go to bed. You, too, if you're hungry, but then you and I are going to have a discussion."

"Do I have to go to bed? It's not even dark yet."

A three-quarter moon was just rising above the treetops. There was only the faintest stain of color left in the western sky. Later, Laurel would wonder what had made her stay. Curiosity, a growing attraction, or a combination of both elements?

The attraction won out as she watched a tired-looking father make supper for his daughter. Frozen lasagna, canned applesauce and buttered whole wheat toast cut in triangles and sprinkled with sugar and cinnamon. Hardly haute cuisine, but probably healthy enough. The fact that he appeared to be a caring father only added to his attractiveness. It was rapidly becoming a major distraction.

After giving her a choice between several frozen dinners, Cody popped two in the microwave and got out a bagged salad. "Wine, milk, coffee or beer?"

"Oh—you choose." She was too tired, not to mention too confused, to think properly. And dammit, she was filthy! She hadn't taken time to do more than wash her hands and splash off her face.

Watching the way his khakis hugged his narrow butt before sheathing what she knew to be muscular thighs, she sighed and slid onto a barstool. *This* was Lee Larkin? This shaggy-haired, shadowy-eyed guy in rumpled pants and a no-brand-name T-shirt was the number one bestseller on every list for weeks at a time, every time he came out with a new hardcover? And again when the same book came out in paperback?

The guy whose mouth she had stared at and wondered....

The guy whose body she had fantasized over in her wildest dreams?

She reminded herself that this was the same jerk who had creamed her right rear fender and then tried to deny her a roof over her head, but it didn't help. She hadn't read him because she didn't care for hard-edged thrillers, but evidently she was in the minority.

She sipped the wine he'd poured, knowing it was the last thing she needed on an empty stomach. Especially when she had some clear thinking to do.

When the microwave pinged, Cody slid the two dinners out, removed the covers, set them directly on place mats, dumped bag salad into two bowls and plopped a package of store-bought dinner rolls on the table. "So...where do we start?" he asked.

Where do we start *what?* Laurel was tempted to ask. She was so far out of her depth she needed a scuba tank. "Why don't you go first?"

"Right. First, Becky, then. Thanks for tracking her down."

"You knew?"

"Trav called as soon as I landed to tell me what was going on. God, you don't want to know what ran through my mind," he said fervently. "There seems to be an epidemic of that going on around here—kids running off." The furrows between his brows deepened. She stared at them, wondering why lines that were lethal to a woman's appearance only added to a man's attractiveness.

"I know," she said softly. "They're both worried sick about Matt, even though he's old enough…"

"Is anyone ever old enough?" Cody said. It was not a question. Arms on the table, he steepled his hands and stared at his long, square-tipped fingers. "Years ago, long before I moved down here, a couple of kids got lost in the woods less than half a mile from here. They weren't found until the next day. It was the dead of winter," he said quietly. "One of them didn't make it. I've been back on the Great Ridge, and even now, after all the changes, it's like another world."

What could she say? At least Matt wasn't really lost, and Becky had been found.

"I'll take you back there someday when it's colder."

She wouldn't be here when it got colder. There was a brief, awkward silence, and then Cody said, "Thank God you found her safe and sound."

"Safe, but I don't know about sound." Laurel poked at the limp vegetables in her mystery dinner. "I put Neosporin on her cuts and scratches, but you might want to check the one on her foot tomorrow."

Toying with his fork, Cody nodded gravely. She thought, I can't believe I'm actually sitting across the table from a world-famous author. Not only that, I think I'm in love with him.

Which was so absurd she didn't even bother to deny it.

Comparing Lee Larkin's celebrity to all the P. Diddy and Britney Spears wannabes she had steered through interviews and fund-raising events was like comparing a five-course meal at the Four Seasons to a frozen dinner.

Cody reached out to snap on a small TV, muting the sound. "I don't know if you've heard any weather news today, but it looks like we might be in for a blow."

"A blow," she repeated, still struggling with the fact that he was a *New York Times* bestseller whose books had been turned into blockbuster movies. How did he get away with it? Publicity was such a wacky commodity. Those who wanted it most couldn't get it, while those who wanted it least couldn't escape.

A few somewhat puzzling exchanges between Ru and Travis came to mind that suddenly began to make sense. "Why is it such a big secret?" Laurel asked as she carefully placed her utensils across the plastic tray.

"The hurricane? It's not, only they've screwed up on the predicted course so many times it's beginning to look like a snail track. First Bermuda, then a course that would take it across the Florida peninsula and into the Gulf, and now they've rerouted it up the East Coast."

Distracted, Laurel tried to visualize the storm track.

She hadn't been referring to the hurricane. Instead, she got caught up in watching his lips form the words.

"Remember Jeanne a couple of years ago?"

She blinked. "Sorry, I've never been much of a hurricane watcher."

"As long as you're in hurricane alley, you might want to check in from time to time. That's why I took you a TV set."

"Okay, I'll watch. Now, can we talk about Lee Larkin?"

Frowning, he looked away. "I don't suppose you could forget you heard that."

"Certainly not. I intend to call up all my friends in the media and tell them I just shared—" she glanced down at her half-empty container "—whatever it was we shared. And if I can borrow a digital camera and a computer, I'll e-mail pictures. I'd like to get one of you chasing after BooBoo. Do you think you could oblige?"

"Your friends in the media," he repeated, turning it into a question.

"I thought you knew—I'm head of public relations for a big fund-raising outfit in New York." Okay, so they were smallish—as in three full-timers and a varying number of part-time employees.

"It just gets better and better, doesn't it?" He sighed, and for some reason, Laurel found herself pitying him.

She carefully folded her paper napkin and laid it across her tray. "Forget I said that, will you? You obviously don't need the publicity, and I wouldn't dream of abusing your privacy."

"No? You'd be surprised how many people lack your scruples," he said bitterly. Looking suddenly as exhausted as she felt, he stood and began gathering up the remains of their impromptu meal, tossing some in the trash and dumping the cutlery in the stainless steel sink. "More wine? We might as well finish it off."

She held out her glass. "Why not?" She couldn't get any loopier than she already was. "Cody, I'm not in the business of writing exposés. I never have been. But you might want to caution Becky."

"How? Tell her Daddy's keeping secrets? She'll want to know why, and it's a bit hard to explain to a child. One of the reasons I moved down here was to get away from all that. It blew the coverage of our divorce all out of proportion, making it hard to get a fair shake when it came to the custody hearings. I was made out to be this big party animal, complete with groupies and at least two mistresses."

"Two? *And* groupies? What are you, an overachiever?"

He chuckled, taking the gibe as she'd intended it. She knew him well enough by now to suspect that he was no party guy. He'd taken his time finishing two glasses of wine. She was pretty sure he didn't smoke, snort or pop pills. She'd seen at close range those magnificent arms of his; he wasn't into intravenous feedings.

As for his sex life…

*Forget it. Just forget about that, it's none of your business!*

*Ah, but don't you wish it were?*

## Chapter 16

They migrated to the large open living area, where Cody switched on another TV set. This one, too, was tuned to the weather channel. "Sit down, they're about to do the tropical update. You might as well stay for that."

As tired as she was, Laurel had a few more topics on her agenda, so she sank into one end of the sumptuous leather-covered love seat and even went so far as to close her eyes. With a little encouragement, she could fall asleep.

Although she could think of a place where she'd rather sleep…

"Wake up. Here, have some coffee and then I'll walk you home."

"Huh? Wha…?"

Laurel blinked and looked around. The TV screen was dark, the lights dimmed, but every single feature on the face in her dreams was as clear as day. "What time…? Sorry," she mumbled. "Told you I was tired."

"Actually, you didn't, but Caroline called, wanting to know if you can come in early tomorrow. She said you've taken on extra duties and she doesn't know how she's going to manage without you when you leave."

When she left. If she'd needed something to bring her back down to earth, that did the job. "She say how early?"

"About nine. Something about composing new copy for the next *Island Breeze* ad and doing something to the displays."

"Hmm. They were a mess after yesterday."

"And you didn't stay around to help because you'd promised to look after Becky, right?"

And look how *that* turned out, she thought guiltily as she glanced around for her shoes. Last time she'd seen them they had been on her feet. "I'd better go home and get some sleep. What'd you tell her?"

"That you'd be there as early as you could make it."

She managed a smile, although the veils of sleep were still clouding her mind, not to mention her judgment. He held out a hand and without thinking, she took it, which meant he was entirely too close when she came to her feet.

Neither of them moved away. "Mmm…thanks." She managed to sound halfway coherent. "My shoes?"

"Laurel." He leaned closer, so close she could see the gold splinters and the darker rims in his irises. "Kiss me good-night, and I'll walk you home. No hanky-panky, scout's honor."

His grin was too tempting to resist. Laurel didn't even try. He tasted like coffee, and she wanted some, but even more than that, she wanted him. This is crazy, she thought. I don't even know this man!

Only she did. In ways she'd never even thought of knowing Jerry. Ways that had nothing at all to do with shared business interests. Ways that had far more to do with kindness and integrity, with shared family problems, shared mutual friends—the kinds of things on which a woman might build a solid, lasting relationship.

But that wasn't what was sizzling through her body now, melting away her resistance like fog under a blazing sun. She had the strangest feeling that if they'd never actually met—if they'd only passed as strangers, their eyes meeting briefly before moving. on—she would have known him in some essential way that transcended all common sense.

*Listen to yourself! That is a lot of hooey and you know it!*

But hooey or not, with his arms holding her, his lips on hers while his aroused body moved against her, Laurel knew she was home at last.

With her arms around his neck, her fingers pushed through his hair, loving the texture, the warmth, loving…

His tongue teased, enticing her to play. His were the kind of kisses that must have led to the world's growing population. With one hand he cupped her breast, the touch of his thumb on her nipple leaving it throbbing for more attention. Her arms moved down his sides to hold him closer and she tugged at his shirt, mindless of what she was doing. If he had lowered her to the floor at that moment and undressed her, she wouldn't have uttered a single protest. If anything, she'd have helped him. And then she would have pulled his shirt over his head, unbuckled his belt and peeled off his khakis and whatever he wore underneath.

Briefs or boxers?

The mind boggled. She forgot to breathe.

It was Cody who ended the kiss by lifting his head. Looking slightly dazed, he huffed out a heavy sigh.

Puzzled, her knees about as supportive as boiled spa-

ghetti, Laurel blinked at him. "Cody? What's wrong?"
She knew for a fact that he hadn't suddenly lost interest; the hard evidence was pressing up against her belly.

His smile was grim, but at least he made the effort.
She caught her breath, bumped her head against his
chest and said, "Well, that's almost better than caffeine."
Her attempt at self-deprecating humor was a pathetic
failure.

"Hmm?" He sounded as if he'd choked on a
chicken bone.

"For waking up, I mean."

"Funny…it had just the opposite effect for me. All I
could think of was bed."

That was another thing she liked about him. That he
could tease her so gently at the same time he was reject-
ing her. She told herself that with issues yet to be settled between them, it was just as well. At least one of
them still possessed a functioning brain.

Trying for some semblance of dignity, she said, "Tell
Becky to wait for me tomorrow and we'll go out again,
and I promise not to take my eye off her." She felt
around on the floor for her mules. "That is, unless she's
grounded."

"You might need to postpone your explorations for a
few days," he said, his voice almost back to normal. "If
Helene maintains her present speed and course, I expect
we'll be seeing the first bands of rain by early afternoon."

"Wait a minute, you mean the hurricane? It's coming
here? I thought it was way out in the south Atlantic."

"That was yesterday." He opened a drawer and took
out a flashlight. "Sure, you don't want to sleep over? I
can't promise you any entertaining ghosts, but I can
offer a dry, comfortable bed."

She backed off, literally and figuratively. Although if he was offering to share his own bed, she was incredibly tempted. "Thanks, but I'm a restless sleeper. Poor Becky wouldn't get a wink of sleep."

"I do have a couple of guest rooms. One's even partially furnished."

She still didn't know if he'd been inviting her into his bed, or merely being a good host, but she wasn't about to take any chances. The survival instincts she had worked so hard to build had holes that rivaled the Grand Canyon. Although come to think of it, a few of those holes had shown up even before she'd left New York.

I do not have time for this, she told herself, mentally erecting a defensive wall around her emotions as he walked her back to her own dark, uninviting house. Besides, she was smarter than that. She didn't do sleepovers, not even when the guy was as tempting as chocolate-covered sin.

Especially not when he was a bestselling author. That would put her in the same category as all those screaming girls—the belly-button brigade, she called them— that flocked around the minor celebrities Jay-bass hired for their events.

"Watch those sandspurs," Cody warned. "I thought I'd dug 'em all out last year, but they came back in triplicate."

And quit being so damned *nice,* she was tempted to say. That just makes it worse!

Against a dark background of dense, scrubby maritime forest, the old house loomed pale and shadowy in the moonlight. Puzzled, she said, "I thought I'd left the porch light on." She tried to recall whether or not she'd left a light on inside. She must have cut them off without thinking, one more sign that she needed to get away from this place as quickly as possible. Too much salt air corroded the brain cells.

"Probably the socket," said Cody. He seemed to have recovered nicely from what had happened between them just a few minutes earlier.

"My thinking exactly." If he could be cool, she could damn well be cooler.

"Salt air's rough on metal."

Not only on metal, she thought wryly. "Can sockets be changed or do we need to buy a new fixture?"

"I'll ask Trav to check it out when he has time. He's better than I am where electrical things are concerned."

All this and modesty, too? She kept the thought to herself. Frustration brought out the petty side of her nature. Always had. When they reached the steps, she turned to face him. "Thank you so much for seeing me home." She smiled all the way back to her molars. "And thanks for going easy on Becky. I think she was more scared of what you were going to say than of being lost."

"Oh, she'll get the lecture, but it can wait until morning. Try the light switch."

She opened the door, reached inside and clicked the switch nearest the door. The porch light came on. "Hmm. It works. I guess I just forgot to turn it on before I left."

A mixture of yellow bug light and pale moonlight shone across the gray-painted porch floor. Cody stepped away and Laurel entered and turned to hook the screen behind him.

Suddenly she felt the small hairs on the back of her neck stand up. "Cody?" she whispered without turning around. "Wait a minute, don't leave yet."

One foot on the top step, he turned and sent her a

questioning look, his face oddly pale in the yellow light. She said, "Wait just a minute, will you?"

She switched on the overhead hall light and winced at its harsh glare. Cody came back to stand behind her as she stopped at the entrance to the living room. He didn't say a word, but she felt his presence behind her. "I don't know," she murmured. "Something just…feels odd."

"What?" he breathed against her ear, stirring tendrils of hair against her cheek. The heat of his body so close behind her seemed to wrap her in security, which was about as dumb as anything else she'd imagined lately.

She shook her head. "I know this sounds crazy, but…" The words trailed off and she reminded herself that hormonally speaking, she was still far too vulnerable. That kiss hadn't helped. She was probably just imagining whatever it was she was imagining. "Everything looks just the way it did when I left here earlier."

Scanning the room, she took inventory. Newspapers on the table, paperback book turned down on a chair arm from last night. The double-hung windows that she'd left open all day were still open. Same thing in the kitchen, plus the jar on the windowsill filled with wildflowers she'd collected yesterday was still there. Which meant that no one had knocked it over trying to climb through the window.

Feeling Cody beside her, steady as a rock, she edged closer until her shoulder bumped against his arm. The tension she felt emanating from his taut body was probably just a reflection of her own. "Look, call me crazy," she said quietly, "but somebody's been inside since I left."

The cup she'd used this morning was still in the sink, waiting until she had a day's worth of dishes to wash.

*Like you expected a burglar to wash your dirty dishes? Smart, Lawless. You're really on top of it, aren't you?*

"Everything's right where I left it, but…" She shook her head. "It just *feels* different. I can't explain it." This was so unlike her, she was almost embarrassed. The one thing she had never been was fanciful—anything but. She was a pragmatist of the first water.

But dammit, *something* was different. Something that didn't involve spooks or specters, or even a big, clumsy dog that could scatter a stack of books with one flap of his hairy tail.

Cody nodded. His eyes moved around the room, lingering here and there before moving on. Then his gaze returned to her face, his expression softening. "You want to wait here while I check out upstairs?"

She grabbed his arm. "Oh, no, you're not leaving me alone."

"Not in any haunted house, huh? Have you heard her lately?"

"My ghost? Not lately, and anyway, she's never any trouble. Not that I believe in ghosts," she added quickly as she followed him up the stairs. "It's only a bunch of old crows. I've seen them over across the creek, they sound just like—just like crows. I guess," she added lamely.

Cody grinned, but sobered quickly as he stepped off onto the second-floor landing. He still carried the flashlight, but once the house lights were on, he'd switched it off. It occurred to Laurel that it would serve as a handy weapon if they ran into trouble.

"Anything out of place?" he asked. They were standing in the door of the bathroom where only a short while ago she had given his daughter a bath and tended her minor injuries. It still smelled faintly of lavender body lotion and coconut shampoo.

Same old rust stains, same old limp shower curtain. Same jars, bottles and hairbrush arranged in perfect alignment. Nothing had been touched so far as she could tell. "This just doesn't make sense," she muttered as she followed him across the hall to her bedroom.

"How about in here?"

She edged past where he stood in the doorway. The shoes she'd worn to work were placed neatly side by side at the foot of the bed, right where she'd left them. Her purse was still on the dresser between the saucer that held her wristwatch and earrings and the...

Her purse... "Oh, no," she whispered. She had a single credit card that she hadn't dared to use in recent months, and about seventy dollars in cash, plus her driver's license, her social security card and her cell phone. Thinking of Ru's story of identity theft, she unzipped all four compartments and looked to see what, if anything, was left.

"It's all here," she said, puzzled. Her cash, and even her social security card, which she knew she shouldn't carry with her, but she did, anyway.

"One of the drawers is slightly crooked," Cody observed. He was standing in front of the dresser.

"It sticks, remember? It takes both hands to open or close it."

"Yeah, I remember."

But had she? Moving past him, she reached for the tarnished brass rings, trying to recall whether or not she'd been in too big a hurry earlier to close it properly. It took jiggling first one end and then the other, but she'd been in a hurry to change clothes and collect Becky from Travis and Ru.

She tugged the drawer open and stared down at the contents.

And caught her breath.

"What's wrong? Laurel, what is it?" Cody's hands closed on her shoulders as he looked from the open drawer to her face and back again.

"Someone's been messing with my things. I never leave them like this," she whispered tersely. She glanced up in time to see his puzzled look as he stared down at the array of neatly folded undergarments. Obviously, he saw nothing amiss, but she knew.

She *knew*. She always folded things in a certain way and layered them in the drawer in a certain order.

As embarrassing as it was to be discussing the arrangement of her intimate apparel with a man who had only to touch her—had only to look at her to trigger a major meltdown, she made a stab at explaining. "Look, I know how I left things, all right? And I know they're not that way now. See? These are all jumbled together." She indicated the back of the drawer where her nightgowns were kept. Those, too, she folded in a certain way, simply because she always had. A restless sleeper, she wore gowns instead of pajamas that twisted around her. Nylon instead of cotton for the same reason. Nor was she about to defend her choices.

To his credit, Cody refrained from making any sexist remarks. He didn't even mention the compulsive orderliness that Peg loved to tease her about. Instead, he picked up a small, lace-covered satin pouch. "What's this, a good luck potion?"

She snatched it from his fingers and buried it under

her nightgowns. "It's called a sachet." So she loved fragrances—that was hardly a crime.

They continued to stand shoulder to shoulder, staring down at her underwear drawer until he said, "You want to check the others?"

She didn't. She wanted to leave, to go back to his house where she'd felt safe and relaxed enough to fall asleep in a chair.

The dresser was a narrow three-drawer affair, the wood something called golden oak that had darkened with age. If she had to go through the other two drawers—and of course, she did—she'd rather do it with him standing by.

Her jeans, tees and camp shirts were folded neatly in the middle drawer, but the minute she opened it she knew that they, too, had been disturbed. Some people folded T-shirts in half, then in thirds. She held them by the shoulders, flipped the sides behind, then layered them into thirds. Same result, different method.

"Everything there?"

How could she make him understand when she didn't understand, herself? "It's all there as far as I can tell, but someone's been messing around. Cody, don't ask me how I know, I just do, that's all." Laurel the pragmatist, freaking out because her neatly folded garments were no longer stacked with military precision, each stack separated from the next. Call her obsessive, but it was just as easy to be orderly as it was to be disorderly. Easier in the long run, because she never lost things, the way Peg did.

"It had to have happened between the time I took Becky home and now," she murmured. "I'd have felt it if it had happened during the day, because I stopped off to change clothes after work."

"Felt it how?"

How could she explain something she didn't understand, herself? "I don't know," she snapped. "I'd have just felt it, all right? Maybe your ghost would have whispered in my ear!" Twisting around she stared up at his face. If he laughed, she might just hit him. "Is that what you wanted me to say? So you can tell me I need to vacate the premises because our rental agreement doesn't cover certified fruitcakes?"

He laid a hand on her shoulder, probably intended to keep her from flying apart. "Shh, slow down. We don't have a rental agreement, remember? Nothing official, anyway. Besides, my ghost is into telling jokes, not pawing through ladies' lingerie."

She let his hand remain on her left shoulder only because warmth was soothing. But damn, damn, *damn,* why did he have to be so *perfect?* Dan would have hooted with laughter, then told her to knock off the screw-top wine. Jerry would have…

Well, he would have held her, she was pretty sure of that. As if his arms alone could protect her from some creep who got his jollies from pawing through her underwear. But he wouldn't have understood, he just wouldn't.

"He d-didn't even take my money," she said brokenly. Not until his arms came around her did she realize she was crying. Embarrassed, she pulled away, wiped her eyes on her wrist and said, "The only time I ever cry is when I'm mad as hell and can't do anything about it."

"Like when you backed into my truck?"

Her sputter of laughter was unconvincing, but under the circumstances, it was the best she could do. His ex-wife must be crazy to have let this man get away. "Does Becky know how lucky she is to have you for a father?"

"You think there's something paternal about this?" Both eyebrows shot skyward. He was still holding her, but it was a different kind of holding than what had happened at his house. Laurel had never before realized that there were so many different kinds of holding, of touching.

"About what?" She pulled free of his arms so she could think and took a step back, coming up against the dresser. She crossed her arms over her chest.

He uncrossed them. "Easy, honey, take a deep breath."

She did. It didn't help. He moved in and she was trapped, just the way she wanted to be, she thought resignedly as his arms closed around her once more.

This was the *other* kind of touching.

She closed her eyes and felt the soft, moist brush of his mouth on hers. What began as a gentle salute quickly escalated into something else as his tongue began a tantalizing dance of exploration. There was something so familiar about the taste of him—about the feel of his hard, warm contours pressed against her body—and not just because it had happened before.

Once again it was Cody who drew back. His eyes were all dark rim and pupil, with little of the gold showing. He was breathing heavily. "Lousy timing," he said gruffly.

"Tell me about it," she muttered. The sensible part of her brain—that long-neglected portion of which she'd been so proud for so long—knew he was right. Her breast was still tingling from his touch, and between her legs she was hot and wet and swollen.

"Becky," she said with a sigh of resignation.

"Becky's fine. BooBoo sleeps on the foot of her bed. He'd bark his head off if she was in any danger."

Laurel raked her hair back with an unsteady hand. "So where was he today when she got lost?"

"Shut up inside the house. I couldn't ask Trav to take on the mutt, too. He went over and let him out a couple of times during the day while Ru kept an eye on Becky, but the mangy idiot still managed to wet down my favorite chair."

If she'd needed something to break the tension, that did it. Covering her mouth, she snickered, then she burst into a guffaw. "Becky told me—she said he—"

"That he's been taught not to do it on the floor." Reaching past her, Cody closed the middle drawer, opened the bottom one and looked to her for confirmation. "How's this one?"

Obviously he was as relieved as she was to be back on safe ground, safe being a relative term.

The gray cardigan that Peg had insisted she bring was folded neatly on top of two long-sleeved blouses and an old GA Tech sweatshirt of her father's she'd kept for sentimental reasons and brought along in case the weather turned cooler. She always folded the sleeves back, then folded the sweater in thirds, the way she did her T-shirts.

Now it was folded in halves.

Enough of this wilting lily act. She'd have to wash every single thing she owned before she could wear it again, but that was her hang-up, not his. "I guess who-ever pawed through my clothes didn't find anything worth stealing. Maybe the labels weren't good enough. Or maybe it's because I usually cut the darn things off because they scratch the back of my neck."

"Or maybe they were looking for something that could have been hidden under a stack of clothing."

Bristling with an excess of emotional energy, she demanded to know what. "The key to a lockbox? I don't have a lockbox. I don't even have a safety deposit box." Because she had to do something, she bent over and refolded her cardigan, then slammed the drawer shut. It went crooked. One end jammed until Cody eased her aside and did the job properly.

So much for her vaunted control. She'd always made it a policy never to lose her temper in public, never to act on impulse. The method that had kept her out of serious trouble all these years involved meticulous scheduling, conscientious planning and scrupulous adherence to all plans and schedules. All of which sounded dull as mud, especially once she'd started dealing with so many "creative" types.

But dammit, it was the only way she could function. Peg teased her, calling her trusty daybook a security blanket. Maybe it was, but until a few months ago it had kept her on schedule and out of trouble.

"You'd better get back to Becky," she said, wanting nothing so much as to tie him to her bed and keep him there for the foreseeable future. "If she wakes up and you're not there, she'll be worried."

How many times had that happened to her—that she would wake up after a bad dream and have no one to call. Her mother would be out at a lecture at a university. As for her father, he could be anywhere from the Far East to the Middle East to the North Sea. Anywhere oil companies might need an innovative and creative software specialist to exploit their natural resources.

"I don't like leaving you here."

"I've been here for two weeks and nothing's happened to me. Women have moods, hadn't you heard?" She beamed him a wide smile, hoping she sounded convincing. Ghosts and spooky feelings she could deal with. What she couldn't deal with was having some guy she hardly knew meddle with her emotions. She knew who she was. Knew who she was supposed to be in love with. All Cody did was confuse her, and she'd never dealt well with confusion.

And now on top of all that, some freak with an underwear fetish was messing around in her things. "Look, nothing was stolen, and now whoever broke in knows there's nothing here worth stealing, right?"

He waited a long time before saying, "Like I said before, I've got two guest rooms going to waste."

She shook her head. "Thanks, but I'll be just fine. I'll lock the doors and stack dishes on the windowsills in case anyone decides to come in that way."

"You won't sleep a wink."

"Not your problem," she said firmly.

"Maybe. Maybe not. But as long as I'm here…"

# Chapter 17

On his way to the front door, Cody turned back to the living room. Frowning, he picked up one of the sofa cushions and examined the corded seam.

Standing in the doorway, Laurel planted her hands on her hips. "Oh, for heaven's sake, you're worse than your daughter. What do you think I'm hiding, pirate treasure? The map to some previously undiscovered archaeological site?"

"Hey, I'm a writer, remember? This kind of stuff is grist to my mill."

He passed it off as a joke, but she was on to him now. She'd seen it with Becky, and even with the dog. He was one of those rare individuals—rare in her experience until recently, at least—who seemed determined to take care of those nearest him. And if he thought slitting her cushions would keep her any safer, he would do it. Even though they were his couch cushions, not hers.

Feeling like an impostor—she was his tenant, not his responsibility—she took the opening he'd offered. "I can see it now, the next Lee Larkin to hit the *New York Times* bestseller list: *Blackbeard's Haunted House,* or *The Treasure Beneath the Shell Mound.*"

"There's an idea," he mused, continuing to examine

each of the worn tapestry cushions until he was satisfied that none concealed anything more ominous than
dust, a few dog hairs and whatever else had accumulated
there over the ages. Evidently none of the previous res-
idents, including Cody, had cared enough to lift the
heavy old upright vacuum onto the sofa to suck up the
debris.

When he'd examined all three cushions as well as the
rest of the sofa, Laurel spoke up. "You really think
there's something hidden in there?"

"Probably not. Hard to meddle with a seam without
leaving some sign of tampering," he murmured absently.
"Not all creeps worry about leaving evidence, but anyone who takes pains to refold and replace everything in
a drawer could conceivably slit a cushion along the
seam and sew it back up again."

"Looking for what? Besides, I don't have a sewing
kit and I've never heard of one being included with burglar tools. I always hide my priceless diamond jewelry
in a cereal box, not my sofa cushions."

"Oh, yeah, no one would ever think of looking there,"
he said sarcastically. Thumbs hooked under his belt,
feet spread apart, he stared at the blank wall.

She waited, wavering between relief and impatience.
He might not have believed her at first, about someone
having been inside her house, but something had evidently changed his mind. Under the overhead light, his
features looked harsh and angular and even more attractive, if that was possible.

"How are you at making lists?" he asked abruptly.

"I have an advanced degree in list making."

"Excellent. What you need to do is to list every single item you brought with you, right down to the road

maps. Then check to make sure it's all still here. I doubt if anything's been stolen, but it's a good first step."

A first step. "Does that mean there's a second step?"

"We'll see, won't we?" His smile was tense, but genuine. His eyes still looked darker than usual, and this time Laurel didn't think it was passion.

She waited, wondering when she would wake up from this particular dream. Would it qualify as a nightmare, or one of those dreams she occasionally had when she went too long without sex?

Then he nodded, as if reaching some conclusion. "We'll need to search your car, too, to see if anything's missing there."

"Besides some paint on my fender, you mean?"

"Hey, don't get personal, I told you I'd deal with that."

The lighter note was certainly welcome. With all the crazy things that were going on in her life, she was having trouble sorting them out. "Right," she scoffed. "You didn't even wait for the police to come and make a report."

"Called 'em from home."

"I see. It's that old low-profile thing again, right? You didn't want to go on record, afraid someone would blow your cover."

He grinned and she wondered how anyone could consider laugh lines and crow's-feet unattractive. "You got me dead to rights. Now, how about collecting whatever you'll need overnight."

Despite the fact that she wouldn't be able to sleep a wink in the house where someone had meddled with her things, she was reluctant to expose herself to temptation. "Don't we need to report it to anyone?"

"Report what? That you got a spooky feeling because your Skivvies weren't organized properly and your sweater was folded wrong?" He shook his head. "Let's give it a little while to settle out. Maybe something else will occur to you."

"What about fingerprints? Seriously."

"Whose? Mine, yours? Trav's, or the couple who rented it before? Now, go get your gear and let's lock up. You can come back in the morning to get ready for work."

Hands on her hips, Laurel stepped back and said, "Whoa. What is this 'go get your gear' stuff? I can lock up and you can go home and be there for Becky if she wakes up in the night."

He gave her a look that suggested patience dangling by a thread. "If Becky wakes up, you'll hear her hollering all the way over here. In case you hadn't noticed, this is a pretty quiet neighborhood."

Laurel wasn't about to remind him about her occasionally raucous ghost, who was probably only a trick of the acoustics anyway. Of course it was. Or noisy birds. Or campers in the Park Service campground just a ridge and a creek away. "All the better. If I need you I can just yell out the window, okay?"

"Are you always this stubborn?"

"Always," she said sweetly, "especially when I know I'm right. I am not going home with you. I'm hardly helpless, you know."

Cody's tolerance had been stretched too far. First the hassle with his publicist, then the frustrating call to his editor regarding scheduling, followed by coming home to discover his daughter was missing.

And now this. He didn't swear. He didn't argue. He didn't even raise his voice, he only looked at her until she caught her lip between her teeth and turned away. Then he snatched her cell phone from the kitchen table,

programmed in his number and made sure the thing
was charged. "Lock up as soon as I leave. Use the ceiling fan tonight, not the air conditioner, it's too noisy."

"Oh, you noticed that?" Her smile was pure saccharine.

Ignoring the remark, he jammed a straight chair
under the knob of the back door and told her to do the
same with the front once he left. "These old paneled
doors wouldn't keep out a determined raccoon, but at
least you'll hear the ruckus in time to call me." He lev-
eled a stern look at her. "Promise me you'll call if you
hear so much as a mouse scratching in the attic."

"Mice? Oh, now I'm really terrified."

"I give up," he muttered, shoving open the screened
door. At the foot of the steps, he glanced back to see her
standing in the glare of the yellow bug light. Hands on
her hips, she looked small and vulnerable and sexy and
stubborn, and if that didn't exceed his quota of adjectives,
Cody told himself as he jogged across her yard toward
his, then he could probably come up with a few more.

Maddening woman. Becky had taken to her right
off, otherwise, he never would've gotten involved. But
the truth was, he owed her. Whatever reason his daughter had for not speaking directly to him, she was over
it. And the reason was Laurel. Had to be. Unless Ru or
Trav had taken up family counseling. With all they had
going on, what with Matt skipping out and Ru trying to
keep from losing the baby, he seriously doubted they'd
bother. Laurel had evidently managed to reassure her.
But reassure her of what?

Sooner or later he needed to find out what had been
going on under all that blond, ponytailed hair, but at the
moment he had another priority. Several, in fact, starting with whoever was messing around his rental. He'd

seen no evidence of intruders, but something had definitely spooked Laurel, and she didn't strike him as a woman who freaked over nothing.

In all the excitement over Becky going missing, she might have forgotten how she'd folded her things, but…

Nah, that didn't make sense. Just because he lived out of the dryer, that didn't mean other people did. Breaking into an old house like that, even with both doors locked, was kid's play. If someone had been inside, it hadn't been vandalism. Whoever it was had been searching for something specific.

Quietly, he let himself inside his own front door, then stood a moment and listened to the house, hearing only the quiet hum of the refrigerator compressor. It was a good place. Good vibes, as his latter-day hippie friends would say. He'd done part of the interior work himself, learning as he went along. So what if not all the window trim was perfectly mitered? He'd wood-filled the discrepancies. As for the door frame that was a quarter-inch off square, he'd planed the door to fit. He'd probably have been better off doing the rough carpentry, but that crew was too fast, too good. Anxious to move in, he hadn't wanted to slow them up.

Hearing no sounds from Becky's room, he quietly climbed the stairs and opened her door. She'd stopped demanding a night-light since Laurel had told her that the lighthouse kept watch over her. Now she fell asleep counting the seconds between the sweeps.

BooBoo lifted his head from the foot of the bed. Becky slept on her stomach, one fist jammed against her chin. Quietly, he pulled the door to, leaving it unlatched in case the dog needed to go out, or Becky woke in the night and called out for him.

On the way to his office, his thoughts returned to Laurel. In spite of a few indications to the contrary, she struck him as essentially levelheaded. She'd been genuinely spooked, but if she had any clue as to what was going on over there, she wasn't ready to talk about it.

It just so happened that he had a few resources, starting with the name of the company where she'd worked until a few months ago. Just so happened, too, that he had damned few scruples when it came to protecting someone he…cared about.

Yeah, he could admit that much at least.

At least he hadn't kissed her again. A smart man didn't start something he didn't intend to finish.

Instead of starting with J. Blessing Associates, he decided to check out the tract of land the four heirs were involved in, in case there were any other claimants. Not that he knew firsthand, having never inherited anything worth more than a buck-fifty, but he'd done enough research to know the damage that property disputes could cause.

It took only a few minutes to check with the tax office. From there he went through land transactions back a few years. It made for tedious reading, but he stuck it out, using shortcuts wherever possible.

One thing quickly became apparent; there were a hell of a lot of Lawlesses in the area. Google the name and it went on forever. Not that many here on the island, but he found several in Terrell County, one in Currituck County and another three in Hyde County, on Ocracoke Island, to be exact. He wondered if Laurel realized that she was surrounded by kinfolk. Something she'd mentioned earlier led him to believe she didn't have any immediate family, just

Trav and a couple more cousins. At least those were the only ones involved in the land deal that had brought her here.

He started a search for J. Blessing Associates. There were half a dozen outfits by that name, or close variations thereof. He narrowed it down to fund-raisers. Then, flexing his shoulders, he removed his computer glasses, polished them on his shirttail and slid them on again.

Some forty-five minutes later he shut off his computer, switched off the desk light and swiveled his chair around toward the wide window that overlooked the old house. With two houses to secure, tomorrow was going to be a busy day unless Helene took a drastic turn away from the coast. From the looks of her latest position, he had a feeling it wasn't going to happen. If he turned in now, he might be able to log a few hours of sleep.

Or not, he thought resignedly, with one last glance at the shadowy old house across the way.

"I looked everywhere. It's not here! Dammit, Jerry, I told you not to let it out of your hands!"

"Calm down. You must've missed it. I put it where it'll be safe and if I know Laurel, she'll guard it with her life."

Kirk shifted the cell phone to his other ear while he fumbled to shake a cigarette out of the pack. "Yeah? Then why wasn't it there? I even felt for loose boards—the place is a real junker, ready to fall down in the next hard wind."

"How the hell do I know? Maybe she didn't take it with her after all. Maybe you just missed it when you did her apartment. Maybe it's in a locker somewhere. Did you look for a key?"

"If she had a friggin' key, she musta had it on her. I

looked in every damned place you could hide a paper clip, and I'm telling you, it's not there!"

After several moments of silence, Jerry Blessing said, "Just find the damned thing, or else start looking for another job."

"Another *job!* What, are you crazy? You can trust her if you want to, but I'm not waiting any longer for my share. If I have to play rough, I can do it."

"Dammit, Candless, don't do anything stupid! We've waited this long, we can wait a couple more days. I've already told her we're ready to start up again. Trust me, she'll be here, and the minute she shows up, I'll ask for—"

"Yeah, well, ask all you want to, but I'm telling you, if you screw up and get caught, I've never heard of this Bank of Curaçao. My name's not on any papers, remember? Just those damned numbers. Why couldn't you memorize them?"

"Oh, sure, just like in the movies." Sarcasm dripped from the words. "I'm supposed to memorize a whole string of numbers and swallow the frigging evidence, is that it? And what about the ATM card, am I supposed to swallow that, too?"

"How do you know we can even trust these bank people? There's been a storm down in some of those islands in case you haven't heard. What if the bank got washed away? What then, smart-ass?"

"It doesn't *matter* if the damned bank gets washed away, everything's done electronically these days! Even if the bank gets trashed, our account's still good."

"Yeah, as long as we have what it takes to get our money out. Okay, I'll give it one more shot tomorrow as soon as she leaves for work, but they say that storm is headed this way now, and I'm telling you, I'm not hanging around for any damned hurricane. And Jerry? Remind me next time I go into a business deal to pick a guy with a friggin' brain in his head. There's not even a Starbucks in this crappy-ass place!"

Laurel lay awake, unable to sleep for thinking that someone had been inside her house. Looking for what? For her?

"Please, dear God," she whispered prayerfully. "Violence makes me sick in my stomach."

The first thing she intended to do once she got back to New York was to schedule a course in self-defense. Nothing to do with guns, though. She would never be able to shoot someone, not even to save herself.

Unless he was threatening someone she loved. Her thoughts immediately flew to Becky Morningstar.

Closing her eyes, she tried counting down from one hundred. She gave up at number fifty-six, her shoulders so tense that her head was barely touching the pillow. Sleep was out of the question. She might as well put her wakefulness to good use. Think, Laurel, think! First your apartment gets ransacked, and now this.

Whatever *this* was.

Who could have broken into her house, entered her bedroom and searched through her drawers? What were they looking for? She had nothing of any real value. Besides, they hadn't even taken her money.

Remembering Ru's story of having her identity stolen, she felt almost sick with relief that her documents were intact, even her credit card. Not that she intended to use the thing until she was certain she'd be able to pay it off, but having it in her billfold had made her feel more secure.

It would take more than a credit card to make her feel secure after this. To think some creep had actually stood right here in her bedroom, touching her things with his bare hands, breathing the air she was breathing right now. She had changed the sheets on her bed, but it didn't help.

"Oh, hell," she muttered. Flinging back the light covers, she sat up just as the lighthouse beam swept past. Through the woods she could see a light in the windows on the second floor of Cody's house. The light went off even as she watched.

What if she were to…?

To what? Jump out of the frying pan, into the fire?

Okay, what if? she asked herself, trying to be objective. Would that be any worse than lying awake in this house knowing something malevolent was out there?

Without giving herself time to change her mind, she quickly tossed a few things into a tote bag. She slipped off her gown, stepped into a pair of jeans and after only the briefest hesitation, shrugged into her old gray cardigan. It was far too heavy for the airless heat, but it represented comfort and security. Crazy or not, she buttoned it up around her neck.

A few minutes later she was standing on Cody's lower deck, wondering whether to ring the doorbell or turn tail and run when the door opened.

"Took you long enough," Cody said quietly.

"How did you know?"

"Common sense. You're not particularly sensible, but you're not stupid. Want something to eat?"

She shook her head, wondering whether to be flattered or insulted.

"Then come watch me eat a smoked turkey sandwich. You can tell me all about what it's like to be in retail and I can tell you how much I appreciate what you've done for Becky."

"You mean letting her get lost today?" She followed him through the open rooms to the marble, steel and wood-paneled kitchen. A glance at the clock on the microwave revealed that it was just past midnight. There was still time to back out without compounding her mistake, even knowing that it was already too late.

"She's a kid, Laurie," Cody said as he took out a covered plate and several jars and set them on the table. "Kids follow their imaginations. I'm starting to discover that Becky's is more adventurous than I'd suspected."

"Inherited from her fiction-writing father?" Suddenly feeling self-conscious, she slid into one of the teak-and-black leather chairs and watched while he spread four slices of bread. "What did she inherit from her mother?"

"With any luck, those genes won't kick in for another few years. Mayo, mustard or both?"

"Both," she replied, since he'd already done the spreading. "Why not?"

"Why? Because the marathon-shopping gene doesn't usually show up until the early to midteens." His easy grin said he was joking. The readiness of the answer said he wasn't. At least, not entirely.

He set out two plates, opened the package of sandwich meat, picked up an onion and held it up for her approval.

She shook her head and he put it back in the plastic bag. Rather regretfully, she suspected.

As he handed her one of the cheese-and-smoked-turkey sandwiches, he said genially, "Now that I've bribed you, how about telling me what's going on in your life that would attract an amateur burglar."

"You're blaming *me?*" She lowered her sandwich. He

bit into his. "Now it's *my* fault that someone broke into my house?"

He shrugged, as if making up his mind whether or not to answer.

But Laurel had learned a few things over the course of being interrogated by professionals. She picked up her sandwich again and studied it critically, fingering it until the crusts were properly aligned. "Incidentally, what makes you think it was an amateur?"

"Answer to your first question," he said calmly, "you left several windows open, including one in the pantry that's easily accessible from the back stoop. There were fresh scratches on the frame. Second question," he continued calmly, "a pro would've known there was a chance something might give him away, so he'd make it look like a common burglary. The place wasn't trashed. Your wallet wasn't lifted. Conclusion, someone was searching for something. Whether or not they found it, that's another question. What do you have that might be of interest to someone else? Or might threaten them?"

Puzzled, Laurel tried to think of anything she owned that was worth the risk of breaking and entering.

"I hardly wear any jewelry," she said slowly. "These earrings that I wear all the time." She fingered a small, delicately patterned hoop. "But they're vermeil, not real gold. My watch came from the drugstore, and my clothes aren't particularly expensive. Nothing worth stealing, at least."

"Go back to the break-in at your New York apartment," he prompted, his eyes watchful under sleepy-looking lids.

She laid her sandwich aside. "I wasn't there when it happened, I told you that. Didn't I tell you that?" Without waiting for a reply, she went on. "See, a few months before that, there was this…this problem at the place where I work." Had she told him about that, or not? At this point, she couldn't remember what she'd told whom. Whatever had happened to her neat, orderly, a-place-for-everything-and-everything-in-its-place brain? "Anyway, by that time I was pretty distracted, looking for work, but not even the temp services needed me. I know, I know—I'm whining. But by the time the break-in occurred, I'd already left to come down here." She forked a dill pickle slice from the jar and nibbled on it. "At least now I'll have another entry on my résumé in case Jay-bass is still shut down when I get back."

"Tell me about that," he said.

"About Carolina's Craft Gallery?"

"About where you worked before and what happened to it—why you ended up coming down here. Step by step."

Laurel thought she might have told him before. She'd given an edited version of what had happened to Harrison and Cleo, Travis and Ru.

"Go on. I'm listening." He nodded, encouraging her to spill it.

And for reasons she would probably never understand, she did just that. Without mentioning Jerry's striking good looks or his obviously privileged background, she described his brilliant business mind and his generosity, both corporate and personal. He had never once bragged about his family, another mark in his favor, but she'd picked up on a few clues. Such as the way he never referred to the valuable antiques he owned as being antiques, but as the little rug from Grandmother Whaley's morning room or Granddad So-and-so's humidor stand.

And of all the impressive paintings he owned, the only one he'd prized enough to protect was a mediocre watercolor that his mother had painted when she was a student at Hollins.

She went on to describe his generosity and the company he'd formed to raise funds for the newer charities that were too small to hire larger fund-raising groups. Briefly, she mentioned the other partner, Kirk Candless. "Actually, I don't know him all that well," she admitted, leaving out the fact that she didn't like what she did know about Jerry's partner and talent scout. "Kirk spends most of his time traveling, trying to coerce celebrities to headline our fund-raisers. We can't afford to pay them—well, we pay all expenses, of course—but publicitywise they benefit by being associated with a good cause. That's where I come in, making sure we get enough publicity without having to spend an arm and a leg on it. What's good for our cause is usually good for their careers."

"Tell me about a few of your causes." Rising, Cody got out a pan, half filled it with milk, and set it on a burner while Laurel tried to think of a way to describe the good works done by J. Blessing Associates.

"To make a long story short, it might be anything from women with small children who need help with day care so that they can find a job, to hurricane relief— we've done a lot of that lately—to reading programs for adult immigrants."

"I thought the government had all that pretty well covered."

She shook her head. "Not enough. Not nearly enough. Anyway, different groups with needs that aren't being covered hire us to help them by raising funds."

"They hire you?"

Trying not to sound defensive, she described the overhead involved in even the smallest operation. "It all has to be covered before the profits can be handed over. I'm good at getting the biggest bang for the buck when it comes to publicity, but the guest celebrities expect to be coddled. And then there's our everyday expenses— the rent and utilities, plus the cost of hiring a hall and catering the affairs."

"And on top of all that, you clear enough to make it worthwhile?"

Laurel took another bite of her sandwich and Cody dumped sugar into the milk and stirred in dry cocoa. "Actually, I don't know all that much about Jay-bass's finances," she said after a few moments passed. "That's why I only had to give a statement and then go in for questioning a couple of times."

Moving with deliberate care, Cody switched off the burner and poured cocoa into two mugs. He handed one to Laurel and sat down across the table. The clock on the range said 12:34 a.m. From somewhere outside came the monotonous call of a chuck-will's-widow, the eastern version of a whip-poor-will.

"Back up a minute," he said quietly. His voice alone, that deep, smooth baritone, leached the tension from her shoulders. She hadn't even realized it was there. "You had to go in for questioning? You had to give a statement? What the hell were you being questioned about?"

"Oh, well…actually, nobody ever said what it was we were accused of. Jerry said it was all part of this Homeland Security thing—that they were suspicious of all the fund-raising groups."

"*They* being our newly consolidated intelligence

folks, right? So were you sending funds to terrorists? Maybe chipping in to buy a few WMDs?"

"Oh, for Pete's sake, if you're going to try to weave one of your goofy plots around everything I say, I'm going home!" She was half out of her chair when he reached over and caught her arm.

"Sorry. I tend to act inappropriately when my feelings are hurt. My plots may occasionally be improbable, but they're almost never goofy."

She settled back in her chair and shrugged. "I shouldn't have said that." Besides, she didn't want to go back home. Home to her temporary haunted house, where someone had broken in and pawed through her clothes, looking for God knows what. "The thing is," she said finally, "I still can't make a connection between my underwear and whatever Jay-bass was accused of. Back at the apartment, Peg said every one of Dan's CDs was taken from the case and tossed on the floor. What on earth is going *on?*"

"That's what I intend to find out," Cody said calmly.

Ignoring his mission statement, Laurel said, "I mean, if I had money, if I could afford to stay someplace else, would I be living in a dump with no central air?"

"Careful, that's twice you've trampled on my tender feelings."

"Oh, pooh."

His eyes twinkled, more gold now than obsidian. She took a deep breath, increasingly aware of a comfort level that was entirely too seductive. If she could just crawl into his bed and curl up in his arms, she'd be out like a light for the next eight hours.

Or not…

Cody interrupted her developing fantasy. "What

about the key to a deposit box? Something that doesn't take up much space? Or maybe to a storage unit in case we're talking about big sums in small bills?"

Well, that certainly brought her down to earth with a solid thud. "I thought I explained that once expenses are taken out, the rest of the take goes immediately to whatever group we're working for. And anyway, I don't have anything to do with the financial end of the business, that's Jerry's department. I wouldn't know a balance sheet from a racing form."

She frowned as something nudged at her brain. A brain that was no longer functioning at peak efficiency thanks to a lack of sleep and an overdose of stress.

"What?" he prompted softly after several moments passed in silence.

"I'm…not…sure," she murmured. "I kept a clipping file on all our events so I could send copies to the agents of whatever celebrity had appeared. Those were confiscated along with everything else in the office, but I remember a few of the write-ups mentioned the sum we took in."

"And?" he prompted again.

She shook her head as if to clear it. "And I seem to remember being surprised a few times at how low the figure was. I mean, math's not my strong suit, but still…"

"You never asked anyone about the discrepancy?"

Slowly, she shook her head. "I'm not really sure there was a discrepancy, but looking back…"

Still frowning, she tried to recall a few times when she might have questioned the difference between the amount spent and the amount handed over to a particular charity. She stared down at the skin forming over her cocoa mug until Cody gently removed the half-empty mug from her hands.

Yawning, she shook her head. By the time he had put away the remains of their midnight feast, she was practically asleep.

"Come on, before I have to carry you up those stairs." His gruff tenderness was almost too much. She'd always been good at important things such as making and sticking to a plan. Only when it came to being coddled did she fall apart, probably because she'd never had a chance to get used to the luxury.

# Chapter 18

"Am I spending the night here?" Laurel knew it was a stupid question before it even left her lips. She had arrived uninvited on his doorstep, bags in hand. "I don't have to, you know. I just couldn't sleep. I thought you might be still up, and…"

Cody scooped up the canvas tote into which she'd tossed a pair of jeans but no blouse; a toothbrush, but no toothpaste—and the book she'd been reading ever since she'd left New York and had yet to finish.

Talk about being in control of her mind.

He led her up the stairs, down a wide hallway, and opened the door on what was obviously a guest room. And she wasn't disappointed, really she wasn't. He said, "Bathroom's though there, Becky's next door, I'll be down the hall if you need anything."

Even in the dimly lit hallway, she knew she wasn't imagining the feverish gleam in his eyes. "Thanks. Remind me to check the cut on Becky's heel in the morning." If he could ignore the electricity that had been sizzling between them with increasing voltage for days, then so could she.

"I looked before she went to bed. No sign of infection. Now, do you have everything you need?"

"Every single little thing," she said brightly. What she really needed was off-limits. About a thousand miles off-limits. "G'night. Oh, and thanks." She stepped into the room, expecting him to close the door and walk away.

"Aren't you gonna give me some sugar?"

Three steps from the door, she halted, turned and stared at him. "Sugar?" She couldn't have heard him correctly.

Cody caught her face between his hands. He was smiling, his sleepy-looking eyes half-closed, but gleaming as if they were lit from within. "'S what I used to say to Becky before she got too grown up." And before she could offer a whimper of protest, his lips came down on hers.

Spontaneous combustion, that's the only way to describe it, she thought dimly. Hot, wet and incredibly sweet. His hands raked up and down her back, then dropped to her hips, pressing her tightly against him. She groaned and twisted in a frustrated effort to get closer.

The bristles on his jaw sent shivers of excitement down her spine, not to mention a rash on her throat that would probably show up tomorrow. His hair felt thick and warm and alive, and when she ran her hands down his back, sliding her fingertips under his belt, he shuddered. Cupping her bottom, he moved her against his erection.

"Now go to bed," he rasped, holding her away. "Or else."

"Or else?" she managed to croak.

"Or else neither one of us is going to get any sleep tonight. We've both got to go to work in a few hours. I've got to look after a kid and a dog while I start hauling out storm shutters."

Well. That was as good as a cold shower, anytime. Thank goodness one of them had a grain of common sense. At least there were no ghosts here, Laurel thought sleepily a few minutes later as she wrapped her arm around a fat down pillow. It was her last conscious thought before a soft snore issued from her throat.

"Lawsy, talk about timing," Caroline exclaimed when Laurel came through the back door at a quarter of ten the next morning. "We get a record holiday crowd and what do they do? They call for a damned evacuation. Ocracoke's going today. I doubt if many of them will stop to shop on the way north. We're next, but by that time, with everything else already evacuated, there probably won't be a vacancy this side of Raleigh."

"You mean we all have to leave? To go where?" If she had to leave the island, she might as well keep on going, Laurel thought. And she wasn't ready.

"Oh, not me. Most of the full-timers stay, especially those on high ground, but they want all the tourists off the island. The power'll probably go off, and with everything closed up tight and emergency services stretched thin, the last thing we need is a bunch of tourists complaining that all the stores are closed and they're out of beer. They might think a hurricane sounds exciting, but believe me, it's hard work, before, during and after."

Laurel listened, her mind racing madly off in ten different directions at once. "Should I go? Should I stay and help out?"

"That's up to you, hon."

By noon Laurel was still undecided. Barely a handful of shoppers had showed up. "I'm so mad," one woman had exclaimed. "I've got two days left on my rental. It's hardly enough to come back for if we have to go as far inland as we did during Isabel. I need a consolation prize, maybe that wire-wrapped opal pendant— oh, and the earrings, too."

Another woman turned out to be a local—a native, judging from her accent. Laurel was quietly pleased at how quickly she had come to recognize the brogue that, according to Travis, had its roots in sixteenth-century England.

Caroline greeted the woman as Miss Maggie. "You going to Elizabeth City to stay with your daughter for the duration?" she asked.

"I reckon not. I've been here for every storm for the past sixty-nine years. Besides, I couldn't move Mama."

"How's she doing?"

"Good days and bad. She's not hurting, she's just slipping away a little more all the time. Let me have one o' those glass things to hang in her bedroom window, she notices things like that. I put a bird feeder outside, and it stays full all day. She likes watching all the activity."

Laurel quickly took out several of the beveled glass sun-catchers. They were costly, but then, they were hand cut, each one slightly different. "It's the bevels that give them that iridescent sparkle," she explained while Caroline went into the stockroom to get a box.

"Laurel, is it?" the older woman asked after peering at her name tag. "I'm Maggie Burrus." The woman extended a weathered, but neatly manicured hand.

Laurel accepted the gesture, responding to the other woman's open friendliness. With her cropped white hair and snapping black eyes, she seemed poised and even attractive despite a wealth of wrinkles and a large, crooked nose.

Maggie tilted her head to one side. "You know, you've got the look of some folks around here."

Not even trying to hide her pleasure, Laurel beamed. "My father was a Lawless." Her name tag read simply Laurel. "I understand that's an old family name around here."

"Oh my, yes—one of the oldest. Used to be all up and down the Banks, from Ocracoke to Chic'macomico. Some went over to the mainland when the Union Forces invaded and took over the island. Others stayed put and rode it out." Leaning against a square wooden column in the middle of the showroom, she warmed to the topic. "Travis Holiday, he's one. His mother and mine went to school together here on the island. I think they were third or fourth cousins. You know how it is— once you pass first or second, you sort of lose track."

Laurel nodded as if she knew exactly what the older woman meant, but the truth was, she'd never even thought about extended family until she came South.

"You're staying in that old house of Trav's, aren't you? The one he sold to that writer fellow?"

As there were no other customers at the moment, Laurel felt free to learn as much as possible from this unexpected resource. She mentioned Harrison, whom the older woman had never met, and the cousin who lived in Vienna, Virginia, whom she had.

"That's the one that bought that cottage with the green roof down near Hatteras." And with a teasing smile, the older woman said, "I guess you've met the ghost, too, by now."

"Tell me the truth—it's just a trick of the acoustics,

right?" Laurel leaned her elbows on the high counter. "Birds, or even sounds from people in the campground? As quiet as it is here—well, compared to where I live, at least—sound travels. I hear the ocean all the time, and it's got to be half a mile away."

"Oh, honey, don't go and take away Miss Achsah's fun. The way I heard it, she deserves the last laugh if any woman ever did. She's buried right there behind where you're staying, over on the other side of the creek. Didn't Travis tell you?"

Laurel shook her head. She'd have been just as happy not knowing that. Of course she knew there was a grave-yard nearby, but knowing something about one of the people buried there was another matter. "I did notice the tombstones," she admitted, "but I haven't gone any closer, it's so grown up around there. And there's the creek…."

"Peter's Creek, it used to be called. Used to be the place where Trent—that's the real name for Frisco—where Trent ended and Buxton began. A few years ago, back in the fifties, I believe, they started putting up road signs, but before that, the post office had renamed half the villages."

A few years ago in the *fifties?* Laurel hadn't even been born then.

"Everybody knew who lived where, either on one of the back roads or the main road or the soundside, or on one of the ridges. Down in Hatteras, where I grew up, it was Up the Road and Down the Road. Then there were the back roads, but everybody knew which one you were talking about."

Laurel could file these legends away with the story of Blackbeard meeting his gory end just a few miles away. Someday she might even share them with her children.

Maggie was wearing white slacks, a gauzy orange tunic and orthopedic shoes. Gazing past a display of art glass and a funky metal sculpture, she frowned as if gathering her thoughts. "You say you thought about looking over those old graves?"

Laurel hadn't seriously considered it, but she only nodded.

"I doubt if you could read many of the markers now anyhow. Marble's soft. The lettering wears away after a while."

"You say the woman's name was…?"

"Achsah. It comes from the Bible, though I couldn't tell you where. Anyway, the way I always heard it told, Miss Achsah married herself three husbands, the first one when she was barely a woman grown. He was a Lawless, so I reckon that's where your folks come in. The next fellow she married after the first one died, they say he drowned when he was out tending his net and a storm blew up. They hadn't been married more than a year when it happened. Achsah was still a young woman, though, and life was hard on widows back in those days, especially widows with young'uns. So she found herself an old widower."

Laurel slipped her foot from her mule and pressed it against the cool wooden floor as she waited for the punch line. There had to be one. Whether or not it bore any resemblance to the truth was debatable. She would never really know, and what difference did it make, anyway?

"Well, the way they tell it, the old coot was a drunkard and real quick to take offense. They told it on him that he beat her for the least little thing. They said she used to wear her sunbonnet pulled down so you couldn't even see her face."

"And she lived in my house? That is, the one I'm staying in now?"

"Not when she died." Maggie shook her head, causing her chandelier earrings to brush against her tanned, wrinkled neck. "She was living up near the Cape on the back road then."

The door opened and three women came in. Laurel slipped her feet back in her shoes and glanced over to see if Caroline was on the floor. Miss Maggie said, "Let me buy that glass piece, and I'll leave you to your work. I talk too much. Reckon it's on account of I don't get out much now that Mama's bedridden."

Laurel quickly handled the sale while Caroline showed the three customers a tray of Michelle Alexander watches. As she handed the package across the counter, Laurel said, "But the laughter—is that supposed to be this Miss—what did you call her? Alice?"

"Achsah. There's been at least one Achsah in every generation around here as far back as I can remember. As for the laughter, they say when she died she was still married to that mean old sot who used to beat her, but when his folks went to bury her in their family graveyard, her first husband's folks—the Lawlesses—they stole the coffin and buried her back there in the woods. That was all Lawless land back then. Now it's mostly been split up and sold off, what with the highway running right through it and the Park Service taking such a big chunk over on the oceanside. Not the old graveyards, though."

Nor the old legends, Laurel thought as she watched the woman drive off in a late-model sedan. Whether or not there was any truth to the stories was another matter.

A laughing ghost?

It could have been worse, she mused as she hung another sun-catcher in the window. She was going to miss this place—these people—when she had to leave.

It was ten past six when Laurel got home to find Becky and BooBoo waiting on her front steps. From the looks of his coat, someone had evidently run out of patience and groomed the dog with a pair of garden shears.

Becky came out to meet her, her sandy legs marked by an assortment of bruises, scrapes and scratches. "Mama's coming back early. Daddy said that's all he needs, but I don't think it is, 'cause he cussed real bad. I was playing with my Platypus game, and I wasn't s'posed to hear him, but I know lots of bad words. Want to hear some?"

As tired as she was, Laurel had to laugh. "No thanks, honey. If you and BooBoo want to wait on the porch, I'll change clothes and we can go exploring for a little while."

"Did you know we're going to have a hurricane?"

"I heard about it, yes." Laurel started unbuttoning her jumper before she got to the front door.

"Do you know alligators eat dogs?"

"Uh…that I didn't know, but I guess even alligators have to eat. I'm pretty sure BooBoo's too big, though, in case you were worried." She opened the front door to go inside. When Becky and the dog followed her in, she didn't bother to tell them to wait outside. What difference did a little more sand make? The stuff seemed to ooze from the cracks in the floor.

"Scatter some pretzels in the kitchen if you want to," she said as she headed upstairs. The dog adored the salty treat and would happily hunt them until he'd found every one. At least it kept him from bounding up the stairs and pouncing on her bed. He had done that once before she'd learned to shut the door behind her whenever he was in the house.

When they emerged some ten minutes later there was a stack of plywood on the front porch. "Storm shutters," Cody announced as he came around the corner of the house. "Have you stocked up on essentials yet? I assume you're staying."

"Essentials," she repeated blankly. Chocolate, tampons, moisturizer and lip balm?

Becky chimed in. "Batteries, milk, water and—what else, Daddy? Oh, yes, peanut butter and toilet paper."

Cody chuckled as he hitched himself up to sit on the porch, giving her a clear view of his broad shoulders and his thick, sun-streaked hair. This was the man who had kissed her to within an inch of consciousness last night?

"Plus or minus a few other items," he said in that rusty voice that never failed to register on her internal radar. "When I bring over a ladder to put up your shutters I'll take care of the buckets in the attic. Might as well start out with empty ones." The attic was reachable only through a trapdoor in the upstairs hall ceiling. "Trouble is, if we get the northeast side, they'll overflow and leak through unless they're emptied every few hours."

The northeast side of what? Thoroughly befuddled, Laurel plopped down in a porch swing. "You want to back up and start all over again?"

"You haven't been keeping up with the reports?"

"I've been working. I do know there's a hurricane on the way. Caroline was complaining today about the evacuation notice."

"I hope that's all she has to complain about when it's over. It's only a cat-one, but that can change overnight. Sure you don't want to evacuate? There's still plenty of time. Leave now and you might even find a vacancy, maybe around Richmond. In that case, you'll probably want to keep on going." Without being too obvious about it, he was watching her closely.

Becky looked from one to the other, as if she were at a tennis match. The expression on her face defied interpretation until she turned and shouted, "BooBoo, get out of that flower bed!" Turning back to where Laurel stood, she shook her head. "I told him and told him not to do that, but he loves to dig in the sand."

Laurel sighed. "Let him dig, the storm will probably ruin our landscaping efforts anyway. Maybe he'll find a few potsherds or a gold coin."

Becky's eyes widened. Cody said quietly, "Not now, honey. Maybe later, all right?"

Lifting her narrow shoulders in a heartfelt sigh, the child turned to Laurel. "Daddy says sometimes storms uncover shipwrecks, so—"

"Miss Laurie has shopping to do, that is, if she's staying."

"You are, aren't you, Laurie? I can go with you and help you get stuff."

"Or you can stay here and help me," Cody suggested.

"Laurie needs me to show her what to buy. We can even get takeout for supper, Laurie, 'cause Daddy'll be real busy, and then right after the storm we can go out and find some more Indian stuff." Her face fell. "Do you think Mama will let me take my sharps home with me?"

Her shards, Laurel interpreted. "If you leave them

here, I'll bet your father will build you a case to keep them in."

"Thanks," Cody said with a wry grin. "My carpentry skills aren't exactly legendary. If you plan to stay, you'd better get on with your shopping, otherwise all you'll find are a lot of empty shelves."

There was nothing like an emergency to take her mind off her aching feet. Plus a few other problems, Laurel thought later. They were on their way to Avon to shop. While she was there she intended to check by the frame shop. Ready or not, she wasn't about to leave Jerry's watercolor in any hands but her own during a damaging storm.

Her mind on a dozen things at once, Laurel headed north on highway 12. She couldn't help but compare Cody, calm and good-natured in the face of imminent danger, to Jerry, whom she had last seen pale, sweating and agitated. Of course, Jerry had had only a few minutes' notice before the enemy stormed his gates.

By the time they'd left on their shopping trip, her bossy, irritating, grumpy, sexy, tenderhearted bestselling author-landlord had been climbing a ladder, carrying a big sheet of plywood to cover her bedroom window. Maybe she should have stayed behind. She could at least have handed him up the storm blinds.

Creeping along behind a row of traffic, she wondered idly what ghosts did during a bad storm. Move inside? Vaporize? Go back to wherever they came from? Did the tide ever come up over the graves, and if so, did that…

"I think Daddy really likes you," Becky said. "Maybe you could marry him, and then I wouldn't have to move to California with Mama and Mr. Everstone. I could stay here and go to school and everything."

"Oh, honey..." Not again, please! A guilt trip, she didn't need.

"I can make my own bed so you won't have to do it. Picola uses Mama's perfume sometimes. She puts it on just before she leaves so Mama won't smell it on her. I've never told," she added piously. "'Cause she's real nice, even if she does make me eat icky stuff."

Sifting through Becky's chatter, Laurel sorted it into neat piles, one labeled Overheard, another labeled Wishful Thinking, still another as Irrelevant.

Marrying Daddy she tried to file as Irrelevant, but it refused to stay put.

"Can Mama come get me even if we have a storm?"

"Becky, I'm not sure, I'm no expert on hurricanes. I guess it depends on how bad it is, and when she gets back to this country."

"I bet I wouldn't like Paris. They eat snails there. I wouldn't have gone even if they'd asked me. I won't like California, either."

Laurel pulled in at the Sub Shop, looked to see if it was still open and cut the engine. The place was surprisingly crowded, probably with evacuees. "Have you ever been to California?"

"No, but I've seen it in the movies, and they have lots and lots and lots of cars and nobody walks anywhere."

Which was probably a slight misconception, but Laurel had enough to deal with at the moment. "What kind do you like?"

"Mmm, I like lots of ham and chicken and bacon and no vegetables. I think Daddy does, too."

They settled on an assortment and Laurel resigned herself to eating whatever the other two didn't care for. She paid for three twelve-inch subs, hoping she wouldn't have to use her credit card to get Jerry's watercolor out of hock.

The frame shop was only a few minutes away, and Becky opted to stay in the car and guard their supper while Laurel ran in to get her painting. It was already starting to drizzle.

"Here you go," the woman behind the counter said, tilting the framed watercolor so that she could see it. "I cut a new acid-free mat and used acid-free backing. It costs more, but it's worth it. That old cardboard that was used for backing would have ruined it in another year or two, especially down here where it's so damp. By the way, I found these between the watercolor and the backing. If you want me to, I can unseal the back and put them back."

The woman handed her an ATM card and paper containing a series of numbers. The card held Jerry's name. Not his mother's.

Laurel shook her head and waited for something to make sense.

# Chapter 19

Standing in the middle of the attractive gallery-frame shop, Laurel studied the ATM card and the scrap of paper. A telephone number? More likely, an account number.

But why on earth would Jerry have had an account in a bank in the Netherland Antilles? The Blessings had obviously had money, but something didn't add up. For one thing, the woman who had painted the watercolor hadn't been a Blessing when she was in college, had she? Jerry hadn't even been a blip on the horizon back then.

Still puzzled, Laurel pulled into Conner's Market on the way home where, under Becky's supervision, she bought everything on the list and several things that weren't. It would never have occurred to her that candy bars, bubble gum and comic books were considered hurricane supplies, but who knew?

A light rain was still blowing when she pulled up in front of her house. A shirtless Cody came out to the car to meet her, his bronzed torso gleaming with moisture above a pair of wet, low-slung jeans.

She managed not to stare, but a retentive memory could be both a curse and a blessing.

He said, "Sit tight, I think we'd better reconsider our plans."

For the first time she noticed her boarded-up windows. "How am I supposed to see if the power goes off?"

"I've got a generator."

"Well, unless it has a long extension cord, it's not going to do me much good."

Becky grabbed two of the bags and slid out of the car while Laurel reached into the backseat for the rest. Cody stopped her. "Becky, take what you can carry and head home with it, it all goes over there. Laurel, you can't stay here. While you've still got lights, run inside and pack whatever you'll need for the duration, then drive on over. My place is on higher ground."

Well, it was, but not that much higher. Laurel eyed the spreading live oaks with branches practically scraping against the eaves and the single pine that, if it fell the right way, would come down on the roof of the old house. There were dangers…and then there were dangers. Too much closeness, especially under extreme conditions, could prove far more hazardous to a woman's health than storm winds and falling trees.

Or at least, to her heart.

Becky cried, "Come on, Laurie, we can play games. I've got RuneScape and Platypus and lots and lots of books."

Which is how once again Laurel, damp and barefoot, found herself standing in the middle of Cody's guest room, hanging a single change of clothes in the commodious closet. This is getting to be a habit, she told herself as a fluttery sense of anticipation began to build.

Cody had insisted on bringing everything in from her car, as well as clearing her refrigerator of all perishables. Did that mean he expected her to stay longer than just overnight? She hadn't thought much beyond the immediate future when she'd packed the watercolor, her best nightgown and a pair of sweats. She'd asked him about it at the time.

"If she continues at her present speed and course, we should be in the clear by morning, all except the tide."

"Tide," Laurel repeated numbly, picturing the recent tsunami that had devastated so much of the other side of the world. Not here, she thought…surely not here.

Picking up on her thoughts—he had an uncanny way of doing that—Cody said, "Tidal waves usually stem from earthquakes, not hurricanes. A lot of the island is barely above sea level, so it gets flooded pretty often. That's why you see so many houses built up on stilts."

"Not mine." She peered through the window at her rental. The old house looked forlorn, rejected and lonely in the premature dusk.

"If the power goes off as it usually does, it could be days before we get service again. In that case, you'll be much better off in a place where at least you'll have lights and running water."

*Sorry, Miss Achsah, but I guess you've seen storm tides before.*

"Laurel? You still with me?"

"Just thinking," she replied. Thinking about the fact that they'd be sleeping only a few feet apart, bumping into each other on the way to the bathroom or the kitchen—maybe even looking for excuses to do just that.

For the life of her, she couldn't figure out what was going on in Cody's mind. He was attracted to her physically—certain signs were unmistakable. As for anything else…

But of course, "anything else" was out of the question. There was Jerry. There was her job. There was a whole life waiting for her back in New York, not to mention the puzzling find that had been tucked inside his mother's painting. Maybe Jerry could shed some light on the mystery.

Checking her appearance in the dresser mirror before heading downstairs, she wondered why the thought of returning to the life she'd left behind such a short while ago no longer seemed so appealing.

"Daddy said supper's ready." Becky poked her head into the bedroom and then came on inside. There were smudges of chocolate at the corners of her mouth.

"I see you've been into the hurricane supplies," Laurel said.

"I thought you meant the candy for me."

"You thought nothing of the kind. What am I going to do without candy if I get scared?" She gave the blond ponytail a playful tug.

"You can sleep in my room with me and BooBoo if you're scared of the storm. I've got the lighthouse. Are you scared of storms, Laurie?" Becky followed her into the bedroom, wriggled her tiny rump up onto the bed and scooted back until she could cross her legs. Her bare feet were filthy.

"I'm—shall we say, respectful?"

"What does that mean?"

"It means I've seen what these storms can do. Not personally, just the news accounts. But I trust your father to do whatever it takes to look after us."

Amazingly enough, she did. John James Lawless had never done a single thing to earn her trust. Occasionally when it was convenient he might collect her and her mother and take them along to Venezuela or China or Saudi Arabia. As he usually traveled on company planes, including a few family members was never a problem. But if her mother happened to be away on a jaunt of her own, Laurel was left behind, because John James didn't care to take responsibility for a young daughter.

She used to wonder why they hadn't simply put her up for adoption. Becky didn't know how lucky she was to have two parents who wanted her enough to fight for her.

"Listen to that wind," she murmured as she dragged a brush through her thick hair. She was overdue a trim.

"What if it blows so hard the lighthouse falls down? Could I have my hair cut just like yours?"

"Do you know how long it's been standing? You'll have to ask your parents about a haircut, but if I had pretty long hair like yours, I'd never cut it off." Laurel headed for the door and Becky scrambled down from the bed and hurried after her. "How long?"

"Your hair?"

"The lighthouse. How long has it been there?"

"Why don't we see if your father has a book about it?"

"He pro'ly does. He has lots and lots of books. Can we hurry up and eat, 'cause I'm really hungry."

"What, after all that candy?" Laurel teased as they jogged down the wide staircase.

"I didn't eat but two pieces, and they were real little. Laurie, are you scared of the ghost? What if she gets lonesome over there and moves into Daddy's house?"

"So you know about Miss Achsah?" They turned into the kitchen, where Cody was setting out drinks. Two glasses of red wine and a glass of milk.

"Daddy told me about her when we used to live over there. He said she laughs 'cause she's happy, so you don't have to be scared, isn't that right, Daddy? And anyway, maybe she's just birds or loons."

The lights flickered, but came back on. Laurel froze, one hand on the back of a chair. Cody said, "Relax, I've got battery lanterns until I can switch over to generator power. Now, who wants Italian, who wants vegetarian and who wants, uh—whatever this one is?"

An hour later they were in the living room, Becky and Laurel sharing the big leather recliner as Laurel read from the book on lighthouses. Cody read the business section of the *Virginian-Pilot,* which served as the local daily.

Hearing a soft purr beside her, Laurel stopped reading and peered down at her young friend. "She's fallen asleep," she said softly to Cody.

"Past her bedtime. She usually flakes out pretty soon after dark, but I guess tonight's special, having you here."

"Not to mention Helene." The wind had taken on a distinctly keening note.

Cody rose and laid aside the newspaper. "I'll take her up to bed. Chances are, she won't even wake up."

"What about her feet? They're pretty dirty."

"Sleep's more important. I'll wash her sheets in the morning if they need it. Or slip on a pair of clean socks. Come on, sugar," he crooned softly as he eased the sleeping child into his arms. From behind the chair where he'd been sleeping, BooBoo lifted his head, then got up, stretched one long leg at a time and followed.

Laurel said, "I guess I should turn in, too."

"Wait, will you? There's something I'd like to talk over with you."

Turning the lighthouse book down on the chair arm,

Laurel stared after the retreating form. Father and child. Both blond, both beautiful in their own way. Both so familiar, so very dear.

And she'd known them for what—a couple of weeks? *Woman, you are just begging for trouble.*

If she were smart, she would pack her bags and evacuate like everyone else with a grain of sense. It still wasn't too late.

"Why don't I go over and stay with Travis and Ru?" Laurel asked when Cody came back downstairs. "Maybe there's something I can do to help out. Trav's family, after all."

Cody crossed to the massive leather sofa and settled down, legs extended and crossed at the ankles. He'd left his shoes upstairs and she stared at his feet as if she'd never seen a naked foot before.

She'd seen more of him than his feet when they were on the beach. As modest as his navy boxers were, her imagination had been more than equal to the task of interpreting what was underneath, especially when they clung to him as he waded ashore.

God, I'm losing it, she thought. "So, why don't I call over there and see if it's all right? Whatever Ru usually does in these circumstances, I can do for her so she won't be tempted to exert herself."

"They're gone." His eyes were closed. He looked tired.

"Gone? Gone where? Did Matt—is he all right?"

"Nobody's heard from Matt, but they left this afternoon. Ru's too near term to risk being stuck this far from the hospital in case the road washes out. I could fly them out, but I can't guarantee my plane won't be damaged. If the dunes break through, the landing strip could be gone by morning."

If the dunes broke through. My God, how many dunes were there between the ocean and Ridge Pond Road? How high were they? "What if Matt tries to call? He'll probably hear about the storm and worry. Even eighteen-year-old boys worry."

Without opening his eyes, he shook his head. "He'll call his cell. They're staying with Harrison and Cleo for the duration."

"And that's *safer?*"

"According to the last position, the storm's going to graze the Outer Banks sometime after midnight before heading out to sea. As long as she stays on track, Harrison's place won't get much more than rain and gale-force winds. At least the roads won't wash out in case they have to get to the hospital in a hurry."

Absently, Laurel eased off her shoes and drew her feet up beside her, thinking about what Ru had said about her three miscarriages and how desperately they both wanted this child. "I guess I'm glad they've gone," she conceded. "I really am. I know they're both worried sick about Matt, but there's only so much worry a person can deal with at one time. Do we need to do anything to their house?"

Cody's slow smile made her toes curl. A lazy warmth unfolded inside her as he said, "No, but thanks for offering. Trav and I took care of everything before they left. While you were at work."

"Not even any buckets to empty?" She felt weepy and aroused and confused as heck.

"Not over there, but you can help me do those in your attic in—" he turned his wrist to glance at his watch "—in about three hours. I'd as soon empty them before the hardest rain sets in. So if you'd like to get a few hours sleep first…"

"I couldn't possibly. Does the wind always sound like this?"

"Wailing like a banshee? Wait'll the full chorus gets started."

Just then there was a loud cracking sound and a moment later, a deep thud. Startled, Laurel sat up and stared at the darkened window. Cody said, "There goes your big pine. I should've had it taken down. Emily weakened it, but when it greened up again, I didn't have the heart to remove it. Then Isabel took a whack at it, and I guess it was too much."

She didn't want to talk about trees, she wanted to talk about this thing that was happening between them, but if she brought it up he might ask, what thing?

Or he might call it friendship, and how could she argue with that?

It wasn't friendship. At least, it was, but it was more than that. She'd had friends before—at least she had whenever she lived in one place long enough. Not a single one, not even Peg, had made her feel this way. Certainly not the so-called friend who had taken her virginity and then bragged about it to his pals.

But ever since the moment when he'd roared into the post office parking lot, creamed her right rear bumper and then blamed her for it, there'd been something about Cody Morningstar that got under her skin.

"Trav's called a conference for when things settle down again."

"A conference?" Tilting her head, she frowned at him.

"Your clansmen. Lyon bought a cottage down in Hatteras a few years ago. Harrison and Cleo usually spend a couple of weeks there in the off-season. I expect they'll want to see how it fared."

They were silent for the next few minutes, listening to the rising fury of the storm. Branches snapped off and struck the side of the house. Wind whined around the eaves. Laurel thought she could even hear the heavy oak branches creaking and groaning as they twisted in the wind. How many storms had those old oaks survived?

And this wasn't even the worst of it, according to the weather guru, only the early bands.

"Tell me about this guy you work for," Cody said out of the blue. "I get the feeling there's more between you two than work."

Which reminded her of something Cody might be able to shed some light on. Leaning back again, Laurel tried to picture Jerry in Cody's position—barefoot, wearing ancient jeans with frayed bottoms and a faded T-shirt, with a dark stubble on his jaw and shadows under his eyes.

The shadows, maybe. Jerry had looked pretty harried the last time she'd seen him. Of course they'd talked since then, but she hadn't seen him in—God, it had been ages. It was beginning to feel almost like another life.

Her gaze moved over Cody's relaxed body. *Laid-back* was a term that came to mind, but it was more than that. Casual to Jerry meant rolled-back cuffs and an open collar on a shirt that was custom-tailored with a white-on-white monogram on the pocket. His Gucci loafers were always polished even in the worst weather, when just dashing from the curb to the front door meant wading through mounds of frozen sludge. She used to tease him about walking on water. He'd never got the joke, but then, one of the few things about him she would change if she could, was that he had no sense of humor. None at all. Oh, he laughed when everyone else did, but she could tell he was faking it.

"We're good friends," she said, wondering how to describe their relationship. Good friends and occasional lovers who'd been headed toward making a commitment when everything had blown up.

"Good friends," Cody repeated softly.

"You implying anything in particular?"

"No, just wondering." He turned to face her then, across some six gleaming feet of pale maple floors. "I don't poach on another man's territory. At least, not knowingly. So if there's something you're not telling me, now's the time to get it out in the open."

Even if she could have spoken, she wouldn't know what to say. He wanted to poach? She *wanted* him to poach!

"We…had a relationship. I thought it would lead further than it has, but then, Jerry has other commitments. Business ones, I mean—responsibilities. And of course, since the trouble…"

"The Late Great Unpleasantness," Cody murmured.

"The what?"

"Past generations of Southerners refer to the Civil War in those terms."

"I heard it was called the War Between the States."

He shrugged, or as close as he could come to it when leaning back against the plump, leather-covered cushions. She tried to breathe evenly, but it wasn't easy. How could she regulate her thoughts, her emotions, when she couldn't even regulate her breathing? All she knew was that for the past several minutes an undercurrent had been building beneath their lackadaisical conversation that had nothing to do with storm winds or falling trees, and definitely nothing to do with war.

"Why don't I...?" She hadn't a single notion of what she'd been planning to say.

He stood up, moving as easily as if he hadn't spent half the day carting sheets of plywood up a ladder and screwing them to her window frames. "Why don't *we*," he corrected softly. "I'd like to sleep with you, Laurel. Sleep being a euphemism." While her brain stuttered to a dead halt, he held out a hand, obviously waiting for her to stand.

To stand and do what? Make a dash for the front door? Follow him to the stairs, to that master bedroom with the king-size bed? What was it the preacher said at weddings...something about "Speak now or forever hold your peace"?

He could have clinched the deal by taking a single step in her direction. Instead, he waited. She probably should give him credit for not forcing the issue, but dammit, she wanted him to force it. To make up her mind for her so that afterward, she could blame it on him instead of her own weakness.

"What about Becky?"

"Becky sleeps like a log." A slight frown crossed his brow and he said, "At least now she does."

There was her out. She could inquire about whatever problems the child had once had, and the moment would have passed.

Instead, she stood and moved a step closer, and that was all it took to ignite a fire that had been smoldering just underneath the surface for days.

# *Chapter 20*

They were halfway up the stairs when the lights flickered again and remained off. In the sudden darkness, Cody swore softly. "Sit here on the steps, don't risk trying to go up or down. I'll light a lamp."

"What about the generator?"

"It'll wait until the worst of the storm moves on."

Laurel sat, clutching the edge of the step as the suffocating darkness closed around her. Moments after she realized that the air conditioner, too, had shut down, a light swept through the small circular window over the staircase—the only one that had been left uncovered.

Her shoulders relaxed. She released the breath she'd been unconsciously holding. And then Cody was back carrying a lamp and a flashlight.

"Want to shower first? We have enough pressure for a quick one."

"I guess I need it," she admitted, chagrined to think she'd forgotten how long it had been since her early-morning bath.

"You need relaxing. Might as well take advantage of the last warm shower, the water heater isn't on the generator." He took her hand, pulled her to her feet and led the way to the carpeted bath that was larger than the bedroom of her apartment, where he began unbuttoning her shirt.

She could hardly swallow, much less speak. When he slid her camp shirt from her shoulders and laid it on the vanity, she resisted the urge to cross her arms over her breasts. Instead, she tugged his shirt from under his belt, her eyes never leaving his face. He looked more than exhausted, he looked as if he were under a severe strain.

No more than she was. Under a thin layer of white lace, her nipples throbbed into hard buds. Her knees felt wobbly; she grew damp with desire. It felt almost as if she was entering a whole new world, as if she had never made love to a man before.

There was love in every touch of her hands as she slipped his shirt over his head. She reached for his belt and when her fingers brushed against the hard ridge near the buckle, he caught his breath audibly.

"I'm sorry," she mumbled, not sure why she was apologizing.

Cody's hand covered hers and he rubbed it against the erection that was threatening the zipper on his fly. She couldn't have moved if her life depended on it. She was frozen there, her hand covering his throbbing erection, while he ripped open the placket of her own jeans and tugged them down her legs.

"Step out," he said, his voice unrecognizable.

She stepped out, first one foot and then the other. "Now you," she said, her voice shivering almost uncontrollably.

He lit an oil lamp and moments later he lifted her, set her inside the burgundy-tiled shower and closed the glass doors. The enclosure was large enough to have held a committee meeting.

"We'd better make it fast before the pressure gives out."

Tilting her face upward, she allowed the lukewarm water to stream over her head. Then Cody reached for a loofah, squeezed on a cedar-scented shower gel and began caressing her back with the soft-rough texture. She arched her back, and when his attention strayed below her waist, she gave up and turned around.

"Cody…" At the sight of his huge erection pulsating from a thicket of dark golden hair, words failed her. All she could think of was having him inside her, moving faster and faster toward the summit they both sought.

Dropping the loofah, he lifted her so that her legs wrapped around his waist. And then he settled her slowly, slowly, neither of them speaking a word.

*Don't slip, don't slip—oh, yes-s-s-ss!*

Good, good, better than good. Her mind shut down as she soared through a world of sheer sensation, unlike anything she had ever imagined, much less experienced.

Not until he sagged and gradually slid down in the corner of the shower did she come to her senses enough to realize they hadn't even kissed. He hadn't kissed her breasts, her lips, much less any other erogenous zone she might have possessed. And yet the climax she had just experienced was beyond description—far beyond anything she had ever before experienced.

Did he know something no other man knew?

Or did it have nothing to do with technique, but with the fact that the sound of hurricane winds, when combined with the scent of lamp oil, made the world's most powerful aphrodisiac?

*I'm in trouble,* she thought just before he lifted her from his lap and stood. *The worst kind of trouble.* "I'm sorry, things sort of got out of hand," he said, reaching down to help her up. The water from the twin shower-heads was barely a trickle now.

She took his hand only because she wasn't sure her legs would support her. What could she say? No apology needed?

She said, "Too late to shampoo?"

"Wait till morning," he said, his voice deeper, rougher than before.

Just then she caught a glimpse of his hardening penis. Act two? She wasn't sure she could handle it, not until she could bring some kind of perspective to what had just happened. She could still hear the storm raging outside, but it was nothing compared to the storm raging inside her head, her still-tingling body.

She managed to rinse off most of the suds as the water trickled down her body, finding creases and crevasses, pooling around her toes before being swept down the drain.

Neither of them spoke while Cody turned off the faucets and held on to her arm as she stepped from the slick tiles to the enormous towel he had dropped onto the floor.

What now, she wondered. Go to our respective corners and at the sound of the bell, come out fighting?

*Oh, God, I think I'm getting hysterical.*

Laurel had never succumbed to hysteria in her entire life, not even close. That's what a logical brain was for—to weed out the irrational from the rational and react accordingly.

"I'm going to check outside first," he said, after wrapping her dripping hair in a thick towel and draping another one around her body.

He grabbed another towel and knotted it at his waist

before leaving her there. She watched his bronzed back and his muscular legs, still damp from the shower, and then she sighed and looked for a deodorant stick. Shaving her legs would have to wait. "Lotion, lotion," she muttered, searching through the toiletries on the blond wood counter surrounding the twin bowls.

No lotion. No dusting powder. Not a drop of water from the lavatory faucets. Later she might borrow a bottle of water and brush her teeth, but right now she only wanted to hide until she could make sense of what had just happened.

She was no stranger to sex. Not overly familiar with it, but then, that was because it had rarely fit into her overall life plan. Plans were important. Once she'd been old enough to make plans, she had been pretty much in control of her life.

Somewhere inside her head, she heard the echo of mocking laughter. This time it wasn't a ghost with an overdeveloped sense of humor.

Scooping up her clothes, she made it as far as the guest-room door by the time he returned. Without a word, he took her arm and steered her to the master bedroom, where he'd lit another oil lamp. "We've got a few hours before we need to do anything. By daybreak we should be in the clear. I'll switch over to the generator and we can survey the damage."

Determined to be every bit as matter-of-fact as he was, she leaned back against the headboard and drew her knees up, wrapping her arms around them. "You think the worst is over, then?"

"Give it another few hours. We're on high ground here, and the house is about as secure as possible, barring a cat-five that hangs around for a couple of days."

So laconic. If she weren't still bemused by what had happened only a few minutes earlier, she might even have been irritated. "I thought hurricanes were supposed to wreak havoc on beaches."

"Some do. Build too close to the water and you stand to lose everything. That's why I built on high ground a safe distance from the ocean."

"Even though you could easily afford to build one of those gigantic beach castles," she said, feeling an irrational urge to needle him.

"Yep."

"Huh!" She felt petty and mean and vulnerable. It was not a great combination. It didn't help when Cody opened the bedside table drawer and took out a foil packet.

And then he took out another one. Laurel's eyes grew round. She looked at him questioningly. He said, "You didn't think we were finished, did you?"

"We're not?" She had hoped not. Else what was she doing in bed with him?

Talk about your whole personality coming unraveled…!

It dawned on her that compared to all the men she'd known in the past—not that there had been that many—Cody was the only real adult. She didn't even try to rationalize that thought, especially when he smiled that lazy-eyed smile of his and took her in his arms.

They both smelled of the same shower gel. If she lived to be a hundred years old, the woodsy, spicy scent would cause instant meltdown. That and lamp oil. And hurricane winds. At that rate she'd spend the rest of her life trying to subdue her libido.

"This time we'll take the scenic route," Cody promised.

He was as good as his word.

Better…

Sometime during the night, Laurel woke to the sound of…silence. For several moments she lay still, waiting for full awareness to sink in. Her first thought was that she was sore in places that hadn't been sore in a long time.

Her second thought was that she wasn't in her own bed.

Her third thought was that she was alone.

She reached across to where he should have been, only he wasn't. She sat up and called softly. "Cody?"

When there was no response she got out of bed, wrapped herself in the robe she saw hanging on the closet door. It was miles too large, but she rolled up the sleeves, wrapped the sash around her twice and then bloused it up so she didn't trip on it.

She tiptoed down the hall to Becky's room. There was just enough light from the Coleman lamp on the hall table to see by when she opened the door. BooBoo bounded down and came galloping toward her, and she caught him before he could skid into the door. "Shh, come on, boy. You need to go outside?"

Was there anything left standing outside? She was afraid to look, afraid not to. Feeling her way, she led him down the stairs, or rather, the crazy Afghan trotted down, then turned around and came back to see why it was taking her so long. He sniffed at the bathrobe and she cuffed him away, wondering when Cody had disappeared.

Was it still night? There were several lamps burning, a Coleman fluorescent one on the coffee table and two old-fashioned, glass-bowled oil lamps, one on the bookshelf and one near the front door. Just as she clipped the leash on the dog's collar, the outside door opened and Cody came in. He was wearing boxers and rubber boots.

Not a good sign.

Without a word to her, he took the leash and led the dog outside. The sky was pitch-black, but evidently the storm was over. The stillness was almost unreal. The word eerie came to mind.

Cody said, "Do your business and make it fast."

Why, she wondered. Because he was eager to get back to bed? With her?

She was still standing in the open doorway, feeling more uncertain by the minute, when he came back. Seeing the tiny scratch on the left side of his neck where her fingernail had caught him, she could have died of embarrassment. Only then he'd be stuck with her remains. Probably bury her across the creek with the woman who might or might not be her ancestor.

Yes, and she'd come back and haunt him, too, she thought with grim amusement. If he thought Miss Achsah was something, just wait until he saw the way she did it.

Unclipping the leash, Cody looped it over the doorknob. "Did he wake you?" There was nothing of the lover who had been both ravisher and ravishee a few hours earlier.

"No, the silence did. The wind's stopped blowing. When I checked on Becky, he acted like he needed to go out, so…"

"Good timing. He might not get another chance for a while."

"Could you tell if there's been any damage? Besides the big pine, I mean?" Wrapping her arms around herself, she followed him to the kitchen. He went directly to the instrument panel hanging on a wall beside the back door and tapped a finger on the barometer. She'd seen him do it earlier, when they'd been unloading supplies.

"Lot of branches, the pine and at least one big oak. Other than that, it's too soon to tell. I emptied your buckets. No point in letting them overflow and leak, though. We'll have enough mopping up to do without that. In a few hours I'll cut on the generator."

Power outages she knew about. They had those even in the city. Generators, she knew nothing about, only what she'd learned from Cody—that they wouldn't supply anything that drew a lot of power, such as ranges and heating devices. And evidently they were death to computers.

"Well…shall we have an early breakfast and get ready to start raking?" she asked brightly. What the devil was going on here? Was this the same man who had made love to every inch of her body three times over the past few hours? Including the arches of her feet and a place at the base of her spine that drove her wild, that she hadn't even known about?

She followed him, thinking that if he was having second thoughts, then maybe she should have a few, too. Too late for anything but damage control, but she might as well get started on that.

In a room just off the kitchen he began fiddling with a ham radio. She knew what it was only because Travis had one, too, and told her how it was used during and after a storm. She shifted her weight to the other foot and waited.

"Why don't you go back to bed, get a few more hours of sleep?" he said. He sounded almost as if they were strangers.

Well, fine. She hadn't asked for any damn commitment!

Wheeling around, she stomped off toward the stairs. "As long as you don't need me any longer, I might as well go home now that the storm's over." Cheap shot, Laurel—really nasty. "Could you lend me a flashlight and maybe a candle?"

Before she even finished speaking, a gust of wind hit the house. It didn't actually shake, but she could feel the vibrations. Shocked, she waited to see if there would be another one.

There was, and then another. And then the whining and whistling was back, louder then ever. "But I thought…"

"That was the eye we were in. Now we get walloped from the other side. Before it's over, the tide will be half-way up Travis's ridge."

"His shed—and what about his boat?"

"Shed's on high ground. We tied his boat off before he left, but there's no guarantee she'll still be there come morning. If you're not going back up to bed, you might want to join me in a pot of coffee. Use the gas ring to reheat it."

She sighed. Her shoulders sagged and she lit the gas ring, then slid into one of the chairs and propped her elbows on the table. The truth was, she wanted to join him anywhere, anytime, in all ways conceivable. So much for careful planning.

Labor Day Monday dawned calm and warm, with a light southwest breeze and a pink and turquoise sky instead of the more common blue and orange spectacle. "It's almost as if the colors get blown up from the tropics along with the storm," Cody said as he joined Laurel on the front deck. It was the first time he'd seen her since she'd gone back to bed, this time in the guest room.

Which was just as well, all things considered. After she'd gone back upstairs he had stayed up monitoring the ham radio and finally grabbed half an hour of shut-eye on the couch downstairs.

Frisco and Hatteras were still under several feet of water, with several roofs blown off and a lot of damage at the marinas. They weren't even recovered yet from the last few hurricanes.

On the other hand, compared to parts of the world where tornadoes, earthquakes, mudslides and avalanches regularly ravaged the countryside, they'd got off comparatively easy this time. He wasn't worried about his own security. His house was well above tide level, even without having been built up on twelve-foot pilings. Not so the old house, but like others of its generation, it continued to defy the weather like a centenarian whose body was in ruins, but whose eyes gleamed with quiet wisdom.

At one time he'd considered replacing it with a small guesthouse or another rental. Since then he'd changed his mind and decided to go on caring for the old relic for as long as it stood. Which might be a pretty big commitment, considering it could well outlast him.

As for the woman who had moved in despite his protests and promptly worked her way into his life and under his skin, that was another matter. They had a choice of confronting the issue head-on, of ignoring it altogether, or tiptoeing around until they were in over their heads.

But this wasn't the right time. There might never be a right time, but he was already committed to the fight for equal rights where his daughter was concerned, and that battle took precedence over everything else.

After the final split, Cody had come close to going off the rails, drinking too much, writing the kind of crap, full of vengeance and violence, that he wouldn't even bother to print out, much less show his agent. He had lived in a hotel for the first few months, but then, knowing no judge would allow him to keep a child in a hotel, he had sobered up, straightened himself out and gone shopping for a house in a peaceful neighborhood, preferably one with a large fenced yard.

He'd found it the second day, only as it turned out, the neighborhood wasn't quite as peaceful as it looked. After a domestic dispute turned sour just two doors down, bringing in a swarm of cops, he'd learned that it happened on a fairly regular basis. This time, though, the guy had shot his wife and then swallowed the gun.

Before the ink was even dry on the papers he'd just signed, Cody had bought out of the deal and started his search all over again. It had been an article in the *Virginian-Pilot* that had inspired him to expand his search to the Outer Banks of North Carolina, half a day's drive away.

He had first seen the place in February, easily the most inhospitable time of year on a narrow barrier island where a northeaster could cover the highway with water, leaving you stranded between villages unless you happened to be driving an amphibian tank.

At the time he'd been driving a BMW. It had been raining hard when he'd left Virginia, but as soon as he'd neared the beach area the cloud level had lowered and the wind speed had doubled. Although he hadn't known it at the time, he had driven head-on into one of the infamous Hatteras Lows, a northeaster that formed just offshore and hung around sometimes for days on end.

By the time he'd crossed Oregon Inlet Bridge headed

south, visibility was practically zilch. Fortunately, there
was little traffic. Not until a few days later had he discovered that blowing sand had pitted his windshield
and stripped his front end down to primer. Most of the
damage had no doubt happened when he'd hit a stretch
of highway covered in what he'd assumed was rainwa-
ter, only to learn later that seawater seeped through the
dunes. A hundred feet farther on, he'd come to a section where the highway had been completely covered
in what, for all he knew, could have been quicksand.

That's when he'd first met Travis Holiday, a retired
Coast Guardsman who'd come along, driving a rugged
SUV, towed him to high ground and then followed him
the rest of the way to make sure he stayed out of trouble.

"If you plan on spending much time down here, I'd
see about getting me something else to drive."

"I'm thinking maybe a boat," he'd joked.

"Yeah, that, too." Early the next morning Trav had
stopped by the motel where Cody had spent the night,
one of the few that had been open that time of year. "You
got a few minutes, stop by my place and meet my wife.
You two have something in common."

Cody couldn't imagine what, which was probably
why he'd taken the time to pull into the long shingled
house on a ridge overlooking the sound. A writer, he
never knew where his next inspiration would come from.

As it turned out, it had been the rescue itself. He met
young Matthew, a tall, quiet teenager who resembled
neither of his parents—Cody learned later that Matt
was a product of Travis's first marriage.

And then Ru told him how Trav had rescued her
when she'd been stranded on the beach under more or
less the same circumstances. "I'd been trying to find the

ends of the earth, and believe me, I found it. It was just like now—the weather, I mean. Like a hurricane that goes on and on and on, until you want to scream. One of the northeasters—not that one—actually cut an inlet just north of Buxton."

He'd liked the couple. Quiet, attractive, intelligent and just enough offbeat to be interesting. They hadn't known him from Adam, although both were obviously readers, judging from the crowded bookshelves.

They'd invited him to stay for lunch, and he had. One thing had led to another, and he'd ended up buying several acres of woodland and an old house. From there he'd gone on to build the kind of house that even Mara, with her superficial values, would find it hard to disparage. Whatever it took, he had been then, and still was, intent on gaining at least a far more generous split, if not full custody. Two weeks in the summer and alternate holidays weren't enough. Becky was changing too fast. Each time he drove to Midlothian to collect her, they had to start all over again getting acquainted.

This time, for reasons he was only now beginning to suspect, the process had taken days, not hours. From the moment Picola had handed her over, warning her to use her sunscreen, to eat her vegetables and not go in the water without her daddy, she had treated him almost as if he were a total stranger. Almost as if she didn't trust him.

He had even stooped to bribing her with her favorite candy, but not even that had helped. She'd been sitting in the backseat for safety's sake, which made talking even more difficult, but dammit, she hadn't even told him when she needed a pit stop. Not even when she'd been carsick. As much as he hated to admit it, the damned dog had actually eased the situation. Using Boo-Boo as an excuse, he had stopped every couple of hours.

Things had still been strained when they'd got home, at least for the first few days. To give credit where credit was due, it was Laurel who had made the difference. Cody had a feeling that someone might have led Becky to believe that he didn't have time for her. More than once she'd asked him why he wasn't working on his book.

"Because I'd rather play when I have a playmate," he'd answered. He worked far into the night after she went to bed, but made little progress. His mind wasn't on the project.

"So what shall we do today? Build a tree house? Track wild animals? Go fishing for supper?" He'd asked her just a few days ago.

"Da-addy, those are boy things. Could you read me a story?"

"You read as well as I do. Tell you what, why don't we write a story. You pick the hero, I'll pick the villain."

"I pick Blackbeard. What's a villain?"

The joint effort wouldn't win any prizes for either accuracy or literary merit. Nevertheless, he'd printed it out, Becky had drawn the illustrations, he'd found her a binder and she slept with it under her pillow.

Things were pretty much back to normal now, so far as their relationship was concerned, but there was one thing that still bothered him. Standing on the deck, looking over the storm damage against a background of small pink clouds and patches of turquoise sky, Cody wondered, not for the first time, if Everstone was the problem. His own impression—granted, it was based on a single meeting—was that the guy didn't make a move that wasn't calculated for effect. If he was on the fast track to the governor's mansion, that wasn't too surprising, but where did that leave Becky? Mara might enjoy the role of an accessory, but not his daughter. No way.

Laurel joined him on the deck. She looked around at the devastation wrought by the past few hours and said softly, "Oh, my…"

"My thoughts precisely." He caught her hand and held it. It was warm and small and capable. She smelled of sleep and his shower gel, and faintly of sex. Or maybe that was just his imagination.

"I took two bottles of water upstairs for teeth brushing."

"I've already switched over to generator power. No hot water, but at least we have the basics."

"Basics are good," she murmured. They were standing by the rail, facing outward. Slowly, Cody turned to look at her. "Basics are…all that's really necessary, actually."

"Hold that thought." Lifting her hand, he kissed her knuckles, then tucked her hand through his arm. Side by side they stood there, looking out over a littered lawn, leaning trees—one big cedar near the edge of the woods was uprooted. The clearing was littered with a mixture of trash, leaves, branches and shingles.

"I moved down here because it struck me as a great place to bring up a kid. Good schools, decent people, close communities—plenty of wholesome activities a kid can get involved in. Times like this, the whole community pulls together. Things like that give a kid a sense of security."

He was about to add that it was also a great place to hide out for a guy who preferred to keep a low profile, when a car with a rusted-out muffler and a bass-heavy radio blaring full blast roared past at well over the speed limit.

Laurel raised her eyebrows, but said nothing.

"Okay, so we have a few boneheads with busted eardrums. All I can say is that this place felt right from the first time I came down here. It still does. I know that sounds crazy, but—" He wrapped an arm around her, drawing her closer to his side.

"I know what you mean," she said quietly. "I've lived in a lot of places before, but I've never before felt a—an *attachment*. I look out at some of these sprawling old trees and feel almost as if I knew them—as if I'd known them ever since they were seedlings." Closing her eyes, she whispered, "I can't believe I said that. Honestly, I'm not a woo-woo type. Ask anyone who knows me and they'll tell you Laurel Ann Lawless is one woman who has her head screwed solidly in place."

He moved around to face her. "Hey, I started it, right? The woo-woo stuff? I remember reading once that we all have a natural home, one place in the world where we truly belong. Trouble is, most of us never know enough to go looking for it, much less recognize it if we're lucky enough to find it."

"Hmm…I'll have to admit, that's pretty woo-woo."

He grinned. "I think that was about the same time I was trying to figure out how big a boat it would take to hold all the books I wanted to carry with me while I sailed around the world."

"What about food?"

"I seem to recall thinking I could stack enough frozen dinners in a locker to last me between ports."

"And you'd operate your freezer and microwave on what—wind power?"

"Hey, I'm not the one who claims to be practical." He rubbed his chin against the top of her head. A flock of birds he didn't recognize flew past, possibly blown in by the storm.

Laurel tilted her head to look at him. "What's wrong with being practical? Okay, I admit it. I'm a walking cliché among my friends. I'm the one who always plans ahead and follows every plan to the letter—the one who believes in a place for everything and everything in its place. So sue me."

No point in mentioning that some of her college classmates used to call her by the derisive nickname of Anal Laurie. She'd thought for a long time that they were calling her Annie Laurie.

He chuckled, and to change the subject she said, "I've lost some shingles."

"Place needed reroofing anyway. Cuts down on the work of stripping it down to the sheathing, although it'll be months before I can get a roofing crew on it. They'll be booked solid now, for the rest of the year and then some."

"Speaking of planning ahead—"

"Were we?"

Doggedly, she continued. "Speaking of planning ahead, I'll probably be heading back to New York in a day or so. My old job's available again—if not right now, pretty soon."

"Tell me about it. You were what, director of public relations for a fund-raising outfit?"

"Oh, well…that sounds a lot bigger than it really is. It's not something I ever studied, I sort of fell into it. I used to freelance for a few small weeklies, writing ad copy and reviewing movies—that sort of thing. The pay was pathetic, though, and when I applied for the job with Jerry, he hired me on the spot. I'll never know why."

Before Cody could comment, Becky appeared in the doorway. "Daddy? Is it over?"

She was wearing Disney-figured pajamas and clutching a cardboard folder under her arm. She held it out and said, "This is me and Daddy's story, Laurel. You can read it if you want to."

## *Chapter 21*

By mid-afternoon Laurel was sore, exhausted and filthy from picking up trash that had either blown in or floated in, and from dragging brush out to the roadside to be collected. Certain parts of her ached for another reason, one she was determined to put out of her mind.

Hearts didn't actually ache, that was only a fable. Something songwriters wrote about and crooners crooned about. Heartache rhymed with heartbreak, June rhymed with moon, and from there it was but half a step to loony tunes. She'd never liked that kind of music anyway, considering it juvenile and about as substantive as cotton candy. Never mind that her favorites among all the old movies she'd collected in video form were love stories.

"So I like fantasy," she muttered as she collected torn shingles that had been caught in the hedge. "So sue me."

Pausing, she mopped her wet face with a dirty forearm, leaving one more streak of dirt. For the remaining time until she left here, she had her work cut out for her if she intended to leave the old house in as good a condition as she'd found it.

After a brief break for refreshments, while Cody took down storm shutters and Becky helped to collect small broken branches, piling them onto a large plastic tarp, Laurel climbed to the attic and began the task of emptying buckets. It was slow going, otherwise they'd have slopped over and leaked through the ceiling.

Cody came in just as she was on her way down the ladder with a full bucket for the third time. He reached up, took the bucket from her and set it on the floor, then he lifted her bodily down from the ladder.

"My job," he said.

"Not while I'm still a resident here," she said flatly. She refused to look him directly in the face, and not just because she looked like something found in a city dump.

*Mistake, mistake, mistake!* Those words had been echoing in her mind all morning, like a smoke alarm that refused to shut down.

"Let's try the brigade system. You slide 'em to the edge of the trapdoor, I'll take it from there."

Without a word she turned and made her way to the far end of the attic, hunched over to keep from scraping the rafters. She slid the blue plastic bucket across the unfinished planks that made up the floor, slopping water over the top as she went.

To hell with it, she thought.

Or as Becky said, "Heck on it."

Kneeling beside the square opening, Laurel waited for Cody to return with an empty. Gazing down on his shirtless shoulders and his cobweb-laced hair as he climbed halfway up and exchanged an empty for her full bucket, she tried not to remember where they'd been and what they'd been doing only a few hours earlier, while the worst of the storm raged all around them, blowing off roofs and flooding half the island.

He'd smelled like cedar and spice. They both had, from his shower gel. Now they were both sweaty and grimy, and it didn't make a speck of difference. If he had reached for her and not the bucket, she would have gladly fallen into his arms.

Yes, and then they'd both end up in the hospital, only with the highway washed out in places, they wouldn't even be able to get there.

"What about your plane? Is it all right?" she asked, needing to keep her mind occupied with impersonal topics.

"Nothing a few hours of work won't take care of. How many more?"

How many more what? "Oh—just four. The ones over by the back chimney aren't as full."

They dealt with the remaining buckets in short order. Cody returned with the last one and handed it up. He was still at the bottom of the ladder when Laurel started down. "Move," she ordered.

Instead of moving, he reached up and caught her around the waist and swung her to the floor. "I need the ladder outside," he said, just as if his touch hadn't burned right through her grimy shirt, giving rise to a swift wave of lust that left her starved for oxygen.

"Sure, take it," she said, quickly stepping away. It was only lust, she told herself. Lust was all she dared admit to. "What's Becky doing?"

"Trying to clean up your flower beds again, or where they used to be before half a dozen limbs and about two feet of rain fell on them. BooBoo's helping," he added dryly.

A little laughter went a long way to relieving the tension. She would like to think the tension was mutual, otherwise she might as well bury her ego in that ancient graveyard back in the woods.

No doubt about it, making love had been a major mistake, one that was probably going to change the direction of the rest of her life. First chance she had, she needed to make a new road map to the future.

"Want to come help me take down the blinds? You can collect the nuts and screws for me."

Don't even go there, the sane side of her brain ordered. *L* stood for left, which stood for logic. Or was it for lust, love and other unmentionables?

Obviously, this was no time to try and plan the future.

Once all the shutters were down and stacked neatly in the back of Cody's SUV to be stored in the shed behind his house, he called for another break. "I suggest we all clean up, get something to eat. Then, once the water's had time to go down, we might do some exploring."

"Can BooBoo and me go swimming?"

"Sorry, scamp, not a chance. Tell you what, though— I need to check on Trav's place first, so while I see how his boat fared, you two can walk along the sound shore if Laurel agrees. As long as you wear your shoes and watch your step," he cautioned. To Laurel he said, "That suit you?"

If he'd proposed taking off for the Straits of Gibraltar, she would have probably agreed, she was that tired. Not to mention that infatuated. Okay, so she'd admitted to lust and infatuation, but that was absolutely *all* she would admit to.

What was it those old maps said about unexplored territory?

*There be dragons.*

Becky was practically jumping up and down with eagerness. "I bet we find a buried pirate ship, don't you? Daddy said storm tides uncover all sorts of stuff. There was a big old shipwreck down at Hatteras last time I was here, but then it got covered up. Maybe the storm uncovered it again, can we go see?"

"It'll be a while before the roads are clear, sport."

"Then can I please get wet all over?"

"In shallow water, and only if Laurel agrees," said Cody. To Laurel he said, "The water's still a couple of feet higher than normal. You might not even be able to get down as far as the shoreline, but watch your step, will you? No telling what gets displaced during a storm tide."

Becky was practically jumping up and down. "Laurel, go put on your bathing suit, hurry!"

"It's still over at the old house. These shorts will have to do."

"Didn't you bring a bag over?"

"Nightgown, hairbrush and toothbrush." She tweaked the child's turned-up nose. "Oh, and Cody, would you take a look at something for me while Becky finds her wading shoes?"

In all the excitement she had forgotten the odd items that had been hidden behind the back of the reframed watercolor. Now she retrieved them from her purse and tucked them in her pocket while she washed her face and hands and finger-combed her hair.

After frowning at her image in the mirror, she added one more thing to her to-do list. Call and make an appointment for a trim as soon as she got back home.

"These were behind the backing on the watercolor I had reframed," she said when she came back downstairs. She handed Cody the note with a series of numbers on it, and the ATM card with Jerry's name on it, not his mother's. "I'm pretty sure those are Jerry's numbers. He loops his eights like a capital *S* and he always crosses his sevens."

"So does anyone else who's ever been to Europe."

Laurel had been several times, but she'd never picked up the habit. "That's his color ink, too." The greenish-blue was distinctive of Montblanc.

Cody studied the numbers, then turned the ATM card over and studied both sides. He said, "Hmm."

"I was hoping a fresh perspective would help. Could it be something his mother sealed inside when she had the watercolor framed? I don't even know when she died, but what if it was something she wanted Jerry to inherit without having to pay inheritance tax? At least, that's the only theory I could come up with."

"Where'd you say you found this?" Cody's eyes were narrowed. He looked less like the Cody who had made love to her until she couldn't walk, much less think, and more like she imagined the hero of one of his hard-edged novels would look.

Laurel vowed silently to buy every single thing he'd ever written as soon as she got back to New York. "It was between the watercolor I had reframed and the original backing."

"He didn't mention it when he gave you the painting?"

She shook her head. "Could it be phone numbers? Credit card numbers? Lottery numbers? Social security numbers?"

"This looks like an area code…and this…" He pointed to the longest string of numbers. "This looks almost like…" He frowned. "Damn, I wish I could go online, but until the power comes back on—"

Becky jogged downstairs wearing her bathing suit

and the rubber shoes she wore to protect her feet from shells. "Come on, Laurie. Can BooBoo come if I promise to wash him off when we get back?"

"You won't get much exploring done if you have to hang on to a leash. Better leave him with me, I'll anchor him to the dock."

"'Kay. Come *on*, Laurie!"

They were almost out the door when Cody's cell phone buzzed quietly. He waved them on and took the call.

This time, it was Becky who hung back. She watched until Cody ended the call, and then hurried back to where he stood. "Was that Mama?"

"No, honey, it was Uncle Travis." He waved Laurel over. "How'd you two like to hear some good news for a change?"

BooBoo was stalking a plastic bag that clung to a denuded oleander. "Maybe she's not coming for me," Becky said hopefully.

"Don't tell me, the Mets just won a three-game series? The price of gas is down? Trav's son checked in and he's moving into the dorm down in Wilmington?"

"No such luck, I'm afraid, but how about Helene Roberts Holiday, born just about the time the eye of the hurricane passed over us."

"You're kidding," Laurel protested. "*Really?* They've had their baby and she's all right?"

"Loud, lusty and all of seven pounds, three ounces, according to her dad. Trav sounds a little shaky, but mother and child are doing fine."

Embarrassing tears sprang to her eyes. She patted her pockets for a tissue, muttering something about leaf mold and allergies. Choking back a small laugh, she did her best to ignore Cody's scrutiny.

"Okay, I admit it—I cry at parades, too. You want to make something of it?"

The slow warmth of his answering smile was enough to curl her toes. Whirling away, she grabbed a broken limb that dangled from a wild cherry tree and gave it a fierce tug. They hadn't yet started on the hangers, only the branches that had broken clean.

"They're not called widow makers for nothing," Cody warned as he lifted and swung her bodily from beneath the battered tree. "We'll talk about your allergies later. Once the power comes back on I'll see what I can find out about your mysterious numbers, but right now I need to check for any damage over at Trav's place." It was the sort of thing Matt would have done if he hadn't disappeared with a single bag and no word of where he was headed.

As it turned out, the Holiday's house came through the storm with only a dozen or so missing shingles, a large uprooted cedar lodged against the shed roof and several broken oak limbs that would have to come down before the next hard wind.

Looking down from the ridge onto the soundside, the scene was totally different, the shoreline drastically changed. Where once there'd been a wide band of white sand, now there were mountains of debris-littered eelgrass. Where yesterday a small pier had reached out some twenty feet over the water, now there were five leaning pilings.

"At least the boat looks all right," Cody said quietly.

"Why is it out there, away from the pier?"

"Notice the way she's tied off between the four pilings? There's enough slack so she'll float on a flood tide, but not enough so she'll beat up against any of the pilings. If he'd left her tied to the pier, she'd have battered against it and then probably ended up in Engelhard when the thing washed away." He glanced at Laurel and said, "You two get on with your treasure hunt while I wade out and start the pump, but watch your footing. No telling what's underneath all that seaweed."

Water, for the most part, Laurel quickly discovered. While she followed the eager child, calling out an occasional warning, her mind wandered in too many directions to focus on any one topic. When Becky raced back to show off a Jack Daniel's bottle half filled with sand and ask if they could break it to see if there was a note inside, she came back to the moment.

"Honey, it's probably no more than a year old. If anyone wanted to send a message they'd use e-mail."

"But Laurie…"

"Look at all the seaweed around the shell mound. If the tide came up that high, I'll bet something interesting washed out, don't you think?"

That got her past the moment. Warning Becky not to race through the eelgrass, she turned to where Cody was just wading ashore. Shirtless and wearing only sneakers and a pair of wet cutoff jeans, he looked like the star of a swashbuckling pirate movie, minus sword, boots and hat. How on earth did a man who spent most of his time slaving over a word processor manage to get those muscles, not to mention the all-over tan?

"Is it all right?" she asked.

"She collected about a foot of water. I left the pump engaged. Did you warn Becky to watch for snakes?"

"Since she saw one the last time she visited the shell mound, she'll probably remember." Together they turned to follow the child, neither of them particularly interested in any newly exposed potsherds and arrowheads.

Was he as aware of her as she was of him? Laurel wondered. She had never been very good at scientific studies. This had all the earmarks of both chemistry and electricity.

A bit breathlessly, she said, "How did people survive down here all these years, with highways flooded and displaced predators ready to pounce every time there's a high tide?"

He grinned, looking both tired and beautiful in the late-afternoon sunlight. "Makes you wonder, doesn't it? Your folks obviously made it, though, else you wouldn't be here."

"In more ways than one," she said. Just then she tripped on a half-buried length of rope. Cody caught her. When they moved on, he didn't release her hand.

*My God, just holding hands with him is enough to reprogram my brain,* she thought.

Already well ahead, Becky called, "Come on, Laurie, let's go before it gets too dark!" BooBoo ran back and forth, barking his silly head off. At least if there were any varmints in the vicinity, they'd have been scared off by now.

Even littered with seaweed it was obvious that much of the shell mound had washed away. Laurel wondered how many other things had washed away since her ancestor had first arrived on the island.

Which led directly to another thought. She had ancestors. She hadn't skipped a zillion or so generations and popped into the world a freestanding unit on September 9, 1977.

It gave her an odd feeling.

"Stick to the track when you head back, and don't stay more than ten or fifteen minutes," Cody warned. He indicated the track they had worn through the mounds of seaweed. "I need to check on a few things inside the house before the power comes on again. You two take care of each other."

She liked the way that sounded. She would like it better if he'd included himself in the equation.

Just before dark that evening the power was restored. They had been back long enough to shower in cool water and change into dry clothes, with Becky chattering constantly over the day's find of a spear point, assorted shells, two arrowheads and five potsherds, three of which were net-incised and one of which was nearly five inches long.

By the time they came downstairs, Cody, his hair still wet from his own shower, had put steaks on to grill. Laurel took out bagged salad and added whatever ingredients she could find for color and texture. She only half listened as Cody explained to his daughter that the largest shard, which was black on the inside, had probably been a cooking pot.

"I bet I know what happened." Becky squirmed excitedly. "Some Indian lady picked it up without using pot holders and it burned her hands and she threw it on the floor and it broke. I saw Picola do that once, only it was a pan and it didn't break, but she said a bad word. Daddy, when I'm twelve, can I say damn?"

"Only in extenuating circumstances," Cody said solemnly, and Laurel turned away to hide her smile. She couldn't bear to think of how much she would miss them when she left.

Which reminded her… "I need to make a call, will you excuse me? The salad's made except for the feta."

Out on the deck, she counted the seconds between sweeps of the lighthouse's beam while she waited for Jerry to answer his cell phone. A few more stars came out as she gazed through the near darkness at the house she had almost come to think of as her own. With a new roof, some insulation, a fresh coat of paint and—

"Jerry? Well, hi, stranger." She closed her eyes in disgust. Talk about gauche greetings!

"Laurel. I was hoping you'd call."

# Chapter 22

At the sound of Jerry's familiar voice, Laurel waited for the goose bumps to prickle. Still waiting, she said, "Yes, well—I thought I'd better let you know that my job here is over. Actually, it ended before it was supposed to because of the hurricane, but I guess you heard about that. Anyway, my rent's only paid up through yesterday so I'll be heading back as soon as the highway opens up again." She waited for a reaction, not quite sure what she expected…or even what she wanted.

"I see."

He saw? What the devil did *that* mean? He'd told her to come on back, hadn't he? "Jerry, have I called at a bad time? I mean, if you have someone there with you, I can call back later. Or you could call me when it's convenient."

"I don't suppose you've seen Kirk, have you?"

Inside the house, Cody had put on a Sarah Brightman CD. Maybe that was the reason she hadn't heard him correctly. "Have I seen whom? Jerry, I think maybe my cell phone's running out of steam. The power's been off, so I haven't been able to recharge it lately. Did you say *Kirk?*"

When nothing happened, she squinted at the little gizmo in the upper right-hand corner. Dead as a doornail. "Well, shoot," she muttered. So much for technology.

Frustrated, she punched in Jerry's number again. If it would just hold long enough, she could give him Cody's landline number and he could call her back on that.

The door slammed behind her as she hurried into the kitchen to read off the phone number. Cody was just taking up the steaks. "You get through all right?"

"My phone ran out of gas," she said irritably, trying to remember where she'd left her charger. Taking a deep breath, she forced a smile. "All this and baked potatoes, too?" The call could wait.

Becky said, "I scrubbed them and punched in the numbers on the microwave. Do you like butter or sour cream on yours?"

"Either—both. Salt and pepper, though, not sugar."

Becky wrinkled her nose and said, "Nobody puts sugar on potatoes, do they, Daddy?"

At least, Laurel thought as they sat down to eat, if she'd accomplished nothing else, the two Morningstars were back on good terms. Whatever had been going on between them the first few days had evidently been settled. She'd like to think she had played a small part in the reconciliation.

*If you marry my daddy...*

Just stop that!

Now, if only she could do something for Trav and Ru, such as finding their son. Cousin or not, she would tell that boy what she thought of him for giving them even more to worry about than they already had.

"I need to go get my charger," she said.

"You're welcome to use my phone. Cell or landline, take your choice."

"No thanks, it can wait." She'd managed to get her message across before the connection failed. That she'd be headed north as soon as the highway was open again. What else was there to say?

Becky wanted to talk about the new baby, and so they did, while they devoured a surprisingly delicious meal. Cody reached across the table and touched his daughter on the nose. "I don't know about Helene, but you were probably the most beautiful baby born over the past five hundred years. Bright red all over, bald, with a lovely pointed head and eyes the color of blueberry muffins—at least I think there were eyes under all those puffy wrinkles…"

Becky squealed, "Daddy, I was not! Mama said I was ugly, but you loved me anyway."

"Your mama's right, hon."

Laurel yawned. Poststorm activities burned up a lot of energy. She would sleep like a log the minute her head touched the pillow. Unless Cody—

Uh-uh. No way. She had enough to forget without adding to her store of memories. "You two cooked, so I'll do the cleanup," she said.

Becky shoved her plate away and made room on the table for her new finds. They were sandy. Laurel thought, So what?

Cody said, "Then if you'll excuse me, I'll go crank up my computer."

"That means turn it on," Becky explained as she arranged her new treasures on the bare teakwood surface.

Laurel hoped he intended to check out the numbers and the mysterious ATM card. What in the world had Jerry's bank card been doing behind a watercolor of a nineteenth-century sailboat tied up at a dock with a windmill in the background?

And now, as if she didn't already have enough on her

mind, there was Jerry's odd question about Kirk. Or had she misunderstood him? What on earth would Kirk be doing here? Searching out talent?

"I don't think so," she murmured. Eyebrows drawn together in a frown, she rinsed the dishes and placed them in the dishwasher while Becky got out her collection of artifacts from previous explorations and aligned them with today's finds.

If only she could remember his exact words. Was it her imagination, or had he seemed more interested in checking on Kirk's whereabouts than on her own? If Kirk was out scouting up talent again, that meant that Jay-bass was off the hook, which was more or less what Jerry had implied.

"Daddy's going to build me a box to keep my stuff in," Becky announced just as Laurel finished rinsing and loading the dishwasher. "He's going to put a glass door on it so I won't have to open it to look inside." Her snaggletooth smile was utterly disarming, freckles, sunburned nose and all.

Laurel filled the detergent compartment and shut the door. "That sounds perfect."

"You can borrow it to look at if you want to, 'cause I'm going to leave it here till next time I come, 'cause Mama says I have too much junk in my room."

"Laurel, have you got a minute?"

She glanced up to see Cody at the head of the stairs. His face was in shadow, but his voice sounded…odd. That was the only word she could think of to describe it. *Odd.*

"Thanks, hon, I'd love to," she said as she squeezed Becky's shoulder and hurried to join him. "What's wrong?"

"Nothing, I hope. Still, it seems odd."

There was that word again. "What's odd?"

"The numbers you gave me? One's a phone number. You know anyone in Curaçao?"

"The island?" She shook her head. "I'm not even sure where it is. What about the other number?"

"How much do you know about money laundering?"

"About *what?*" According to a few of the early news reports that was one of the things J. Blessing Associates had been semi-accused of. Totally baseless, she was sure of it. Jay-bass, funding terrorist groups? Laurel had dismissed it as the usual cheap-shot speculation by the gutter press.

"Money laundering, as in cleaning up dirty money and making it respectable." Once in his spacious corner office, he gestured to a leather armchair and she dropped into it, her mind galloping off in several directions at once.

"I know what it means," she said with a vague wave of her hand. "In general terms, at least. I don't know the details, but I guess it probably happens a lot. In fact…"

He waited, hips leaning against his desk, legs crossed at the ankles. Finally, his silence sucked the words from her, just as he no doubt intended.

"Jay-bass—this company I work for? Did I tell you about how we were shut down and interrogated by all these CSI types?" She knew she'd half-explained to Harrison and to Trav and Ru, but how much had she told Cody?

So much for having a steel-trap mind. Hers had obviously rusted in all this salt air. "I was questioned before I left town. I wasn't ever accused of any crime, but looking back—thinking about the kinds of questions they asked…"

She frowned at a yellow legal pad on the wide desk, trying to recall the details of what she'd been told, what she'd been asked.

"Go on," he prompted quietly.

"The thing is, I've always been so good at details. Everyone said so, even if it wasn't always meant as a compliment."

What she wasn't quite so good with were subtleties and nuances. Her mind simply didn't work that way. "All I can tell you is what I told the two men who questioned me," she said finally. "Frankly, I was shaking so hard I could barely talk. Nothing like it had ever happened to me before. I've never even had a traffic ticket."

Cody lifted his hands, palm outward. "Hey, your record's safe with me. I never even reported you for reckless driving."

"Oh, shut up," she said, but it helped to lighten the atmosphere. "Anyway, I wasn't involved with finances. We raised money for small charities that couldn't afford to hire the big-name fund-raisers, but it was strictly a gate-plus-donation affair, so we always knew right away how much we'd taken in. At least Jerry did. By the time the actual event occurred, my part of the job was finished. I was usually planning the next campaign. But..."

"But?" he prompted when she continued frowning at the legal pad, trying to recollect just what it was that had bothered her when she'd thought back to the last few affairs.

She shook her head. "I don't know. There was something there but it's gone now."

"Give it a shot. Stream of consciousness. Just start talking and let it flow."

Her eyes widened. "No way!"

"About your job, I mean," he said, and she wondered how good he was at reading minds.

"Starting where? Okay, we usually shoot for a certain demographic. Disposable income and as far as I'm concerned, lousy taste in entertainment, but if you tell anyone I said that, I'll deny it."

"Scout's honor, my lips are sealed."

What they were was soft and sensitive and tempting.

Back to business. "The take was usually good, but certainly nothing to get the IRS all churned up. Although looking back, I don't think it was the IRS who questioned me. And anyway, I'm pretty sure Jerry filed all the appropriate tax-exempt forms."

"FBI? CIA?"

She shook her head. "I don't honestly know. I was so scared I couldn't think straight. They weren't wearing badges, but from some of the acronyms I heard, I think some branch or branches of Homeland Security were involved."

"Jesus."

"He wasn't there. At least, if he was, he didn't look anything like his pictures." Laurel closed her eyes and groaned. The only time she shot off her mouth this way was when she was truly nervous, which had happened rarely once she'd been old enough to take control of her life.

"Let me tell you a little about how it's usually done, see if anything sounds familiar." Cody uncrossed his legs and moved around to the desk chair. "The simplest form is grabbing the cash and stuffing it in a stump hole. In other words, skimming off the top and stashing it away where no records are kept. Curaçao happens to be one of those places."

"Offshore banks, you mean. Everybody knows about those." Although she admitted to being a bit cloudy on the details.

She waited, knowing she probably wasn't going to like what she heard. While he might be a bestselling author with a vast source of information, that didn't mean he couldn't be mistaken. Besides, if it were that easy to find out what was going on, Jay-bass would have been off the hook by now.

"Criminal organizations—"

"J. Blessing Associates is not a criminal organization!"

As if she hadn't interrupted, Cody continued to speak. "Criminal organizations have various ways of placing money into the system and spreading it out into any number of legitimate outlets. It's called layering. By the time it finds its way back into the system, it's clean money. I have a feeling whoever hid these numbers worked on a much simpler system."

"Simple...how?" She was calmer now. Marginally.

"Simple like underreporting proceeds, skimming off the top and stashing the money in a safe place until you're ready to claim it."

Something settled inside her like a lead weight. She didn't want to believe it, couldn't allow herself to believe it. "Cody, I know these people. They're nothing at all like that." At least she knew Jerry. Kirk was another matter. Could he have been doing something like that without Jerry's knowing? Had Jerry discovered it and that was why he'd asked if she'd seen him?

Feeling confused and dejected, she slumped in her chair and stared at her clasped hands. "After all the time I spent there, don't you think I would've noticed if something like that were going on?"

Instead of answering, he stood and moved behind her to place his hands on her shoulders. With firm, almost painful movements of his thumbs, he massaged the place between her neck and her shoulder where the muscles had turned to granite.

"You're tense as a bowstring," he murmured when she groaned and tipped her head back. Evidently it never occurred to him that his touch might be responsible for some of that tension.

A warm breeze drifted through the open windows, bringing with it a mixture of mysterious odors. Mostly mud and crushed greenery.

"Laurel?" His voice was barely audible. Drawing her out of her chair, he turned her in his arms and propped his chin on her head. If there was any passion in the gesture, it wasn't obvious, but then, passion wasn't what she needed at this moment.

What she needed was security in a world that had tilted on its axis. Someone to hold her, to assure her that everything would be all right even though she knew it probably wouldn't. Her priorities had been knocked for a loop. She had a feeling her past was not going to lead to the future she'd imagined.

So where did that leave her?

Before she could dismiss the question as unanswerable, the phone rang. This time it was the landline, not the cell phone.

Cody sighed heavily, released her and reached for the instrument. "Go to bed," he mouthed.

She was almost out the door when she heard him say, "You're sure? Did you check out—"

Unable to help herself, Laurel lingered in the doorway. If it had to do with Ru and the baby, she wanted to know. If it concerned his personal affairs, he could close the door.

Instead, he crossed the room, the phone still held to his ear. When the coiled line had stretched almost to its limit, he reached out and drew her back inside. For a moment she'd been afraid he was going to shut the door in her face.

By the time he hung up the phone several minutes later, Laurel knew less than nothing about who had been on the other end, much less what they had discussed. Cody had mostly listened while the other party did all the talking. She waited for him to speak first, startled to realize she was shivering.

"Okay where do we start," he muttered. It was not a question. Opening the legal pad, he turned to a fresh page and started jotting lines she couldn't read upside down. Finally curiosity got the best of her.

"Who? Who called, what's it about, and how does it affect me?" When he went on scribbling, she said, "Or does it affect me?"

Cody looked up. "Okay, here's what we know so far. Your guy, Blessing, has a record in Montana."

"Jerry? I don't think so, he's from upstate New York."

"So he traveled. Juvenile record's sealed, but once he came of age he started building a career for himself, mostly petty stuff. He did some jail time in Knoxville and—"

"Knoxville? But Jerry doesn't even like country music." The minute the words left her, she could feel her face flaming. How stupid could a woman be? City dweller with a degree in journalism, semisuccessful career woman—not that being a PR specialist for J. Blessing Associates was the career she'd envisioned for herself.

"Strike that last remark, will you? Tell me what else you've learned."

Cody nodded and continued. "Looks like this outfit you worked for is just the latest in a long line of Blessing's con games. This time, he came close to being legit—might even have started off that way, but in the end, he couldn't resist skimming."

"Skimming and stashing," she repeated numbly. "Couldn't it be some other Jerry Blessing? Lots of people have the same name."

Cody toyed with the pencil, twirling it between his fingers. "He left a trail a blind man could follow. Too cheap to buy good papers, probably. You tell me, I don't know the guy. You do."

She did. At least she'd thought she knew him. "Pride, probably. He loved his name. He said it led to his calling, that he'd been blessed by having a wonderful family. That's the reason he felt he had to pay back for some of his…blessings."

"The name's real. The rest is phony. I'll have Lyon print out a copy if you're interested."

"No thanks. So, where did you learn all this? Is it public knowledge now?"

"Your cousins make up a pretty interesting brigade. Lawlesses for law and order?" If he expected her to laugh at his attempt at a joke, he could think again.

At least he had a sense of humor. She almost wished he didn't so she could mark down his score. In every category he was over the top. "So what do we do now, call the police?"

"Now we wait. If Blessing's still free, and I'm assuming he is, since he called you?" He made it a question, so she nodded. "Once we get the landing strip cleared off, I'm picking up Harrison and Lyon in Manteo. We'll convene down here and work out the next step. Trav won't leave until Ru and the baby are able to travel, which should be about the same time the road's clear. Couple of bad washouts north of Rodanthe."

"But why? I mean, not that I don't want to see them. I haven't even met Lyon yet, but why now? Why here?"

"As for why now, the sooner the better. As for why here, I can't leave Becky alone and Lyon needs to check out his property for damage. You'll like him, by the way. For a government type, he's almost human. I expect you'll have more in common with his wife, but that'll have to wait. Right now, we need to clear up the matter of why you keep attracting undue attention."

"I do? I mean—what do you mean exactly?"

"You said your apartment was broken into right after you left Manhattan? You said you felt like you were being stalked shortly before you left?"

She nodded. "Either that or I imagined it. When I was in Conner's the other day I had that same spooky feeling, but it turned out to be a woman who thought she recognized me. I mean, who stalks people in a community grocery store?"

"Who breaks into houses to rearrange underwear?"

"I swear to God, if I find out Kirk's been chasing me, I'll wring his scrawny neck." She got up and began pacing. She wasn't a pacer; she prided herself on being cool under fire. Trouble was, she'd never really been under fire until the Jay-bass mess broke.

"What makes you think he might have followed you?"

"Nothing except that Jerry asked if I'd seen him. We got cut off before I could ask him about it."

"Call back?" He held out the phone, but she shook her head.

"I'm no good at pretending. I wouldn't know what to say." She took a deep breath, designed to calm her down, but the faint scent of a cedar-and-citrus aftershave had the opposite effect. "So what next? A ghost I can live with, but not a stalker, especially if it's Kirk. It's all about those numbers, isn't it? That's what he was looking for."

Cody settled back in his black leather chair. "The next step's up to Lyon. This isn't exactly his territory— that is, I seriously doubt if national security is involved in this case, but he has contacts and he knows the drill."

"Tomorrow, you say?"

He nodded. "I suggest we both get some sleep before the party starts."

As if she would be able to close her eyes, Laurel thought as she led the way. When she paused at the door of the guest room, Cody shook his head and lifted his eyebrows. That was all she needed to follow him to his room.

Or maybe not all, but it was a very good start....

# Chapter 23

By the time Cody got the call telling him Harrison and Lyon were on their way to Manteo, all three properties—Travis's and both of Cody's—were completely clear of storm debris. Two neighbors had pitched in with chain saws and rakes. Now on both sides of the highway, mountains of brush, ruined furnishings and drowned appliances were beginning to appear, waiting for pickup to begin. Farther down the highway she could see water surrounding several of the lower-lying homes.

Lawless land, fortunately, was mostly high ground.

"This one weren't bad a-tall," said one of the neighbors, wielding a rake to drag out trash that had floated up under the house. "She come up to my middle step, but Alex come right in the house. 'Pends on which side we get, how high the water'll come up in the sound."

Having watched the coverage until the power went off and having had the dynamics explained to her by Cody, Laurel knew more or less what he was talking about. A few more years and a few more storms, she thought, and she would be an old hand.

"Only thing not flooded is my wife's family graveyard over yonder. It's right by the creek, but it's on a ridge."

"Your wife's family? Someone said the woman who used to live in the old house is buried over there."

"That would be Miz Achsah. I guess you already heard how, after she died, her first husband's family stole her body from her third husband's folks and brought her back home. All this used to be Lawless property. I think Miz Achsah was some kin to my wife, maybe her great-grandma's sister. Fact, I think she's got a picture of the two of them walking home from down the dock, carrying a couple of croakers."

"Croakers," Laurel repeated blankly.

Bill grinned, his bushy white mustache tilting at an angle. "Fish. Prob'ly about ten cent a pound back in those days. Come over when you have time, I'll see if my wife can dig out that picture. Be funny if it turned out you and my wife was kin." With a casual salute, he headed down the driveway, avoiding the worst of the puddles.

Laurel stared after him, her mind spinning with visions of a Norman Rockwell Thanksgiving, family gathered around a turkey-laden table. One of them her great-grandmother, or was it two greats? Before she left she needed to get a delineated chart of just who was who in the Lawless family.

"Where do you live?" she called after the big man who was already halfway down the driveway.

Bill thumbed toward the soundside. "Over yonder, couple of houses down from Trav. Two boats in the front yard. I'll see if Sara can dig out those old pictures. If she don't have 'em, her sister will—Mary lives just over on the other side."

Laurel was still standing there, a bemused look on her face, when Cody emerged from the house wearing sunglasses and a Braves baseball cap that shaded the upper part of his face. He hadn't taken time to shave, but even sweaty and bristly he looked better than anything Hollywood had produced in a long, long time.

*Renée, Nicole, Julia—eat your heart out!*

"Kid knows her way around a computer better than I do," he said, shaking his head. "Time for you to quit the busywork and get cleaned up. I don't want your folks thinking I've been working you too hard."

Laurel wiped a damp arm over her equally damp forehead. "Cody, guess what. I'm almost sure now that I had a great-great-grandmother."

"No kidding. I thought you'd been found in a cabbage patch."

Ignoring his teasing remark, she said, "According to Bill, the woman who used to live in your old house was his wife's great-great-grandmother—the one who's buried just on the other side of the creek? If Miss Achsah is related to me, that means his wife's probably my cousin, too."

"Sorry, can't help you there. I'm not up on the local genealogy, but on a small, isolated island, whoever washed ashore probably tended to stay right here. Some of the oldest families must go back three, four hundred years. Maybe more, since nobody back then was keeping score. Too busy trying to survive."

"What about since then? I mean, surely there are family Bibles, that sort of thing? Travis mentioned a local genealogist." Suddenly, exploring her roots seemed far more important than finding out what was going on with Jerry and Jay-bass. She could always find another job if she had to, but family was something else. Until recently she had never even given it much thought, being too busy trying to survive. Now it was almost like an exploding galaxy.

"Just think," she said, bemused, "I'll have people to exchange Christmas cards with every year. They'll send pictures and newsletters… I'll want pictures of baby Helene and Jimmy, even though he'd only be a cousin by marriage, and of—" She started to say, of Becky, but broke off just in time. Then she said it anyway. "If I give you my address, you could send pictures of Becky. In a few years she'll be a teenager."

"Yeah, that's what I'm afraid of," Cody said dryly. He reached out and plucked a dead leaf off her damp T shirt. "Take a break, Laur, you've done more than enough. We should be back before dark but if there's any delay, I'll call." Earlier he had checked out his plane and inspected the condition of Billy Mitchell Airport's single landing strip. "Tell Becky to stay close and keep the mutt out of the woods. With all this flooding, critters have a tendency to stray."

"Don't worry, we'll stay in the clear. While Becky's busy with her computer I'm going to run over and open up my windows so things can air out inside." The old house might be his legally, but suddenly, she felt a very personal sense of ownership. This had once been *her* family's property.

She watched him swing up into the driver's seat of his SUV and set out along the potholed, half-flooded driveway. He waved once and she waved back. She was still standing there, wondering when her life—not to mention her priorities—had turned flipside up, when he reached the highway and stopped.

Knowing she needed to open up the house and then start packing, she willed herself to move. This dithering wasn't like her.

Oh, and then she'd better change into something decent to meet her cousins. Meanwhile, she could pack the car and be ready to leave first thing in the morning. She needed to go back where she belonged. The trouble was, she no longer knew where she belonged. As illogical as it was, she'd grown far more attached to an old ruin of a house on an island filled with people who might or might not be her tenth cousin a jillion times removed. An island where there was no public transportation, no sidewalks, where instead of a friendly neighborhood bodega, you had shops that sold crab-cake sandwiches, shrimp baskets and the kind of barbecue that was unlike any she had ever had when she'd lived in Texas.

Where it wasn't unusual to find family graves in the front yard, some so old the stones could no longer be read. How many of those graves held the mortal remains of her ancestors?

She thought about the vast, beautifully landscaped cemetery near Atlanta with their neat bronze markers. *Mama, you'd have liked this place,* she thought. And who knew—her father might have liked it, too. She'd never really known either of them well enough to know their true preferences.

Hearing the sound of a laboring engine, she glanced toward the driveway, suddenly aware of the fact that after several minutes she was still standing in the same spot, yard rake in hand, a dozen or more half-finished plans drifting around in her head.

The Range Rover backed up the driveway and

stopped near the break in the hedge. Cody climbed out, leaving the door open, and jogged across the yard, his face looking grim behind those aviator sunglasses.

"Forget something?" she asked, her voice only half an octave or so higher than usual.

"Yeah, I did." He removed his sunglasses and hooked the wings into his hip pocket.

Crazy or not, she knew even before he reached for her what he'd come back for. She took three steps into his arms, face lifted, eyes closed. He caught her and held her so close she could feel the buckle of his belt digging into her stomach. She barely had time to breathe before he was kissing her as if he was starving and she was his last hope of survival. Eventually the threat of oxygen deprivation forced them apart.

With a shaky smile, he gazed down at her, eyes glinting like wet agates. "That's a down payment. Stick close until I get back, will you?"

Breathlessly, she said, "Snakes and alligators?"

"Those, too."

And with that enigmatic warning echoing in her ears, she watched him drive off.

Becky had set aside her laptop. She was munching on pretzels and watching TV, tossing an occasional broken pretzel to BooBoo, who snarfed up every grain of salt on the pale wood floors.

Still bemused, her thoughts chaotic, Laurel leaned against the back of the couch. A dozen years ago she had envisioned herself as an embedded journalist, reporting her story with a vaguely foreign accent while bombs and rockets lit up the night sky behind her.

What ever happened to all those dreams…?

Shaking her head, she turned away, wondering if Becky would be all right for a few minutes while she finished packing her car. When she heard a twin-engine plane pass directly overhead, her thoughts flew to her favorite scene from *The English Patient.*

She shook her head. Time to grow up.

Becky called over her shoulder, "That's Daddy's plane. He doesn't like for me to fly with him 'cause I get sick in my stomach, but sometimes I do it in cars, too."

"You'll outgrow it," Laurel assured her. Maybe the power of suggestion would help. Mental Dramamine. "I'm going to run across the way for a few minutes. Want to help me make potato salad when I come back? Your company will need to eat and I doubt if any of the restaurants are open."

"I know how to use a paring knife, but Picola says I cut off too much potato with the peelings."

"Then I'll peel and you can get out the other ingredients. If you need me, you know where to find me."

It was almost dark when Laurel heard the twin-engine plane coming in over the sound. Leaving Becky playing RuneScape on the kitchen table, she'd gone over again to close the windows she had opened earlier, in case it rained. She was on her way back when she saw the plane fly directly overhead, as if the pilot knew she was standing there, her heart beating faster than any hurricane winds.

Had that kiss meant anything at all? What about last night and the nights before that?

Play it cool, Lawless. Never let 'em see you sweat. Somebody famous had said that, but possibly not in these same circumstances.

Okay, she could be cool. *How nice to see you again, Harrison, how are Cleo and Jimmy? So you're Daniel the Lyon. I'm not sure if we're seconds or thirds, but I'm delighted to meet you.*

Last of all she would nod to Cody. Coolly. As if she hadn't already made a total mess of her life by falling in love with a world-famous author who'd once been married to the most gorgeous woman in captivity, if Ru could be believed.

Consider it a trade-off, she rationalized. Lost a heart, found a family.

Watching the small plane disappear behind the trees as it came in for a landing, she wondered if she'd looked so desolate watching him leave that he'd taken pity on her.

Uh-uh. No way. She freely admitted to being a lot of things—a control-oriented, technologically-challenged neat freak among them. But no one had ever called her a victim. She didn't need pity, what she needed was…

Actually, she didn't need one damn thing. Wants didn't count.

Over a supper of sliced ham, canned peas, potato salad and the dinner rolls she'd found in the freezer, they talked politics, family relationships and hurricane damage. According to Cody, they had circled over Lyon's cottage in Hatteras village on the way to the landing strip. "It'll be at least another day before the water recedes enough to drive down," he said.

"One of the locals looked it over and reported no structural damage as far as he could see," Lyon commented. He was attractive in a weathered way, as if whatever it was he did for the government had taken a toll.

Not until Laurel served dessert, a store-bought cake piled high with canned peaches and whipped cream, did anyone bring up the ATM card and those mysterious numbers that apparently represented an offshore bank account. But that was only after Lyon, at Laurel's insistence, named every single movie his wife had ever appeared in—all four of them.

"I saw that!" she exclaimed at the last title mentioned.

"You and a couple of dozen other fans," he said dryly.

She liked the way he could look so stern and at the same time, those brilliant blue eyes would twinkle with humor. Really, for an intelligence officer—he was deliberately vague about which of the seventeen or so branches of intelligence he worked for—her cousin Lyon wasn't at all scary.

When she said as much to Cody and Harrison, they laughed and told her that players above a certain level rarely needed to use overt intimidation.

"Then I must have been questioned by the custodial staff," Laurel responded. "Is there a group called Intimidation-R-Us?"

"Actually, I believe they're headquartered in an abandoned coal mine in West Virginia," Lyon retorted solemnly. She was just catching onto his droll sense of humor, something he shared with Harrison and Travis, if not with her father. Not that she'd known her father well enough to know if he even had a sense of humor.

Once Becky was settled for the night, having previously covered all the news of wives, new babies and prospective new babies—and yes, Cleo and Harrison were definitely expecting sometime around Valentine's Day—they got down to business.

It was Lyon who said, "There's a lot I can't tell you, but I can tell you this much—Blessing's been under observation for the past eighteen months. He's a pretty small fry in a damned big pond—more like a tadpole in the Pamlico Sound—so nothing was done about it until recently when he or someone in his organization slipped up and made a larger deposit."

"Larger than what?" Laurel asked while the others simply nodded. Harrison leaned forward, his elbows on the table. Cody leaned back, arms crossed over his chest, eyes half-closed. He looked as if he was napping, but Laurel knew by now that looks could be deceiving.

"Humor me," she demanded. "Cody explained, but I'm still behind the curve when it comes to money laundering, or whatever it is we were accused of."

"Not you personally," Cody said without opening his eyes or uncrossing his arms. He reminded her of a big golden lion dozing in the sun. "I have it on the best authority you're in the clear." He nodded toward Lyon.

"I am?"

Her newest cousin nodded. "You checked out so near broke you're totally in the clear." He winked at her.

Laurel discovered that she quite liked being teased by family, even brand-new family she hardly knew. Even when it was about something this serious. "Well. I'm embarrassed, but I guess I'm relieved, too. Tell me all about money laundering, but keep it simple. My one-cylinder brain doesn't handle the complicated stuff too well."

"I'll withhold judgment on that," Lyon said as he rose and poured himself another cup of coffee. Glancing around the table, he said, "No refills?" Setting the pot back on the heater, he rejoined them at the table. "'Kay, here goes." He ticked off the points on his fingers. "First, there's something known as The Federal Bank Secrecy Act—BSA for short—that requires paperwork to be filed on any deposit over ten thousand dollars. The law's been in effect for decades." Another finger went up. "BSA feeds into a national database that has programs designed to flag suspicious deposits." And another one. "Certain law officials are trained to spot any patterns that might indicate illegal activity." He lowered both hands and looked at her then, his irregular features reminding her fleetingly of her father. "Your guys made one small slipup, but it was enough to attract attention."

"Just for one entry? Couldn't it have been a book-keeping error? For Pete's sake, you mean to tell me anyone who ever deposits more than ten thousand dollars gets brought in for questioning?"

Lyon started to explain why certain patterns raised a red flag while others didn't when Cody interrupted. "Who'd have a reason to search her place? Here and in New York? Any warrants? Any of your guys sniffing around?"

After a brief pause, Lyon shook his head. "No warrants on file. If she's attracted attention, it's not from one of ours. You mentioned it before."

He had? Laurel looked from one man to another around the table. "Hey, I'm right here, you don't have to talk about me in the third person. What did Cody tell you, anyway?"

"Just that there've been intrusions at both places where you've lived recently and that you've occasionally had the feeling of being under surveillance."

Surveillance. "I wouldn't exactly put it that way. That is, I never actually saw anyone, so it could be just my imagination." She was aware of feeling both grateful and alarmed that Cody had taken her fears seriously. It would've been nice if he could have assured her that it was all in her mind.

# Chapter 24

It was just past midnight when Laurel went upstairs. Cody wouldn't hear of her sleeping in the old house. Not that she'd argued too strenuously. Tonight she could do without laughing ghosts. So after a generic good-night to all, she quickly ran through her bedtime routine and climbed into bed, where she willed herself to fall asleep.

She hadn't mentioned that she'd been planning to leave tomorrow. Now that Lyon was here with his expertise, all she had to do was decide what to do with an amateurish watercolor that had probably not been painted by anyone's mother after all. She'd heard enough to know that the Jerry Blessing she'd thought she knew didn't exist. Probably never had. To think she had not only slept with him, she'd even expected to marry him.

Now what? Lose her pride, offer to pay more rent and see if Cody offered an alternative? Go back to New York and try to fit back into her old life, minus Jerry and Jay-bass?

So much for a lifetime spent coloring inside the lines.

Over a breakfast of bacon, high-test coffee and scrambled eggs, the three men continued to plan her immediate future. It was Lyon who said, "She's better off down here where it's easy to keep an eye on her until we round up all the players."

Cody nodded and said he'd see to it.

*He would?*

Harrison said, "We've got plenty of room. Cleo would love the company—so would Jimmy."

"See to what?" Laurel exclaimed. "Are you talking about *me?*" She had woken about four in the morning and been unable to go back to sleep. Watching the light-house beam sweep across the window, she'd tried again to make plans for the future, only to give up in frustration. Jay-bass was probably history, no matter how things turned out. All her winter clothes were in her apartment, neatly stored in labeled boxes under the bed. Or possibly not so neatly, as Peg had had to repack them after the break-in.

"We can keep a closer eye on you here," Cody explained. "Just until things are settled. After that, it's your call." While his gaze continued to rest on her, she tried vainly to read his thoughts.

"My call," she repeated. "You know what? I used to think all the calls were mine to make. Is that a hoot, or what?"

When nobody hooted, she said, "Okay, for now, but I'll owe you another rent payment." Which meant she would have to see if Caroline could use her for the next few weeks, or however long it took to get her life back on track.

The day after Thanksgiving was known as black Friday in retail circles, supposedly the busiest day of the year. Where would she be come Thanksgiving? Probably not at any Norman Rockwell–type celebration.

Her dismal thoughts were interrupted by Cody's cell phone. He tipped his chair so far back to reach it that any other man would have crashed to the floor. Not Cody, Laurel thought bitterly. Men like Cody never fell. Only women like her fell—women who drew up neat little life plans and expected a Doris Day finale, with all the loose ends tied up by the end of the third act.

Cody was frowning as he spoke into the phone. "Wait for low tide, about four this afternoon. There's at least a foot of water at the S-curve now. Some of it's saltwater seepage." He sounded less than thrilled to hear from whoever had called. "Right, then we'll expect you late this afternoon. If you've got a choice, rent something with four-wheel drive."

He ended the call, grimaced and nodded to the two other men. "Whenever you're ready, we might as well head out." Turning to Laurel, he said, "Mara and Everstone are on their way from Norfolk International. I doubt if she'll take my advice, so in case I run late, I'd appreciate it if you'd see that Becky's reasonably presentable. No point in handing her any ammunition."

"You're trying the custody thing again?" Harrison asked.

With a fleeting look of grim satisfaction, Cody nodded. "This time I've got a better than even chance of getting a split decision."

It was just past noon when a silver sedan with rental plates pulled up in the front yard. So much for waiting for low tide. The men weren't yet back. Laurel had been French-braiding Becky's freshly shampooed hair. She crossed to the sliding glass doors, left open to catch the light breeze, and looked out in time to see a dead ringer for Ava Gardner emerge from the passenger side. "I think that's your mom," she said to the child.

Becky's lower lip was already thrust out. "I don't want to go back with her."

"She's probably worried about you after the storm."

Hearing a loud shriek from outside, Laurel's first thought was that the woman had seen a snake. Handing Becky the scrunchie, she said, "I'd better go let them in. You come on down, all right?"

"My God, what's *happened* to you? Oh, darling, who *did* this to you?" The words were accompanied by Boo-Boo's frantic barking.

Not a snake then. Laurel hurried downstairs in time to see BooBoo lunging against his running lead. "Down, boy!" she shouted, as if "boy" ever obeyed a single command.

"What happened to my baby?" the Ava Gardner look-alike cried. "If Cody did this, I'll kill him, I swear I will." She turned to the man who was just now emerging from the car, "He'd do anything to hurt me, didn't I warn you?"

Laurel checked out the man who must be Becky's new stepfather. Tall, with thick gray hair and a Lincoln-esque face, he was wearing flawlessly tailored slacks with a white oxford dress shirt, the neck open and the cuffs turned back.

Had to be the politician, she thought, amused for no real reason. Bleached teeth, tanned face, thick gray hair not simply barbered, but expensively styled. She'd learned to recognize the difference.

Laurel came halfway down the outside stairs with Becky lagging three steps behind. "How do you do, I'm Becky's next-door neighbor, Laurel Lawless," she said. "Cody's not here, but we're expecting him any minute now."

Becky muttered, "I don't wanna go home, I wanna stay here with you, Laurie."

"Go get any toys you want to take home with you," Mara ordered. At closer range, Laurel decided the woman was almost too perfect. Her face had that chin-tight look that hinted at a recent lift.

Becky didn't move. Mara glared at the flight of stairs that led to the first-floor deck and said, "Isn't there an elevator? My God, what was he thinking of?"

"High tides," said Laurel. "Or maybe a low-tech version of a stair-climber."

"I see he hasn't wasted any time collecting another set of groupies. If I'd known that, I would never have let my daughter come down here."

Laurel refused to dignify the remark with a response. Once inside the house, she extracted her hand from Becky's and said, "Show your mother where your things are, honey. I'll gather up your games."

Mara looked around. "My God, he doesn't even have carpets."

"Carpets collect too much sand." Laurel didn't know if it was true or not. She really didn't care.

Becky raced past and climbed the freestanding stairs.

"Becky?" Mara called after her.

"You said to go pack my things!" the child yelled back, and Laurel groaned silently, wishing Cody was here to manage his own affairs.

"There are some things downstairs on the washer and a pair of shoes on the back deck," she said. "I'll put them in a plastic bag if you'd like."

Halfway up the stairs, Mara looked over her shoulder. "Don't bother. Whatever she needs, I'll buy when we get home. I must say, you're older than his usual choice."

Instead of firing off the response she was tempted to make, Laurel said, "I'm a neighbor. I've enjoyed getting to know your daughter. Her suitcase is on the closet shelf. She probably can't reach it."

"Know your way around, I see? Well, take it from me, if you're expecting a commitment, don't. Cody tolerates Becky, but there's only one person he really loves, and that's himself."

Laurel took another deep breath, wishing she could just walk away. Waiting a full minute before following the stunning brunette to Becky's room, she arrived just in time to see Mara snatch handfuls of shorts and T-shirts from the dresser drawer and throw them down on the bed.

Without speaking, Laurel retrieved the suitcase from the closet, opened it and began folding the small garments and packing them neatly while a tearful Becky looked on.

"I can't find my pirate book, Laurie," she sniffed.

"We'll find it. Or you can leave it here with your treasures, since your father plans to build you a case for them."

Becky took a deep, shuddering breath. "Aw right, but tell him to make me a shelf for my books, too."

"There's a wet bathing suit on the clothesline. Shall I put it in the bag with the other things?" she asked, her voice carefully calm.

"Oh, just leave it," Mara snapped. "I'll buy her another one."

Becky said sullenly, "I want to wait for Daddy. I'm not going till he says I have to."

"Nice try. Go get in the car, young lady."

Even angry, Mara Everstone was beautiful, her black hair thick and lustrous, her skin a testament to good genes and relentless care. Laurel was suddenly aware of her own sunburned, disheveled appearance.

Mara snapped the suitcase shut. "Is there a decent restaurant around here? We left Norfolk without stopping."

"Probably none you'd like," Laurel replied evenly. "I expect they're all still closed, anyway."

Laurel carried the small suitcase outside while Becky clutched two games and several books, one of which was a library book. Laurel didn't say a word. Cody could make a donation to the library to replace it. At this point, it was the least of her worries.

Everstone was leaning against the car, a high-end model that was probably going to need some extensive care after plowing through all the saltwater reported to be still standing on the highway. It was a wonder they'd made it at all.

Mara said, "Get in the car, Rebecca."

"I'm not going till Daddy gets back." Lower lip thrust out, arms clutching her precious possessions, the child stood defiantly on the bottom step.

"Rebecca…"

"I don't have to go with you! Daddy said——"

"Your father has nothing to say about it. He's already more than used up his visitation rights. Clyde, would you put that child in the backseat and buckle her in?"

"What about BooBoo? I'm not leaving him here, he'll run away and get snake bit."

Obviously, the woman hadn't considered the dog when she'd left Norfolk in a rented sedan. Now she looked the animal over as if uncertain he was worth bothering with in his present state. "Oh, God, he just lives to make my life difficult. What did I tell you, Clyde? You see what I've had to put up with?"

Laurel was wondering how to keep them from leaving short of throwing herself bodily across the driveway when she caught sight of a familiar-looking dark green SUV turning off the highway onto Ridge Pond Drive. Thank you, God, she whispered silently.

Becky ducked under Everstone's arm and raced toward the Rover, crying, "Daddy, Daddy, Daddy, tell her I don't have to go! Tell her I didn't talk while you were working, 'cause I didn't, did I? Not even once. I promise I won't ever bother you if you'll let me stay."

She wouldn't *talk?* She wouldn't *bother him?* My God, Laurel marveled, could it really be that simple? No wonder the child had seemed almost afraid to speak directly to her father. Deliberately or not, Mara must have warned her against being a nuisance.

Looking grim, Cody got out and swung his daughter up onto his hip. Her skinny, mosquito-bitten, briar-scratched legs wrapped around his waist. To Laurel he said, "Sorry I didn't make it back sooner. Everything under control?"

Lyon and Harrison emerged slowly from the SUV and stood back, obviously reluctant to break into the tense tableau.

"It is now that you're back," Laurel murmured. Slipping past him, she joined the other two men.

Harrison said quietly, "Fireworks?"

"A few. Lyon, is your house all right?"

"Yard's still flooded, but other than a basketball standard that floated across the front steps, we're in good shape."

"You might as well come on in. I'm eager to find out if you've learned anything else about—you know."

As the two strange men—attractive men, at that—approached, Mara changed demeanors the way a chameleon changed colors. Cody made the introductions and Everstone became the instant politician, complete with two-handed handshakes and flashing white teeth.

Urged on by an impulse that sprang out of nowhere, Laurel said, "If you'd like, BooBoo can stay here for now, isn't that right, Cody? He obviously won't fit in your car. Maybe you can pick him up when you bring Becky back for her next visit." Her smile was every bit as wide and insincere as Clyde Everstone's. Anything for the sake of peace. There were too many issues on the table.

"If BooBoo stays, I'm staying, too," Becky declared. Wrapping her arms tightly around her father's neck, she buried her face against his shoulder.

"Oh, God, I don't need this," Mara declared dramatically once Lyon and Harrison moved past to go inside.

It was Everstone who smoothed over the situation. "Darling, why don't you get in the car. Becky, you need to go home now, but in a couple of weeks maybe you can come back for one last visit with your father before we move out to California. You'll like California."

"No I won't, I hate California!"

"Don't be in too big a hurry to leave Richmond," Cody said. "I'm seeing my lawyer on the eleventh to re-open custody hearings. He'll be in touch." He brushed a kiss on Becky's head. "Honey, you need to go home and pack your winter things. We don't get much snow down here, but it gets plenty cold. And hey, next time you come, Trav's new baby will be here. Maybe Aunt Ru will let you hold her."

"What about Matt? He promised to show me how to take a motor apart."

"He promised *what?*"

The question went unanswered as the visitors drove off, taking a tearful Becky with them but leaving the bedraggled, half-shorn dog behind. Laurel watched from the first-floor deck, feeling more than a little tearful herself. Was it possible to fall in love with a child in such a short time?

A few minutes later, Cody joined her, looking tired and distracted. "Come on inside, I'll make coffee."

"What about Harrison and Lyon?"

"They can have some, too. They're probably up in my office, hacking into my computer and editing my work in progress."

Laurel's eyes widened. "They wouldn't!"

The lines in his weathered face deepened momentarily as he flashed her a familiar smile. "Just kidding. Lyon's downloading some data he requested last night."

"Do you really have an appointment with a lawyer about the custody thing? Can you do that unilaterally?"

"Mara will be there, count on it. The house is already on the market and Everstone's got to hit the campaign trail running if he plans to be on the ticket."

"What about Becky?"

"A kid makes for a great photo op, but Becky's the world's worst traveler. Besides, she'll be in school."

"There are schools in California," Laurel reminded him.

"The schools here are some of the best in the state. I checked it out."

"What makes you think Mara will let you have her?"

"She won't. Not a hundred percent, but if she plans to travel with Everstone, she'll have to hire a full-time nanny, which gives me a definite advantage, since I can be a full-time daddy."

"I'll keep my fingers crossed."

They stood on the first-floor deck and watched as a few early stars popped out. Cody's arm was around her shoulder, his hip pressed against hers. "Did you know it's a proven fact that there are three times as many stars over the Outer Banks as anywhere else in the Northern Hemisphere?"

"Who says so?"

"Me."

"Hotshot fiction writer. Some authority you are."

He knuckled her under the chin. "Hey, let's show a little more respect here."

Just then the beam from the lighthouse swept over them. "See, there's one of the more important navigational stars right there," he said solemnly. "Laurie?"

Turning around, he leaned against the railing and drew her into his arms. In the light shining out through the wide glass doors, he no longer looked tired. "Laurie, we need to talk. It's too soon, I know. You don't know anything about me, but—"

She placed her finger over his lips. "Shh. I know more about you than you think, and not just from reading your biography on the back of your books."

"Thought you hadn't read me," he teased, his voice several degrees deeper than usual.

"I haven't, not yet, but I read your book jackets. According to your bio, you've won all sorts of awards and you live on an island where you're currently at work on your next novel."

"Did the bio happen to mention that I grew up in Oklahoma, mostly on my own, and that I muddled around trying on different careers until I found one where I could pick my own hours and not have to wear a necktie to work?"

"I don't believe that was mentioned." Her heart rate had doubled. Deep, calming breaths weren't even a possibility.

"What about all the mistakes I've made and the lessons I'm finally starting to learn late in life, you read anything about that?"

"Um…don't think so. I could go back and check, though."

His face moved closer, blocking out the billion or so stars and a quarter moon just rising in the east. "Don't bother. I'll give you the condensed version."

His lips had just brushed over hers and were beginning to settle down to a serious exploration when the sound of the sliding door on the upper deck caused him to break away, swearing under his breath. "Your damn family. I see I'm going to have to run the gamut before I can even declare myself."

"Declare what?" she asked, no longer even trying to breathe.

"Hey, are you two coming upstairs anytime tonight?" Lyon called down from overhead. "Got something you're going to want to see. Two things, in fact."

One of the two things, when they trooped up the outer stairs and joined Lyon and Harrison in Cody's office, came almost as an anticlimax.

"Picked this up on your scanner," said Harrison, grinning broadly. "It came in while Lyon was busy digging into his official sources on your laptop. Pretty smart, not hooking up the one you work on to the Internet. Some bad stuff out there."

"Come on, come on—what'd you find out?" If Cody was impatient, Laurel was no less so. She had a feeling they'd been on the verge of something important— something that involved plans for her immediate future.

"This guy Candless? Seems he was a little late evacuating for the storm. They found his rental in a washout just north of Rodanthe, buried up to the rearview mirror."

"He's dead?" Laurel gasped, covering her mouth with her hand. She despised the man, but that didn't mean she wished him dead.

"Car was empty. Apparently he broke into a cottage and stayed there until the storm was over. When the highway crews started coming down to repair the damage, he hid out in the back of one of the trucks. They discovered him when he climbed into the cab looking for food. Poor guy was starving." Harrison chuckled, while Lyon shook his head.

"Trapped by a box of Krispy Kreme doughnuts."

"You said two things," Cody reminded them. "That's only one."

"Oh, yeah. Lyon, you wanna tell him?"

"Seems a young cousin of ours has up and joined the Coast Guard without telling his folks. He wanted to wait until he'd made the grade. Now he's waiting for an opening in boot camp." Lyon grinned, looking younger than his admitted fortysomething. "Waiting at my house, according to Jazzy. Matt showed up yesterday, hoping I'd break the news to Travis for him."

"Jesus," Cody muttered. "Why the devil didn't he just speak out and say what he wanted to do?"

"Beats me." Lyon shrugged. "Probably because Trav was so dead set on his getting a degree."

Harrison nodded slowly. "Yeah, but Matt wants to be a diesel mechanic, at least that's what he said last summer when I asked him about his plans."

"The Guard's got a great school for that. I think it's in Yorktown, I'm not sure. Anyhow, Jazzy said the poor kid's scared stiff Trav's going to boot him out."

"Yeah, well…he's only following in his old man's footsteps. That's pretty flattering, when you think about it. Give him time, Trav'll come around. He's got another kid to worry about now."

"Let's hope he waits until this one's cut her teeth before he enrolls her in any college." Harrison chuckled, then stood and yawned.

It was almost eleven by the time the other two men turned in after making plans to fly out early the following morning. "I promised Jimmy I'd take him fishing," Harrison said.

Lyon chimed in with, "Yeah, and I promised Jasmine an autographed Lee Larkin book. How about it, Cody, do I get the family discount?"

"Hey, everybody else on the island might be kin, but last I heard, we're not related."

"Not yet," said the gray-haired director of operations of one of the lesser-known intelligence groups. "I give it about what…two weeks?"

Early the next morning, while Cody flew his two guests to Manteo where Lyon had left his car, Laurel straightened up the kitchen, stripped beds and put a load of laundry on to wash. Then she went across to the old house and stood in the open door, inhaling the mustiness, the dampness and hints of long-ago living.

To go, or to stay, that was the question. Didn't some famous person ask a similar question?

Probably not about the same thing.

"Are you here?" she whispered. She'd never been into the woo-woo beliefs of a few of her classmates. Even her mother, who loved nothing better than exploring old burial mounds, scoffed at the New Age stuff.

"If you can hear me, I intend to clean off your grave before I leave. It's the least I can do." She waited for any confirmation, audible or otherwise. Maybe a whiff of frigid air or the sound of a tapping table. How did ghosts communicate, anyway? Was life on the other side one big joke?

"All right, just so you know I mean you no harm."

Oh, yeah—as if she could do anything to harm a woman who'd been dead for more than half a century. "You know what I mean," she muttered, and quickly set about checking the contents of the refrigerator and opening more windows.

Cody got back shortly past noon. By then, Laurel had the house as clean as she could make it and her car was all packed. It was called hedging her bets. She heard a plane fly over and knew without even looking up that it was his twin-engine Cessna. She barely had time to shower and clamp her hair back with a tortoiseshell clip before she heard him drive up.

"That was quick," she said by way of greeting.

"No point in lingering." His eyes were all over her. Even with the baseball cap and sunglasses he wore when he flew she could feel them. "I see you fed the mutt," he said.

"One bowl of dog chow and one of those fancy bones for dessert." She'd brought him over with her and tied him to a porch post, with kibble, water and his favorite bone.

"He'll probably be a permanent resident, you game for it?" Turning, he walked out to her car, opened the door and lifted out her big suitcase. He set it on the edge of the porch.

She felt her palms grow damp. "Um, actually, I haven't had much experience with dogs," she admitted in her Minnie Mouse voice. "Cats, either, for that matter."

"What about husbands?"

Her heart stuttered, stopped, then doubled its pace. "What about them?"

"You ever had one of those?"

"Cody, there's a lot you don't know about me."

"Hey, life's a learning experience." Without the sunglasses, he looked far less confident. Looked almost vulnerable, in fact. "I'm game if you are."

Holding on to the porch support to keep from hurling herself in his arms, she said cautiously, "To start with, I'm a left-brain person. I like logic and order. You're obviously one of the creative right-brain people."

"See, that's what I mean." He moved up the steps and reached for her hand, tracing her knuckles with his thumb. "My shortcomings are your long-comings and vice versa. I toss a handful of silverware into the drawer, you come along and sort it out. I live out of the dryer, you sort and fold and put things away."

"You work crossword puzzles in ink and then toss the papers on the floor. I check to see how many mistakes you've made, fold the papers and put them in the recycling bin."

"See, what'd I tell you? We're a natural. You came down here to find your family, right? Me, I come with a ready-made family."

By this time they were in the living room. Laurel reached to pick up one of the games Becky had left behind when Cody caught her hand and drew her down onto the sofa. "Some stuff can wait, some can't. Laurie, we've got something good going on between us. I'm game to try for something more—something permanent—if you are."

With her heart in her throat, she couldn't have spoken if her life depended on it. Amazing, she thought, that after little more than two weeks he looked more familiar than her own face in the mirror. He even smelled familiar—a mixture of coffee, healthy male sweat and the pine-scented bath soap he favored. Did that add up to pheromones?

Who knew. Who even cared?

"Come on," he crooned softly. "It can't come as any great surprise."

She nodded vigorously. "Yes, it can. Does, I mean. I mean, what do you mean?"

He sighed, his breath stirring her drying hair against her face. "For a wordsmith, I'm not doing so hot, am I?"

"Try words of one syllable."

"'Kay, here goes." He cleared his throat. "I love you. Will you be mine?"

She closed her eyes, afraid to speak for fear the sound

of her own voice would bring her out of her dream. "Yours and Becky's?" she ventured.

"That's two syllables." He tugged her closer until she was snuggled against his side.

"Cody, until a few weeks ago I thought I was in love with Jerry Blessing. You see what a screwup I am when I put my mind to it?"

"Hey, I was married to Mara. You wanna talk mistakes, I can match you two for one. See, what I've discovered now that I've matured is that it's what's inside the box that counts, not the pretty wrappings." He grinned. It looked more like a leer. "I like what's inside your box—I like it a lot."

"But not my wrappings?" She couldn't help it, she had to laugh. Once started, she couldn't seem to stop.

"Wha-a-at?" Cody said.

"Nothing," she gasped. "Everything." Sobering enough to sound halfway coherent, she said, "Tell you what, why don't we give it more time? I'm new at this business of acting on impulse."

He nuzzled her throat, finding the place that sent goose bumps streaking down her flank. "You need more time? You got it. How about a week from now we take off for—"

"Whoa. You skipped the part about asking my family for my hand. That is, if you still want it after two weeks."

"Both hands plus everything that comes with them," he declared fervently. Somehow her shirt had come unbuttoned. She felt his nimble fingers fiddling with the snaps at the back of her bra.

"You do know that any children we might eventually

have will inherit dozens of cousins," she said with a
catch in her breath.

"One of your biggest attractions," he said just as he
lowered her onto the cushions. "Stability and all that.
Never had much, myself, so we'll make do with yours.
Now, enough of the proposals, let's get started on chapter one."

*Everything you love about romance...*
**and more!**

*Please turn the page for Signature Select™*
*Bonus Features.*

## Bonus Features:

## Author Interview
### A conversation with
# DIXIE BROWNING

*A former newspaper columnist, USA TODAY
bestselling author Dixie Browning has written more
than 100 category romances. Recently we chatted
with Dixie about her writing career, family and her
favorite things.*

4

**Tell us how you began your writing career.**
I began when a friend grew tired of writing her
weekly art column for a local paper and handed it
off to me. As an artist, an art teacher and an
eternal optimist, it never occurred to me that I
didn't know how to write. I took over the column,
went on to write several art-related articles for
various publications, and a year or so later
Harlequin ran a short story contest. (I had just
been introduced to romances at the time.) I
entered, even though I'd never written fiction.
Not surprisingly, I didn't win any prizes, but I was

hooked on writing by the time I finished my entry and went on to write two complete manuscripts, both of which were published in 1977. I continued to write on my secondhand manual portable typewriter, and a few years later when Silhouette was born, I had another manuscript ready to go. I was out of town teaching a watercolor workshop when a Silhouette editor called my home to say she wanted to buy my manuscript. That was before the days of cell phones, so needless to say, by the time I had called all my family and friends, my long-distance bill was astronomical.

**Was there a particular person, place or thing that inspired this story?**
The Lawless stories—all of them—were inspired by the territory itself.

Northeast North Carolina was settled so early in our country's history that it has a "feel" all its own. Roots go deep; families tend to remain in the region. Gene pools intermingle, and going back a few generations, one can find scores of cousins. Here in the South, especially in a small area that was isolated for hundreds of years, "second cousin on my mama's side, third cousin on my daddy's side," is often a reality.

I've always been drawn to the rich, flat, alluvial farmland on the mainland nearest the Outer Banks. Mama's folks came from that area; Daddy's from the Outer Banks. The Lawlesses came from the same region, and like the rest of us, sooner or later, they return. As they do, I'm waiting for them, ready to get to know them and share them with you.

**What's your writing routine?**
Sometime between 7:00 and 8:00 a.m., I stoke my inner muse with a healthy breakfast of homemade granola, followed by a pint of high-test coffee. Then I head for the computer and write until midmorning, at which time I get dressed, stretch a few cramped muscles, and go back to work for another few hours. Occasionally when I'm pushing a deadline I'll write in the afternoon, but my mind is always fresher early in the day.

**How do you research your stories?**
I usually try to write about places I know, but in a pinch, I have widely scattered friends—(some more scattered than others!)—who can answer questions. I subscribe to fashion magazines to keep me up to date...although I have to admit, I can't picture one of my heroines wearing some of

the outfits that pass as high fashion today. Does that make me old, obstinate and provincial? You betcha!

**How do you develop your characters?**
They more or less develop themselves. Consciously or otherwise, I'm sure most are patterned after people I've known. Occasionally I might see someone who snags my interest, and without ever speaking to this person I might create an entire persona based solely on appearances. Sooner or later they'll show up in one of my stories. Sometimes in more than one, but I'll never tell.

**When you're not writing, what are some of your favorite activities?**
Reading! Watching Braves baseball games on TV. Painting—I'm currently working toward a two-woman show.  I garden a bit—flowers and shrubs—but I'm lazy and gardening is hard work, so I leave the serious stuff to my husband. I do like to cook, though. Rarely by recipes; I can't abide having to follow instructions. Needless to say, I've had some spectacular failures.

**If you don't mind, could you tell us a bit about your family?**

You can read much of my own background in the Lawless family history. A few names have been added, the branch from which the Lawlesses sprang, but it's up to you to decide who's real and who's fictitious. Speaking more immediately, I have a husband. Sorry, ladies, but I married the most wonderful man in the world. He's just imperfect enough to keep my ego from suffering by comparison. Our son is one of the most fascinating men I know, our daughter, the most generous, nurturing woman in the world. Our beloved daughter-in-law is my best painting buddy. We also have two grandchildren who are suddenly no longer children. What shall I call them...grand-adults? Along with dozens of cousins, both here and over on the mainland, I have two sisters who live within shouting distance on the same wooded ridge overlooking the Pamlico Sound.

**What are your favorite kinds of vacation? Where do you like to travel?**

My favorite vacation is to stay right here, with stacks of books-to-be-read, friends and family dropping in and a beach walk to look forward to each day—usually with one or more members of our family. I did my traveling years ago and thoroughly enjoyed every bit of it, both foreign and domestic, but my nest is just too comfortable to leave.

**Do you have a favorite book or film?**
I couldn't possibly name a favorite book. There are hundreds, if not more, of wonderful writers who are constantly at work to feed my reading habit. Movies? I rarely go to a theater, but I did enjoy *Whale Rider, The Natural* and *Cold Mountain.*

**Any last words to your readers?**
Read! Teach your children to read, too. It's the easiest, safest and cheapest escape when you really, really need to get away from it all. It's like stepping into someone else's life for a few hours. You'd be amazed at how much you can learn—or maybe you wouldn't—from fiction. And remember, even with the most hair-raising thriller, you're guaranteed a safe return.

# Recipes

*Here are a few homegrown recipes from my own kitchen.*
—Dixie Browning

### FRIED FISH

Mama fried the best fish I've ever tasted. Her method was simple, but a bit un-PC. Salt the fillets and let them stand for 15 or 20 minutes while you heat bacon grease in a cast-iron frying pan. (Okay, if you insist, canola oil, but for goodness' sake, season it with a bit of bacon grease!) When it's piping hot, but not quite smoking, dredge your fillets in cornmeal and place them in carefully, skin side up, waiting a minute or so after each one to allow the grease to get piping hot again. Warning: it'll spatter, so stand back. You might want to drop a few newspapers on the floor in front of the stove. After about 4 or 5 minutes, turn the fish and

brown on the other side, then drain on a
paper-towel-covered newspaper and prepare to
enjoy.

## UGLY MUFFINS

These are tasty and healthy. They evolved because
I crave chocolate, but I'm diabetic, plus
weight- and health-conscious.
(Fried fish notwithstanding.)

2 cups mashed baked sweet potatoes or
canned pumpkin (*not* pumpkin pie mix)
2 cups whole wheat flour
1 tbsp baking powder
1/2 tsp baking soda
1/2 tsp salt
7 envelopes of pink sweetener (add another
one if you use canned pumpkin)
3/4 cups cocoa
1 1/2 cups (approx) water

Mix dry ingredients thoroughly, then add raisins,
chopped nuts, chopped dried apricots or the
dried fruit of your choice. The amounts are up to
you.

Now add the mashed sweet potatoes or pumpkin

and mix thoroughly. It's hard going, but once you have it more or less thoroughly mixed, add about a cup and a half of water with a dash of vanilla and stir some more. The batter will be stiff, but it's a good upper-body workout.

Finally, spoon batter into PAM-sprayed muffin tins and slide it into the oven. About 30-35 minutes at 350°F should do it. Touch the tops, and if they're springy, they're done. Granted, they'll be dense and even a bit chewy (like chocolates!) and ugly as homemade sin, but they're healthy and delicious and worth the trouble. I refrigerate mine after the first day or so—that is, if there are any left.

For variety, leave out the cocoa and use your favorite spices, instead.

## PONE BREAD

Unless you're from the eastern part of the state, you probably haven't had this. It's my mama's recipe, and we used to have it on Sunday, usually with gravy—never with butter.

- 3 cups cornmeal
- 5 cups boiling water
- 2/3 cups cold water
- 1 tsp salt
- 2/3 cups flour
- 2/3 cups sugar
- 2 tbsp molasses
- 2 tbsp shortening

Scald meal in boiling water. Add remaining ingredients except shortening. Stir and let stand overnight. Melt shortening in heavy iron Dutch oven. When it's piping hot, pour melted shortening into batter and stir, then pour batter back into pan. Bake 2 hours at 375°F, then cover and bake another hour at 300°F. Let cool in pan and serve cold with or without gravy. It's a dense, mildly sweet corn bread, probably something like Indian pudding. I've never had that, so I'm not sure.

## PECAN PIE

This is possibly the finest pecan pie anyone ever baked. It's my ex-son-in-law's recipe. (Don't ask!)

2 tbsp butter
1/2 cup light brown sugar
3 eggs
1/2 cup dark corn syrup
1/4 tsp salt
1 tsp vanilla
1 1/2 to 2 cups pecans
1 tsp Courvoisier

14

Preheat oven to 450°F. Melt butter, stir in sugar, beat in eggs one at a time, add other ingredients and pour into a 9-inch pie shell. Bake at 450°F for 10 minutes, then lower heat to 350°F and bake 30 minutes or until set.

## MAMA'S HATTERAS-STYLE CLAM CHOWDER
(Warning: no tomatoes, no cream, no milk!)

Fry 2 or 3 pieces of cubed bacon or salt pork in heavy pot. When brown, add a pint of ground clams and juice, (or about 3 cans of minced clams if you haven't been clamming lately) 1 chopped onion and black pepper to taste. Most

people down here use *lots* of pepper!  Bring to a
boil and add a pint of hot water and 4 potatoes,
diced. Simmer until potatoes are soft. For a
thicker chowder, cook longer or add another
potato. Serves 4-6.

## GARDEN GUMBO FOR TWO

At the end of the summer we usually have too
many tomatoes, although the okra is beginning
to play out. Here's one of the ways I use what Lee
brings in from the garden.

Fry 2 slices of bacon, remove from pan, drain and
set aside. In bacon fat, sauté 2 or 3 thinly sliced
okra pods, 1 medium onion or 2 or 3 green ones,
a cup or so of cubed leftover ham and/or half a
pound or so of raw shrimp. When onion is clear,
peel (if you're fastidious) one giant, juicy tomato.
Chop and add this along with half a cup of
Chablis, a bay leaf (or if you're here on the island,
wax myrtle leaves will do just fine) and a grind or
two of black pepper. Simmer 15-20 minutes and
serve over cooked rice with bacon crumbled on
top.

# Old Naming Patterns

The following naming pattern was once a common practice. Though not an invariable tradition, it often gives a clue regarding the names of grandparents whose names are sometimes elusive in genealogical research.

The first son was named after the father's father.

The second son was named after the mother's father.

The third son was named after the father.

The fourth son was named after the father's eldest brother.

The first daughter was named after the mother's mother.

The second daughter was named after the father's mother.

The third daughter was named after the mother.

The fourth daughter was named after the mother's eldest sister.

Before the year 1910, no birth or death certificates were issued in the state of North Carolina. What records escaped fire, war, storms and the emergence of new counties were augmented by family Bibles and word of mouth. As there were relatively few families living on the Outer Banks in the mid to late 1600s and the early 1700s, many of the bloodlines crossed and recrossed, mingling in the early days with the native Algonquin population. Thus, beyond the first few generations, relationships become increasingly convoluted. A newcomer with roots on the island can spend many years searching old graveyards, old family Bibles and untangling local legends.

Laurel Ann Lawless Morningstar will never know the full extent of her family ties, but will content herself to know that here she belongs. She has finally come home.

# Author's Journal
## History of the Lawless Family

John Lyon Lawless, son of Robert and Sarah Lawless, was born January 6, 1737 somewhere in England. The exact location is not known. John L. was shipwrecked on Hatteras Banks, along with two brothers, one of whom was Robert, who later became an inlet pilot.

On December 25 of 1762, John married Margaret Haywood, born November 15, 1745, granddaughter of George William Haywood, who was an officer under Edward Teach (Thatch) also known as Blackbeard. Haywood was said to have been given title to Ocracoke Island, possibly for testifying in court against his former employer, by the English king.

John and Margaret had four children; a daughter named Margaret and three sons, Zachariah, Robert and Reuben, all of whom married into local families and begat numerous offspring. Zachariah, born March 7, 1786, served in the militia of North Carolina during the War of

1812 three years after marrying Elizer Wilhelm. Their descendants include three sons: Levin, Edmund Dailey and Allen, and three daughters: Comfort, Courtney and Delaney, all of whom married into other local families and went on to produce many children.

Of those sons, Edmund Daily Lawless, b. July 10, 1820 to Zachariah and Elizer, married Sally Gallins, born Feb. 22, 1825, daughter of Zorababel and Margaret Ballard Gallins. The children of Edmund Dailey and wife Sally are, in order of birth: Robert Lyon, Margaret S., Edmund Dixon, Zorababel G., Mary H., Crissy Jane, Ethelbert Dozier and Elizer A. Lawless. It is said that Sally Gallins Lawless, carrying in her arms the infant Edmund Dixon Lawless, (who grew up to become a lighthouse keeper), was the last person to walk across Hatteras Inlet before it was cut by a northeaster, in or about 1849.

During the War Between the States, before Federal forces invaded and took control of the island, a few of the Lawless men sailed with their families across the Pamlico Sound to the mainland of northeastern North Carolina. Among them was Robert Lyon Lawless, who later became known as Squire Lawless and amassed a fortune, much of which was lost when his whiskey-making industry was finally destroyed by government agents. It is said that the only route to his still, located deep in the swamp, was Milltail Creek.

Squire Lawless set two men, each holding a lantern, on opposite sides of the creek. If the light was briefly blocked, that meant a boat had passed between them and one of the two watchmen would run ahead and warn Squire of either a customer or a revenuer.

Squire Lawless married three wives, one of whom gave birth to a son, John James Lawless, who married and had three daughters and a single son. One of the daughters married Calvin Travis Holiday, who became the grandfather of Travis Lawless Holiday. John James Lawless, Junior, worked his way through three years of college in the Texas oil fields before dropping out to specialize in oil-related computer software.

Of the three daughters born to Squire Lawless and his second wife, Rodantha, one is believed to have graduated from a New England college, where she went on to teach for many years. Another died when the bite of a greenhead fly became infected. The third daughter, Dorcas, moved back to Hatteras Island and married into one of the local families.

Ethelbert Dozier Lawless, (b. December 5, 1856 to Edmund D. and Sally Gallins Lawless; d. Dec. 5, 1936) became an assistant keeper of Cape Hatteras Lighthouse. There he met and later married Achsah Wilhelm, daughter of Achsah Mariah S. and lighthouse keeper Bateman A. Wilhelm.

Side note: Achsah Mariah Wilhelm Lawless, twice widowed, twice remarried, was reported to have been mistreated by her last husband. At her death, the family of her first husband stole her body and reburied it in the Lawless family graveyard, near present-day Lawless land.

The children of Ethelbert, light keeper and sea captain in the West Indies trade, include E. D. Lawless, Jr, who died at age four months; Elida D., who married Robert Gallins, (grandparent of Daniel Lyon Lawless); Lula D., who married Octavius Farrin, grandparents of Harrison Lawless.

Little is known of the other direct descendants of Ethelbert Dozier and his first wife, Achsah Mariah, other than their names. A search among the family records of other original families on the Banks may provide clues, for the Lawless daughters tended to marry local men, among them fishermen, inlet pilots, teachers and boatbuilders.

After the death of his first wife, Achsah, Ethelbert, known as Captain Dozier, sailed into the port of Wilmington, NC, where he married a woman by the name of Margaret Douglas, whom he brought home and left in charge of his young family. Margaret and Ethelbert had no issue.

# THE LAWLESS FAMILY

## A Family Tree